Tempting
TALK

SARA WHITNEY

Tempting Talk

Tempt Me, Book 3

Copyright © Sara Whitney 2020

Published by LoveSpark Press, Peoria, IL 61603

Cover art: Deranged Doctor Designs
Developmental Editor: Sue Brown-Moore
Editor: Victory Editing
Sensitivity Reader: Salt and Sage Books

First Edition: March 2020

ISBN: 978-1-953565-02-0

To the authors of Heart & Scroll,
for your feedback and your friendship.

And to the Omegas.
What a privilege to be in your company.

**She's not just breaking her own rules.
She's setting them on fire
and pushing them off a cliff.**

Rock deejay Mabel Bowen's all play, but only at work. She learned the hard way that dating just isn't worth the risk to her public reputation, so she's happy spending her nights alone—until she meets an accountant with Clark Kent charm and Superman muscles.

Jake Carey's all work, and then a little more work. He grew up broke and never took the time for relationships as he scrapped for every promotion. Yet he finds himself setting aside his spreadsheets every time the morning show host with the maple syrup voice comes around.

When work becomes pleasure, all bets are off. Friendly coffee turns into flirty lunches, and then a scorching night out obliterates all of their previously drawn lines. Can Jake convince the woman who spins words for a living that the numbers add up on this once-in-a-lifetime love?

Tempting Talk is a 2019 RWA© Golden Heart© finalist.

CONTENTS

ONE

It was six a.m., and Mabel Bowen wanted to make some radio magic.

"You ready?" she asked.

Her cohost lifted his oversized coffee mug and tipped it straight back, his Adam's apple bobbing as he swallowed. With a smack of his lips, Dave Chilton plunked the now-empty mug on the countertop and raised a challenging brow. "I am now." He shook out his hands and stretched his neck to either side. "Let's see if you can keep up, Bowen."

"You're so on." She met his grin with one of her own and settled her headset over her ears, repositioning herself to sit cross-legged in the chair that faced him over the radio-station control board.

"Here we go in three... two..." With a flourish, Dave flipped on their mics to start the day. "Good morning, friends and foes! You're listening to Dave and Mae in the Morning on 105.5 WNCB, the Brick, where *we just rock.*"

Although Dave's voice would be booming through the speakers positioned in the halls of the radio station, their snug soundproof studio kept the two of them cocooned from the outside world while they unleashed their mojo. Cohosting a morning radio show meant lousy hours, but playing daily verbal tennis with her best friend more than made up for the early alarm.

"You know what else rocks?" Mabel spoke into the shock-mounted mic positioned next to her lips but kept her eyes on Dave as they got the show underway. "We're here to ease you out the door on this glorious Wednesday morning in July. Dave, what can the residents of our fair city expect weather-wise today?"

"Hot."

Her lips quirked at his flat tone, but she kept her voice drily sarcastic. "Wow, so specific. And tomorrow?"

"Also hot."

"Uh-huh. Sure, sure. And then on Friday?"

"Hot again," Dave said. "It's summer in Beaucoeur, Illinois, people. Brace for hot!"

As he spoke, Mabel's body gave an involuntary shiver; outside, it was pushing eighty-five with the sun barely up, but inside, the studio air-conditioning was waging its usual war to send her into hypothermic shock. She twisted in her chair, taking care not to dislodge her head-phones, and snagged the emergency cardigan she kept stashed in a cubby on her side of the console. She started to pull the purple sweater on as she straightened but froze with one arm in and one arm out when she became aware of three pairs of eyes peering in through the big window that separated the recording studio from the greenroom beyond.

She recognized station owner Kirby Richardson, of course, but the two men flanking him were new. New and apparently there to redefine the word *hot*. She hastily shoved her arm through the remaining empty sleeve but couldn't tear her gaze from the two best-looking humans to ever set foot in this building. The instant Dave cut their mics to play the first song of the morning, she addressed him out of the side of her mouth. "Hey, uh, Dave?"

He looked up from the press release in his hand and followed the discreet tilt of her head toward the window where the onlookers continued to gaze in at them. He swiveled his head back toward her and voiced what she was thinking. "Our new buyers?"

"It's either that or we're newly enrolled in a male-model delivery service."

"No money in the budget for that," Dave said as she snuck another peek. All three had turned their backs to the studio and were surveying the jumble of furniture crammed into the greenroom where the deejays hung out between shifts.

"Behold, our new corporate overlords," Dave muttered.

Kirby had announced last week that he'd finally found a suitable buyer for the station, allowing him to retire to his beloved golf course and bringing an end to a stressful and uncertain time for the station staff. Of course, these new owners ushered in an entirely new source of stress and uncertainty, but she and Dave were prepared to go down joking.

"Looks like they're here to kick the tires," she said.

"Mess around under the hood."

"Poke us with their dipsticks."

Dave's lips twitched at her lame innuendo, and as she twisted her face into a broadly comic wink to drive the punch line home, one of the new owners turned, and his assessing gaze landed on her. Blood rushed to her cheeks at his bold stare, but no way was she backing down. She lifted her chin and studied him right back through the thick glass.

Tall. Thick black hair. Strong square jaw. Suit that cost more than her car. Muscular body filling out that suit with—

Nope. Her brain was galloping away from her toward an entirely off-limits target. She swallowed the excess saliva suddenly pooling in her mouth and forced her eyes away from what was clearly Superman in his Clark Kent persona. She glared down at the show notes crumpled in her tight fist, willing herself to project breezy nonchalance instead of unsettled awareness.

"Wonder what they're talking about." Dave's whisper interrupted her rampaging thoughts. She risked another glance up and was relieved—or was that disappointed?—to see that Superman had joined his blond friend to contemplate the grimy whiteboard listing the station's remote broadcast schedule for the next month.

"Oh, probably our slovenly deejay habits." Even though the booth was soundproof, she kept her voice low as the blond man gestured emphatically toward the carpet. "Archibald, my good man, these surroundings simply *will not* do!"

Dave snorted and then replied in a peevish whine. "How can we be expected to work with people who labor in such appalling conditions?"

She gave an answering sniff. "Just look at this couch, Percival. Is it... My word, is that *velour*?" She pressed a hand to her chest as the two suits walked past their admittedly atrocious sofa. "Why, my tailor would be beset with the vapors were I to sit upon it and introduce this fine suit material to such low fibers!"

She and Dave burst into laughter at the precise moment that Superman looked up and met her eyes again. Her pulse fluttered in her throat, and she swallowed hard. He looked effortlessly cool with one hand tucked into his pants pocket, nodding thoughtfully at whatever Kirby was saying.

Effortlessly cool and utterly off-limits. She had rules. And besides, the music break was over, and she and Dave were back on air in five seconds. Thankfully, she had years of experience in shoving away the real world as soon as the On Air light lit up. But while Dave shuffled papers for their upcoming events segment, her traitorous eyes flicked to the greenroom once more. Superman was watching her again, and the moment he noticed her noticing him, he spun around to rejoin the conversation his buddy was having with Kirby.

Ridiculous to feel self-conscious, yet there it was. No way was she going to let him catch her looking at him again. Besides, he was *off-limits*. The reminder was what she needed to force her eyes back to Dave, whose fuzzy brows arched above his glasses in a question.

"All good?"

"Absolutely. Let's go." She filled her lungs and exhaled hard to jettison the distractions plaguing her brain. The instant Dave turned on their mics and launched into one of the bits they'd prepped that morning, her awareness of the men beyond the recording faded and she was in it again, the entirety of her focus now on Dave, their show, their connection.

Two hours later, her insides were warm from all those good morning-radio vibes as she and Dave signed off for the day. Once they were clear, they exchanged deejay fives—air slaps that didn't require lazy radio hosts to get out of their chairs and actually smack palms—and then they both jumped when a knock on the big studio window startled them. It was Blondie, grinning like a kid tapping away at fish in an aquarium. He gestured for them to step into the greenroom to join him and Superman. Kirby was nowhere to be seen.

"Shall we?" Dave asked.

She lifted her chin. "No other option. They're between us and the exit." But her heart pounded harder than it should have as she stepped through the door Dave held open. She pasted an artificially bright smile on her face and prepared to impress the new bosses with her professionalism and complete lack of distractedness.

Blondie spoke first.

"Dave and Mabel, hello! I'm Brandon Lowell from Lowell Consolidated Media, the new owner of this station. I'm here to check out the lay of the land."

With his dipstick. She swore that sometimes if she thought a joke hard enough, Dave could actually hear it. His small chuff of laughter told her this was one of those times.

Brandon turned and gestured to Superman. "This is Jake Carey with Black, Phelps, and Suarez out of Chicago. He's the accountant here to sort out the books."

Jake inclined his head, but unlike their through-the-window staring bursts, he kept the eye contact brief before nodding to Dave and then focusing his attention on Brandon.

"Would you two have a seat?" Brandon pointed at the

greenroom couch like a king commanding his subjects. "I'd love to talk a little bit about what you see for your future here at WNCB."

"Oh no, not the velour," Dave muttered, and Mabel bit her lip to contain her nervous giggle.

Although the battered couch was comfortable enough for a deejay who needed a quick nap between shifts, it was also covered in a number of suspicious stains and tended to sag toward the middle. When she and Dave settled in, they ended up shoulder to shoulder and sitting much lower than Brandon, who stood in the middle of the room to address the peasants, while Jake leaned against the greenroom desk. Its uneven legs wobbled under his weight, but he just shifted to accommodate the instability, the navy suit fabric stretching taut over his thighs. Wishing she could be so unflappable in the face of unco-operative furniture, Mabel surreptitiously tugged the hem of her skirt as close to her knees as she could get it and fought the urge to fluff the headphone divot out of her hair.

"Congratulations on having the second-most popular morning show in this market!" Brandon boomed once they were settled. "You two are a big reason that Lowell Consolidated purchased your station. That and the fact that WNCB was one of the few independently owned radio shops left in the US."

Mabel studied him as he spoke, wondering why he didn't leave her as flustered as his partner. He was handsome enough with blue eyes and sharp, clean features. But her eyes slid over to actual Clark Kent three feet away from him to confirm that yep, Brandon came across as a lesser specimen of manhood. A little less imposing, a little less handsome. A little... less. Meanwhile, Jake had assumed enough control over the rickety desk to cross one ankle over the other, looking artfully posed and a little bored.

It wasn't like her to let broad shoulders and thick, shiny hair distract her. Ditto that long stretch of neck running from Jake's jaw down to his crisp white shirt collar. That was *definitely* not worth a second glance. And—

Oh God, Brandon had been talking this whole time. She refocused in time to hear him conclude. "So that's why I'm here for the time being, to observe your work and make some decisions about the future. At some point next week, I'd like to sit in the booth to watch you run your show."

She and Dave nodded in agreement, not that they had any choice in the matter. Then all their heads turned when the greenroom door opened and Skip Stevens, the dayside deejay, entered to start his ten a.m. shift. With his deep voice, bald scalp, and droopy jowls, he'd always reminded her of a basset hound. Skip's hangdog expression looked especially hound-like today as he took in the tableaux: she and Dave sitting like chastised children on the greenroom couch, Jake lounging on a desk that was trying its best to buck him off, and Brandon beaming toothily at all of them.

"Oh hi," Skip said, mopping at the sweat on his shiny dome. "This is... Are you...? Yeah, I've got to get on the air." He dove into the studio like it was the last available Uber in a ten-mile radius and had the headphones over his ears and the On Air sign illuminated with remarkable swiftness. Apparently unperturbed by the interruption, Brandon clapped his hands together, barked,

"Excellent!" and pulled his phone from his pocket, exiting the room without a goodbye.

"Good meeting," Dave muttered, freeing himself from the pillowy embrace of the couch after a short struggle. She'd started to lever herself up too when Jake flowed off the desk and extended his hand to her.

Mabel's first instinct was to recoil; everything about him was big and beautiful and overwhelming. What if she touched him and they both burst into flame? But that was silly. When had that ever happened to anyone in real life? And besides, he was off-limits.

By then she'd hesitated long enough that a touch of confusion crept into Jake's friendly expression, so she hurriedly shoved her hand into his and let him pry her up from the quicksand couch.

Had she been worried about bursting into flame? The jolt she experienced when his hand closed around hers was so much more intense than that. His bare palm, warm and a little rough, settled against hers like a lightning strike, all sparks and tingles. Her pulse jumped, her breathing hitched, and she'd bet her mother heard the gong of imminent grandchildren all the way up in Minnesota.

Mabel didn't know how long she stood there holding his hand. Maybe a few seconds. Maybe a few decades. All she knew was that at Dave's loud "ahem," she dropped Jake's hand and prepared to launch into a competitive round of "ignore the crackling chemistry."

Then she snuck a glance at Jake's face and saw... nothing. No emotion, no spark of interest. Just an unreadable stare and a murmured "Nice to meet you both" before he pivoted sharply and left the room.

She watched him go in baffled silence until Dave gave a low whistle.

"Well, good thing *that* wasn't weird," he said.

"Shut up." She brushed her hand down her skirt where the skin still tingled and pushed the memory aside so she could focus on the rest of her day.

TWO

"Enjoying the radio business so far?"

Jake Carey looked up from the spreadsheet he'd been studying and glared at Brandon's feet, which were kicked up on the desk and perilously close to his file stack. "The coffee's lousy, the books are a mess, and this janky chair's trying to kill me."

"Yep, it's nonstop glamour," Brandon said cheerfully, lacing his hands behind his head.

Jake stood to stretch out his spine, sparing a thought for his expensive ergonomic chair sitting unused behind his desk three hours north in Chicago. But no sense in dwelling; after half a week in Beaucoeur, he was resigned to his fate. For the next few months, he'd be surrounded, not by the glass, chrome, and leather of his high-rise accounting office but by the low ceilings, wood paneling, and lingering scent of cigarette smoke at WNCB. Was someone at the station in the habit of ignoring the No Smoking sign on the wall, or was the smell baked into the ancient carpet from the hedonistic years before the practice was banned? Either way, the scent reminded him of visiting his grandma in her South Side apartment as a kid, when she'd ply him with cookies and smoky hugs.

Frankly, he'd kill for either of those creature comforts at the moment; three days removed from his normal gym-office-home routine in Chicago left him feeling tense and twitchy. Of course, Brandon wasn't helping things.

"So, why haven't you made partner yet, Jakehammer? We all thought you'd manage that before you were twenty-five."

His onetime college roommate flashed a grin that set Jake's teeth on edge. They might not have seen each other much in the nine years since graduation, but Brandon still knew how to jab a thumb right into Jake's vulnerable spots, starting with that idiotic nickname he'd been using nonstop since Jake had arrived in Beaucoeur on Wednesday.

Good thing he'd retained the lessons from his years as a scholarship student at the University of Chicago. Fake-it-till-you-make-it generally worked with his wealthier classmates, and since heir-to-the-Lowell-media-empire Brandon had been the leader of the privileged brigade, Jake responded with a smirk of his own.

"Don't worry. I'm planning to dazzle you with my work on this sale and convince you to bring all the accounting activities for Lowell Consolidated to Black, Phelps, and Suarez. You're my golden ticket, man."

Brandon just nodded as if he'd predicted what Jake would say. "That's exactly why I hired your firm. Nobody in our class worked harder than you. And hey, you could be my golden ticket too. This transition goes smoothly, and my old man might finally retire and let me take over the company. If that happens, I'll make up new accounts just for you to audit."

"Deal." Jake dropped back in his chair, imagining the next few months. Straighten out the books, get a handle on Lowell's accounting needs, and head home with a fat new contract for a major media conglomerate. That had to be enough to win the partnership he'd been vying for since joining BPS straight out of college. It was the only future he'd ever envisioned for himself, and he wanted it so badly his bones ached with it.

Dave Chilton's voice crackled through the speaker near the office ceiling and intruded on his thoughts. "We got an email this morning, Mae," the man said over the final notes of the boppy rock song the morning show had been playing.

"Oh yeah?" Mabel's disembodied voice had Jake sitting up straight, the last of his partnership daydreams popping like a soap bubble.

Dave continued, "It's the question we most often get asked, which makes me wonder: why are people so interested in our relationship?"

"Oh, our relaaaaaaaationship," Mabel replied, the purr in her voice sliding along Jake's skin like the softest velvet.

"Mmmm. That woman has a *fine* radio voice," Brandon murmured.

"Shhh." Jake didn't want Brandon's voice intruding as he listened to the blonde he'd met on Wednesday.

Said blonde briskly replied, "You'd think that two people who spend as much time together as Dave and I do have some kind of wild history. But the boring truth is, Dave and I are friends who met in college. We're not married. We're not dating. We *never* dated—"

"I mean, have you seen Mae?" Dave's voice interrupted. "She's hella scary in that tall Valkyrie way. I was never attracted to her. *Yuck.*"

"Dave needs his eyes examined," Brandon muttered.

"Dude." Jake sent him an irritated glare and tilted his head toward the speaker where the deejays' back-and-forth spilled forth. Brandon widened his eyes and held up his hands in a silent apology.

"Yuck?" Mabel scoffed. "You were unattractive first! I wanted to *not* date you first! Folks, did you know that Dave dresses as a werewolf for Halloween every year just by wearing shorts and a tank top? Do you need the number of a good waxer, Wolfie?"

Dave bellowed out a Chewbacca roar, then said, "You're one to talk. Mae once sent a date to the ER with a rash when he got too close to that prickly 'stache of hers."

"My lady 'stache is *magnificent,*" she shot back, and Jake tilted his head to revisit his memory of their first meeting. No upper-lip hair, only a wide, expressive mouth and miles of tanned skin.

"What you listeners need to know," she said, "is that when Dave sweats, it's slightly radioactive. I once saw a droplet roll off Dave's nose and land on a spider. Friends, that spider then bit a passerby, who immediately shot webs out of his wrists and crawled up the side of a building."

Jake chuckled softly as Dave countered, "Good thing I have a lovely wife who doesn't mind my jokes—"

"—or his radioactive sweat—"

"—and Mae, while also lovely, hasn't found that special someone. That someone who won't mind that she doesn't know that Spider-Man's web shooters are mechanical, not biological."

"Nerrrrrd," she interjected, but Dave barreled on.

"So if you're interested in our gal here, send us an email with your bio, photo, and likely parole date."

Mabel gave a gusting sigh that made the hair on the back of Jake's neck stand at attention even though it was nothing more than a voice coming from a speaker. "My special someone's out there somewhere, and in my heart of hearts, I know he'll get sprung early for good behavior. Aaaand after the break, we'll run down the community events scheduled for this weekend, so stay tuned."

A Smashing Pumpkins song kicked up, and Brandon nodded to himself. "That girl is good. They're gonna make me so much money."

There was a conversation Jake should be interested in pursuing. It's why he was in Beaucoeur after all: to make this station profitable. Yet his brain refused to focus on the numbers.

That girl is single.

The thought materialized like the sharp clang of a bell. *Single.* Sure, it'd only taken listening to one show for him to develop an appreciation for her fast wit, but that was just part of his job here, right? He closed his eyes, pinched the bridge of his nose, and sucked in a breath, picturing that empty partner office on the fifty-sixth floor of his building, waiting for him to fill it. The image helped push thoughts of Mabel's voice from his mind, and he exhaled slowly, calm back in place.

"Everything okay?" Brandon was looking at him with curiosity.

"Yep." Of course. He was reliable, work-first Jake Carey. The same as always.

"So who'd you leave behind in Chicago?" Brandon

spoke as if Jake's thoughts were printed above his head. "Wife? Girlfriend? Boyfriend?"

Thumb, meet another tender spot.

"Not even a potted plant," he said flatly. "The job keeps me busy." Which was true, even if it wasn't the whole story.

Brandon just sighed. "God, you workaholics wear me out. At least I've got an ex pestering me about shared custody of the dog." He pinned Jake with his sharp blue eyes. "Is it worth it?"

Brandon's suddenly serious tone was a 180 from his normal flippancy, and Jake didn't even have to think about the answer. "For a partner's salary? Of course it's worth it."

Worth not pledging a fraternity in college so he could spend all his free time taking course overloads to graduate faster. Worth not investing time in his dating life, searching for relationships with the potential for more. Worth every skipped vacation, every weekend in the office, every family holiday where he'd paid for the meal but hadn't gotten there in time to eat it while it was hot.

Fuck, it *had* to be worth it.

"What a drag." The man across from him shook his head as he tucked his phone into his pocket. "In your next life, I recommend being born rich."

Jake huffed a laugh. How perfectly ridiculous and perfectly Brandon. "Sure. I'll get to work on that."

He might not have been born rich, but he'd busted his ass, and now he had a fat 401(k), a condo with a view of Lake Michigan, and enough in savings to allow him to sleep soundly at night. A BPS partnership would be the keystone in the life he'd been building from the moment he'd realized as a teenager that he wanted more for his worn-down mom and his hungry, big-eyed sister than constant money worries and a shitty walk-up apartment in one of Chicago's bleakest neighborhoods. And if that required spending a few months in an extended-stay hotel in downstate bumblefuck, so be it. Nothing was going to knock him off course.

"Knock, knock."

How? How did she summon goose bumps with only a handful of words? His shoulders tightened when the woman with the sharp brain and the supple voice invaded the office. He dragged his eyes to the doorway to confirm that the blonde he'd met on Wednesday still vibrated with the same bright energy he'd first glimpsed through the studio window.

Single. The word resurfaced with another clang, and his palms started to sweat. Thankfully Brandon took up the talking banner while Jake wrestled his accelerating heartbeat under control.

"Well, hello, Morning Show Mabel." Brandon leaned back in his chair and looked at her like a predatory cat. "What can we do for you?"

She stepped into the office, her eyes bouncing between Jake and Brandon.

"Do either of you have jumper cables in your car?" She gestured over her shoulder, presumably toward the parking lot. "The station van's dead again, and I usually use Kirby's cables to jump it, but he's gone, and Dave's at an appointment, and Skip's on the air, and all the ad reps are out of the office doing God knows what, so which of you is gonna be my hero?"

She ended her flood of words with a smile-grimace that Brandon met with a *grimace*-grimace. "I'm sorry, did you say the station van's dead *again*?"

Now Mabel was full-on grimacing too, and she slanted another gaze at Jake. God, she was pretty—and that was *before* she ran her tongue over her lower lip, flipped her hair over her shoulder, and resumed torturing him with her velvety voice.

"Yeah, uh, we need to jump it on occasion," she said apologetically. "Usually after it rains. Or snows. Or if it's unusually dewy. Did that... not come up before the sale?"

"It did not." Brandon leveled a cool gaze at her, and she bit her lip. "Hopefully the human capital performs better under damp conditions."

"Everything but my hair!" she chirped nervously, smoothing a hand over the golden mass hanging past her shoulders. "So, uh, cables?"

She glanced toward Jake again, and he forced himself to rally with a *smile*-smile. Brandon was being a dick, which meant it was up to him to be the decent person. The decent person who was laser focused on his job and his job only, like usual, no matter how much he enjoyed listening to her radio banter.

"I've got cables," he said, surreptitiously swiping his damp hands down the front of his pants.

"Well, thank God," she said with a breathy laugh. "Come white knight for me?"

No. Yes. *Fuck.*

"Yeah. Sort it out, Jakehammer," Brandon said with a wave of his hand, blissfully unaware of Jake's struggle to find his equilibrium. His eyes dropped to his phone yet again, and his thumbs started flying. "My ex apparently wants to start another text fight about whose weekend it is with the dog."

"Jakehammer?" Mabel tossed a playful look over her

shoulder as they exited the office and headed down the hall.

"I beg you, do not."

Her voice was as decadent off the air as it was on. Only three days working on the periphery of a radio station and he already understood why some people made this their career. The job-centric thought summoned the calm, professional competency he was known for in Chicago. Of course there, he was usually examining audits instead of searching for battery cables.

"Where's the van?" He stepped ahead to hold the door open for her, wincing at the blast of summertime heat.

"Around back." She pointed. "We always keep the spot next to it open in case it needs a jump."

She stopped short when they reached the far end of the parking lot and he hit the unlock button on his Jeep.

"This is *yours*?" she asked as she clambered into the passenger seat.

"Yes." He slid behind the wheel to find her eying the interior with unabashed interest. Although his Jeep was obviously a decade old, he kept it looking like he'd driven it off the lot that morning.

"Huh." Her finger traced the immaculate dashboard.

"What?" He fired up the engine and backed out of the spot, starting to suspect that his ride wasn't impressing her with any kind of professional anything.

"It just…" She flapped a hand toward his suit-covered chest. "It doesn't really fit your whole 'I earned a million dollars before breakfast and made three assistants cry' vibe. Don't you guys all drive, like, black Audis?"

"I've never seen the point of spending money on a luxury car," he said stiffly. Three of his coworkers did in fact drive black Audis, but the thought of spending money like that physically pained him. Far better to funnel it into rainy-day funds for his mom and Finn.

His mom and Finn. *That's* why he was here. He needed to push away any other considerations, including the woman next to him smelling like a fancy garden, to get his job done. *Work-mode Jake, activate.*

He circled the building and eased into the spot next to the van plastered with the Brick logo, then shucked his jacket, rolled up his sleeves, and grabbed the jumper cables. As he got to work hooking the clamps to the two batteries, Mabel's words refused to stop tumbling through his brain. Once she got the van's engine turned over, she joined him on the sunbaked asphalt where they stood in silence until he asked, "Is that really how I come off?"

Her eyes snapped up to his.

"Hmm?" She bundled her hair into her fist and lifted it off her neck. "Oh, the fancy-businessman-driving-an-old-Jeep thing?"

At his curt nod, she dropped her hair with a shrug, gesturing toward him. "Your suit looks like it cost more than your ride. I made assumptions."

"I've never once made an assistant cry. Wouldn't dream of it. That's a hard job." He kept his eyes on the motor of his Jeep. When he was fifteen, his mom had answered phones for a slimy insurance agent who sent her home in tears at least twice a week, so he'd picked up an after-school job bagging groceries. It added enough cushion to the household budget that she'd been able to search for a less stressful position. The day she quit the insurance job, the tears she'd cried had been happy ones and he'd figured out the best way he could contribute to the family.

"So, how are you liking the glamorous world of radio?"

The echo of Brandon's question jolted him back to the present. "Why does everybody keep asking me that? You guys sound like a cult."

She pressed her hands together as if in prayer and bobbed her head. "The cult of radio. You're in it now, bub."

"Clearly." He stepped forward to unhook the cables from the now-purring engine. "It's fine. It's a job. One that'll land me a partnership hopefully." Then he'd be back in Chicago, and she'd be here using that voice to stroke the eardrums of everyone within listening radius.

"I hope you get it soon then. You don't want to fall behind on your car payments." She patted his Jeep's bright green front quarter panel with a grin, and he bit back the urge to laugh.

"Careful. This Jeep is the longest relationship I've ever had."

"Ooooh." She caressed its panel again, then her phone pinged, and she fished it out of her pocket with a groan. "Shit, I've gotta go. I'm supposed to be doing a live remote at the Beaucoeur Public Library's north branch in forty." She clambered back into the van and cranked down the window. "Thanks for your help."

"You bet," he said. Then he shoved aside his detached professional competency for a second. "And hey, Mabel?"

She popped her head out the window, blue eyes round with curiosity. "Yeah?"

"Dave's right. Spidey's web shooters are definitely mechanical."

Her mouth dropped open for a split second before she

tossed her hair with a shout of laughter. "Another nerd! Oh, you're gonna fit in *fine* around here."

Then she slammed on a pair of sunglasses, reversed out of the spot, and roared away, leaving him staring after her on the boiling asphalt, the cables dangling from his hand and her laughter echoing in his head.

THREE

"Oh good, you're goofing off. That means you can help me out."

Mabel looked up from her phone and narrowed her eyes at Dave's wife in mock outrage. "That's it? No hello? No 'so good to see you, old friend'? Just 'you're lazy, please help me'?"

That earned her a smile from Ana Chilton. "Hello, old friend. So good to see you. Can I steal a moment of your very valuable time for a project that's kicking my ass?"

"Duh." Mabel levered herself off the greenroom couch with a grunt and shoved her phone in her pocket. "Whatcha need?"

"My husband, for one thing."

Mabel jerked her head toward the studio where Dave was conferring with Skip about which local artists to promote on New Music Wednesday next month. Ana walked over to the window and waved until he spotted her, and Dave unfurled such a delighted grin that Mabel had to swallow past a hard little ball of envy in her throat.

Not that she wanted Dave, of course. But had any man ever been that delighted to see *her* on the other side of a pane of glass?

No. That answer was a definite no.

"Hey, baby." Dave exited the studio to greet his wife with a kiss, squeezing the sturdy brunette close. "How'd I luck into a workday visit?"

"I'm here to shamelessly use your brain." She rested her hand on his cheek briefly, then tossed a look at Mabel over her shoulder. "That one too. She's clearly not busy."

"Hey!" Mabel protested. "I was staying abreast of current affairs so I'd be able to contribute on air tomorrow."

"She was on Twitter," Dave said.

Dammit. "*Anyway*," Mabel said, "what's up?"

Ana shrugged out of her blazer and dropped it on the back of the desk chair. "Work put me in charge of the questions for our women's shelter fundraiser in two weeks. I need to see if actual humans can answer the things I'm pulling together. And you two are close enough approximations to humans for me to test them out on."

Dave rubbed his hands together, competitive glee lighting his thin face. "Excellent. We'll crush it."

"This isn't a competition, darling. Nobody's winning anything today." Ana's voice held the saintly patience she'd perfected with their two toddlers.

"Okay," Mabel said, "but you'll also tell us how supersmart we are if we can answer them all, right?"

Ana rolled her eyes. "You'll have the gratitude of Beaucoeur's largest social service agency for helping us make trivia night a success."

"All right then." Dave grabbed the pages Ana held

out, his eyes moving across the words. "Pssht. Child's play."

He grabbed a pen from the desk and got to work jotting down answers while Ana leaned toward Mabel and said in an undertone, "So. The guys from Lowell Consolidated."

Well, that brought things back down to reality.

"Oh, um," Mabel began, "the guys have only been here for what, a week and a half? And Brandon promised no big changes—"

Dave looked up from the paper with a scoff. "Sure. They bought us, and now they'll let us do business as usual. Seems likely."

Her optimistic, everything-rolls-off-my-back-like-I'm-a-Slip-'N-Slide partner sounded so gloomy, and it killed her. "Hey, it'll be fine," Mabel told him. "Maybe Lowell'll pump a bunch of money into our show, pay for some billboards or something."

"Guys, no." Ana interrupted them. "Dave, quit listening for a sec. I want to talk to Mabel about their hotness. I bumped into them on the way in today, and they are just... so, so hot. No offense, dear."

She patted Dave's shoulder, and he shrugged and turned back to the questions. "Doesn't bother me if you objectify my new bosses."

"Excellent," she said, sighing dreamily. "Because Brandon's at, like, *peak* hotness."

"I don't think we should obj— Wait, *Brandon*?" Mabel twisted her face in confusion. "Jake's clearly the hotter one."

Ana screwed up her face right back. "I guess, if you prefer your men dark and handsome and terrifyingly square-jawed."

"Um, I thought everybody preferred their men dark and handsome and terrifyingly square-jawed." Mabel did anyway. She *definitely* did.

Ana just sniffed. "Some of us prefer more refined features."

"Oh, you poor thing. You enjoy refined male beauty, yet you ended up with this troll." She jerked a thumb toward Dave. "Do you make him wear a lucha libre mask around the house?"

Dave reached for Ana's hand and lifted it to his mouth for a kiss. "That lucha libre mask is a very important part of our lovemaking, what with my wife's Mexican heritage."

Ana yanked his hand away. "Oh my God, do not drag my heritage into your weird mask fetish."

"Are you calling my mask kink weird?"

"Eww, David! I was *kidding*!" Mabel hollered, slapping her hands over her ears. "Can one of you hit me over the head really hard so I forget the past sixty seconds?"

The Chiltons' evil laughter didn't stop until she wrestled the sample trivia questions away from Dave and grimly set to work answering the ones he'd left blank, but even with their combined efforts, a few questions remained stubbornly unanswered.

"I give up," she announced.

"I don't." Dave slid her a glance, then shouted toward the hallway. "Hey! Can I get a consult from our in-house accountant?"

"What are you doing?" she hissed, but her grinning partner just ignored her to address the man who materialized in the doorway.

"We're working on some trivia questions and could use help from an expert."

"Uh, sure." Jake Carey stepped warily into the deejay's natural habitat, eyes drifting over the yellowed station promo posters and pinned-up leis from a long-ago party tacked to the far wall before landing on her and then Dave. "As long as it's about banking reform, I should be helpful."

Mabel let loose with an embarrassingly loud guffaw, then clapped her hands over her mouth, leaving Dave to say smoothly, "Actually, it *is* about banking reform."

Jake glanced at his watch and then shot them a confident smile. "Okay. Hit me."

Still giggling a little at the absurd coincidence, Mabel read off the sheet, "Which 2002 law created the Public Company Accounting Oversight Board to cut down on fraud?"

"The Sarbanes-Oxley Act," Jake said immediately.

This time Ana was the one to burst into shocked laughter. "He's right!"

"Seriously? Who remembers Sarbanes-Oxley?" Mabel demanded.

"Accountants," Jake said drily. "Accountants remember Sarbanes-Oxley."

"Shoot." Ana stood and snagged her blazer. "I need to run. But I'll let the trivia committee know that we're on the right track for difficulty and range of topics. Thanks, all."

"I'll walk you out." Dave grabbed his wife's hand, and they strolled out of the room, leaving Mabel alone with Jake, who made no move to leave.

"What else you got?" he asked, leaning forward to look at the list.

Was that a little competitive streak coming out? Okay then. She looked down at the last of the unanswered questions on the sheet. "I don't suppose you know what pop artist recorded a song featuring the line 'She's like so whatever'?"

One corner of his mouth lifted into a smile as he reached for the paper. "Don't you guys do music for a living?"

Her eyes drifted down his arms, which were covered to the wrists by his shirt and suit coat. Pity. After he'd rolled up his sleeves to jump the van, she'd practically had an out-of-body experience ogling his exposed forearms. Accountant Jake Carey had *goooood* forearms.

"We do music, but Dave doesn't listen to pop and I'm drawing a blank." She garbled the words in her haste to get her mind onto a safer topic, one that didn't involve this man's muscles.

Jake pressed his thumb against his lips in thought, and her eyes followed the motion. Nice lips. Lucky, lucky thumb. "I do believe that's Avril Lavigne's 'Girlfriend.'"

As soon as he said it, her vapor-locked brain unstuck, and she yanked her eyes away from his mouth to hum the song quietly to herself. Yep, that lyric was in there.

"You're right," she said in wonder. "I was just schooled in music by an *accountant*."

He shrugged. "I have a younger sister. Also, 'Sk8er Boi's' a bop."

She burst into a startled laugh, and his chocolate-brown eyes met hers, lit with a spark she hadn't seen in him before. But when Dave walked back into the room, that warmth vanished, and she watched him turn back into corporate-accountant guy, the man with the gorgeous face and the holy-shit body covered in an expensive suit.

"I'd better get back to work. Glad I could help."

"Thanks," Mabel called after his retreating back, and

only someone who knew her well would pick up on her unusually husky tone. Unfortunately, Dave knew her better than anybody.

"Aren't you two adorable," he crooned. "Just don't get us fired this time, huh?"

His words hit her like a bucket of cold water, and her chin snapped back. "Jesus, Dave."

He winced. "Sorry. Too far?"

"Too fucking far." A dart of pain bloomed in her heart, and she crossed the room to stand in front of the bulletin board plastered with take-out menus and old concert fliers.

Dave followed her. "Hey, come on. It was a joke. You know I don't blame you."

"Why not? *I* blame me." She used her pinkie nail to straighten an ancient Pearl Jam poster on the wall, but when Dave stepped closer to her, his shoulder nudged it off-kilter again.

"You went out with a guy you were interested in. You didn't know he'd trash you to the station manager when you ended things."

She laughed bitterly. "The station manager who happened to be his father and who threatened a humiliatingly public firing if we didn't go quietly."

"So we went quietly, and now here we are." Dave gestured toward the greenroom.

"Yes, here we are," she agreed, taking in the broken-down couch, threadbare carpet, and sagging blow-up palm tree decorated with a string of snowflake lights. "Exiled from paradise—"

"Gainesville, Florida, wasn't exactly paradise."

"Well, it was definitely a larger market and closer to the beach."

"I still say we should've sued," he said darkly.

"Probably." The helpless anger swept over her again even though it had been almost five years since she'd dumped the wrong guy and opted not to pursue a no doubt soul-killing legal battle against him and his father.

"Are you really not happy here, Mae?" Dave straightened his glasses where they perched on his long nose, then studied her with concern. "Because I think Beaucoeur's been pretty good to us."

She hugged her arms to her chest. "Oh sure. Cool job, nice coworkers, devoted listeners. Your kids were born here, and I finally figured out all the light switches in my house. What more could we want?"

All true, but she still felt unsettled. Why was it so hard to admit to Dave that despite all the good in her life, she had a hole in the middle of her chest?

Fear. That was her problem. She could interact with fans all day long and rattle away on the air while thousands of people listened, but she was too scared to go looking for a relationship after the fallout from her last one close to half a decade ago. So she'd just learned to tune out the loneliness that always throbbed in her heart.

And then goddamn Superman had strolled into her station, hauled her up off a couch, and dialed up the volume on all that loneliness. But Jake was involved with the new owners, so he was an extra level of not-for-her. Of course, no way in hell was she going to tell Dave any of that. Since he was still looking at her in concern, she shot him a carefree grin. "It's all good. And at least we're not playing Celine Dion for a living."

As she expected, he gave an exaggerated shudder. "*Light rock.* Perish the thought." Then he turned serious again. "But you made heart-eye emojis at the accountant, which isn't something I see every day. Just... keep your mind open, okay? Who can say where you'll be when you meet the right person?"

Mabel nodded, not wanting to continue this discussion by pointing out that accountant Jake was the last person she should risk jumping back into the relationship pool with. No, she had every intention of tamping down the loneliness and throwing herself into work like she always did. No more heart-eye emojis, no matter how handsome the accountant in question might be.

FOUR

The clattering buzz of Jake's phone yanked him out of his numbers hypnosis, and he blinked at the time on the screen when he slid his thumb across it to answer. How was it after seven already?

"Hey, man. What's up?"

Everybody had a friend who preferred to call instead of text. For Jake, that was Milo Markowitz, college-buddy-turned-corporate-legal-counsel for a Chicago imports company.

"My dude! You up for dinner?"

Jake shook his head. "Seriously? I'm in Beaucoeur. I've been down here for almost a month." And he hadn't even made a dent in the station's fucked-up files or all of Brandon's special projects, which was why he was still hunkered down in his temporary office instead of enjoying the marginal comforts of his hotel.

"Huh. I could've sworn you said you'd be done by now."

Jake laughed grimly. "Not even close. I'm here until the media company's done with me. They've got me going through all kinds of shit I've never analyzed before. Audience shares, ratings numbers for their stations across the country, putting together how it all relates to ad revenue. It'll be a few more months at least."

Not that he was counting or anything. Beaucoeur was fine for a downstate city, but he'd run back to Chicago that same day if he got the call to come home. He'd just prefer to do it with a partner plaque on his office door.

Milo grumbled. "Well, now I have to find some willing woman to be my Friday-night dining partner."

"Riiiiight," Jake said. Milo, with his wildly curly hair and pretty-boy face, never had trouble finding a date. "I'm pretty sure you won't be eating the Purple Pig's chorizo alone tonight."

"No doubt," Milo said. "And if you're going to be gone from the mahogany halls of Black, Phelps, and Suarez for much longer, maybe I'll have to visit you. Bring a little culture to the sticks."

Jake wasn't sure what culture Milo claimed to possess other than an encyclopedic knowledge of baseball stats and a deep, abiding love of Greek food and beautiful women. Still, he'd welcome a visit from his buddy. "Sounds great. Pick your weekend."

Milo rang off with a vague promise of "soon," no doubt already thumbing through his mental Rolodex for an evening chorizo companion. Jake, meanwhile, had at least two more hours of work to do before he was comfortable knocking off for the night, and a tiny bit more coffee might help him cross the finish line. At this time of night, he was the only one in the station other than the Goth-y overnight deejay who drifted silently around the darkened hallways during her shift like the ghost girl from *The Ring*. She'd scared the shit out of him the first time he bumped into her after hours, and he peered cautiously down the hall to make sure he wasn't in danger of her sneaking up on him again tonight.

The coast was clear, so he made for the kitchen. Other than spooky Tracy, he enjoyed working at the station after dark, with nothing but the low hum of the broadcast from the wall speakers to disturb him. But once he reached the coffeepot, rows of phantom numbers obscured the water-stained surface of the machine, and he rubbed his eyes. In some ways, Beaucoeur was no different from Chicago. His office wasn't as swank, and his mattress wasn't as comfortable, but his days focusing on spreadsheets to the exclusion of the people around him were the same, as were his long hours, late-night caffeine intake, and rushed, solitary dinners before he fell into bed to do it all over again the next day.

"Can you make it pour with your mind?"

Mabel's amused faux whisper snapped him out of his trance, and his stomach clenched. "Yes. It's the first thing they teach us in business school." God, since when did he tell dad jokes? He was hopeless.

She brushed past him to reach for the carafe. "Well, at my college radio station, we only learned how to tap a keg, so let's handle this the old-fashioned way. May I?"

The fancy-garden scent of her hair mingled with the smell of coffee as she extended the pot toward him, and he held out his mug for her to top off. They'd fallen into this routine over the past several weeks. Exchanging pleasantries in the hall, which often stretched into short conversations that left him with a dry mouth and damp palms. Chatting over coffee as he floated up out of his body to watch with a mix of horror and amusement as he tripped over his own words.

It was fair to say that the lovely Mabel had him totally flustered.

"Are you telling me you can drink coffee this late and still function tomorrow?" she asked as she poured.

"Cast iron." Her eyes tracked his movements as he patted his stomach. At this point in the day, the coffee tasted like lukewarm hate, but he swallowed a mouthful anyway, in part to have something to do with his hands, which suddenly felt awkward at the ends of his arms. "What brings you by the station tonight?"

A date? Had she been on a date?

"Where else would I be on a Friday night?" She gestured around the kitchen with the pot before returning it to the machine. "Actually, I was almost all the way home from book club with a few girlfriends when I realized I'd forgotten something."

She spun in a swirl of blond hair and floaty skirts to rummage through the refrigerator as that fucking bell clanged in his head again. *Single.* She hadn't been on a date, and other than the nightside deejay, it was just the two of them alone in the station right now. His heart tripped at the idea as she wheeled back around with a yellow-and-white-striped box in her hand and reverence on her face.

When she lifted the lid with a flourish, he asked, "Cupcakes?"

"The *best* cupcakes," she said. "One of the ad reps brought them back from the Cakery, and I meant to grab them on my way out today."

"The best, huh?" The desserts reminded him of home, and he slid his phone from his pocket and pulled up his camera app. "Do you mind?"

"Not at all." She posed like a game show host, flashing

her pearly whites as she displayed the box and its contents.

Once he'd captured the shot, she set the box on the break room table and downed half a chocolate cupcake before he'd finished sending his text.

"Heaven!" she crooned around her mouthful. After she chewed and swallowed, she pointed. "Help yourself."

"You sure?" At her nod, he selected a plain vanilla cupcake from the assortment, leaving her the red velvet. She looked like the red-velvet type. "Thanks."

She leaned a hip against the table. "So you're an amateur cupcake photographer too?"

"Nope," he said as he peeled away the wrapper. "A friend's boyfriend just opened a bakery, and she'll want to see the downstate competition."

"Ooh, the big-city accountant has a friend with a bakery? Tell me more." She licked a smear of chocolate icing off her finger and looked at him expectantly.

"Josie's actually my sister's best friend," he said. "I sort of inherited her."

Another clang sounded in his brain. *Josie.* There'd been a time when he cared that Josie was single, just like he cared that Mabel was single.

The hand holding the cupcake fell to his side in recognition. How had he been so slow to recognize it? The nervous jokes, the sweaty hands, the pressure in his chest that was equal parts anticipation and fear. And this wasn't like with Josie after all. *This* was Asha Abebe all over again.

"Well?" Mabel pointed. "Are you gonna smash it or eat it?"

"S-sure. Sure." Mechanically, Jake lifted his hand and

took a bite, his heart hammering too hard for him to taste anything.

He'd spent three months with Asha in their accounting capstone study group senior year before he'd figured out that panic attacks weren't causing his anxiety to spike when he was around her; it was his attraction to her that was causing the kind of down-low tingles he'd never experienced before. After he'd sorted it all out—*hi, hello, I'm Jake, and I'm a demisexual*—he'd rushed in and fallen hard. Asha was the first woman he'd slept with, the first woman he'd *wanted* to sleep with, and he'd loved her enthusiastically and with his whole heart until the day two years later when she told him she'd accepted a job in Munich. She'd asked him to come, but how could he abandon his career, leave his mother and sister to fend for themselves? She made her decision without ever consulting him, and their relationship fell apart immediately.

He'd survived the pain of that loss, but it had left him wondering if Asha was his only shot at love. This though, with Mabel? He was experiencing the same riot of emotions, the same jangled nerves and hyperawareness. In fact, if anything, it was even more intense. After all, Asha hadn't had that *voice*.

"What did you think? Positively orgasmic, right?"

The word reverberated in the space between them—orgasmic, orgasmic, *orgasmic*—and pink marched across her face while he struggled to reorient himself in a room that seemed to spin around him as he focused on her mouth. Her kissable mouth.

His eyes snapped down to his hand, where all that remained was the empty cupcake wrapper. Her mouth, her voice, her words... Was it really happening again?

Was his world about to tilt on its axis again after seven years? Queasy excitement flooded his veins.

A relationship. He was thinking about a relationship with her. Mabel. The woman with honey in her voice.

Panic has entered the chat.

Then a miracle happened. "Oh my God!" Mabel dropped her face into her hands with a wail. "Forget I said that. Rewind! Rewind!"

Her palpable embarrassment chased away his own mounting anxiety. This bright, funny, confident woman was just as awkward as he was right now, and the realization allowed him to regain his footing. He cleared his throat and clenched his fist around the empty cupcake wrapper. "Tell you what—the next time I'm in Chicago, I'll swing by Have Your Cake and bring you some of Erik's cupcakes for a taste test. See which is more, ah, orgasmic."

A bleat of laughter erupted from her throat. Yes, the woman with a voice richer than the icing he'd just consumed laughed like a barnyard animal, and he liked her even more for it.

"Hey, what are you doing tomorrow night?" She rubbed her fingers against her skirt as the pink returned to her cheeks. Before he could respond, she said in a rush, "A group of us are going to that trivia night thing you helped out with. We're not competing, but it'll be fun just to hang out and watch. And all the drinks you buy help the local homeless shelter."

She smiled hopefully up at him, but the panic edged back in, and he was shaking his head even before she'd finished speaking. Wanting to spend time with Mabel, wanting to go out with her, *touch* her, all that ran counter to his work goals. Trivia was a no-go, for so very many reasons, yet somehow, when he met her bright eyes, his lips started to shape the word "sure."

Then, thank Christ, his phone dinged with a text from Susan Suarez asking for a numbers update on one of his projects. Saved by the motherfucking bell.

"Sorry." He gripped his phone and pushed out the excuse. "Saturdays are when I catch up on my email backlog, and it's even worse than usual since I've been gone from the Chicago office."

Disappointment flitted across her face, and he forced himself to ignore it.

"Sure. I get it." Her shoulders lifted and fell on a sigh, and then she picked up the box with the remaining cupcake. "Well, I'd better call it a night. See ya."

With a small nod, she spun and headed out the door, taking all the vitality from the room with her. Which was fine. His job was simple: keep his head down, keep his eyes on his spreadsheets, keep the partnership in his sights. This... this would pass. It *had* to pass, and his life would get back to normal again.

FIVE

Two more minutes. Two more minutes and she'd be out the door.

Mabel gathered the stack of ad copy she'd marked up and headed toward the main office, hoping to drop it on Brandon's desk while everybody was gone for lunch. Then it was home to shower and hope for a smoother day tomorrow.

When she stepped into the room, however, she was dismayed to discover it wasn't empty; Jake's handsome face was furrowed in concentration as he stared at his laptop and rhythmically drummed a pen against the desktop. For one cowardly moment, she considered backing out of the room so he wouldn't spot her; the embarrassment over him turning down her trivia invitation last week was still fresh. But she must've made a noise because his eyes flicked up from the screen and immediately back down. Then his pen-tapping slowed, and he dragged his eyes back up to her face again.

"Well, hello." His voice was warm with amusement, and the corners of his eyes crinkled.

"Hi," she said, pushing confidence she didn't feel into her voice. Despite radio being, well, *radio*, she normally put effort into her appearance at work. But this morning she'd woken in a panic to find that her phone was dead and she had twenty minutes before she was due on air. While her ego could normally absorb a day of roaming the WNCB halls greasy and unshowered, that was *before* the hottest guy she'd ever met had started working down the hall from her, all tall and good-smelling. She might not allow herself to date him, but that didn't mean she'd lost her vanity.

When his lips twitched in amusement, she groaned. "I know, I know. I'm a walking dumpster fire."

"Did I say anything?" He leaned back and crossed his arms over his chest, his mouth curling as he took in her limp ponytail, her makeup-free face, and worst of all, her sleeping ensemble.

"You didn't have to." She huffed her way across the room and dropped the stack of papers onto the corner of Brandon's desk, cursing herself for not shoving the damn things under the door and running. "I overslept. This is me in my natural state."

She'd burst into the studio with seconds to spare that morning in the shirt she'd slept in, a tiny pair of lime-green running shorts, and battered floral gardening clogs. At least she'd managed to scrounge a cleanish sports bra from a gym bag in her car to wiggle into at a stoplight.

"A Minnesotan, huh?"

She plucked at her threadbare Mankato East T-shirt, which featured a cartoonish drawing of her high school's cougar mascot.

"Oh, you betcha." She hadn't felt self-conscious sitting across from Dave all morning, but Jake's scrutiny made her want to squirm. Then again, was she really going to let a lack of mascara hold her back? She was tougher than that.

"I thought Minnesotans were a punctual people."

He flipped his laptop closed, and she took it as a sign that, not only was he not bothered by her dishevelment, but he was open to a longer conversation. Sacrificing a little vanity was a small price to satisfy her curiosity about this guy with the pricey haircut and the unpretentious vehicle, so she plopped into Brandon's chair. "We are, but when I ditched my accent, I was required to give up all my other Minnesotan ways. Goodbye, hotdish."

He snagged a clear plastic blender bottle off his desk and took a swig.

"Is that your lunch?"

He looked down at his hand, as if surprised to be holding something in it. "Yes. Why?"

She wrinkled her nose at the grayish mass inside. "Don't tell me you're one of those guys who doesn't stop for lunch and just powers down a protein shake so he can 'get right back to it.'" She adopted a macho tone for that last bit and laughed when he paused with the bottle halfway to his mouth. "Oooh, you are."

He finished the motion and took another swig, allowing her to eye the play of muscles rippling under his jacket. What she wouldn't give for a little of that Clark Kent X-ray vision right now to see what delights were hidden by the layers of fabric. No wonder his palm had been rough against hers when he'd helped her up from the couch during their first meeting. She'd bet all the loose change in her purse he'd earned those calluses in the gym.

She tilted her head playfully. "Don't you know that you're missing out on a whole world of restaurant lunch specials and inane coworker chitchat? Don't your fellow numbers people at wherever you work—"

"Black, Phelps, and Suarez."

So serious about his big fancy job. "Sure, them. Don't you ever grab lunch with Black? Or Phelps or Suarez?"

He leaned back in his chair, looking fractionally more relaxed than when she'd walked in. Good. He should take a little time for himself during the day. From what she'd been able to observe, his work hours were long, intense, and rarely interrupted except by maniacs forcing cupcakes on him.

"Ha. No. Black pretty much lives full time in France, and Phelps wouldn't be caught dead dining with us rabble. Susan Suarez took me to lunch on my first official day and then not again for the past nine years."

He took another drink, and she considered leaving him to his lunch. She should really slide right out that door and on home. But he seemed... lonely? Was she reading him right? He was alone in a strange city with only Brandon for company after all; if she were him, she might welcome some friendly conversation over the noon hour. She might be a grubby little urchin, but she was a good talker.

"So did you start there straight out of college?"

He swirled the contents of his bottle and raised his brows as if daring her to mock his lunch again. She let it go without comment. "Actually, I started interning there the summer before my sophomore year of college. So I've been with them in some capacity for twelve years." He must've seen the math on her face because he added, "That makes me thirty-one, if you're wondering."

More like *dirty*-one. Did he have any idea what it was doing to her as he swiped his thumb across his lower lip to catch an errant drop of shake? She cleared her throat and reminded herself of how quickly a bad work relationship could detonate in the middle of her life. This man's mouth was not worth the risk.

She forced a light tone. "Thirty-one? So ancient, whereas I'm a mere twenty-eight."

"A veritable baby." He saluted her with his bottle.

Even though he was forbidden office fruit, her perverse brain was apparently on a mission to drag more information out of him. "You went to school in Chicago?"

"University-of. And high-school-of before that."

"The fancy suburban kind?"

He drained the last of his shake and closed the spout on the lid with a snap. "Definitely not. The underfunded, lucky-to-have-enough-textbooks-for-each-kid kind."

His voice was matter-of-fact, and she struggled to imagine this shiny, healthy example of manhood growing up in a hardscrabble neighborhood. "Really?"

"Yeah, I did it all. Begging for scholarships, working every part-time job I could find, constantly worrying about helping Mom make rent so we didn't get booted from another apartment." He shrugged. "It was incentive to work hard. To not get distracted."

Something from their conversation that first week clicked into place. "To drive an old Jeep. To make partner," she said softly.

His eyes found hers. "I want my mom and my sister to have a safety net if they ever need it." His expression darkened. "They refuse to let me send them checks directly anymore, so everything I don't need for living expenses goes into three savings accounts: one for me, one for Mom, and one for Finn."

"Wow. Generous." She pulled her legs up and crossed

them underneath her. "My dad covers my Starbucks expenses when I'm home for a visit. Says it's all he has left after four years of out-of-state tuition."

Woof. Privilege, party of Mabel. Thankfully, Jake smiled at her upper-middle-class joke, which returned him to his previously relaxed expression.

"Hey, coffee expenses add up. You don't want your dad to go broke." Then he leaned back in his chair, and his tone shifted to confessional. "Anyway, it's almost more of a habit than anything else. Mom and Finn are both settled and happy, and if all goes well, this is my last assignment before I'm promoted to partner, and then I *really* won't have money concerns."

She tilted her head, searching his face for excitement at the prospect but seeing only grim determination. "Will that make *you* settled and happy?"

"It better," he said immediately. Then his brow creased. "I mean, of course it will. It's the only thing I've had in my sights for as long as I can remember."

He fell silent and stared down at his closed laptop, leaving her to sort through the Jake Carey pieces she'd uncovered: impoverished childhood, expensive suits, solitary lunches, utilitarian vehicle, laser focus on work. And did she dare add a hint of loneliness to that list? Did he also know what it was like to be busy and fulfilled at work while also feeling like you were missing something *important*?

"Who *are* you?" The question slipped out as she tried to fit all the pieces of him together.

"I'm Batman."

He growled it in a Christian Bale voice, and she replied without thinking. "Nope. Superman."

"Superman?"

Damn. She hadn't meant to say that out loud, but now she couldn't ignore his arched eyebrows. So she tossed her hair and brazened it out with her best smirk. "You just seem like the kind of guy who accidentally wears his underpants on the outside."

His lips twitched. "Not even once. Try again."

Oh hell. She'd already called cupcakes orgasmic and asked him to a social event that he couldn't have turned down faster. What did she have to lose? "When I saw you through the studio window for the first time, I... thought you looked like Superman."

A slow grin spread across his face, and he lifted his chin, giving her a delicious view of that sharp jawline. "It's the hair, isn't it? Dark-haired guys always get the Clark Kent comparison."

She sighed, resigned to spilling her whole tawdry thought process. "It's the hair. It's the jaw. It's the shoulders." She waved her hand from the top of his head down his torso. "You've got the whole superhero package."

His grin widened, and he rubbed his chin in a show of deep thought. "Superhero, huh? I don't know about that. It's probably only a *little* above average."

Mabel looked at him blankly, then mentally reviewed what she'd said.

Oh God. *Package.* She slapped a hand over her mouth with a giggle. "What are you, twelve?"

"Guys are gonna guy." He shrugged. "Sorry. I'm sure you're used to a more sophisticated level of conversation on a date."

The word *date* did something funny to her nether regions. What kind of woman did Jake spend his free time with? Whomever she was, Mabel would bet she'd never schlep to work in beat-to-hell gardening clogs. As she was picturing what kind of posh creature he'd probably escort around Chicago, he rolled his empty shake bottle between his palms, smile gone.

"Not that this is a date, of course," he said gruffly.

"Of course not. I don't date people I work with," she said automatically, grateful for the reminder. He was so easy to talk to that she could almost forget everything, including her hands-off rules and the fact that she was sporting last night's bedhead.

When he looked at her curiously, she followed his lead and shared more than she normally would with someone who wasn't Dave. "Actually, I don't date, period." She pressed her lips together and considered how much she should share. "Bad experience at my last job. It's... hard sometimes for women in the public eye."

His face softened for a split second before he saluted her with the bottle. "Here's to not dating. I don't take the time for it either." The statement was said matter-of-factly, with no more emotion than he might say "It's supposed to rain today" or "Curling's my favorite sport," and she felt a burst of pity for the singles of Chicago at being denied Jake's devastating smile lit by candles across a white tablecloth at a fancy restaurant.

"Ah, that explains why you picked such a disappointing restaurant for lunch." She gestured around the low-ceilinged room, and he laughed.

"True. And the dress code is *so* lax."

The thrill she experienced at drawing a joke from him had her leaping to her feet to continue their playful sparring.

"What, does this not do it for you?" She put her hands on her hips and spun to give him the full 360-degree view of an outfit that she wouldn't even wear to the gym on a day when the air-conditioning was broken and she was guaranteed not to run into anybody she knew. When she rotated back to face him, his face was alive with laughter, his expression... interested. And *that's* when she became aware of just how short her shorts really were and how clearly she could see the outline of her hot-pink sports bra through the worn cotton of her shirt. His eyes were slow to lift from her legs, and when they did, she held his gaze with her own, practically begging him to explain why he made her want to break her own rules.

And then Brandon came crashing through the door.

"Ah, Mabel. Hello." He stopped dead when he got a look at her. "Wow, you're a mess. No offense."

That derailed her buoyant mood.

"Well, gee, why would I take offense at that?" She folded her arms over her chest, all traces of her playful confidence draining away.

Jake, who'd turned his attention back to his laptop when Brandon walked through the door, didn't bother looking up. "Pretty bold criticism from a guy with a coffee stain on his tie."

Brandon looked down at the blotch on his burgundy-striped silk and gave a cry of distress.

But Jake wasn't done. "Not that it matters. Mabel looks beautiful no matter what she's wearing."

He looked up and gave her a tiny, private smile that made her breath catch in her throat. How unfair to say the perfect thing and then look at her like *that* while Brandon was in the room with them.

Wait, what was she doing? *He. Was. Off. Limits.* She had to get out of there before she forgot that and blew up her work life yet again. She couldn't risk that for herself, and she definitely couldn't risk it for Dave and Ana.

Time to go. Way past time to go.

"I marked up that ad copy like you asked," she told Brandon stiffly. "If you want anything different, let me know." She backed toward the door, not wanting to give him the same twirling fashion show she'd given Jake. "Okay, uh, I'll see you guys tomorrow."

She slid out without waiting to see if Jake looked up from his work again to acknowledge her departure.

SIX

"Is Brandon around?"

Jake looked up from his screen, blinking a bit as his eyes adjusted to take in Mabel's head poking around the doorframe. "Nope. He's in Detroit all week."

"Excellent. Got a second?"

No. Absolutely not. He was swamped, and the last time they'd talked, she'd somehow extracted truths about his life that he never talked about—*plus* he'd made a dick joke, a lame one, to the funniest woman he'd ever met, and now all he could think about were her long, tan legs in those shorts from the day before. Smart, funny, pretty? He'd recognized that on day one. Sexy? Sexual? Someone he was attracted to? Those feelings were rapidly climbing the charts, to use a metaphor she might appreciate. And there was no denying the bolt of pleasure he experienced to know that, unlike last time she'd come to the office, this time she was here for *him* instead of being on an errand for Brandon.

Don't overthink this, Carey. He waved her in, and she slipped inside and shut the door behind her.

"When I crashed your lunch yesterday, you made it clear that you're not usually a stop-for-lunch guy"—she looked pointedly at the day's shake poking out of his bag —"so I brought you a sandwich."

She held out a paper bag and said coaxingly, "Roast beef. Lots of protein. Something best enjoyed with both hands."

Surprise at her gesture kept him from reaching for it right away. Nobody had ever brought him lunch unprompted. But she must've misinterpreted his expression as displeasure because she rushed to add, "It's cool if you're busy. And you don't have to eat it or anything. I can always give it to Dave the human garbage disposal."

Let her give his two-handed protein sandwich to Dave? No way.

"Thank you. That's so thoughtful." If he wanted to, he could wolf this down just as quickly as his usual protein shake and be back to working on the stack of reports for Brandon, no problem. But he found himself pointing to the chair at the other desk. "Join me?"

She hesitated, indecision on her face. "I mean, we're at work," she said. "It's just coworkers having lunch, right?"

Interesting. Did she feel the need to justify spending time with him the way he did her? And were they actually coworkers if she worked for the station and he worked for BPS? He didn't think so but didn't want to chase her away by debating the point, so he just nodded.

Her brow smoothed, and she grinned. "Okay then. I'll go grab my salad."

That day marked the first in a string of lunches with Mabel that left Jake with a feeling of bone-deep contentment he hadn't experienced in... well, ever. For the first time in his professional life, he didn't hesitate to put aside his work to enjoy some company in the middle of the day. Sure, the station's financial records were still the most disorganized clusterfuck he'd ever seen, Brandon kept throwing new projects his way that added to his never-ending workload, he was struggling to juggle his existing Chicago-based clients from a distance, and every night he fell asleep on scratchy sheets that smelled faintly of bleach in a hotel room with drapes that never quite closed enough to block out the streetlights. But he was also spending an hour every day with a woman who made him laugh, whose syrupy voice made him shiver, and it felt like wading into a warm ocean after years of frigid self-denial on the shore.

On a rainy Thursday afternoon in early September, Brandon was occupying his desk over the noon hour when Mabel strolled into the office, a first since Jake had started sharing lunch with her. Dave had joined them a few times, and occasionally so did Skip, but so far they'd dodged the Brandon bullet.

Today, however, instead of vanishing at the stroke of noon, Brandon shocked them both by asking, "Mind if I join your little lunch club?"

Fuck yes, Jake minded. This was his Mabel time. But that was clearly not an acceptable response, so he slanted a glance at the blonde in the doorway, who smiled weakly and said, "Um, sure?"

When Brandon turned his attention to his phone, Mabel shot Jake one of those comically exaggerated grimaces that he saw her and Dave exchanging often, and an ember sparked to life in his chest at the realization that he'd become the recipient of one of those conspiratorial looks.

Once they were all settled at the desks, Brandon surprised them both by providing nonstop entertaining stories about Lowell's other stations while they ate.

"No way," Mabel gasped, setting down her turkey wrap. "They did not have a live alligator mascot."

"Hand to God," Brandon said placidly, smoothly selecting a California roll with his chopsticks. "I made them relocate it to a gator preserve as a condition of the purchase. Alabama's wild, man."

"And here I thought our nonstarting van would be a deal breaker." Mabel giggled.

"Child's play," Brandon said. "Have I ever told you about our Idaho station? Talk about crazy."

"Idaho," Jake said skeptically.

"More like Ida-*whoa*." He grinned and popped more sushi into his mouth as Jake and Mabel groaned over the painful pun.

After Brandon polished off his bento box, he stood and gave them a jaunty salute. "All right, plebes, I've got a round of golf with the mayor." He glanced at the window where rain spattered against the glass. "Or maybe just a round of drinks at the clubhouse. Anyway, thanks for letting me crash today."

After his exit, Mabel cocked her head toward the door. "I had no idea he was funny."

Jake balled up his sandwich wrapper. "He keeps it under wraps most of the time. As I recall, Lowell Senior doesn't appreciate much levity from his son."

"Poor guy."

She held out her paper bag, and Jake tossed the remains of his lunch into it, then took the whole bag from her and chucked it into the garbage. "Yeah, I don't know if

I'd go that far. I doubt he's crying himself to sleep on his monogrammed pillowcase every night."

Mabel's pink lips formed a delighted O. "He does *not*."

"Cry? I can't confirm or deny. But he definitely had his initials embroidered on his bedding when we were roommates freshman year."

The revelation had Mabel doubling at the waist in laughter. "Noooooo!" she howled.

"Don't you dare tell him I told you," Jake said as she shook with mirth. "That strikes me as something he doesn't want his minions to know."

"Oh my God, amazing." She straightened to wipe tears from her eyes, and as she moved, an angry red scrape on the inside of her wrist caught his eye.

He moved to look closer. "Did you lose a fight with Dave?"

"What?" She twisted her arm to examine it herself. "Oh this. No, I lost a fight with the greenroom couch. A nail worked loose in the frame again."

She pulled her sleeve back down, but the long scratch still filled his vision, bothering him in a way that he wasn't able to articulate. Then he was bothered that it bothered him in the first place.

Life was so much simpler when he stuck to work.

Mabel, though, seemed unburdened by any tangential thoughts. She grabbed her phone, shot him a broad smile, and chirped, "Well, I need to record some new ads, so I should bail."

"Okay," he said. Then a horrifying scrap of truth came spilling from his lips. "You make me wish I had a healthier work-life balance, woman."

She froze in the doorway. "Oh yeah? Well, you make

me wish..." Her voice trailed off, and though every part of Jake was on alert for how she'd finish that sentence, she disappointed him, lifting one shoulder with a small smile. "You make me wish I didn't have commercials to produce this afternoon." And with that she was gone.

In truth, his work-life balance right now was healthier than it had ever been. He could attribute it to the slower pace of life in Beaucoeur, but the two months he'd already spent at the station was only part of the equation. The other part—a big, big part—was Mabel herself. In Chicago, work kept him so busy that he rarely got to know anyone well enough to build the emotional connection he needed to pursue a sexual relationship. Here though, he had the luxury of time to spend with Mabel, the woman who made him laugh, who made him tongue-tied. The woman who made him feel things he hadn't felt in years. *Years.* His excitement over that potential almost made him dizzy if he thought about it long enough.

Still, he had a job to do and a partnership to chase, so he pushed the upheaval of his thoughts aside and returned to his numbers. But no matter how diligently he applied himself over the next hour, the rows refused to cooperate. His mind kept wandering back to Mabel. Why couldn't he let their last exchange go?

After a frustrating two hours, made even more frustrating when Brandon returned to conduct a loud phone call with the home office from the desk next to his, he realized what was pecking away at his brain: the station furniture. He'd grown up in a house with a couch that would tear a hole in every pair of pants you owned if you weren't careful to avoid the spring poking out of the cushion. No amount of duct tape had been able to contain it, and his mom couldn't afford to replace it. He'd been devastated at sixteen when he'd sat down on it without thinking and ruined his only decent pair of jeans, the ones he'd saved up forever to buy. That scratch on Mabel's arm had brought back all the helpless anger over his situation that he'd felt growing up.

The station furniture might check a childhood-trauma box for him, but a decade and a half later, he was in a position to do something about it. He looked across his desk to Brandon, who was tapping away at his laptop on... honestly, Jake had no idea what occupied Brandon's days.

"Mind if I take the Lowell credit card out for a spin?" he asked. "Your new employees are in dire need of decent furniture in that biohazard they call a greenroom."

Brandon's brows arched, but he fished his wallet out of his back pocket without hesitation and tossed a shiny black card on the desk next to Jake's coffee. "You really are a full-service accountant. Knock yourself out."

"Thanks." Jake pocketed the card, glad Brandon hadn't pressed him on the issue. He wasn't ashamed of how he'd grown up, but he didn't particularly enjoy discussing it either.

He had a corporate card and *carte blanche*. The most efficient option was to pick a few things out online and get them ordered. But he wasn't able to focus on his laptop screen, so he pushed it aside and set out to find Mabel. If he was doing this, he might as well go all the way.

He walked down the hall to stand outside the secondary recording booth, where he tucked his hands into his pockets and enjoyed the show as Mabel spoke animatedly into a microphone. Her expressive face and broad gestures pulled a smile from him, and she grinned back when she caught sight of him on the other side of the glass. As soon as she flipped a switch and the RECORDING sign in the hallway snapped off, he crooked a finger to summon her into the hallway. She wrinkled her nose at him in adorable confusion but slid the big headphones off and stepped through the heavy door.

"What's up?"

"Come furniture shopping with me tomorrow."

She looked at him like he'd suggested they rob a bank. *"Furniture shopping?"*

"Yes. Furniture shopping. For the greenroom." It *was* an odd request, but for reasons he'd rather not explore, he wanted to buy the damn stuff in person, and he wanted her with him when he did it.

"Why me?"

Because I like you the best. And he didn't just mean out of all the deejays; he meant out of all of them. Everyone he'd met in Beaucoeur. Maybe everyone he knew in Chicago, even. But that was a bit too fucking honest, so he deflected. "Because I didn't want to pick out furniture with Dave."

That satisfied her. "Smart. He's got lousy taste." Then she narrowed her eyes and put her hands on her hips. "Wait, what's wrong with the furniture we have?"

"I won't abide a couch that draws blood," he said, eyes falling to her wrist. And this time he gave in to temptation and touched her, grasping her wrist with one hand and brushing the fingers of his other hand along the skin next to the scratch on her arm.

Instant electricity. It leaped from her skin to his, and his nerves jangled to life as if they'd been jump-started with the cables he'd used on the station van that first week. His breath caught in his lungs as everything about Mabel was suddenly magnified by a thousand. The sweet scent of her skin, the golden glint of her hair, the heat of her arm in his hand. He felt the snap of the molecules around them surging to life and pulling at him, whispering that this woman who'd so enchanted him with her voice and her mind was also the person he wanted to kiss. Undress. Claim.

Unaware that a whole new galaxy was unfurling in his mind, Mabel nibbled on one corner of her lip before slanting a smile at him. "Let's do it. You're in good hands with me."

His fingers involuntarily tightened at the implications, and he abruptly broke contact.

"After your show tomorrow. Be ready." He clipped off his words and spun away from her, striding back to his office to give himself some distance. He powered down his laptop and shrugged into his suit jacket, desperate to get out of the building and wrestle his body under control. But there was Brandon, lying in wait.

"Hey, before you go, I reviewed the analysis you did on revenue during the different on-air shifts, and I based this proposed schedule revision around it. What do you think?"

Brandon slid a colorful grid across the table, but Jake shook his head. "I'm a numbers guy, not a radio guy. I have zero useful input on your programming decisions."

Brandon tapped a finger on the paper. "Yeah, but you've been looking at trends for the different shows and know where the weak spots are. Just take a quick look."

He impatiently scanned the sheet. What he saw at first made no sense, and then Brandon's plan clicked into place and drove every last distracting sexual thought from his mind. "You're separating them."

Brandon slouched lazily in his chair. "I am."

"Are you sure you want to do that?" Jake frowned down at the paper. "Mabel and Dave seem like a pretty great team."

"Not sure about anything yet, but consider the numbers, Jakehammer." Brandon offered him a patient smile.

His analytical mind whirred into motion, and he nodded slowly, working it out. "They're the most popular show by far. You think that splitting them up and moving Mabel to afternoon drive will keep the good ratings going all day."

Brandon shot a pair of finger guns at him that set Jake's teeth on edge. "That's the hope. I want all my plans in place before I announce any changes, but right now it seems like the best solution to shake things up."

Jake kept staring at the grid. "Are you sure about this? They seem stronger as a duo."

Brandon flicked his fingers, brushing away Jake's words. "Your only job here is to tell me if I stop making money. And I don't want any unnecessary drama before the announcement, so not a word to anyone."

Jake clenched his jaw. "I'm aware of my professional confidentiality requirements, thanks." *Fucker.* He let the paper slip between his fingers to land on the desk in front of him. "I'm out. See you tomorrow."

Before he left the building though, Jake was drawn back to the recording studio, where he discovered that Dave had joined Mabel in the booth. He watched through the glass as they spoke into the mics, making goofy faces and feeding off each other's energy. A whisper of envy curled through his brain. Sure, he had friends in Chicago. Work friends and friends from school. His sister and her social circle. Milo. But Mabel and Dave had the most natural partnership he'd ever seen.

Then his envy vanished in a wave of unease. Brandon wanted to pull these two apart? These good partners *and* good friends? The thought was monstrous. His chest clenched, and he spun away from the window. He needed to get a grip on himself before their outing tomorrow.

SEVEN

This was a bad idea. She should put up a token effort to get out of it.

"Honestly," she said when Jake arrived in the green-room to collect her, "the furniture's fine. There's no need—"

He shot her a censorious look and, without breaking eye contact, walked up to the desk and applied the lightest bit of pressure to the front corner. It tilted crazily, and all the contents started to slide toward the edge. "Fine, you say?"

"Ugh, point taken." She snatched up a pen that rolled across the surface on the way to the floor. "Let's do it."

Not like this was a punishment. She was playing hooky on a sunny Friday in September, and she was doing it with a gorgeous guy. A gorgeous, off-limits guy, but still.

"Want me to drive?" She jangled her keys at him, but he shook his head.

"Driving helps me learn the city better, but I'll take a furniture store recommendation if you've got one."

"Sure," she said, snapping her seat belt on as the Jeep

roared to life. Skip's voice poured from the radio, introducing the next set of Brick music, and she turned to him with a grin. "Aww, you listen to the station in your car?"

He slid on a pair of sunglasses, hiding his eyes from her. "Of course. What did you expect?"

She rooted through her mess of a bag in search of her own shades. "I don't know, NPR maybe? Or, like, aggressive jazz?"

"Jazz? You think I'm a jazz guy?"

He sounded so genuinely offended that she reconsidered her flippant assessment. "It just goes with your fancy suits and super-serious numbers job."

"Wow," he said. "Jazz and suits and numbers. You make me sound like a real Renaissance man."

She flicked her eyes sideways and played with fire. "I'm sure it's a turn-on for the ladies." She heard the flirtiness in her tone and couldn't bring herself to regret it despite it being a clear violation of her rules.

"Mmm, yes," he said drily. "As we've discussed, chicks dig my twelve-hour workdays and single-minded pursuit of a partnership at my firm."

He didn't elaborate further, and because her wrist still burned with the memory of his fingers pressing into her skin the day before, she kept pushing when she should be changing the subject. "Okay, but what about high school? I know you don't date much now, but I bet the prom queen/cheerleader set loved you back then."

His laugh didn't hold much humor. "That's a *big* no."

She gave a theatrical gasp and clutched her hands to her chest. "Were the girls at your high school all tragically robbed of the power of sight?"

"Not really their fault." His eyes didn't stray from the road. "I didn't try very hard with any of them, and I was busy with my after-school jobs." He flicked his gaze over to her. "Also, it took a while for me to grow into my nose."

Mabel studied it, straight and high-bridged. "It's a good nose."

"Well, *now*," he said with a faint smile.

"That reminds me so much of Dave." She looked away from his profile to stare at the road. Time to pull it back in. This was a work outing, and ogling the driver could only lead to trouble. "He was scrawny when we met in college. I swear, I could've beaten him up and taken his lunch money when we got paired up on a project in our first radio class."

That pulled a bigger smile from him. He glanced over at her while they waited at a stoplight, but she only saw her own reflection in the mirrored lenses of his aviators.

After a moment, he asked abruptly, "Have you ever done the radio thing without Dave?"

"You mean like when he's sick?"

"No, I mean have you ever had a show on your own, full time?"

Mabel settled back in her seat, always glad to chat about her partnership with Dave. "Never. We were lucky and landed a great Florida market shortly after gradua-tion, then moved here after that job... came to an end."

Please don't ask why, please don't ask why, please don't ask why.

But he merely *hmm*ed in response and dropped the subject, and she forced herself to remember every humili-ating detail of her departure from the Florida station. It was getting far too easy to let herself imagine that it could be different with Jake.

When he put the Jeep in park outside the sprawling furniture warehouse, she fished a baseball cap out of her purse, pulled her hair into a ponytail, and settled the hat low on her brow.

"Are we undercover today?" he whispered, exaggeratedly looking left and right.

She laughed, glad that animated Jake had decided to rejoin their conversation.

"I sometimes try to keep a low profile in public," she confessed.

He peered over the rim of his sunglasses. "Right, because you're kind of a big deal."

"No!" Mabel felt her cheeks warm. "It's just that occasionally a fan notices me and posts about it on social media. I've had bad experiences with rumors when I'm with a guy, so—"

"Say no more, rock star. We'll go incognito," Jake said easily. "Let's do this."

But he didn't make a move to leave the Jeep, and neither did she. The late summer heat intensified as Jake's smell, that good, clean male smell, surrounded her. Without meaning to, she leaned toward him, wondering if she'd feel that jolt again if she touched his skin.

She inched closer to the hand resting on his gearshift, imagining what would happen if she slid her pinky against his. But at the last moment, he cleared his throat and popped his door open.

"So are we going to spend some money that doesn't belong to us or what?"

The intimate mood broken, she swallowed and said brightly, "Absolutely. Lead the way."

Thank God one of them was remembering to keep it professional.

Inside the store, Jake headed straight for the couches. "I'm thinking leather, something you filthy deejays with your long hippie hair and your disgusting coffee can't ruin."

"Hey, we all get our mandatory hose-downs once a week, whether we need it or not," she said, matching his nonserious tone.

He laughed, then pointed at a plush blue sofa. "Sit. I want to make sure this one won't leave a mark on your otherwise flawless skin."

The breath whooshed from her lungs, and she plopped gracelessly on the cushions. The one-two punch of Jake's commanding tone and the implication that he thought her skin was flawless—that he'd thought about her skin at all—was doing things to her insides.

"Nah, it's too cushiony. Let's try the next one," he said, reaching down and hauling her up. He didn't even grunt as he did it, which she took as a compliment, and the touch of his hand set off the jangle of nerves she was coming to expect when they made skin-to-skin contact. It made focusing on anything but him a chore.

Good thing he was apparently unruffled by it all and there to herd her through the store inventory. After a few tries, they decided on a black leather couch with just the right amount of firmness, and then they moved on to recliners because, as Jake explained, "Every room needs one."

She snorted. "You're such a *guy*."

He extended his arms to his sides in an invitation for her to examine his decidedly masculine figure. "Thank you for noticing."

Good God, had she. All afternoon, the only thing she could think about were those broad shoulders in that slim-cut button-down. She blinked a few times and pivoted sharply toward the recliner section. "Then you definitely need to make this decision." She pushed him toward the row of identical-looking chairs and ignored her sudden desire to suck on his bottom lip.

This attraction was a problem. He was a problem. But she was in no hurry to cut their shopping trip short, especially when, with each model he tried, he shed a bit of the reserve he carried with him. By the time he made his final recliner selection, he was grinning like a kid.

"On to desks," he said. "That one in the greenroom is a menace."

When they reached the office section, he made her sit at each one and pretend to type so he could "assess the aesthetics."

"Happy?" she asked when they'd settled on a finalist.

"Not quite. Hop up."

She looked at him in confusion, so he put his hands on her waist and swung her up onto the desktop, then seated himself next to her.

"Seriously?" Her voice was breathy, and her heart thundered at the proprietary way he'd put his hands on her body.

"What?" He looked at her with wide-eyed innocence, his shoulder pressing against hers. "It might need to support two people on occasion."

She was so close—*so close*—to asking if he was implying what she thought he was implying, but he'd already stood up to arrange delivery details with the saleswoman.

"They guaranteed delivery within two weeks," he said as they walked back to his Jeep. "And the delivery guys promised they'd take the old couch straight to the dump so no other deejays will be harmed by the biohazards living between the cushions."

"Funny, funny guy," Mabel replied, her mind spinning with excuses to extend this shopping trip a bit longer. Her own rules didn't allow her to date Jake, but at the same time, she wasn't ready to end this outside-the-office contact. If she could just prolong the afternoon, she'd get to spend a little more stolen time with him without making her question whether those no-dating rules were helping her or holding her back. Because right now all she wanted to do was take those rules and set them the hell on fire.

She bit her lip and took the plunge. "Hey, you wanna use Brandon's card to buy us some lunch?"

He didn't answer right away, and Mabel started to worry that she was having a better time than he was until he looked over at her with a slow smile. "Brandon *absolutely* needs to buy us lunch." He fired up the car. "Point me to your favorite spot."

"Rule breaker!" she exclaimed, heart beating faster. "I was wrong. The Jeep might suit you after all."

EIGHT

"You've been holding out on me."

Mabel grinned up at him. "What, that human beings occasionally eat outside during the work week?"

"Yep. Exactly."

They shuffled forward a step as the line inched closer to the kabob vendor.

"Frankly, it's inexcusable. All this time I've been in Beaucoeur, and you've never once dragged me here." He gestured to the lines snaking across the sidewalks outside the county courthouse where a half dozen food carts offered various culinary delights to be devoured alfresco on the public square.

"Honestly, I was worried you'd burst into flames if I exposed you to direct sunlight." She looked at him over the rim of her sunglasses, and their eye contact threatened to stretch past an acceptable length of time until she blinked and looked forward with a playful toss of her hair. "You know, like a gremlin."

"It's a risk you take with accountants." In truth, he did feel a little like he might burst into flames, but it wasn't from the late-September sun beating down on his head and roasting him inside his suit. It was from the nearness of her body to his as they crept closer to the front of the line. With Brandon's plans weighing on him, he'd tried to keep a wall between them when they'd set off that morning, but the sheer enjoyment of time spent with her pushed those concerns to a corner of his mind almost immediately, leaving his keen physical awareness of her front and center.

He already knew she was smart. He already knew she was funny. And now he knew just how much he wanted her. And that was a hell of a thing to grapple with in the midst of scores of hungry Beaucoeurians. So naturally he looked for an opportunity to touch her.

"You're missing part of your disguise," he said. She'd ditched her hat, and he tugged a lock of her hair. As an excuse for physical contact went, it was flimsy, but it was all he had. And damn, her hair was soft between his fingers.

She straightened her Rolling Stones tank top and pointed one gold-sandal-clad foot with a grin. "The hat didn't match the ensemble." She took a step forward, leaving him free to glare at the dude walking past who couldn't keep his eyes off her bare legs under her denim skirt.

"People might recognize you and get the wrong idea about us," he said when he caught up with her in line.

"Please, have you seen you?" Her teeth flashed white against her tan skin as she smiled wolfishly. "I *wish* somebody would think we're dating."

The smell of spicy meat faded into the background, and he forgot to be annoyed with the fidgety guy behind him as her words ping-ponged around his brain. She'd made it clear weeks ago that she didn't date—some kind of bad experience, and a public one at that. So she had to be joking around. But God, imagine if she wasn't. Imagine if he could return the compliment, tell her that her hair was sunshine and her eyes were robin's eggs and her lips were the softest temptations he'd ever seen. Imagine if he kissed her.

Oh fuck, imagine if he kissed her.

The line shifted again, and he swallowed back the need pounding through him to give the stout, mustachioed man behind the cart his order. Once his hands were full of kabob and soda, it was easier to be his usual friendly self again. Mabel guided them to an unoccupied bench at one corner of the grassy square, where they proceeded to devour their food and discuss whether the original cast of *Barbarian Time Brigands* was superior or if that honor belonged to the cast of the reboot. As their debate escalated, pressure built in Jake's chest and expanded until breathing almost became painful.

Happiness. It was happiness swelling under his rib cage and putting pressure on his lungs. He was many things in his life: reliable employee, devoted son, overprotective brother, loyal friend. But happy? That wasn't part of his résumé. Yet here he was on a weekday afternoon, sitting in an outdoor plaza that offered a glimpse of the Illinois River. He'd ditched his coat and loosened his tie, and Mabel was pressed against his side, beaming up at him as she spoke. He couldn't think of a time when he'd felt more pure contentment with exactly where he was in life.

He crumpled up his wrapper and wiped his greasy fingers on a too-small napkin, determined to chase this unusual feeling. "So tell me, local citizen. Why is your town called *Beaucoeur?*"

The twitch of her lips gave him pause.

"What's so funny?"

"Oh my God, your accent!" she laughed. "*Somebody* took French…"

He tipped his head in acknowledgment. "I thought it would impress girls." A pause. "It didn't."

Mabel shook her head. "Well, we've already established that the girls in your high school didn't know what they were missing. But to answer your question, we actually pronounce it 'Boe Core' around here. It's named for the French fort-slash-trading post established along the river here in the 1600s."

"'Beautiful heart,'" he translated. "That's nice." His accountant's brain wasn't often seized by the poetry of words.

Mabel hummed an agreement, then tipped her face up to the sun. "I love being outside this time of year, even when it's hot. It's the end of September, which is practically October, which is basically the dead of winter, so I need to soak up as much warmth as I can before Illinois becomes a frozen tundra."

She slipped off her sunglasses, closed her eyes, and reclined her body toward the sky, which meant Jake could stare as much as he wanted at the dip of her collarbone, the curve of her cheek, the swell of her lips. He didn't even care that he was uncomfortably warm in his suit.

Then her eyes opened and she smiled that bold smile of hers—not the plastic, for-the-public one he'd watched her take on and off like a scarf or a pair of earrings all day, but a big, generous, eye-crinkling smile that he'd only seen her give Dave. He'd bake under the September sun in a wool overcoat and long johns if it meant spending more time with Mabel like this.

Then she sighed. "We should probably head back. I've got a couple of things to wrap up today before my obnoxiously early bedtime."

The mention of her schedule jostled the new schedule to the front of his mind, and he fished for more information about just how badly she'd take a possible work upheaval. "Those hours must suck." *Be more obvious, idiot.*

"Yeah, the four-thirty alarm's the low point of my day, and I miss out on lots of things. Primetime TV, moonlight strolls, going to the movies after the sun goes down. You know, traditional adult human activities." She smiled and took a final sip of her iced tea.

"You don't ever wish for a different shift?" He held his breath as she shrugged, hoping she'd be interested in a change.

"Sure, I occasionally think about what a normal schedule would be like. It'd be nice to live like the rest of the world, but right now it's *so, so, so* worth it to do what I do with Dave."

And there it was. The pinprick to the happiness balloon in his chest. This lively, lovely woman would be crushed when Brandon upended her work life, and he wasn't allowed to breathe a word to her.

Before he could fully spin out into full-blown career guilt, they were interrupted by a twentysomething guy who stopped short when he walked by their bench.

"Holy shit, you're Mae Bell."

Jake felt Mabel's body go stiff before she relaxed into a self-consciously casual pose.

"In the flesh!" she chirped.

The kid's eyes widened, and Jake didn't blame him one bit for looking like he was staring directly into an event horizon after suddenly coming face-to-face with Mabel. He felt a little like that himself most days.

"Oh cool! Is Dave here too?" His eyes traveled over Mabel's shoulder to land on Jake.

She instantly leaped to her feet and put her back to him, facing the newcomer. "Nope. We aren't actually attached at the hip. It just seems like it sometimes. Wanna grab a selfie?"

As the kid juggled the foil-wrapped burrito and soda in his hands to reach for his phone, Mabel guided them a few steps away, and Jake shoved his clenched fists into his pockets. She hadn't been joking, of course. Here she was going out of her way to keep from giving anybody the wrong idea about her private life. Then again, the privilege of actually *being* part of her private life wasn't all bad.

The thought pulled his eyes back to her. She was goofing off for the camera while the kid grinned broadly and slung his arm around her shoulder and Jake quietly marinated in jealousy.

Before Mabel and the kid parted ways, he said, "See you at the bar on Saturday?"

"Wouldn't miss it!" she called as he strolled off.

Once he and Mabel were alone again, they deposited their trash in the nearest garbage bin, then turned toward the side street where he'd parked his Jeep.

"Bar on Saturday?"

"Yeah. Dave plays in a band, and they've got a show on Saturday." She nudged him with her hip. "We've been promoting it on air all week, if you'd bother to listen."

He hip-checked her right back, heart bumping hard at

the contact. "Oh, I heard it. I was just waiting for you to ask me to show up."

When he glanced at her out of the corner of his eye and saw her smile, he couldn't help it. He turned to face her, and she leaned in to create a pocket of stillness in the middle of the busy lunchtime crowd.

"Would you meet me there on Saturday?" she asked. "It could be fun to do something outside work."

Her expression was nervous and hopeful, and it was all he could do not to kiss her right there. Instead, he reached for her hand.

"I'd love that." He ran his thumb over her knuckles, and they both shivered.

The ride back to the station was quiet. Jake spent the drive picturing all the things that could develop that weekend and hoping like hell that Mabel was too.

NINE

Mabel couldn't pick an outfit on Saturday, which wasn't at all like her. Usually she was dress and go, but tonight she tried on basically everything in her closest, waffling over which ensemble was best before settling on the first thing she'd put on twenty minutes earlier: a short black skirt and a loose-fitting sparkly silver top that draped over one shoulder. It required a strapless bra, but the effect was worth it.

She started to tug on flats, then reconsidered and reached for a pair of impractically tall, impractically red heels. She almost never wore them, but if not now, when? She slid them on and checked herself out in the mirror.

"You're dressing for yourself," she told her reflection sternly. Her reflection didn't look 100 percent convinced though, so to shut that hussy up, she dug into the back of her makeup drawer for the tube of candy-apple red that she used sparingly. But tonight cried out for red—for herself and no one else. *Certainly* not for Jake.

But when she smiled at her ruby-lipped reflection, it was Jake she was picturing, trying to blend in with the dressed-down Beaucoeurians in his usual suit and perfectly knotted tie. She absolutely shouldn't be imagining him getting a good look at her in this eye-popping outfit, but making safe, smart decisions where he was concerned had become impossible. Something between them had shifted during their shopping trip. His usual warmth and good humor were still there, but it had all been overlaid with a sharp intensity that she'd never seen from him before. It left her breathless with anticipation and desperate to know what was going on in his orderly brain.

Maybe those flats were the smarter choice after all. They'd keep her grounded, remind her that she was a practical woman who didn't throw caution to the wind with any guy who caught her fancy. Then again, Jake wasn't just *any* guy. He was her friend and her biggest temptation, and she still wasn't sure what to expect tonight.

The crunch of Ana's tires in the driveway brought an end to her shoe debate. Looked like she was headed out in the killer heels.

"Va-va-voom." Ana winked as Mabel climbed into the van.

"Thanks!" she said, buckling her seat belt. "And thanks again for the ride."

When the Moo Daddies played a show, Dave generally caught a ride with Skip so they could set up early, and Ana picked up Mabel so the Chiltons could escort her home at the end of the night—never a bad idea when she was going to be surrounded by fans and alcohol.

"My pleasure." Ana glanced at her once more before reversing out of the driveway. "You all dressed up for Jake?"

Mabel crossed her arms over her admittedly generous neckline. "Can't a woman look good for herself?"

"Of course." Ana smiled a Sphinx smile and let the subject drop until they were a block from the bar. "So let me just say, if all that"—she circled her hand over Mabel's body—"doesn't convince Jake to sneak you away for a quickie tonight, he's legally dead."

Heat twisted low in Mabel's belly, but she forced out a flat laugh. "Hardly. He touched my hand on Thursday, and I almost hyperventilated. We're not... I mean, I'm not..." She groaned. "Okay, I like him, Ana. Really like him. Like, *a lot*." As her best girlfriend, Ana would understand how significant that was.

"Nothing wrong with that," Ana said as she wedged her car into a spot in the back corner of the overflowing parking lot.

"It's not that easy," Mabel protested. "You of all people know that. I mean, did you *want* to move away from Florida?"

"I love you," Ana said with a sigh, resting her fingers on the door handle, "but you've got to stop using that as an excuse to keep yourself shut down."

She slid out of the van, forcing Mabel to scramble after her. "I don't!"

"You do." Ana eyed her under the buzzing fluorescent lights illuminating the outside of the squat bar. "Jake's just working here short-term, right? And then he's back to Chicago?" Mabel grudgingly nodded, and she laughed. "Well, that's perfect. Get your beak wet, *chica*!"

"*Beak?* Yuck."

Her friend patted her shoulder. "Stop overthinking it and stay open to new possibilities." Then she turned and headed toward the bar.

Mabel took a moment to collect herself. She'd been veering between elation and indecision since she'd impulsively asked Jake to meet her tonight, and she still wasn't sure how she wanted the evening to end. It couldn't possibly be as simple as "not technically coworkers, so remove clothes immediately," right? The thought heated her cheeks despite the early-autumn chill in the air. Weeks and weeks of lunches and laughter and chemistry for miles, and here she was contemplating that forbidden leap.

It was madness. And it *thrilled* her.

"You coming?" Ana asked from the entrance, and Mabel scurried after her, no closer to making up her mind.

Once they were inside, Ana headed off to find Dave and the band in a room at the back where they were fidgeting and tuning up while Mabel walked to the bar to see if Jake had arrived yet. The Moo Daddies had become a popular local cover band since they formed a few years ago, so she wasn't surprised to find the Elephant already packed with fans of all ages. Her eyes swept over the groups of Rayman College kids, the middle-aged couples on dates, and the clusters of gimlet-eyed women near the stage, vying to be the chosen lady of the night for the Moo Daddy's famously beautiful drummer, Aiden. No Jake to be seen, although she had no idea what his civilian clothes looked like. Maybe all he owned was suits.

She leaned against the bar and traced her fingers over the mosaic of broken pottery as she waited for the three women next to her to scoop up what looked like two dozen bottles of beer for their table.

Once the crowd had thinned, Tammy the bartender shot her a gap-toothed grin. "Hey, Miss Mae. The usual?"

"Absolutely!" she chirped. She needed to sand down the edges of her nerves.

Tammy, a tan, leathery woman who could be anywhere between forty and seventy, owned the Elephant with her wife, Joanne, the free spirit responsible for the bar's weird, artsy vibe, from the mismatched vintage-kitsch glassware to the Jackson Pollock-esque walls in the bathrooms. Tammy flipped her graying-brown ponytail out of the way as she set to work on Mabel's favorite drink, a Harvey Wallbanger. She knew it was a silly thing to pick as her usual, but the vitamin C in the orange juice always made her feel virtuous about the vodka.

Ana joined her as she waited for Tammy to grab the juice from the fridge.

"The band's all ready to go, and they saved us a table up front. Skip's already sweated through his shirt." She wrinkled her nose, then brightened at spotting something over Mabel's shoulder. "Ooooh, can we invite those guys to sit with us? *Guapísimo*."

Mabel turned to see that the crowd at the bar had shifted to reveal a group of extraordinarily buff men who knew how to put the free weights at the gym to good use. "*Guapísimo* indee—" she started to agree. Then her voice compressed into a strangled croak.

Holy hell. The guy with his back to her was the one she'd been looking for since she walked in, and Lord have mercy, he looked *good*. His soft, broken-in jeans hugged his long, strong thighs, and the arms of his gray T-shirt curved around the bulge of his biceps. The muscles of his back flexed as he brought a beer bottle to his lips, the fabric pulling across his broad shoulders, and Mabel swallowed a whimper.

"Good luck!" Ana whispered before disappearing, leaving Mabel to snatch up the glass that Tammy had just set in front and down a big swig.

At that moment, as if his Mabel-senses started tingling, Jake turned and cocked his head, shooting her a lazy grin. "Well, hello." He leaned an elbow against the bar top and ran his tongue along the inside of his lower lip as his gaze traveled down her body. "Looking good there, Mae Bell."

She almost dropped her glass. "H-hello," she managed to squeak. "You look, um... casual."

He threw his head back in a laugh while she absorbed every devastating aspect of weekend Jake. His body was both leaner and thicker than she expected, if that were possible. As well cut as his suits were, they didn't do justice to the way his wide shoulders tapered to his trim waist, and they cruelly concealed the muscle definition that his T-shirt was revealing: biceps, pecs, traps, the whole deal. She bet he had a six-pack under there. Maybe even an eight-pack. He oozed sex appeal in a suit and tie, but his weekend wear may have just annihilated her last defenses against him.

She swallowed hard as her eyes traveled to his face, where he was watching with amusement as she ogled him. Oh, fuck her luck, he had a hint of dark stubble on his jaw. She was doomed.

"Wow," she said faintly, gulping another slug of her drink and trying to rally. "Did you feel weird leaving home without a tie?"

He leaned close to mock-whisper, "Would you believe that I still feel weird with one on?"

She assessed him briefly. "Nope. I think you were born with a tiny power-stripe around your neck."

He laughed again, his white teeth practically glowing in the dim bar lighting. "Ties took some getting used to, believe me."

She nervously rattled the ice cubes in her glass and pointed toward the stage. "We've got a table waiting for us up front."

"Lead the way." He grabbed his beer bottle off the bar.

"Miss Mae?" Tammy's voice stopped her. "Here. I think you'll need this."

She slid another Harvey Wallbanger across the bar to her and sent a pointed look toward Jake. Mabel flushed and hoped her brain-scrambling waves of lust weren't obvious to every single person in the vicinity.

"Thanks," she muttered, finishing her first drink and plucking the second one from the bar. She was keenly aware of Jake's presence behind her as she led him across the crowded room. Between fans of the station and fans of the Moo Daddies, much of the crowd tonight knew who she was, so she nodded and smiled when people waved to her, trying to tamp down her nervousness at being someplace so public with Jake. Where was his head about tonight? She had no idea if he was as confused about the possible shift in their dynamic as she was. So far he'd been his usual friendly self, if a little loose with that hot gaze on her body earlier. But that wasn't an answer either way.

By the time they were settled into their seats, Dave and the band were onstage and Mabel had sucked down most of her second drink in an attempt to keep her mouth occupied so she wouldn't blurt out any of the things she wanted to say. Things like, "Isn't it a little hot for all these clothes?" and "Why can't I stop thinking about kissing you?"

Thankfully, the band launched into "Rockin' in the Free World" and kept her from saying anything unwise. Dave played lead guitar and sang while Skip played bass and Aiden Murdoch, who had the body of a Greek statue and the morals of an alley cat, bashed the drums. By the end of the night, Dave would be wasted but still nailing every song, Skip's cue ball head would be glistening with sweat, and Aiden would have picked out the lucky lady of the night.

As the crowd went wild after the first song, Jake turned to her and hollered, "They're really good!"

"I know!" she hollered back with a grin.

He glanced down at her half-empty glass and jumped to his feet. "Be right back."

As soon as he was gone, Ana leaned across the table and yelled over the music, "My God, his arms are huge. Are you seriously telling me there have been no quickies at all?"

Mabel frantically shushed her. "Stop! Nobody's having any quickies!" At least they wouldn't be if she couldn't get a handle on what they both wanted. Ana merely leaned back in her chair with the delighted laugh of a happily married woman, the lucky bish.

Jake returned within the span of one song with a beer for himself and another Wallbanger for her, and the simple brush of his fingers when he handed her the glass almost sent her over the edge.

She was a boat tossing on choppy waters, the churn courtesy of her fear over dropping the last of her protective walls. But if not with Jake, then what man would ever be enough? He was worth the risk. She was almost positive of it.

As the band plowed through its first set—covers of the Red Hot Chili Peppers, the Beatles, Cage the Elephant, a little bit of Alice Cooper—more and more people arrived, and the place got even noisier, making conversation impossible. Mabel sipped a fresh drink, this one courtesy of Ana, and willed herself to relax as the tingle of good booze spread through her midsection. She was in a packed bar while her best friend did what he loved, his eyes shut tight as his fingers danced across the strings of his guitar. At her table was his lovely wife alongside the man Mabel liked far more than she should, given the circumstances. There was no reason she couldn't just float on this lovely cloud of vodka and music and energy from the crowd.

Jake looked relaxed too, sprawled in his chair with his long legs stretched in front of him. This loose, smiling man was night and day different from the tailored number cruncher she'd met in July, and a rush of affection for him flooded her chest when she realized he was watching her watching him.

"What?" she yelled over a particularly raucous version of "Mary Jane's Last Dance."

"Nothing," he yelled back. "I just can't get over how amazing you look tonight."

His eyes raked down her body again, and his thumb circled the rim of his beer bottle in a way that shouldn't be suggestive but was somehow the hottest thing she'd ever seen another human do. And just like that, her heart launched into overdrive. That dumb organ in her chest had no chill. She was officially No-Chill Mabel, and No-Chill Mabel wanted to reach out and take what was right in front of her.

Then he made it worse by straightening in his chair

and leaning toward her, bringing his mouth close to her ear. "And my God, you smell good."

She choked back a small moan as all her southern parts clenched in anticipation. She leaned in, eyes fluttering shut, and—

"Mae Bell! Where are you? Somebody find that woman and tell her it's time to sing!" It was Dave, slightly drunk and yelling into the microphone.

She jumped away from Jake and said shakily, "Can you hold that thought? Dave will pester me until I do this."

"Do what?" Jake sounded confused.

"You'll see." She flashed him a grin, drained her glass, and bounced from her chair.

TEN

Jake watched transfixed as Mabel climbed onto the stage. His curiosity over what she was planning to do up there fled when her step up pushed that already short skirt even higher, making it look like she was at least 80 percent leg. She walked behind the drum set and grabbed a spare microphone from the kit stashed there, then turned around and winked at him like they were the only two people in the bar.

"I know nobody here needs any introductions, but what the hell, I'm gonna do 'em anyway," Dave yelled over the cheers. "This is Mae Bell. Lots of you know her as that horrible woman who badgers me on the air every morning. Well, tonight she's gonna be our backup singer. How's that sound?"

The whole place roared as Mabel performed a straight-faced beauty queen wave. The lights illuminated her hair, turning it into a golden nimbus, and her silvery top glittered under the stage lights as it hung off her left shoulder, which he'd been fighting the urge to kiss, to lick, to bite, all night long. His mouth went dry.

Dave counted off the song, and the band launched into the B-52s' "Love Shack," with Mabel doing her best girl groupie impression, shimmying along and belting out the chorus. The song reached its peak when everything came to a dead halt as Mabel squinched her eyes shut and belted, "Tiiiiin rooooooof! Rusted!" and the audience went nuts.

At the end of the song, she dropped into a small curtsy and started to set the mic back down, but Skip caught the back of her shirt. "Not so fast. Dave, you ready for a break?"

"You know it," he said, mopping at his sweaty face with a handkerchief. "Fill in for me, Mae?"

She stepped up to grab the mic from him with a *faux* shocked expression. "Me, pass up the chance to torture an audience? Never."

The laughter from the crowd was drowned out as the band launched into the opening strains of the Kings of Leon's "Sex on Fire," and Jake's brain stopped working entirely. He forgot where he was, forgot *who* he was. Forgot he was the guy with no room in his life for relationships. It was all he could do to keep from turning into a cartoon wolf and unfurling his tongue across the table while Mabel performed.

Was a visiting record-label exec going to steal her away from her radio career because of her singing? Probably not. But the joy she exuded with Dave and his bandmates was infectious; she was having a blast, and that energy was what the crowd responded to.

Dave's wife caught his attention during a short break as Mabel conferred with the band. "Isn't it crazy how comfortable she is in front of a crowd?"

He rested his elbows on the table and gestured toward the stage. "I had no idea she could do... *that.*"

Ana nodded sagely, then leaned closer to him. "She likes you, you know. She's been completely closed off to any relationships since her last one, and she'd kill me if she knew I was telling you this, but it was a relief when I noticed her blushing every time she talks about you."

She talks about me. Jake wanted to pound the table in triumph. Instead, he stayed still and waited for Ana to deliver some kind of warning about not hurting Mabel, which he assumed was coming.

"And?" he prompted when Ana didn't continue.

"And nothing." She blew Dave a lazy kiss when he saluted them from the stage. "I just wanted to tell you I appreciate your resurrecting her optimism in men. Or her libido at least."

Libido. Jake's eyes fluttered shut at the thought that Mabel might harbor libidinous feelings for him, and he didn't open them again until Mabel spoke into the mic one more time.

"Thank you all so much!" She strutted across the front of the small stage. "We're going to wrap up my portion of the night with something a little slower to make sure you're good and ready for Dave to come back."

She nodded to Dave, who made a few quick gestures to the rest of the band, then held the mic close to her lips. "My last song tonight is dedicated to..." Her voice trailed off as she looked right at Jake with a private smile on her face, and everything—the crowd, the band, the lights, all of it—receded into the background as her gaze held his. Then she snapped out of her reverie, apparently remembering she was onstage in front of hundreds of people, and tossed her hair back to expose her bare shoulder before turning to the crowd at large. "To all of you, for letting me have the stage for a few songs!" Then she counted off her final number, Sting's "Fields of Gold."

"Ooh, I haven't heard this one in a long time," Ana whispered. "It's one of my favorites."

Jake could see why. Mabel's voice soared over the melody as the stage lights played across the wistful expression on her face. He felt his heart twist. If this woman was willing to let him into her life, he wouldn't hurt her for the world.

And then the song was done, and Mabel held out her arms as if she could embrace everyone in the crowd as they roared their approval. Dave announced a fifteen-minute break for the band, after which they'd play their last set. Before Mabel exited the stage, that underwear model they had playing the drums slid out from behind his kit to spin her around and dip her so low that she squealed and laughed as her hair brushed the floor. Jake hated him for the entire fifteen seconds it took.

While Mabel climbed off the stage and accepted high fives from the tables she passed, Ana excused herself to say hello to Dave, leaving Jake alone to try to collect himself. But by the time Mabel collapsed into the chair next to him, he was practically vibrating with the need to put his hands on whatever parts of her she'd allow.

"So." She tilted her head toward him, looking almost bashful. "That's a thing I do from time to time."

Her eyes were bright, her cheeks pink. God, she was beautiful.

"I don't know what to say," he said. "You were fantastic."

She shook her head. "Either you're being kind, or you have your beer goggles on."

"Beer goggles are for eyes."

"Beer ear goggles then," she amended with a laugh.

Time to make it clear to her where he stood. He'd danced around it enough tonight, and he couldn't take it anymore. He had to touch her, this talented, laughing, vibrant woman. He slid his hand beneath the yellow silk of her hair, curled his fingers around the nape of her neck. She stilled under his touch, eyes fluttering shut, and he asked the question pushing against his brain. "Did you drive yourself here tonight?"

But at his words, she pulled away, eyes wide. "I need... I need a sec," she mumbled, leaping to her feet and heading toward the restrooms.

Fuck. He pushed too far, too fast. She wasn't ready for this, and why would she be? His sexual floodgates were open, but she could very well still think of him as some guy from work. Blowing up their friendship was the worst possible outcome to the night. He had to apologize, make this right, even if it killed him to do it. This kind of connection was so rare for him, the first in almost seven years. By some miracle he'd come to this strange town and found the woman who woke him up to all this hot, heady possibility. But if she wasn't ready, or if she didn't return his big, pulsing feelings... Well, that would fucking suck, wouldn't it? He just needed to figure out what she was thinking.

He stood and followed her down the hallways to the restroom, reaching for her arm once he was close enough. "Mabel, I'm sorry." The instant his fingers touched her wrist, she whirled around.

"Don't." Her voice was too loud in the hallway, and she said more quietly, "Don't apologize."

She really *wasn't* interested. He swallowed his flash

of bitter disappointment. "I didn't mean to push for something you're not ready for. I respect the hell out of you. You're the best, funniest person I've ever—"

She laughed wildly. "Wait, you think I don't want this?" Her tongue darted out to wet her lower lip, and she crossed her arms over her stomach. "*All* I want is this, and it terrifies me."

"Why?" He immediately took a step back, giving her space.

She studied him with worried blue eyes. "We cross this line, there's no going back. Is that what you want?"

"*Yes.*" A simple word, but it burst from his throat, raw with emotion. "I want my hands on you. I want my mouth on you. I want..."

The feral expression on her face shut down his words, and they stared at each other in charged silence for a long moment until they moved toward one another at the same time and crashed together in a kiss. She pushed him backward until his back hit the wall, then flattened herself against him, fingers digging into his shoulders and hips bumping against him as she chased his tongue with hers. His senses flooded with the smell of her, the taste, the incredible fucking feeling of having Mabel in his arms at last, warm and pliant.

She broke their kiss with a moan, and he pressed his thumb gently into the soft underside of her jaw until she met his gaze.

"I'm being honest when I say that I've never been more turned on in my life," he said.

His already hard cock twitched with satisfaction as her lips fell open and her eyes darkened.

"Did you drive yourself here tonight?" He repeated

his earlier question, and she shook her head, apparently robbed of speech. "Ana and Dave drove you?"

She nodded.

"Okay if I take you home?"

She nodded again.

"Okay if I take you home *right fucking now?*" he growled, sliding his thumb down her neck to her exposed shoulder.

"God, yes," she breathed. "Let's go."

ELEVEN

The joke in Beaucoeur was that everything is fifteen minutes from everywhere else. How long to get to the library? Fifteen minutes. The movie theater? Fifteen minutes. The mall? The office? The gym? It's all fifteen minutes.

The fifteen minutes it took to get from the Elephant to Mabel's house were the longest fifteen minutes she'd ever endured. Neither she nor Jake spoke much. She felt swathed in a layer of gauze, the beat of her heart muffled in her chest. Her head was spinning from a mix of alcohol, adrenaline, and excruciating awareness of the man sitting next to her, breaking every traffic law to get them to her house that much faster.

She was having trouble focusing on more than one part of him at a time. His strong hands, one gripping the steering wheel, the other sliding along her bare leg. His scent, that delicious masculine mix of soap and Jake. The muscles in his arms, straining against his shirt and making her speculate about what the rest of him would look like when she finally peeled off his last layers. Her body hummed with excitement. Excitement and arousal.

"Turn here. I'm the fourth house on the right. Park in the driveway."

Those were the first words she'd spoken since they left the bar, and she was surprised at how hoarse her voice sounded. She could tell herself that it came from all the singing tonight, but she knew the truth: lust had left her throat rough, her head spinning. Her lips still stung from the intensity of their first kiss, and she needed more. She needed to spend hours exploring his mouth, and thankfully, they had nothing but time to do just that.

Jake parked his Jeep, and they tumbled out and raced up the stairs of her front porch. She fumbled with her keys, laughing as she almost dropped them before disengaging the lock and tugging Jake in after her.

Once the door was shut behind them, all their rushing fell away and they stood facing one another. In her heels, she barely had to look up to meet his eyes, dark and thick-lashed. They were usually full of intelligence and humor, but tonight his eyes reflected her own want back at her.

He took a step toward her, and she took a step back, unexpected nervousness flooding her. She took two more steps back as Jake took two more forward until she bumped against the wall. His eyes traveled across her face for a moment before he reverently ran two fingers down her cheek. At his gentle touch, her nerves fled and her hunger flared. He must have seen the shift in her eyes because he bent his head, and before she could overthink it or talk herself out of it, she tilted her face up and met his lips with hers.

They fell into each other then, kissing and touching. He ran his hands down her arms, and she slid her fingers under the hem of his shirt, moving them up his back. His skin was as warm as she'd imagined, his taut muscles flexing under her fingers. He licked along her lower lip, sliding across the seam with his tongue, and she opened her mouth to let him in. He kissed her urgently, only breaking the contact to move his lips down to her neck, grazing his teeth along her bare shoulder.

"I've been wanting to do that all night," he rasped, pressing kisses against her skin. The heat of his breath made her shiver.

She let her head fall back against the wall as he slid her shirt farther down her shoulder, and her breathing hitched when he ran his big hand along her collarbone and then trailed his fingers down. He hooked a finger around the wide neck of her shirt and slowly, agonizingly slowly, pulled it down over her breast. When he ran his thumb over her nipple where it strained against the fabric of her strapless bra, she made a noise deep in her throat that made him smile wickedly and press himself against her. God, he was hard. She rubbed against him, wanting that delicious friction even through the layers of their clothes, and he groaned and pushed her bra down, gazing at her exposed breast for a moment. Then he met her eyes with such a rapturous expression that she had to laugh.

"And I've been thinking about this all night," he said, voice rough.

"Mutual. So mutual," she panted. "Touch me *please*." And he did, stroking her nipple first with his thumb and then with his tongue until she was writhing against him. He continued teasing her with his mouth as his hands moved down to grip her hips, holding her against the wall while he tilted forward and ground himself against her. She rocked against his cock until he groaned and moved his head up to claim her mouth again, giving her the opportunity to sink her hands into his hair. Of course it was as thick and soft as she'd imagined. Not a single part of him was turning out to be a disappointment.

After a series of long, drugging kisses, he broke away to command, "Bed, couch, floor. I don't care, but it needs to be now."

Mabel put a hand on his chest and pushed him back a step. "This first." She grabbed the hem of his shirt and started to pull it over his head. Once he realized what she intended, he helped her by lifting his arms so she could tug it off and expose his torso. She tossed the shirt to the floor, and he held still as she looked her fill.

"You... you're perfect," she breathed.

And he was. Solid muscles curved along his arms, and his thick, defined chest lifted and fell with his heavy breaths. God *damn,* but her guess had been right; he had a full six-pack. She stepped forward and stroked a hand along his pectoral muscle, then followed the path of her hand with her tongue, loving the salt taste of him, the crispness of the dark hair that dusted his chest. She reached down and gripped the thick ridge of his cock through his jeans, then looked up at him with a wicked smile.

"I was right. It *is* the whole superhero package."

He huffed out a laugh, but his eyes were closed, his hands clenching and unclenching. "I mean it, Mabel, I'll pull you down on the floor right here and—"

She giggled and tugged him forward. "The couch," she said, stumbling a little as she moved into the living room. "Lights on or off?" She reached for the light switch in the living room, missing it on her first attempt. With a frown, she tried again, but the switch was jumping around more than she expected.

She felt Jake go still behind her.

"What's wrong?" She leaned against the wall to control the slight rotation the living room was doing around her. Maybe kicking off her high heels would help. She flipped her left shoe off but almost tumbled over when she reached down to pull off the right one. When she straightened, she found Jake frowning, and he'd stopped touching her, which was all wrong.

"How many drinks did you have tonight?"

Mabel grimaced at him, swaying slightly even though she'd kicked off those death trap heels.

"I don't know, *dad*," she said. "I had one or two at the bar, you brought me a couple, I had one onstage..."

Her voice trailed off when she saw the hunger on his face fall away, replaced by something that looked an awful lot like dismay. He stepped toward her, and she raised her arms to twine them around his neck. If they could just start kissing again, she was sure she could put that hot, needy look back on his face.

Instead, Jake ducked away from her arms and tugged her bra and then her shirt back into place.

"What... what are you doing?" she asked stupidly, reaching out to touch the miracle of his chest again.

Jake trapped her hand against his body and held it there, drawing her closer and placing a kiss on top of her head. "I'm going to hate myself for this maybe forever, but you've had a little too much to drink for me to be comfortable doing anything more than kissing you, sweetheart."

Mabel struggled out of his grip. "What? No! I want you. I want this. I've wanted this for weeks!" She felt herself starting to wilt, an unsteady whine creeping into her voice.

"The feeling is so much more than mutual. You have no idea." Jake's laugh was strained. "And we can pick up where we left off as soon as possible, I swear. But I don't want this to happen when you're out of your head."

He cupped her face and ran his thumbs along her cheeks, kissing her gently when she started to protest. "You wouldn't like me very much tomorrow if I didn't stop this now. I definitely wouldn't like myself anyway."

Mabel wanted to object, but her tongue felt too thick in her mouth for words and all she could manage was a mewl of distress.

"I'm disappointed too, believe me. Just... give me a second." Jake released her and leaned against the wall, tipping his head back to take a few deep breaths while he surreptitiously adjusted himself in his jeans. With a hard exhale, he bent down to snag his T-shirt from the floor. "Okay, you lush. Time for bed."

That muffled feeling that had been wrapped around Mabel ever since they left the bar had thickened since she'd gotten home, and it was getting harder for her to think or even stand upright. She pointed down the hall to her bedroom and let Jake lead her there after she almost veered into a wall when she tried to move under her own steam. In her bedroom, she indicated the cat sleeping on the end of her bed.

"Thass Tybalt." She crossed to her vanity to remove first her left earring, then her right one. "Hope you two get along."

Jake perched on the edge of her bed and applied himself to scratching Tybalt under his chin while she unzipped her skirt and let it fall to the floor.

Behind her, Jake muttered, "Christ."

"Don't usually drink like thish on show nights," she tried to explain to the two Jakes who were somehow both sitting on her bed, but the words felt like lead in her mouth. "Or any night, really. You make me nervous."

She giggled a little and snaked her bra out from under her shirt, dropping it on the floor on top of her skirt. She now stood in front of the Jakes in just her silver sequined shirt, which she tugged down to keep her black lace underwear from peeking out underneath.

"And you," Jake said tightly, "make me feel many, many things. All of them good, in case that matters to you at all in the morning."

She nodded blearily and started to slide her arms out of her shirt, but he scrambled off the bed to stand in the doorway.

"Fuck. Just... wait until I'm gone to change into something better for sleeping." He laughed shakily and ran a hand through his already mussed hair. "Gotta be honest, I'm at my breaking point here."

But she was barely listening to him. Fatigue pulled at her, and she yawned so widely it made her lose her balance as she listed to the bathroom to brush her teeth and haphazardly wash her makeup off. That completed, she staggered toward her bed and crawled under the covers, no longer concerned about what she was wearing or where the two Jakes were. The dizzily spinning world went black shortly afterward.

MABEL WOKE up close to noon the next day with a pounding head and a world of regret, but her fervent desire for the sweet release of death outweighed any embarrassment she should be feeling about the way the previous night had played out. Unfortunately, she also felt too wretched to relive any of the nicer parts of it.

Rolling over, she stared blearily at her bedside table until her eyes focused on the folded note six inches from her nose. She smiled through the pain in her temporal lobe.

Leaving tonight was the hardest thing I've ever done. To be continued. SOON.

—Jake

Mabel rolled to her back and clutched the note to her chest, which was still covered in silver sequins. Then she staggered out of bed to retrieve her phone from her purse in the living room. A few texts were waiting for her. From her mom: *How was your concert last night, sweetie?* From Dave: *Good show, dollface.* From Ana: *Seriously, that man is so hot, and he likes you too. DO NOT HESITATE.*

Mabel shook her head in consternation, then winced. No head shaking just yet. In fact, she might still be a wee bit tipsy. It didn't stop her from sending a *thank you* to Dave and a *super fun* to her mom. Ana she ignored because she wasn't ready to unpack last night quite yet. And then she tapped out one more text: *I have detailed, ambitious plans to do extremely dirty things to your body, but maybe not today. Thx for taking such good care of me last night. XO*

Then she pulled those damn scratchy sequins off, rolled over, and dropped back to sleep, a smile on her face and Tybalt a warm ball at her side.

TWELVE

Jake got to the station early on Monday, although he was only early by normal-person standards, not Mabel's and Dave's. Since it was seven a.m., nobody other than the morning-show duo was around. He was dying to stop by the studio to check in on Mabel, but he forced himself instead to head straight to his office and boot up his laptop. After a miserable ten minutes, he admitted that he couldn't concentrate on work. What awful fucking luck. They'd finally been alone on Saturday and had actually admitted that they were desperate for each other, and he'd been so turned on he couldn't see straight. He'd had no idea she was so tipsy when they left the bar; it wasn't until he saw her stumbling into the living room and fumbling with the light switch that he'd started to put it all together. What kind of guy would he be if he hadn't gotten her safely to bed, patted her cat's head (*not* a euphemism, sadly), and shown himself out?

Turns out he was the kind of guy who went back to his lonely hotel room, got himself off in the shower, and then ended up staring at his laptop screen thirty-six hours later, desperately fighting the urge to burst through Mabel's door to demand a do-over of Saturday night that ended with both of them satisfied and smiling.

Searching for a distraction, his eyes drifted across the spray of paperwork on Brandon's desk, which pulled his mind back to the *real* problem facing him. "Goddammit." He shrugged out of his suit jacket as if it were the cause of his current frustration.

The coat, of course, was blameless; what was threatening to choke him was residual guilt over not telling Mabel what Brandon was planning. He'd been pushing the concern aside as much as he could, reasoning that he was professionally obligated not to get involved. But the guilt was expanding and getting heavier, like a wool blanket soaking up water. He'd tasted her lips on Saturday. He'd experienced her want, seen her vulnerable, curled a hand around the nape of her neck briefly as she'd sunk into sleep. And he'd been so turned on the whole time that he had no idea how he'd had any blood in the rest of his body to walk himself out of her house for the drive back to his hotel.

He hadn't been lying when he told her at the bar that he'd never been more turned on in his life. Mabel made him light up, made everything in his body fire at once: his brain, his heart, his dick. He was counting the minutes until he could touch her again, but before that, he had to either get this secret off his chest or bury the guilt in the farthest reaches of his fevered brain.

He was staring into space, reminding himself that his entire career relied on him keeping his mouth shut about Brandon's plans, when he heard a rustle and a click and looked up to see Mabel easing the office door shut behind her. She was dressed in a plain, fitted black T-shirt and jeans, her long hair plaited into two braids.

"Hi," she said, sounding a little cautious. "I've got eight minutes. Dave's playing 'American Pie.' It was the longest song we could think of."

"Smart," he said lamely, content to simply drink in the sight of her.

Their brief silence was broken when they both started to speak at once.

Mabel laughed and plowed ahead. "I am *so sorry* about Saturday. I swear, I don't usually end my nights stumbling around like that. I can't believe you had to babysit my drunk ass."

Jake stood and came around the desk to stand in front of her.

"Consider me on call for all your drunk babysitting needs." He reached out to take her hands. "And I apologize for everything that went down at your place. I don't want you to think that I'd ever take advantage of a woman who's been drinking, or—"

"Jake." She cut him off with a groan. "You barely got to second base, and then you watched the world's saddest strip show and went home alone. I think that's the opposite of taking advantage."

She grinned sheepishly, and the pressure constricting his chest slowly loosened.

"So we're okay?"

Mabel stepped closer and tightened her fingers around his. "We'll be okay once we finish what we started on Saturday."

And with that he was fully erect, which Mabel clearly discovered when she leaned against him for a kiss. She gave a satisfied *hmmmm* and rocked her hips forward.

Jake groaned. "Sweetheart, if you don't stop that, we're going to finish what we started *right now*, and I don't think Don McLean writes a song long enough for that."

Still, he wasn't ready to quit kissing her, so he tugged her back and sank into the softness of her mouth until Mabel pulled away, breathing unsteadily. She dropped her head to his shoulder, giving it a quick, sharp bite through his shirt. He hissed and thrust against her again, wishing for her tight heat all around him. Why hadn't they both called in to work today for a do-over?

She took a step back and toyed with the end of one blond braid. "Want to get dinner tonight? Not lunch, and not at the office. Dinner, in public. And then other stuff in private."

He couldn't think of anything he wanted more.

"My evening is yours. Although I'm guessing your dinnertime is more like late afternoon thanks to your sleep schedule."

"You'll get used to my rock 'n' roll lifestyle," she teased, dancing forward for one more quick kiss. "I love being able to do that."

"Agreed." He hooked a finger into the waistband of her jeans and pulled her into him again. Good Lord, the things that woman could do with her tongue.

"Who would've thought I'd meet such a good guy during a corporate takeover?" She laughed as she slithered out of his arms, sounding so carefree that something in Jake's chest shifted.

He grabbed for her hand, turning her back toward him, and opened his mouth before he could have second or third or tenth thoughts. "We need to talk," he blurted.

"There are things I need to tell you. About me, about us. About your—"

She gently tugged her hand away. "Sorry, but I have to go. Song's ending." She pointed at the speaker over his shoulder on the wall.

An uncomfortable mix of relief and queasiness swamped him; she'd cut him off before he could say the word *job*, which would've skated him right up to the edge of professional malpractice. And now he had a few more hours to decide whether to jeopardize his own job for her.

"Okay. We'll talk tonight."

"Okay." She smiled and slipped away, and sixty seconds later her cheerful voice came through the wall speaker, teasing Dave about the groupies he'd attracted at the show on Saturday night.

Jake managed to resume his work with more focus this time, until the door opened again and Brandon breezed in, setting down his briefcase.

"Good news, buddy. Today's the day we shake things up. I've already called the staff in for a meeting as soon as the morning show's over. You'll join, right?" Not pausing for an answer, Brandon barreled on. "It's all the changes we've been discussing. I've already talked to Roman, and it's all coming together. By the way, you've got the final numbers on the trip, right?"

Jake's stomach dropped. Today? This was really goddamn happening *today*, when he was on the cusp of starting something real with Mabel? When he'd just come *this close* to violating every ethical obligation he had to warn her about what was waiting for her? His heartbeat thundered in his ears, and he stared numbly at the feckless rich boy in front of him until Brandon snapped his fingers impatiently. The sound jolted him to life, and he flipped through folders on his desk until he found the one with the projections he'd worked up.

Brandon flipped it open and ran his eyes down the rows of figures. "Looks great. Thanks."

"Don't do this, man."

Brandon lifted his brows in surprise at Jake's rushed words, but fuck, he had to try one more time to convince him to change his mind. Given Brandon's general obliviousness about the emotional nuances of anyone but himself, he almost certainly had no idea that Jake and Mabel were anything more than lunch buddies, and Jake preferred to keep it that way. With effort, he adopted a just-us-guys tone. "I mean, think about it. All these changes aren't going to be good for—"

"Nah, I got this." Brandon's voice was final. "You do the numbers, I do the radio, remember? Trust me."

That was that. Discussion over.

Brandon pulled out his phone to take a call while Jake's mind spun in circles, chasing a solution. Something drastic. He could quit the account. Resign in protest.

The thought—so tempting, so *decisive*—danced across his frontal lobe before he dismissed it with a jerk of his head. Where the actual *fuck* had that come from? Quit the account? Jeopardize his job, his promotion, his future? He slumped back in his chair, clenching his head in his hands. None of the decisions he'd made since he came to Beaucoeur would make any sense to anyone who knew him in Chicago. Taking long lunches. Losing his focus. Considering quitting over a woman he'd known for a couple of months.

Get a fucking grip, man. This wasn't the end of the world. Sure, Mabel wouldn't be happy with the changes, but she'd understand that the decision hadn't involved him. And they were in a good place. At dinner tonight, he'd explain that his job literally forbade him from giving her a warning and that Brandon had brushed off his attempts to change his mind.

It would work out. It had to.

THIRTEEN

Having been summoned by a nervous, sweaty Skip, Mabel and Dave walked into the conference room, which was filled with their grim-faced coworkers. Brandon sat at the head of the table, finishing a phone call, Jake to his right.

As she and Dave slid into seats at the opposite end of the room, she bit back a smile at Jake's somber, I'm-a-fancy-big-city-accountant expression. He was *so damn cute*. Relief that they were still moving in the same direction after the tumult of Saturday night displaced her apprehension over this meeting. Maybe she could convince him to skip dinner entirely and go straight to her place after work.

With an obnoxious clearing of his throat, Brandon called the meeting to order and interrupted her pleasant train of thought.

"Thank you for coming in this morning, and Skip, thanks for voice tracking the next hour so we can all meet. As you all know, I've been acting as the general manager since Lowell Consolidated Media officially acquired this radio station back in July, and I'll continue to do so for the next few months until I hire a full-time replacement and return to Lowell headquarters in Detroit." His gaze swept the room, taking in the expectant faces of his new employees one by one. Then his voice sharpened. "Now, let's talk about some changes."

Mabel gripped her hands together tightly in her lap and exchanged nervous glances with her coworkers. Their period of post-sale calm was about to end. The question they'd all been worried about for months was how much turmoil Brandon was about to introduce.

"Starting this week," Brandon said, "we'll put out a recruiting call for female fans of the show to join our team of Brick Babes. They'll dress in station shirts, show up at our public events, mingle with the fans, give everyone a good time."

The implication of what Brandon was saying moved slowly through Mabel's brain. "Wait, so—"

Brandon interrupted her. "The Babe program is a huge success at several of our other stations, particularly with male listeners. We can increase the number of station appearances, drive up overall attendance, goose alcohol sales at the bar events. It'll be a crucial extension of the station brand."

Dave sniffed from the seat next to her. "Let me guess," he said. "Only the hottest women need apply? No T-shirts larger than an extra small will be available?"

"You got it." Brandon pointed a jaunty finger gun at him. "It's pandering, but dammit, it works."

Tracy, the raven-haired overnight deejay, leaned forward now, tatted-up arms crossed over her chest. "Are you saying we're going to pack our events with women in tight T-shirts to get more men to show up?" Disdain dripped from her voice.

"Now, now, no judgment. Nothing wrong with a group of attractive ladies mingling with fans. Men are our main listener demographic after all." Brandon beamed like a barker at a carnival. "Tell your friends at the body-piercing studio. Our listeners love a good septum ring."

Tracy's hand flew up to cover the barbell in her nose. She and Mabel exchanged appalled glances as one of the advertising staff muttered, "You've *got* to be kidding."

Brandon plowed ahead. "The Brick Babes are a key part of this next bit of exciting news. The station's organizing a trip to Jamaica in January for its listeners. The Babes will go, and some of the deejays too, interacting with listeners for the five-day trip. Lowell has arranged events like this for its other stations, and it's always a huge success. The station splits the profits with the travel agency that organizes it, we give away an all-expenses-paid trip for one or two lucky listeners while the rest of them book at a set rate. Our ratings go up, our fans get access to their favorite deejays and a bevy of hot women in a tropical climate, and a lucky few of you will get a paid vacation in January. It's win-win."

Brandon looked around the table, obviously expecting enthusiasm. But Skip looked like he was witnessing a slow-motion car crash, and Dave was so tense that Mabel could practically feel him vibrating in his chair.

"And what about playlist control?" Dave asked. "Will we still be choosing our own music?"

Brandon hesitated, which Mabel took as a bad sign. "Within reason," he said finally. "But before I answer that, I want to talk about some staffing changes."

The tension around the room ratcheted even higher,

including with Jake, if Mabel was reading the strain around his eyes correctly.

"You've all met Jake by now." Brandon gestured to the man at his side, and yep, Mabel had read his expression correctly. He was braced for something bad. Oh God. "For the past several weeks I've had Jake combing through the station's numbers: ratings, polling results, ad dollars, appearances. You name it, he's looked at it, quantified it, and put it in reports for me. I can tell who's performing well and who could be better. So let's start with Roman. Would you like to make your announcement?"

Across the table from her, the afternoon-drive deejay stood up and ran a trembling hand over his suspiciously black hair. "I'm calling it quits, boys and girls. I've had thirty-two good years at this station, and I'll miss you all. But *Mr. Lowell*"—venom crept into Roman's voice as he cut his eyes to Brandon—"made it clear that the station's heading in a direction that I just can't follow. Good luck, pals. It's been a joy."

With that, the Brick's longest employee turned and left the conference room, squeezing Tracy's shoulder on his way by.

Tracy was the one to break the stunned silence. "So who's going on afternoon drive?"

Their resident black-clad curmudgeon sounded uncharacteristically hopeful, which Mabel understood immediately. Tracy liked the night shift, which suited her hard-edged persona, but this would be a higher-profile gig and better hours to boot, so of course she'd be interested.

"Well, let's start with who's staying put. Tracy, we're increasing your on-air time, so you'll start broadcasting at seven p.m. rather than eight p.m., and you'll run until midnight. Skip, your shift will end at three p.m. rather than four p.m. But the big change we're making is splitting up Dave and Mabel, keeping Dave on mornings and moving Mabel to afternoon drive, three to seven p.m."

That announcement prompted gasps around the table followed by a heavy silence, which Mabel broke a few seconds later with a sharp laugh. She glanced at Dave, expecting him to join in her incredulity over what was obviously a bad joke, but his stricken face dried up her laughter. She whipped around to face Brandon.

"You're kidding, right? I mean, Dave and I are a team," she said, flicking a finger back and forth between the two of them. "We're the *morning show*. It's what we were hired to do."

"Not kidding," Brandon said. "And as a reminder, your contracts don't specify what shows, shifts, or partners you're assigned to, only that you're an at-will employee of WNCB who's got a two-year noncompete with any competitor broadcast outlet in a forty-mile radius."

Mabel's jaw dropped as the reality of what Brandon was saying sank its claws into her brain while he kept talking.

"Jake's analysis showed that you and Dave draw the highest ad dollars and appearance fees. It just makes sense to share that wealth and have one of you anchoring each of our key time slots."

She slowly swiveled her head around to look at Jake, whose face had leached of all color.

"*Jake's* analysis led to this decision," she said woodenly.

His shoulders lifted as he took a deep breath. Looking directly at her, he said, "I'm the accountant on the job, and I ran the numbers, yes. It was Brandon who—"

She recoiled from his words as Dave cut him off.

"It doesn't matter what the numbers say. Mabel and I were hired as a team, *to be* a team, and to think that either of us will be as strong without the other is shortsighted."

Brandon's calm mask finally slipped, and he spoke with a clipped tone. "Dave and Mabel, we're not done. The rest of you I'll meet with one-on-one at a later date to discuss any additional changes."

Like rabbits sprung from a snare, the dismissed staff bolted from the room, happy to be clear of the storm that was about to burst. Skip paused in the doorway with such a sympathetic look on his hangdog face that she could barely control the sob threatening to tear from her throat.

It was now two against two, Brandon and Jake at one end of the table, Mabel and Dave at the other end, and she realized too late that this was how those relationships should have stayed from the beginning. Us versus them. Corporate versus employees. Suits versus jeans. Maybe then she'd only have her anger to deal with, because the added lash of betrayal made everything so much worse. And the most horrible part was, she *knew* better. She'd already learned this lesson once. Who was to blame but herself?

"Let's save us all some time," Brandon said, all traces of his smile gone. "This is a done deal. It's got the most financial upside, and the station's earnings are going to come under far more scrutiny now that you're owned by a company that actually exercises fiduciary oversight. And don't think I don't know why you two had to leave the Gainesville station. This place has been good to you when you didn't have many other choices available to you."

Cold horror trickled down her spine, and she snarled

and leaned forward in her chair, ready to launch herself across the table.

But Dave dropped a steadying hand on her shoulder and spoke in his most even tone. "Brandon, you've been in radio for years. You know a morning show works best with two people."

"I agree." Brandon beamed as if Dave were the brightest student in a class of dullards. "And that's why we'll rotate the Brick Babes through the show as revolving cohosts."

"What?" Now Dave was the one yelling. "You want me to host with the *Brick Babes*?" He pronounced the last two words as if he were saying "fungal infection."

"Damn right," Brandon said. "You can have different ones on the show until you find one who clicks. That pairing of host and hot girl drove our Pennsylvania morning show to number one in its market."

Helpless rage overwhelmed Mabel, and even though fury was making her hands tremble, she forced herself to address Jake, who was now visibly sweating in the air-conditioned room. "You're awfully quiet. Anything to add?"

He winced as if her voice was a lash against his skin, but he clenched his jaw and said nothing.

Brandon rolled his eyes. "Look, I'm not lying. You and Dave are the biggest draws by far compared to the other on-air talent, and the new Babe cohost at the Pennsylvania station has been immensely successful based on their ratings and ad sales numbers."

Mabel's lungs squeezed as Brandon's net closed around her, and she fought to keep her tears at bay.

"This doesn't make any sense," Dave said. "Neither of

us has ever hosted on our own before. We're better together."

Brandon shrugged, bored and above it all. "It's either this or option B."

"It can't possibly be worse than this," Dave said grimly.

Brandon smiled that not-quite-a-smile again, and his overly jovial voice should've warned her that they were going to hate what was coming next.

"I've looked at the Beaucoeur market. You're a rock station, but you've got competition from others in the area with similar programming. There *is* a major programming niche that's been entirely ignored so far, so while option A is to remain a rock station and maximize our most valuable on-air assets by splitting up the two of you, option B would be a complete format conversion to a light-rock station."

Dave inhaled sharply, and honestly, if this wasn't her life being scattered to the winds, Mabel would find it all hilarious. This was karma kicking them in the teeth for always joking that playing Celine Dion for a living was a fate worse than death.

She could practically hear the hamster wheel of Dave's brain spinning away as he tried to puzzle out the least-horrible option, so she took the choice from him. Resting her hand on his arm but not daring to look at him for fear of breaking down, she addressed Brandon. "What you're saying is, I move to afternoons or the station goes light rock?"

"Smart *and* pretty. No wonder Jake's so smitten." Brandon smirked, Jake paled, and Mabel's skin prickled as if someone had dumped a bucket of ice water over her head. "Yes, that's what I'm saying. I'll give you a day or two to think on it."

"No need." Mabel exhaled slowly and willed herself to treat this like any other public appearance where she needed the protective armor of her radio persona. "If Lowell Consolidated needs me on afternoon drive to keep this a rock station, then I'll be delighted to make the move."

"Mae, you don't have to do this," Dave said in a low voice. "We can figure something else out."

"Good luck finding a job in this market." Brandon sounded bored. "Oh, and don't forget those noncompetes."

But Brandon's horrible smugness faded to background news when a realization hit her like a sledgehammer to the midsection.

"You knew." She gasped and turned to Jake. "Asking me if I've ever done a solo show, wondering if I'd be happier with a later shift. You dropped hints, and I was too stupid to catch on."

Jake flinched at her furious tone, and suddenly she didn't want to hear another word from anyone in that room.

Sparing a last glance at Brandon, she ground out, "I'll do whatever you want me to do, and you can both go to hell." Then she fled from the room, raced down the hall, and slammed through the front door of the building. Fifteen seconds later, the door crashed open behind her and a strong hand closed around her elbow, pulling her around to the side of the building so they were out of sight of curious onlookers.

As soon as they rounded the corner, she wrenched her arm out of Jake's grip. "How could you do this?" She didn't shriek it, but it wasn't too far down the volume scale.

Jake retracted his hand immediately, and although he spoke through a clenched jaw, his voice was gentle. "I tried to change his mind, but he's the owner. I'm just the numbers guy, and I don't even work for Lowell. Mabel, you have to know that I didn't want this for you."

But she was thinking back to the conversations she and Jake had shared, those stolen lunch hours that had been the bright spots for her over the past several weeks. The suspicion that had surfaced in the conference room unfurled in her brain. Had he been softening her up for Brandon's announcement? Lulling her with his jokes and his smiles, sure that she'd happily agree to whatever his boss wanted? The idea curdled in her stomach and soured every happy memory she'd made with him.

"I trusted you! You made me trust you!" She blinked away tears, refusing to cry in his presence. "You touched me. You kissed me. You..." The thought of making herself so vulnerable to someone plotting against her turned her stomach, and she shook her head frantically, wishing she were anywhere but right there.

He spread his hands in front of himself in a helpless gesture, his eyes pleading. "I had to keep his plans confidential. I had no choice. My job requires—"

She laughed bitterly, cutting him off. "You had choices. You could've told me. Or better yet, you could've stayed away from me, could've kept things professional. That news was always going to be devastating for me, but this? Us? This makes it so much worse."

He started to reach for her, but she sidestepped him and backed away, unwilling to endure his touch when she was hurting so badly.

"I *knew* how bad office relationships are, but I liked you. I fell for you, like an idiot. And now?" She sucked in a deep breath and willed herself to calm down, modulating her voice to mask the pain in her heart. "This is over, Jake. Too bad you didn't fuck me when you had the chance." Then she lifted her chin and let him glimpse the cauldron of disgust boiling away in her chest. "Then again, I guess you kind of just did."

Ignoring his stricken expression, she turned and walked away to fall apart in private.

FOURTEEN

Fuck. Fuckfuckfuckfuckfuck. Jake stood paralyzed behind the radio station, listening as Mabel's car roared out of the parking lot.

"Fuck!" he roared in frustration, pivoting to slam his fist into the brick wall of the building once, twice, three times. Pain exploded across his knuckles, but he welcomed it. The throb and sting chased away the memory of the loathing he'd seen in Mabel's eyes before she left. Panic crawled up his spine at how badly this had gone.

He was cradling his hand to his chest, not caring that his torn knuckles were oozing blood onto his favorite suit, when Dave found him a few minutes later. Without a word, he joined Jake in leaning against the sunbaked bricks.

"Any idea where Mabel was headed?" Dave asked without preamble.

His head snapped up. "Listen, man, I am so sorry about—"

Dave cut him off. "Save it. I'm pissed, but not at you." A beat. "Mostly."

He nodded in understanding and offered Dave the explanation he'd tried to provide to Mabel. "I wanted to give her a heads-up. Of course I did. But I'm legally bound by the confidentiality clause in my contract, and the Lowell account is huge for us. Which I realize sounds like a bunch of excuses, but..."

"No, I get it," Dave said. He was as placid as Mabel had been murderous. "You did what you had to do for your job. Nobody can blame you for that."

"Mabel sure did." God, why hadn't he made her listen?

Dave shrugged. "She's a tiger, that one." Then he dug into his back pocket and produced a handkerchief, which he handed to Jake. "Do something about your hand, dude. I can't handle that much blood."

"Thanks." He wrapped the clean white cloth around his screaming knuckles, the pain momentarily distracting him from the shitshow of his life. "Why do you have a fucking handkerchief?"

"Because I'm a fucking gentleman," Dave replied calmly.

Jake laughed weakly and rubbed his uninjured hand over his eyes, then answered Dave's initial question. "I don't know where she went, and I was left with the very strong impression that I won't be privy to that information again. Ever."

A childish part of him, the part that had briefly hoped Mabel would be understanding about today's announcement, now longed for Dave to tell him that it was all going to work out. That she'd call him tonight and ask him over for a drink or plan to meet him for lunch the next day so he could apologize and explain.

But Dave didn't say any of that of course. Because they lived in the real world. Because Jake had let himself be distracted by Mabel. Because this was what he deserved for trying to prioritize something other than work.

"This change is going to be hard for her," Dave said, apparently unaware of Jake's frantically churning mind. "And not just because she's apparently being replaced on the morning show by a rotating cast of bimbos—which I'm not at all excited about, if Brandon ever cares to ask. But hosting afternoon drive solo, when her whole career she's been part of a morning duo? That's a huge change. And with you wrapped up in the Lowell side of things..."

Dave trailed off, flopping back against the wall. They were roughly the same height but couldn't have looked more different: Dave, whippet thin and clad in jeans and a Zoso T-shirt, and Jake, in an athletic-cut suit to accommodate his shoulders and arms. Yet they were both torn up about the same woman.

"You know her better than I do. What's my best option?" He needed to figure out his next step. "Does she go for the big gesture, like apology flowers? Or does she reassess after a cooling-off period?" When Dave didn't answer right away, Jake grudgingly added, "I like her, man. I don't want to walk away from that. She's not just some hookup—"

Dave held up a hand with a grimace. "Oh God, please stop. I'm not her father, and I'm definitely not getting into the middle of this." He slanted Jake a look before continuing. "I don't know how much she's told you, but you should know that we had to leave our last station after the only major romantic relationship in her life imploded and made things uncomfortable for us on the job, so she was already gun-shy before all this went down." He rolled his head against the bricks to meet Jake's gaze, pity in his eyes. "I don't know that there's much you can do at this point to fix things."

His heart hurt to learn that Mabel had been burned by a man she trusted in the past, but somehow he managed a nod. "Thanks."

"Anytime. Hey, Spider-Man's web shooters. Biological or mechanical?"

Everything was too shitty for Jake to process or even care about the abrupt change of topic, so he answered on autopilot. "Biological's cooler, even if they're mechanical in the comics."

Dave shook his head as he pushed off the building. "Too bad. You guys were perfect for each other." He ambled back toward the entrance, calling over his shoulder, "I don't want that handkerchief back, by the way."

Jake stared after him in miserable confusion, then sighed and followed him back inside, heading straight for the spare office. Brandon was there, tapping away at his computer. Other than raised eyebrows, he didn't acknowledge Jake's poorly wrapped fist.

"Not a great meeting," Brandon said, "but they'll come around. It's always rocky at first, but once you implement the changes and give it some time, everyone falls in line."

"Yeah. Great," Jake ground out. He crossed the room to grab a banker's box from the stack in the corner and started tossing his laptop, notes, and file folders haphazardly into it. Time to cut his losses.

"Going somewhere?" Brandon asked mildly.

"Back to Chicago. I'm done here."

Brandon laughed. Jake was really starting to hate that sound.

"I don't think so. We have an agreement that you'll be here until the transition's over. And it's far from over."

"Right." He slammed the box down, not caring that he was crushing the sides. "I can do all that work from Chicago."

Brandon crossed his arms. "No, I need you here."

Jake picked up the box and slammed it down again just for the violence in the motion. Better the box than Brandon's jaw. "And *I* need you to treat the staff here with a little more respect, maybe give them time to process everything without dumping every single change on them at once."

He brushed aside Jake's concerns. "They're pissed now, but I made the best choices for the station, and they'll be humming like a well-oiled machine by Christmas. You'll see."

Brandon's smug calmness infuriated Jake even more. "Then I guess it was all worth it." He snatched the box and moved toward the door. "You've got my cell phone. Call me in Chicago the next time you need me to help you justify an unpopular decision."

He'd almost made it when Brandon's voice stopped him.

"Thing is, I strongly prefer that you do the Lowell work here since this is where I'll be."

Jake paused in the doorway and clenched his hands around the battered box, then gritted his teeth and slowly pivoted to find Brandon tiredly running a hand across his forehead.

"Look, I'm sorry." Brandon's sigh deepened the

creases across his brow, and if Jake weren't ready to vibrate apart in rage, he might be more sympathetic to the toll this seemed to be taking on the other man. "You got caught in the crossfire of a personnel decision, and for that I apologize. But I want us to work together for the next few months so you can get a feel for what Lowell needs from your firm moving forward."

His firm. His partnership. The reminder was as painful as Jake's knuckles hitting that brick wall. The partnership was what mattered, was the only thing that *ought* to matter.

As if sensing his hesitation, Brandon offered a small, conciliatory smile. "Hey, better in Beaucoeur than at Lowell's Michigan headquarters, right?" His eyes flicked over the cramped office before returning to Jake. "Honest to God, *I* prefer it here most days, even if every last employee hates me."

Brandon's whole body seemed to deflate for a moment, but just as quickly he straightened his posture and looked at Jake with the usual shrewd calculation in his eyes. "Whaddya say, buddy? Give me a few more months here to get a lock on the accounts, and then we'll both head home?"

Jake shifted the box to his left hip and plunged a hand in his hair. What a clusterfuck. His unwavering work focus had shattered into a mess of emotions at the worst possible time in his career. He blamed Brandon—was fucking *furious* with Brandon—but he blamed himself too. No matter what, he knew without a doubt that he couldn't keep working in this building, where he'd be reminded of Mabel and the hurt he'd caused her every day.

"Fine," Jake said slowly. "I'll stay in Beaucoeur, but

I'm renting an office where I can work without distractions. You and I can meet whenever you want to discuss progress, but I need space to manage my other accounts too. And don't worry; I'll send Lowell an invoice for the rent each month."

Both of them knew the real reason Jake was asking for an off-site office, but Brandon simply inclined his head. "Sure thing, Jakehammer. Shit, sorry. *Jake*." He leaned a hip against the desk and crossed his arms over his chest. "For what it's worth, I didn't know that you and the lovely Mabel had gotten so serious or I—"

"Oh, fuck right off if you think we're ever discussing *that*." At Jake's growled words, Brandon wisely fell silent. "You have my number. Text when you want to set up our first meeting." Without another word, Jake snatched up the battered box, turned and left the office. On his way to the exit, he passed Skip in the hallway. The man's jowly face held none of its usual affability as he took in the blood-soaked cloth swaddling Jake's fist and the crumpled banker's box in his hands. How closely had Skip followed the farce that was his apparently not-so-private dance with Mabel over the past months?

Probably pretty closely, so he might as well hold nothing back. Clearing his throat uncomfortably, he said, "I'm headed out for the day. If... if anybody asks, please let them know how sorry I am that things unfolded the way they did."

Skip's stern expression didn't twitch, but his voice was warmer than Jake expected. "If it comes up, I sure will."

Jake made it two steps before Skip's voice stopped him. "Oh, and I'd skip the flowers. She'll just stuff 'em down the garbage disposal."

Jake froze with his back to Skip, shutting his eyes

against the hurt the words summoned. Without turning around, he said hollowly, "Thanks for the advice."

Anger and regret battled in his chest as he drove back to his hotel, navigated the parking lot, and entered the lobby.

"Welcome back to— Wow, what happened to your hand?" The desk clerk's question stopped him.

Jake bit back a groan. All he wanted to do was retreat to his room, but he'd been raised too well to be rude to the woman in the pixie cut.

"Oh, uh, I had a little slipup." He kept his hand by his side, not wanting to prolong the conversation as she winced sympathetically.

"Looks awful. Do you need Band-Aids or anything? I'm Thea, by the way. I've noticed you coming and going all month. Jake, right?"

Thea leaned over the counter for a better look at his hand, testing the tensile strength of the fabric covering her upper body. He needed to get out of there before somebody got hit with flying buttons from her shirt.

He started to walk on, then paused midstride when a thought struck him. He might not be able to force Mabel to listen to his apology, and he might not have any say in his city of residence for the foreseeable future, but he *could* control his living arrangements.

"I need an apartment with a month-by-month lease," he told Thea. "Got any suggestions on where I should look?"

Her bright-eyed expression dimmed. "Oh, you're checking out?"

"Well, I can't keep living on takeout and minifridge food." His attempt at a smile was probably ghastly, but it was all he had left in his tank.

"Oh sure. I understand." *Her* smile was plenty sincere as she pulled out her phone and scribbled something on a scrap of paper, then leaned the top of her body across the desk again to push it toward him.

"Here. My landlord's number. It's a nice complex on the north end of town. Mostly young professionals, not many kids. Clean, quiet. Flexible leases."

"Sold," Jake said. "Thanks."

"My number's on there too. Maybe we'll end up on the same floor!" she called hopefully after him, but he was already crossing to the elevators.

In his room, he punched the landlord's number into his phone and explained his situation: temporarily in town, immediate move-in preferred. The man agreed to meet Jake in an hour, so he ended the call and prepared to head back out.

Living in a hotel had been a respite from his real life. He'd been able to leave the pressures of promotion and partnership up in Chicago and enjoy spending time with a pretty girl. Moving into a regular apartment would force him back into a routine: up early, gym, office, home, cook dinner, early to bed. Focus on work. Forget about anything personal. It's what he did up north. It's the stability he should be craving. So why did it sound so fucking empty?

Two hours later, Jake's credit had checked out and the property manager was showing him around the apartment complex. It was big for Beaucoeur—six buildings, twenty units in each—and he had his choice between the two available furnished apartments that were in move-in condition: one was a first-floor apartment that faced the parking lot, and the other was a fifth-floor apartment that faced the lake in the center of the complex.

Fifth floor. No contest.

Jake followed the property manager into the apartment and took thirty seconds to examine the kitchen, living room, bedroom, and bathroom. White walls, beige carpet, tan countertops. It was all clean, functional, and lifeless. Perfect for the way his downstate life was shaping up, in other words.

"I'll take it," Jake said. "Month-by-month lease."

"You got it." The manager awkwardly shook Jake's uninjured left hand. "You might need to hit a furniture store to pick up an extra lamp or two, maybe something for the walls. Want a suggestion?"

Like he gave a shit about the bare walls. "Nah, I'm good." Furniture stores were all tied up with memories of Mabel.

Some emotion must have flashed across his face, because the manager shot him a knowing grin. "Ah, I see how it is. You got a girl to help you decorate."

Great. Now even strangers were rubbing it in.

"No. No girl," Jake replied evenly.

"Oh, gotcha. Sure. Bitches, am I right?" The manager sized up the situation without missing a beat. "Come back to the office and we'll get the paperwork finished. Then the place is yours for as long as you need it."

Jake started to follow him out when his phone buzzed. His heartbeat kicked up, but he played it cool. "Actually, can I meet you down there? I need to check my messages."

The manager vacated the apartment, leaving Jake to turn into a thirteen-year-old, scrambling to pull his phone out of his pocket to see if it was her.

It wasn't, and disappointment lodged in his chest at the notification that he'd missed a call from Milo, the only man under the age of thirty to still leave voicemails. Today's asked, "Why aren't you back in Chicago yet? I need somebody to share this new bottle of Glenfiddich with."

That sounded like the perfect end to this shitty day; too bad he was three hours south. He grabbed a seat on the couch, the thumb on his noninjured hand moving slowly across the screen as he texted back: *Sorry. My exile continues.* After he hit Send, he let the phone fall to the cushion next to him and dropped his head into his hands. He was supposed to be having dinner with Mabel tonight. Instead, he'd be sucking down a protein shake alone in his hotel. For the first time in ages, it really did feel like exile.

Swallowing his disappointment, he opened a browser on his phone, into which he'd started searching good local restaurants to take a date, and googled a different number. After a quick phone call, he headed down the five flights of stairs with a hand swaddled in white cotton and a heart swaddled in misery to sign a lease on an apartment he didn't want in a town that was suddenly much less inviting than it had been twelve hours ago.

FIFTEEN

Mabel slowed to a walk at the end of the running trail, her chest heaving. She'd stormed home from the station and immediately changed into stretchy clothes, then set off on a punishing run to empty her mind through copious amounts of sweat.

It had worked for a time, particularly since September was reluctant to let go of its summertime temperatures. But now she was on the cooldown jog back to her house, and the fury, fear, and betrayal started edging back in. Before the emotional tide threatened to engulf her again though, she spotted Dave's car parked in her driveway. She bumped her pace up to a lope as she approached his driver-side window. It was down, and he had his seat reclined and his eyes closed.

"Been waiting long?" She grabbed the doorframe and startled him upright.

"Long enough that I was worried I'd become one of those dogs that has to be rescued from a car in the mall parking lot when their owners forget them on a summer day."

He adjusted his eternally askew glasses, and Mabel rolled her eyes.

"You have a spare key, weirdo. You could've waited inside."

He got out of the car and followed her onto the porch. "My God, what have you been up to? You're disgusting."

Mabel unlocked her door and ushered him in. "I went for a run."

"In *hell*?"

"I'm not that sweaty!" Then she spied her reflection in the entryway mirror and winced at her blotchy red face and the tank top glued to her chest with dark patches of sweat. "Okay, maybe I am that sweaty. Help yourself to whatever's in the fridge while I take a quick shower."

In ten minutes, Mabel was clean and clothed in cutoff sweatpants and an oversized Rayman College T-shirt, her wet hair turbaned to keep it from dripping everywhere. Dave was stretched out full-length on her couch, resting a bottle of beer on his stomach.

"I made you a mojito." He pointed in the vicinity of the table next to her overstuffed chair, and she settled herself in cross-legged and reached for the sweating glass, moaning when the sharp aroma tickled her nose.

"You brought your own fresh mint! You, sir, are my bestest friend."

They held up their glasses for an air clink since they weren't sitting close enough to actually touch beverage containers, and Dave waited until Mabel had swallowed her first gulp to ask, "You doing okay?"

"Not even a little." She rattled the ice in her glass. "You?"

"Been better," Dave said. "I filled Ana in. She's outraged on our behalf and is already writing an angry letter to the Lowell CEO. My telling her that the CEO is That Arrogant Asshole's father didn't stop her. Oh, and that's his official name now, by the way. All capitalized."

"Suits him," Mabel said darkly.

They both drank in silence for a moment, then she sighed. "What are we going to do? I'm no good without you."

Dave twisted his neck to peer up at her from his reclined position.

"Bullshit. You carry me, Mae. You always have. What partner could I have who's smarter or funnier or quicker on her feet?"

His praise both warmed her and reminded her of their new reality. "Sounds like you'll have your choice of Babes. Whoever she is, she'll be dumber but more stacked. Both crucial qualities for radio." She took another sip, letting the sharp alcohol roll across her tongue as she reflected on what she'd just said. *Bad feminism, Mabel. Very bad.* "Okay, that's not fair. The women who apply might be great. They could all very well be smart and funny and... Nope, I can't do it. I'll try not to be a total bitch about them, but it feels wretched to be told I'm getting replaced by somebody hotter."

Tears filled her eyes at the admission, and Dave rolled over to face her.

"Don't do that," he chided. "They're just propping up the morning side with cheap filler so I have somebody to riff off. That Arrogant Asshole obviously values you or he wouldn't be putting you solo during drive time. It's a compliment, even if it came off as an insult. Trust me. Everybody in that room today knows you're sexier than any of the bimbos they'll trot out for their public appearances."

She gave him a watery smile. "You're sweet, thanks. But if you're trying to seduce me with words, you should know that I prefer bald men with neck tattoos."

"Damn," Dave said. A pause and then, "Speaking of people in that room today—"

"Don't," she snapped, unwinding the towel and letting her wet hair slither around her shoulders. She'd rather deal with a soggy T-shirt than explore that wound again. "We can talk about the show, we can talk about the station, we can talk about That Arrogant Asshole, and we can speculate about the required minimum cup size to be a Brick Bimbo—I'm thinking triple-D—but we're not talking about *him*."

Then the doorbell rang, and Mabel's traitorous heart leaped in her chest. She smoothed her expression before Dave could catch the brief hope that flared on her face. As furious as she was, she still longed for Jake to be standing on her porch so he could explain that it hadn't actually been him who'd reviewed the numbers, looking for ways to move her around like a chess piece on a board, who'd lied to her by omission during the weeks she'd been sinking farther and farther under the pull of his easy charm and his clever mind and his stupid good looks.

But it wasn't him of course. A teenager in a red Lehman's Floral polo shirt stood on the porch holding a potted orchid, its delicate woody stem studded with the most vivid purple blooms she'd ever seen.

The girl smiled broadly. "Before I hand this over to you, the sender wanted me to say this." And here she consulted a note: "Please don't throw the pot through a window until you've read the card."

Mabel had, in fact, been considering that very action.

"For what it's worth, he sounded really sorry on the

phone," the girl confided, handing over the orchid and bounding down Mabel's front steps.

Mabel kicked the door shut behind her and carried the plant gingerly into her living room, holding it in front of her as if it might spit venom into her eyes if she shook it too much.

"So he went with the flowers after all." Dave drained his beer and swung into an upright position.

"You talked to him?"

"I did. What do you want to know?"

Everything, of course. How he'd looked and sounded and smelled when he said it. But at the same time, she didn't want any of that to matter to her. She settled on a lie. "Nothing. I don't care."

She walked around her living room in a circle, unsure of where to deposit her gift and finally setting it down in the middle of the coffee table directly in front of Dave.

"You going to open the envelope?"

She grabbed the small rectangle from the pot and turned it over in her hands before putting it back and slumping to the couch. "Oh, inevitably. I'm too curious not to. But I might cry when I do, and I don't want you here for that, so I'll wait." Whatever was inside wouldn't fix anything, but she'd still read every word of it.

Dave patted her shoulder and ambled to the kitchen to drop his empty bottle into the recycling bin, then plopped back down on the couch.

"He practically broke his hand punching the building after you left, bled all over his fancy suit."

He punched the wall? He bled for her? The thought sent a thrill tingling through her veins, which was actually kind of a messed-up reaction. But hell, it was kind of a messed-up day.

"For what it's worth," Dave continued, "I think he probably did the best he could for us under the circumstances. And that's the last I'm going to say about it, because it's not my job to get you laid. Yuck."

"Yuck," Mabel repeated faintly, the memory of Jake's big hand on her breast rising up and threatening to cut off all her oxygen.

"And listen, there's no shame in being interested in a guy who looks like Superman."

She huffed a soft, surprised laugh. "You think so too?"

"I'm not blind." He wiggled his brows. "And not one of the low-rent TV Supermen. One of the classy movie Supermen."

"Hey, some of my favorite Supermen are TV Supermen!" she objected, grateful for the temporary distraction.

"Reeve or bust," he said. "Anyway, I'm glad you took a chance with him despite it all. It was brave."

"It was stupid," she muttered.

"Brave," he repeated staunchly. "Say it with me."

She rolled her eyes but did as he asked. "I'm the brave little toaster."

"There you go!" He grabbed her shoulder and shook her gently until she laughed. How'd she get lucky enough to have Dave in her life?

He released her and leaned back to prop his feet on her coffee table, and only her affection for him in that moment kept her from ordering him to take his filthy shoes off first.

"*Anyway*," he said, "back to more pressing issues. What are we going to do about the show?"

Mabel took another sip of her mojito as she considered it. "We could intentionally suck. Both of us, separate shows. Tank on purpose."

Dave was already shaking his head. "No way. We both have too much professional pride for that."

"Do we?" Easy for Dave to say; he was staying on the morning show. "At the very least, I could play deeply shitty music. Nothing but Nickelback."

Dave said nothing, just stared levelly at her, and heat crept across her neck as she gave a little growl and slammed her empty glass down on the coffee table. "Fine. I key Brandon's car then."

"Pretty sure it's a rental."

She leaped to her feet and threw her arms into the air. "Join me in my sociopathy, won't you?"

"That sociopathy's all you, darlin'."

She flopped back down on the couch, exhausted defeat dragging her back to earth. "Okay, best case? That Arrogant Asshole's plans fail and neither of our shows gets the listeners he's anticipating, and his world crashes down around him and his failures taste like bitter ash in his mouth. This would have the happy result of moving me back to the morning show, where our ratings will rebound."

"Worst case," Dave said, leaning forward and getting into the game, "I utterly fail on the new morning show with Ashley or Jezebel or Bobbi Lynn Sue, but that's okay because she gets me to leave Ana for her and we live happily ever after above the motorcycle repair shop where she and her five huge brothers work, while you thrive in your afternoon-drive shift, becoming ever more famous until you're picked up by KIIS FM in LA. You move to California, become a deejay to the stars, marry a closeted Scientologist, and Bobbi Lynn Sue and I never hear from you again."

Mabel tilted her head back in exaggerated thought.

"Yeah, that's obviously the worst of the worst-case scenarios. You're right."

"But seriously," Dave said, "realistic case is that we have to go along with what Brandon's asking. Do the best we can and hope that he sees it's not working and puts us back together. And if he doesn't, after a certain period of time has passed, then we decide if we want to start looking for a new station that'll fix what's obviously a horrible mistake or if we want to keep going on separate shows."

Mabel nodded, pressing her lips together to keep them from trembling. A tear slipped down her cheek, and she swiped it away. What he said made sense, and she *hated* it.

"I don't know how to do this job without you," she choked out, resting her head on Dave's shoulder. He wrapped his arm around her.

"I know. Me either. And by all means, rub that wet hair all over my shirt."

Once she was all cried out and her chest felt as hollow as a corn husk, Dave stood to leave. She picked up the orchid pot and followed.

At his questioning look, she said, "I can't keep them here, but they're too beautiful to suffer because they were paid for by an untrustworthy liar. Think Ana would enjoy them?"

Dave accepted the plant without argument.

"Oh, but wait..." Mabel's voice trailed off and she heaved a sigh. "Never mind."

Dave rolled his eyes. "I'll leave the card, you big diva." Promising that he'd see her in the morning, he left with Jake's apology gift.

Alone in her silent house, Mabel set the white envelope on the coffee table, vowing to ignore it for as long as she could.

She lasted four minutes.

Dear Mabel, the card read. *I will always regret the role that I played in what happened today. I will never regret that playing that role allowed me to meet you.*

Jake

Dammit. She was going to have to forgive him eventually.

Forgive him but keep her distance because she never wanted to feel like this again.

SIXTEEN

Like the besotted idiot that he was, Jake listened to every last hour of the morning show on Tuesday, feeling sorry for himself and regretting everything. Mabel sounded cheerful, if a little flat, as she discussed the upcoming split with Dave, and relief and disappointment tangled into a knot in his chest. Relief that she'd come through yesterday okay and was performing like a pro. Disappointment that she didn't sound as gutted by their swift, furious falling-out as he was.

As he listened, he packed up the belongings he'd scattered around his hotel room since July, which took all of six minutes. He kept himself busy for the rest of the show by reading the responses to Dave and Mabel's announcement as it spread across social media.

@Ginab2_1, to @wncbfm: *Don't care who Dave's on the air w/but he needs to stop dressing like such a slob, IMO*

Shelby, on the station's Facebook page: *I've been crying since you announced the split. Please don't do this PLEASE*

@Nutz69, to @wncbfm: WHO THE FUCK CARES CAN YOU GUYS PLAY AIROSMTH

Toby, on the station Facebook page: *congrats to maybell but that lady would be tons hotter if she'd cut her hair short and call me*

That level of public scrutiny made him uneasy. No wonder Mabel had been so careful about hats and sunglasses during their first outing. He wouldn't be able to handle the pressure. Also, that last guy was deeply mistaken, as absolutely nothing about Mabel would be improved by cutting off her hair.

The duo gave a cheerful sign-off, and Jake suspected that not a single listener would ever guess the behind-the-scenes turmoil that had gone into those breezy four hours. He snapped off the in-room radio, slid his laptop into its carrier, and shouldered his luggage. When he shut the room door behind him, he imagined himself leaving all his longing for Mabel behind. Forgotten in a nightstand. Abandoned in the corner of the closet. From now on, he was all about the job.

The sharp-eyed Thea—Christ, had the woman been on duty for twenty-four hours straight?—spotted his bulging suitcase when he stepped off the elevator, and she had his final bill printed and ready to go by the time he made it to the desk. "Here you go! Easy checkout, right?"

"Right," he replied with 90 percent less perk than she exhibited. "Hey, thanks for the tip about the apartment."

He was turning to leave the hotel for the last time when she executed her famous across-the-desk lunge.

"I know I gave it to you before, but here's my number in case work ever lets up." She winked at him and pressed a slip of paper into Jake's hand with such force that her red-lacquered fingernails dug painfully into his palm.

He looked down at it blankly before offering her a vague thanks, leaving the hotel, and tossing his luggage into the back of his Jeep. It wasn't until he'd cranked the engine that it dawned on him: the overly friendly Thea was *interested* in him. He groaned and thumped his skull against his headrest. That was the last thing he needed. His emotional turmoil over Mabel was already crowding out the work worries he should be addressing without adding a stranger's romantic hopes on top of that. At least he was officially checked out of the hotel and could avoid any conversations about *that* in the future.

He shoved the paper with her number into the cup holder he designated for trash and pointed the Jeep in the direction of the station. Yesterday he'd hunted down a tiny office in one of the high-rise bank buildings in downtown Beaucoeur. He'd be able to move in by next week, and all he'd need to do was supply a desk and chair. Until then, he'd operate out of his apartment after a quick stop by the station today to collect a few files he'd accidentally left behind during his storm-out yesterday. If he didn't bump into Mabel, he'd be okay. Probably.

When he walked through the door, there was no sign of her, but he was greeted by an unusually hassled-looking Dave at the front desk, phone tucked under his ear.

"Judy out sick today?" he asked when Dave hung up.

"Today and every day. She quit yesterday."

The dour, gray-haired receptionist with the penchant for cat sweatshirts had up and quit? "No shit."

"She didn't like working for the new management," Dave said. "Sorry."

Jake shrugged. "*I'm* not the new management. What are you guys going to do?"

The phone rang again, and Dave looked down at it in distaste. "Find a new person as quickly as humanly possible, I hope. I've got way too much shit going on in my life to deal with this, but there's nobody else around who can take care of it during the day. Certainly not my partner, because she hightailed it out of here the instant the mics were off."

Because of you, Dave's look said. Jake stood up straight and accepted the silent rebuke.

"I'll talk to Brandon," he promised, but Dave was already picking up the next call.

The man himself glanced up from his laptop when Jake entered the office.

"So Judy apparently—" he began, but Brandon cut him off.

"I know, I know." Brandon jammed his fingers in his normally immaculate blond hair, and Jake didn't bother to hide his smirk.

"Things not going as smoothly as predicted?"

Brandon pulled his hand away with a grunt. "I'll take anybody. Find me a warm body for that receptionist position and she's hired."

Who the hell did he know in town? Brandon would just have to unfuck this one himself. "FYI, I rented an office in the Capital Bank Building downtown. I'll work from there but will still be at your beck and call for updates and meetings. I assume that will suffice?"

"That will suffice." Brandon leaned back in his chair. "Were you listening this morning?"

"I was. They did well."

"Told you they'd fall in line."

Jake pressed his lips together to stop his first response, which wasn't diplomatic. "I'm getting the office set up today, and I'm billing the furniture to Lowell."

Brandon reached into his back pocket, pulled out his wallet, and handed Jake his credit card.

Mouth tight, Jake pocketed it. "I'm buying the expensive shit."

"Dad would want you to have the best," Brandon said with a vague wave of his hand. "He always did like you best of my college friends."

Well, *that* was news to Jake; he'd only met Brandon Lowell Sr. a handful of times when the man had flown in to Chicago to visit his son. Then again, Jake had been the one busting his ass with his books or his internship while the rest of his friends became one with their red Solo cups. And there it was: yet more incentive to redouble his efforts to secure his partnership. Mabel was the red Solo cup he should have resisted.

He pulled out his phone to shoot Brandon a text. "Here's the office address if you need it. When you've got paperwork for me that can't be digitized, just let me know and I'll swing by and pick up."

After hours, of course. Anything to avoid temptation. If he laid eyes on Mabel right now, there was a possibility that he'd forget all his best intentions, throw her over his shoulder caveman-style, and force her to listen to his apologies until she forgave him or kicked him out.

His next stop was the furniture store, which was zero help. He passed the couch section and smiled at the memory of Mabel dramatically sinking onto each of them, swooning Southern-belle-style, to test them out. Then he lingered over the desk they'd picked out for the station. He'd wanted to tug her down onto the desktop in the middle of the showroom that day and kiss her silly, and he'd imagined making similar use of it in the station green-room if they could ever steal a few minutes alone.

His thwarted hopes had him spinning away from the radio-station desk to examine the fussy oak desk next to it. God, he hated furniture shopping.

"Can I help you with anything, sir?"

Jake turned and did a double take. He wasn't a short guy, but the employee who greeted him had him beat by several inches. The man was obviously a weight lifter, with tree-trunk thighs and bowling-ball arms straining against the khaki and cotton covering him. He wore gauges in his ears, the dark skin of his arms was covered in tattoos, and his tight, curly hair was shaped into a subtle pompadour. In short, Robbie, according to his name tag, was the single most memorable salesperson Jake had ever encountered.

He recovered quickly. "Hi. I need to outfit a small office. Desk, a couple of chairs."

Robbie's eyes flicked to Jake's slim-cut suit, skinny tie, and patterned-silver belt buckle. "Seems to me you're a modern guy in a traditional line of work. I think you might like this one." He pointed to a sturdy steel desk with clean lines and ample drawer space. "It's based on the midcentury steel-tanker models."

"Sold," Jake said. "Now point me to chairs."

Robbie indicated a line of office chairs against the wall. When Jake tried to buy the first one in the line, Robbie insisted that he sit in each one to check for comfort, and after a few tests, Jake begrudgingly admitted it was smart to find his best fit.

"I'll take that and two of those blue upholstered chairs for guest seating. And don't bother; I'm not going to sit in those. They'll be fine."

As Robbie jotted down a few notes, a man with a big belly, a mean mouth, and a name tag identifying him as the floor manager moved behind them and pointedly cleared his throat.

Robbie's eyes closed briefly, and then he said with artificial enthusiasm, "What about accessories? Credenzas? Plants? Art? We've got a fine line of coordinated decorative items for any office."

The manager offered Robbie an unctuous smile. "Good boy." He patted Robbie's broad back before stalking way.

Robbie's massive shoulders had tensed when the manager approached him, and they gradually eased as the manager's pungent cologne started to dissipate. Although Jake had recently learned a few things about dealing with a difficult boss, he still didn't feel bad enough to buy any accessories for his new workspace. "Nah. It's just going to be me in there. I don't need anything else."

"Got it." Robbie looked up from the notes he was making. "I don't mean to overstep, but this isn't the way most people usually outfit a new office."

"It's only short-term. I'm on loan from Black, Phelps, and Suarez in Chicago, consulting for a local company."

"BPS?" Robbie looked surprised. "They do work this far down south?" At Jake's equally surprised look, Robbie shrugged. "What, a black man can't know about the biggest accounting firm in the state?"

Jake's mouth dropped open, and he'd started to stammer an apology for his assumption when Robbie's face split into a grin. "Nah, I'm messing with you. It's cool. I wrote a paper on BPS for my senior project." He pointed a thumb at his chest. "I majored in accounting at ISU."

"And you're selling furniture now?"

"Mostly delivering it. They prefer to keep me off the sales floor when possible." Robbie scratched the back of his neck. "My extracurricular herbal activities have made certain types of employment unattainable for me unfortunately. The, uh, ones that require drug testing."

Jake looked Robbie over. "You any good with computers?"

"I'm a fast typist who can spell."

"How are you with people?"

"You're still talking to me, aren't you?"

"You clean when you come in to work?"

"Always," Robbie said.

"How much do you bench?"

"When my shoulder's healthy, 360."

"Think you'd be content with an office job?" Jake asked. "It's not accounting; it's administrative work."

"Would I have to deliver king-size mattresses to eighth-story apartments with broken elevators?"

"Uh, no," Jake said.

"Then I'd be very content."

"You okay babysitting a bunch of radio deejays?"

"Only if they're more interesting than the people I work with here."

Jake laughed. "All right. I'm game if you are."

And that's how Jake left Sheridan Furniture with a desk, three chairs, and one new, hulking radio-station receptionist.

SEVENTEEN

Misery is an excellent sleep aid, Mabel had learned over the years. When her prom date her junior year stood her up because his ex-girlfriend took him back the morning of the dance, Mabel cried for two hours and then slept for fourteen. After an ugly breakup over breakfast in the college cafeteria, she shuffled like a zombie through her classes, then crawled to her dorm at three o'clock and didn't leave bed until the alarm rang the following morning.

Monday night, in keeping with tradition, Mabel downed a truly enormous glass of wine for dinner and was in bed by six. She cocooned herself in her blankets, Tybalt at her head, and let the exhausting flow of emotions wash over her.

Tuesday... happened. She walked through it like a phantom, not connected to her body or immersed in the world around her. She and Dave announced their show changes, and she said words into the microphone when he stopped speaking and it was clearly her turn, but five minutes after their show ended, she couldn't have repeated a single statement that she'd voiced on the air. She went straight home afterward and drifted around her house before heading to bed while the sun was still up and soaking her pillow with tears.

Wednesday morning was better. She was back in her body and in touch with her senses. Everything was sharp, heightened. She was devastated by her impending separation from Dave. She was pissed at Jake even though, deep down, she knew he'd been in an unwinnable situation. She was irritated with herself for her overly dramatic reaction, because hello, she and Jake weren't even an official couple. They hadn't made any promises. For God's sake, she'd spent the bulk of their time together trying to resist his charm and good looks. And overlaying all that, of course, was blinding rage at Brandon. *That* emotion was virtuous and true.

She pulled into the station parking lot and sat in her car for a moment. She could do this. She'd keep it professional no matter what happened, starting today. She'd be professional in her demeanor and professional with her coworkers. Wait, what was Jake? Coworker? Supervisor? Corporate spy?

Whatever. Professional.

She arrived before Dave that morning—one of the benefits of an even more outrageously early bedtime than usual—and headed straight to the break room to start the coffee, staring dully at the *drip drip drip* of the liquid into the pot. After pouring two cups, she scooped up the mail in their slots and walked down the hall to the studio, stopping short when she entered the greenroom.

The new furniture had been delivered yesterday afternoon.

She sucked in a breath and forced herself to enter the

room, gingerly placing the coffee mugs and bundle of mail onto the shiny new desk that she and Jake had flirted over the week before. She thumped the top once, wondering, as she had during their shopping trip, if he'd pictured the two of them testing how sturdy it actually was. The thought had thrilled her at the time, stealing her breath in the middle of the furniture store, but now it wrapped constricting bands around her chest until she had a hard time breathing.

Dave arrived as she was glumly staring at the new couch.

"We picked this out together," she said in lieu of a greeting. "He liked that it didn't have a million pillows."

Dave picked up one of the coffee mugs and took a long, loud slurp before answering. "A couple of things: First, good morning. Second, you've known him for less than three months. I've seen people deal with the end of a thirty-year marriage better than you are. Third, he isn't dead. He's just an accountant."

She wailed and flopped face-first onto the couch, the leather cushion muffling her voice. "Hello, he's a *hot* accountant. And he's the first guy I've liked in ages. Years, maybe. I'm entitled to a mourning period."

"Well, get over it. We've got a show." Dave snapped his fingers like a fussy kindergarten teacher, and she complied with a grumble.

They entered the booth and took their usual seats, Dave in front of the control board and her across from him, and started sorting through their mail. In addition to the usual ad copy and record-label promos, they'd both received a stationwide memo from Brandon that made bile creep up the back of her throat.

"We're supposed to start advertising for Brick Babes

today," she said, reading. "And of course all applications go directly to Brandon." She screwed up her face and made a full-throated retching sound.

"We still planning to be good soldiers?"

She briefly allowed herself the thought of throwing a good old-fashioned temper tantrum on the air. A good ol' bout of cursing, shouting histrionics. Then she looked across the board at Dave, crossed her eyes, and saluted him. "Good soldier, reporting for duty." No sense spending the rest of their time together wallowing in depression.

This resolve carried her through the next few hours on air. Dave made the announcements at the bottom of every hour, and Mabel was quick to jump in with her excitement about the Babes helping the station grow in an exciting direction and the joy of new opportunities and finally she'd get to sleep in and blah blah blah. Her stomach hurt the whole time, but she kept her energy up and a smile on her face. Her freshman-year audio prod professor had drilled it into her head that audiences could hear if a deejay was smiling, and that lesson had stuck with her for going on a decade now.

The studio's voicemail had filled up the day before following their initial announcement, and the volume of calls didn't let up on the second day. Twenty-four hours later and the callers were still incredulous, sad, or affronted on their behalf. Dave and Mabel took turns answering them off air and checking the voicemails.

Lies, lies, and more lies wallpapered the studio that morning, and a part of Mabel's soul shriveled with each "No, no, it's fine! I'm excited!" she delivered.

The morning rolled on, and the calls kept coming. One woman wept as she told Mabel that she and Dave were the best, most loving couple she knew. "Oh, but we're not..." Mabel started to explain, but the woman's sobs drowned out her words.

"It's all going to change!" the caller cried before hanging up.

Mabel held the receiver away from her ear to stare at it for a moment before setting it back on its cradle. "Hey. Let's have a *little* fun and play some of these on the air."

Dave's thin lips twisted into a slow grin. "Let Brandon know that the listener reaction isn't dying down after all?"

"Exactly," she said primly. And they still kept it professional, selecting voicemails from callers who weren't *too* angry or upset. They even played one message from a man who drawled, "Thank God. Now that dumb chick won't hold Dave back no more."

Mabel strapped on her Valley Girl tones immediately. "Ohmigod, dumb? That's the *nicest!* Most people just call me ugly, which is, like, so *obvious.* But this guy noticed that I have no brains to go with my no talent, which makes him the *best!* Call me back and give me your number, dude. I think we should date!"

While she was speaking, Dave held up the memo and pointed to the Brick Babes paragraph, raising his eyebrows at her. She gave him the go-ahead sign and a massive eye roll.

"And bad news, guy who's never gotten laid: I may be losing my smart, beautiful, talented partner to the afternoon show, but I'll be joined very soon by a new feature here at 105.5: the Brick Babes. Ladies, have you ever wanted to get up close with the sweaty lumps of humanity who are your favorite deejays? Do you like the thought of free T-shirts and mingling with crowds in loud bars during public appearances? Well, do we have the opportunity for you!"

Dave ran down the pitch for women to represent the station at its public events and even join him on the morning show. And although he kept his voice upbeat, his expression was resigned. Mabel made monster faces at him the whole time.

When ten o'clock came and they finally handed the show off to Skip, they agreed that those four hours were even harder than the ones they'd done the day before.

"Best not to think of it as a countdown. Just enjoy the rest of the week." Dave pulled her into a one-armed hug that she allowed herself to sag into.

Talking about her departure from the show for two days straight had taxed her more than she'd expected, and she was weary down to the roots of her hair despite all the sleep the night before.

Dave gave her one more squeeze and then released her. "Oh hey, would you mind reviewing some of the cuts that came in last week? Brandon wants something good for New Music Wednesday, but I've been super backed up."

"Sure." Mabel pulled back to look at him. "Everything okay?"

"Hope so, yeah. Just been busy with family doctor appointments. It should be fine." Dave squeezed her one more time and then slid out of the room before she could ask any more questions.

Alone, Mabel shifted her weight from foot to foot in the greenroom, looking at the new furniture. Brandon hadn't seemed *completely* unreasonable over the past few weeks. She nibbled on the edge of her thumbnail as she considered. Would it be possible to bargain with him? She could offer to do both shows while they found someone else for afternoons. Or they might let her stay on mornings if she took a pay cut. No, she couldn't slash her already meager salary. Maybe she could take on even more advertising work if she stayed on mornings so Lowell would get their money's worth out of her?

Options about what she could offer in exchange for leaving her work schedule unchanged dogged her steps as she walked down the hall toward the main office. But when she stopped in front of the closed door, she couldn't bring herself to knock.

Begging Brandon to help her? No. Never. Her temper surged as she revisited the memory of Monday's conference-room meeting. She'd rather die of thirst in the desert than take even one sip from Brandon's flask.

Maybe she could talk to Jake instead.

Fuck. No, that wouldn't work either. She shouldn't have anything to do with him until she wasn't torn between lunging for his eyes and licking his neck.

She'd better give it another day. Or ten.

EIGHTEEN

"It's not the hot girl I was hoping for, but I kind of love the bouncer vibe." Brandon folded his arms and gave Robbie a once-over while the new receptionist answered the calls that rolled in over the noon hour on Wednesday. He'd dressed for his first day in a button-up shirt and suspenders, which upped the station's cool quotient by a few degrees at least.

"He'll be great," Jake said. For all he knew, Robbie'd be a train wreck on the phones, but it felt good to take a leap of faith and give someone the benefit of the doubt. The benefit that Mabel hadn't offered him. It wasn't that he was angry with her. He was just bitterly disappointed at how it all turned out.

"Already better than furniture," Robbie said after he ended the call and leaned his elbows on the reception desk that was three sizes too small for him. "That's a low bar though."

"Keep it up." Brandon flashed a distracted thumbs-up. "Can you show him around? I've got calls."

After Brandon was gone, Robbie shook his head in

wonder. "So I work at a radio station where a BPS accountant gives tours. This is wild."

"Radio. So wild," Jake said flatly. "Okay, the tour leaves now."

He guided Robbie through the various offices, warning him about the sacred pact of the ON AIR signs: no mortal soul dared enter the studio when they were lit. The last and most important stop was the kitchen.

"Pretty standard," he told Robbie. "They tend to have fresh coffee going all day long since somebody's always on the air and needing the caffeine."

But the Brick's newest employee wasn't looking at him anymore; his eyes were fixed on the doorway. Somehow Jake knew who'd be there even before he turned around. Was it her perfume? Her shampoo? Her very essence, calling to something primal within him?

Fuck, he needed to get out of here. This was why he'd rented his own office.

He turned slowly, but Mabel's eyes flicked right past him and settled on Robbie.

"Hi," she purred. "Rumor has it you're our new receptionist. I'm Mabel."

She stepped into the room and extended her hand. The stab of hurt he felt at being so thoroughly dismissed vanished when Robbie's brown eyes widened and he lurched forward and shook her hand mechanically, his enormous paw dwarfing hers. He nodded his head but didn't return her greeting.

"Welcome aboard." She eased her hand out of Robbie's grip and looked at him expectantly, but the man seemed to have lost the power of speech.

The silence in the kitchen stretched interminably, and Jake was about to take over the conversation just to end the sheer awkwardness, even though Mabel was doing her best to pretend he wasn't there, when the Brick's newest employee suddenly found his tongue.

"I just want to say I'm your biggest fan," he blurted, voice unnaturally loud. "I've been listening to you since I was in high school, ma'am."

Mabel's head snapped back, and her eyes narrowed fractionally. Jake watched in amazement as she stalked up to Robbie, who edged backward until he bumped against the fridge.

"Come again?" she asked, looking up, up, up into his face. She was tall; Robbie was so much taller.

Robbie had to clear his throat twice before he managed to squeak out, "I said—"

"Oh, I heard you." She smiled wolfishly and planted a hand on her hip. "But ma'am is for grandmas and women who wear novelty holiday vests." With her free hand, she gestured down at her short skirt and striped tank top. "Do I look like a grandma? Or a woman who wears novelty holiday vests?"

"No, ma— Uh, Mabel. You don't."

"Good. Good," she said, standing on her tiptoes to lean as close to Robbie's face as possible. "Then I'm going to make you a promise right now: if you ever call me ma'am again, I'm going to make you regret it. And you won't like my techniques. Or maybe you will. Let's hope you never find out."

Robbie gave a small, strangled moan.

"Excellent!" The seductive menace in her tone vanished, replaced by her usual chipperness. "Welcome to the station!" Without a single glance at Jake, she spun on her heel and breezed out the door.

Neither man moved or spoke for a second.

"I don't know whether I'm frightened or turned on," Robbie whispered.

"You and me both."

"I need a drink." Robbie exhaled hard.

"You and me both."

At the end of the workday, they jumped into Robbie's car and headed to the diviest Beaucoeur bar Jake had ever seen, a subterranean retreat next to a comedy club and a sad-looking strip joint. He gingerly seated himself next to Robbie at the long sticky bar, terrified that he might have to learn the condition of the restrooms at some point. But he needed alcohol to wipe away the memory of Mabel's husky, sexy threats. Bad enough to be in the room when she delivered them, but worse not to be their intended target. His body had lurched to life and begged for her to whisper vague promises of retribution into his ear.

Fuck, he was a mess. "What's on tap?" he asked the grizzled bartender, who merely shrugged and poured him a glass of yellow-gold liquid. Jake accepted it with only mild alarm, and by the third drink, the tightness in his chest had eased.

"I mean, I knew she worked there and that at some point I'd meet her, but I didn't expect her to be so beautiful, you know?" Robbie said.

"I know. She is," Jake agreed, possibly a little too emphatically. He stared down into his beer, hiding the misery on his face while Robbie regaled his bar buddies with the tale of Jake swooping in to rescue him from his life of furniture drudgery. By the end of the story, the assembled men were hailing Jake as a hero and insisting on buying his drinks for the rest of the night.

Things were getting blurry around the edges when

Robbie returned to singing Mabel's praises, this time with the help of a few other patrons.

"Yeah, I saw her at a broadcast they were doing at a bar last year," the squat guy next to Robbie said.

Jesus, did everybody in this town know who Mabel was?

The guy ran his hand over his shaved dome, looking depressed at the memory. "Tried to get her to party with me, but she turned me down. Really nice about it though."

Jake's own memory was much sharper. "Yeah. She's... she's really great." He sighed. "Her voice is so... God, it's just so..."

He didn't finish the sentence. Robbie shot him a curious look, then gestured to the bartender for another round.

By midnight, Jake was well and truly wasted, and maudlin didn't even begin to cover how he was feeling about his romantic entanglements in this Podunk town.

"Okay, new friend. I've got an Uber on the way. Time to go," Robbie said, slinging a huge arm around Jake's shoulder and helping him stumble up the stairs to street level. The sun had been up when they'd descended to the lower-level bar, and now Jake was seeing Beaucoeur after hours. The neighborhood was hopping, cars packing the parking lots of the nighttime establishments and clusters of people loitering outside, having a smoke.

With a pang, Jake recalled leaving the Elephant with Mabel on Saturday. He'd wanted to ravish her in the middle of the bar, long before they ever reached his Jeep. If he had, maybe they'd have had a different ending.

Fuck, he was too full of beer and regrets for thoughts like that. It had drizzled while they'd been underground, so he did his best to focus on the reflection of the stop-lights glimmering on the damp street as they flipped from green to yellow to red.

Thankfully, their driver pulled up before Jake was completely overtaken by melancholy. He and Robbie tumbled into the vehicle, and fifteen minutes later arrived at the shabby little house Robbie was renting with two of his buddies.

Before he climbed out of the back, Robbie gripped Jake's shoulder with his giant paw and, tears in his eyes, said, "Thanks for giving me a chance, buddy." Then the man and his pompadour rolled out of the car and up the front walk.

When the driver turned to Jake, he was gripped with an unsettling realization: they'd only given the driver Robbie's address. Worse, Jake couldn't *quite* remember where he lived. He'd checked out of his hotel that morning, but he hadn't officially moved into his new place yet, and his beer-addled brain refused to cough up the street name of his short-term rental when the driver asked for it.

"It's, uh, big apartment thing," Jake mumbled. "Like one hundred some units? Got trees and a parking lot? S'brick. Something with flowers."

Jake brandished his new key at the driver, who peered at it, muttered something about drunk idiots, and pointed his vehicle north. He deposited Jake in the central court-yard of the Mayflower Apartments, which did look vaguely familiar. He thanked the man and turned in a bewildered circle, baffled as to which of the six identical buildings was home. Time for trial and error.

The metal exterior doors to each building were locked, and his new key fit the second one he tried. Once inside, he rode the elevator up to five, slumping against the wall for support and praying he was correctly remembering that his new apartment was on that floor. When the doors slid open, he stumbled into the quiet hallway and swayed left, then right.

Shiiiiit. He had no idea what number his apartment was, and the hallway stretched impossibly long in either direction. He rested his forehead against the wall next to the elevator and tried to force his useless fucking brain to think. It was probably one of the doors that didn't have a floor mat or wreath or some personal touch. He was a sad single guy with no friends or personal connections after all. No friends, no wreath. This all felt so much worse than it did in Chicago.

Jake rolled off the wall and lurched down the hallway to examine the two undecorated doors in the hallway. They were side by side. "Convenient!" he said loudly and then shushed himself.

He groped in his pocket for his key and inserted it into the lock of the door on the right. He tried twisting it a couple of times, but the handle refused to budge.

Okay then. It must be the other one. Trial and error! But before he could pull his key out of the lock, the door swung open to reveal a woman in a short robe, wielding an irritated expression and a can of pepper spray.

"What the hell do you think you're— Uh, Jake?"

He peered at her blearily. "Hey, I know you. Right? I know you?"

She blinked in surprise but didn't release her hold on the pepper spray. "Thea. From the hotel. What are you doing here?"

He pointed to his keys, which were still sticking out of her lock.

"Just moved in. I think."

Thea's face cleared in understanding. "Oh sure. The apartment next to mine's been empty for a while. I wondered if you might end up in that one. And wow, are you drunk. Here," she said briskly, extracting his key and plugging it into the neighboring door. It swung open immediately. "There you go."

She pushed him inside and stepped in after him. Jake staggered a few steps into his apartment before realizing that his luggage was still in the back of his Jeep, which was parked in the radio-station lot. Well, shit.

"Um, are you... moved in?" She looked around his bare living room in confusion, but at least she'd pocketed the paper spray.

Jake scrubbed a hand through his hair. "Yeah, s'fine. I've got more stuff to bring up tomorrow."

She frowned. "But what about your bed? Is it made? Do you have towels and—"

Exhaustion suddenly enveloped him, and his limbs became too heavy to stay upright. He had to ditch this friendly stranger.

"Thanks for your help." He pushed as much authority to the surface of his drunkenness as possible. "Got it from here."

She looked longingly around his apartment, no doubt still wanting to be useful, so he stretched his mouth into a wide yawn. She took the hint and cheerfully wished him a good night before bouncing out the door, which he swiftly locked behind her.

He listed into the bedroom, where of course the mattress was bare. Then he located the bathroom, which had no toothbrush, soap, or towels waiting for him. "God-dammit!" he roared, then clapped a hand over this mouth. No need to summon more assistance from next door.

Whatever. Sleep beckoned. He located some folded bedding in a closet and grabbed the comforter, then shucked his clothes and, clad in nothing but his boxer briefs, rolled himself into a blanket burrito on the bare mattress.

He was about to drift off into an uneasy drunken sleep when he remembered what he'd been trying to forget all night. He and Mabel had been in the same room today, and she'd completely ignored him. Unless...

He groped on the floor for his phone, which was still in the pocket of his pants. No notifications. Mabel hadn't called or texted. And why would she? He knew how furious she was with him.

That didn't stop him from throwing his phone across the room though.

NINETEEN

Thursday after the show, which was full of more announcements about the deejay shake-up and Brick Babe auditions, Mabel walked down the hall to the main office and steeled herself to bargain with That Arrogant Asshole. Acid bubbled in her stomach thanks to all the rage she was swallowing, but the inevitable ulcer would be worth it if she could just stay with Dave.

She took a deep breath and stepped inside. The office was empty. And not just empty, but unusually clean. Jake's desk was devoid of laptop, paperwork, notes, everything.

"He's not here." The voice behind her made her jump, and she spun to find That Arrogant Asshole surveying her from the doorway with a blandly amused expression. "Your righteous indignation drove him away."

He pushed past her into the office, setting an armload of papers onto Jake's bare desk. Mabel felt like she'd been caught sneaking the last donut from the box, but she had to know.

"What do you mean? Is he back in Chicago?" Her

heart jumped to her throat at the thought that he was gone. He'd been here yesterday. Had she missed the chance to say goodbye by pointedly ignoring him and the devastated look on his face?

Brandon smiled thinly. "Luckily for you, he rented an office downtown."

Oh hell, why'd she have to be so relieved to hear it? She should *want* him safely out of her city. What was wrong with her?

"Good shows this week." Brandon dropped into his office chair and eyed her speculatively. "Very professional, both of you."

She narrowed her eyes. "Yes. You may have noticed that we are, in fact, professionals."

He lifted his hands in a "down, killer" motion. "I'm aware. It's why I was so surprised about you and Jakehammer. I truly thought you'd both be smart enough not to get... tangled."

He twined his fingers together to illustrate his point, and her throat threatened to close up. Bad enough that things with Jake ended. Worse to infinity that her boss knew about it. Memories of her dismissal from Gainesville made her hands ball into fists at her sides. "That's not what—"

He cut her off. "No harm done. You and Dave are both doing exactly what I need you to do. Oh, and speaking of things I need you to do, you guys and Skip will need to knock out some voice tracking this week. Tracy quit this morning."

"What?" Mabel's mouth dropped open, all other thoughts vanishing. Surly, spiky Tracy had up and left? "Why?"

"You, I think," Brandon said. "She was anticipating a

She wandered back to the kitchen and leaned against the sink, crossing her arms in thought. Of all the things she had to accomplish today, locating the guy she was pissed at—was she still though?—should take a back seat. She chewed on the last of her remaining nails, which had taken a beating over the stressful few days she'd endured, and reasoned with herself. He was probably fine. He was a grown-up and she wasn't his mommy. Then again, Jake was new to Beaucoeur. What if he somehow ended up in the wrong part of town? Anything could've happened to him: robbery, assault, hit and run. People even got stabbed sometimes, or shot. Was he okay? Should she... No. She shouldn't text him.

"You are being ridiculous." She said it out loud, hoping the words would banish the unease in her stomach. No luck though, and she spun out of the room to pace down the hall. Jake's absence had apparently activated the mutant strain of worry-itis that she'd inherited from her mother. After all, he didn't know anybody in town, so who else would care enough to look out for him?

Not that *she* cared, of course.

"Morning."

She looked up to see Robbie's impressive frame wedged behind the front desk. How had she managed to miss him before, looming over his keyboard like a steroidal gargoyle? She pressed pause on her hunt for Jake to talk to the new guy, hoping like hell he'd gotten all the fanboying out of his system after the day before.

"Hi, pal! How's the first week going?"

Robbie flashed square white teeth the size of domino tiles. "Just trying to stay awake. Jake and I had a wild night last night. Not smart with a new job."

Mabel stared blankly at him for a beat. "*My* Jake?"

Something flickered in Robbie's eyes, and she quickly waved her hands in a decisive "no no no" gesture. "Not *my* Jake. I just mean... the Jake that I know?" *Making it worse, Bowen.* "Where is he? Is he okay?"

Robbie's face took on a distinctly pitying look. "He's fine. He Ubered home. I'm guessing he's sleeping it off."

The worry in her stomach dissipated, and she pressed a hand to her chest. "Ah. That explains the Jeep." Well, so much for any pretense that she didn't care if Jake lived or died. She did care, way too much. And that wasn't good.

While she'd been working through every stop on the wheel of emotions, Robbie's position had shifted to the sympathy head tilt. Did he know the deal with her and Jake? Before she could think better of it, she blurted out, "So did he hook up with anyone last night?"

Good Lord, Robbie's head now tipped so far to the side in sympathy that his ear was practically resting on his shoulder—impressive for someone with a neck that thick.

"I mean, I'm asking for his sake. He's new in town, so it would be good for him to meet people, um, outside the station." She looked heavenward, hoping a stray bolt of lightning would crash through the ceiling to end her time on Earth. "Gah! Forget I asked!"

"He didn't," Robbie finally assured her. "It was a big group of guys. He was pretty wrecked by the end of the night."

She sniffed and refused to feel bad for him. *She* was the victim here, not Jake and his cold accountant's heart and his frustrating accountant's code of ethics.

Robbie shifted in his seat, then cleared his throat. "Hey, so do you know how this fax machine works? Apparently Brandon's father prefers his financial updates via hard copy, not emails."

Grateful for his change of subject, Mabel came around the desk to help the least likely receptionist in the universe get acclimated to the WNCB way of life.

———————

THE WEEK HAD MOVED TOO QUICKLY. Mabel kept telling herself to cling to the memories and savor every moment and other Pinterest-worthy clichés, but despite her best efforts at slowing time, here it was Friday, her last day on the air with Dave. They'd spent the week gamely pitching the changes, pitching the Brick Babes, pitching the Jamaica trip, pitching her new afternoon gig. My God, had they been cheerful. Perky. Downright chipper. The unsuspecting listener would never have an inkling about the eye rolling and vomit faces happening behind the microphones.

On Friday, Mabel arrived at work at five a.m., a little earlier than usual, only to find that Dave was already there and with a box of still-warm donuts, no less.

"You, I may or may not miss," she told him. "Your delivery of early-morning breakfast pastries? That I'll miss." She selected a strawberry fritter dripping with thin white icing.

"Such a pastry slut." Dave folded her, sticky fritter fingers and all, into a quick hug. "Maybe it won't be so bad. Neither of us is being shipped overseas. We'll still be working in the same actual building."

She nodded and took a bite of her now slightly smushed pastry. She wanted to believe Dave, but her private fears were too loud. This split was actually going to work well for the station. Dave would thrive in a show with a rotating cast of hot cohosts while she settled into a new afternoon-drive routine all alone. Alone at work, alone at home, alone forever. Poor lonely Mabel.

Sadness threatened, so she selected a cream-filled long John and ate her feelings.

And then they did their last show. They laughed all the way through it, teasing, bantering, and taking occasional phone calls from listeners excited about the upcoming changes. Even That Arrogant Asshole would have to admit that they'd been the perfect corporate drones for him.

In no time, a slightly bewildered Mabel was thanking the listeners for five amazing years, telling Dave she loved him, and instructing them all to tune in at four p.m. starting Monday.

As soon as Dave shut off their mics to hand the show over to Skip, she burst into tears. She gave herself exactly sixty seconds to cry, then she wiped her eyes, blew her nose, offered Skip an apologetic smile, and threw herself onto the couch in the greenroom.

"Skip says the Brick Babe applications are already coming in," Dave said gloomily, flopping down next to her. "Apparently Brandon's making Robbie take a photo of each one and printing them out as part of their application packet."

"Chaaaarming," she drawled. "How's he going to pick the on-air candidates?"

Dave shrugged. "That Arrogant Asshole works in mysterious ways. But I'm guessing it'll be an ineffable combination of hair height and cup size. I do know that they're going to do some sort of audition at a bar in a couple of weeks."

Mabel wilted a little at the thought. "Is it too early for a drink?"

Dave checked his watch. "It's 10:16."

"So... that's a yes on the drink?"

He snorted. "That's a *hell* yes. The Elephant? We can get burgers to go with the booze."

"Hear, hear. Let's drown our sorrows in catsup."

On their way out the door, Dave told Robbie, "I'm taking this one for some beer and grease therapy."

"Smart." They were almost out the door when Robbie's gravelly voice stopped them. "Oh, Mabel, would you be willing to drop off some station paperwork? It needs to get delivered sometime before Monday morning."

"Sure." She reached for the manila envelope. She occasionally ran errands for the ad reps when they were busy, and frankly, she'd welcome any distraction from her job woes. "Where's it—" Then she read the address and immediately thrust it at Robbie. "No way."

"Nuh-uh. No take backs." He stuffed his hands in his pockets. "Besides, Brandon specifically asked for you to do it."

"*Did* he?" She forced the words past her clenched jaw.

Dave peeked over her shoulder and snorted. "Yeah, that's all you, kitten."

Mabel groaned and tucked the envelope under her arm, embarrassed at the maneuvering that had just taken place.

"Fine. But you're buying lunch," she said, pointing at Dave as they walked to their cars.

TWENTY

After the boozy disaster that had been his Wednesday night out with Robbie, Jake decided to lie low in his new apartment for the last two days of the week, feeling miserable and making major inroads on the piles of work that were accumulating as he waited for the furniture to arrive at his new office. As part of his back-on-track mandate, he resolutely kept the radio off for Mabel's final show. It killed him, but not having her lush voice in his head was imperative to finding his equilibrium again.

On Friday afternoon, he took a break from reviewing a new file for one of his bigger Chicago accounts and laced up his running shoes. After six hard miles of nothing but the burn of his lungs and the slap of his shoes on the cement, he thundered up the five flights of stairs to his door, scoured out and the closest to peace that he'd been all week. Chest heaving and sweat dripping from his drenched hair, the only thing he wanted in that moment was a shower. While he was fitting his key in the lock, the door next to his swung open and Thea emerged in a fluttery, flowery dress.

"Oh hi!"

He collapsed against the door and employed his precious remaining oxygen to gasp out, "Hey. How's it going?" The smile he offered her was probably more of a grimace, but at least he made the effort.

"I'm great! You?"

"Great," he panted. He grabbed the hem of his T-shirt and swiped it across his damp face so the sweat would stop stinging his eyes, but when Thea's gaze zoomed to his exposed stomach, he immediately let the material fall. The person he wanted ogling him had been full of cool indifference the last time he saw her.

So much for his runner's high.

Thea's eyes widened, and she blinked a few times before dragging her gaze back up to his with a broad smile. "Hey, so I'm headed to a winery with some friends. Want to come along? Be a chance to meet some people in town."

God, no. "That's a nice offer, but I'll have to pass." He tried to sound regretful.

"I can wait if you want to get cleaned up first."

Her eyes flitted down to his chest, then popped back to his face, which needed another wipe-down, but he'd be damned if he'd give her another show. "Thanks, but still no. I've got a ton of work." That even had the benefit of being true.

Her disappointed frown was there and gone in an instant. "Your loss! Oh hey, you're working with the radio-station people, right? So do I apply to you?"

She tilted her head while he frowned at her in confusion.

"The Brick Babes!" she clarified. "I'm great with

people, obviously, so I'd be perfect if you need someone to talk about the station at bars and things like that."

Hell. This was actual hell. "Actually, I'm not the one—"

She leaned in. "Between you and me, it sounded like what the station's looking for are girls to flirt with guys at public events. And that's something I do anyway, so I thought it'd be fun to be officially sponsored. Plus you get free drinks and free shirts! What's not to like?"

Would this conversation be as painful if every part of Jake's body *wasn't* drenched with sweat? Probably. "I know lots of women are excited about it, but my boss is the one who—"

"And I'd love to meet the deejays! Dave, on the morning show? He sounds soooo cute when I listen!"

Even in his weakened state, he didn't have the heart to squash the hope in Thea's bright, eager eyes. "Tell you what, I'll put in a good word for you, but I'll have to shower first to do it."

Another lightning-bolt smile. "Oh! Ha! Sorry to hold you up. Rude of me. I'd hug you, but you're super gross. 'Kay, the wine is calling. Enjoy your night! Thanks for the reference."

With a little wave, his Energizer Bunny neighbor turned and bounced down the hall. Brandon was going to love her.

He finally let himself into his air-conditioned apartment, pulled off his shirt, and walked straight to the kitchen sink, sticking his head under the faucet to rinse the sweat out of his eyes. He grabbed a clean towel to mop up his face and was headed toward the shower when someone knocked on his door. Suppressing a groan, he pulled it open.

"Listen, Thea—" he began, but the words died on his lips.

"Hi— Whoa." Mabel leaned back to take him in. "Bad time?"

He couldn't have been more shocked if he'd opened his door to discover the ghost of Abraham Lincoln standing there, and his heart rate accelerated as if he were still sprinting uphill. "No. Uh, no, it's fine."

Her eyes snapped to his chest, and her teeth dug into her lower lip. Right. Fuck. Shirtless and glistening was no way to talk to someone he couldn't be in a relationship with, so he hurriedly tugged his shirt back on, wincing as the clammy fabric met his chest and back. "What are you doing here?"

"Right." She snapped her gaze back to his face, and fuck *yes*, her cheeks were glowing pink and her eyes were glassy. Not so indifferent now, was she?

But no. He'd left his Mabel feelings behind in the hotel, remember? The emotional ones *and* the sexual ones. He was focused on getting back on track now, even if he had to shut down a part of himself to do it.

"Um, Brandon asked me to deliver this." She brandished a manila envelope. "Station stuff. He oh so helpfully provided your address. I'm not a stalker, I swear." She laughed weakly, but he didn't join in. Having her in his new space was seriously throwing him off his game plan.

"Thanks." He threw the envelope on his kitchen table, and common courtesy reared its head even though he knew it could be trouble. "Do you want to come in, have a seat?"

"No, I... I'm not staying." But she stepped over his threshold anyway, eyes darting all around his barren apartment before finally settling on her feet. She took a deep breath and blurted, "I was worried about you on Wednesday. Your Jeep was in the parking lot, but you weren't there. Robbie had to fill me in on your boy's night out."

What's that? The woman who pretended he was invisible during their last encounter actually cared if he lived or died?

He shouldn't push the issue, but, well, he'd seen the way she looked at his chest. "You were worried? But you hate me." He took a step toward her, not bothering to hide the challenge in his tone.

She shook her head. "I don't though. That's the problem." She lifted her head, and her lips tugged downward.

"I'm sorry, Mabel. *So sorry.*" It seemed he hadn't left his emotions behind after all. But she deserved this apology, just like he deserved the pain of knowing he'd caused that frown on her face. "I hate that I hurt you. I wish it could've been different, but—"

"But you couldn't tell me, could you? Because of your CPA Hippocratic oath."

He blinked as the rest of his apology was rendered moot. "Yes, actually. The penalties for violating confidentiality are no joke. My hands were tied."

"So Brandon tells me."

More blinking. She was going to think he had an eye problem. "Brandon?"

"Tall, blond, kind of an asshole?" She scowled, then her face softened. "He explained the trouble you could've gotten in if you'd said anything to me. It was... weird."

"I imagine." He rested his hands on his hips as he tried to picture what *that* conversation must've been like.

Mabel interrupted his thoughts by pacing toward his

kitchenette, her sandals slapping against the tile. "Here's the thing: you didn't trust me. I thought we were building something. Why didn't you think I could keep a secret?"

He followed her but kept the round kitchen table between them as a buffer. "Habit. I never mix personal and professional. Never had anybody I was even slightly tempted to break the rules for before." He blew out a breath and braced for honesty. "And part of me worried that you'd go straight to Brandon and get me fired. So yeah. I guess I'm not used to trusting anybody but myself to keep my career safe."

She wrapped her hands around a chair back and studied her knuckles. "Okay. Fair point. I suppose I'm the same with my career."

Sadness still clung to her, and all he could do was say it again. "I'm so sorry."

"For what though?" She let go of the chair and paced back to the living room.

He shook his head in confusion, the whole time drinking in the sight of her. In her short green dress, she was the only spot of color in his newly beige world.

She crossed her arms over her chest and leveled a look at him. "Are you sorry for not telling me? Or for hurting me when I found out?"

His mouth snapped shut, but apparently his face gave away the answer he didn't want to say out loud, because she huffed out a bitter laugh.

"So you're sorry for hurting me, but you still think you did the right thing by not trusting me."

He could lie. He *should* lie.

But no. He at least owed her honesty now, even if it killed him. "I apologize. I'll apologize every day for every-thing, but the thing is, I *did* do the right thing." Disappointment moved across her face and landed like a blow to his gut, but he forced himself to continue. "Confidentiality is part of the job. I've sacrificed so much to get where I am, and I can't just throw it all away."

The length of his apartment separated them, and he keenly felt every foot of that distance. He moved toward her, desperate to make her understand. "What I'm doing with Lowell right now is going to get me a partnership, *finally*. I couldn't jeopardize that, couldn't jeopardize my whole life. Not even for whatever we are."

"Whatever we *were*," she whispered.

Her defeated tone stripped away the last of his pretenses. All his promises to himself about recommitting to work and pushing aside his hopes for a relationship fell away when he looked at her. He still wanted her, and he wouldn't, *couldn't*, walk away from those feelings yet, not after he'd lived without them for as long as he had.

"We were amazing." He closed the distance between them to stand in front of her. "We could still be amazing."

Bam. The temperature in the room jumped twenty degrees. The tips of his running shoes brushed against her purple-polished toenails as she tipped her head up to meet his eyes.

"No. We can't. I have to stay away from you." But even as she spoke the words, her body swayed toward his.

"Why?" he rasped. "I mean, I know *why*. I work for Lowell, I wasn't honest with you, you've had bad past experiences. But that's done now; the decisions are made. Why keep fighting this?"

She shook her head slowly. "Because... because it's not safe for me." She probably didn't mean to give away what she was thinking, but her hand drifted up to press against her heart.

He covered it with his own, relishing the press of his skin against hers. "I'm not dangerous."

"You are." Her voice cracked in the quiet of his apartment, and she shook off his hand, spinning to make a restless circuit toward his kitchen. "I let myself start to care for you, and then you couldn't even meet my eyes in that meeting. I get that you had no choice, and I get that it's irrational for me to be angry with you for that. But you hurt me." She folded her arms. "I just... I don't think we're a good idea."

He ran his hands through his still-damp hair and let them fall to his sides, panic surging in his chest. "So, what, we keep it professional then? Ignore all this chemistry?"

His heart slammed against his ribs as he watched the animation drain from her face to be replaced by remote politeness. She was closing the door on their relationship, this door that almost never opened for him, and all he could do was stand by and watch her do it.

"Yes." She lifted her chin. "From now on, it's professional Mabel or no Mabel at all." She twined her fingers together at her waist as she waited for his answer.

He sucked in a deep breath. "Nothing at all then." He fought to speak through the despair that threatened to suffocate him.

Silence followed his words until Mabel broke it with an unamused laugh. "Okay. I get it."

"No, I don't think you do."

She didn't know about him. He hadn't explained what it meant for a demisexual to fall for someone. How rare it was, how deep his feelings ran. How after Asha, he'd believed that he'd never find another woman who would draw this out of him. Not until Mabel came along with her voice and her wit and her body. Fuck, what if he never found that again? What if this was his last chance? What if she was the one, his *person*?

But he clenched his jaw and said nothing. Telling her any of that now would just pressure her, manipulate her even, and he'd never do that to her. But he could touch her one more time, and so he did. He cupped her jaw and stroked his thumb over her cheek and down across her lower lip. She gave a shuddering sigh and closed her eyes, leaning into his palm as he struggled to find the words to explain without explaining why he was making this choice.

"Just for a little while, I can't..." He inhaled hard. "Seeing you but not being able to touch you is too hard right now."

He needed time to grieve, to lick his wounds. But when he searched her face for some indication that she understood that this was the opposite of a rejection, her features were an expressionless mask.

She pulled away abruptly and spoke with a crispness in her tone that he'd never heard before. "Message received. I'll steer clear if I see you around the office. Bye, Jake."

She turned and walked out of his apartment without another word.

This is what he should want. It's what the Jake of three months ago would've wanted. But it wasn't what he wanted now, not that it mattered. Still, he'd respect her decision and go back to his solitary, work-focused life. He survived his last breakup. He'd survive this too.

She was gone, and he was alone, his sweat drying to a sticky film on his skin.

TWENTY-ONE

Mabel's eyes snapped open at four forty-five a.m. on Monday. She hadn't set any alarms, but apparently her body no longer needed external stimulus to get her out of bed that early.

"This is a terrible superpower," she grumbled to Tybalt, who lifted his furry head from the foot of the bed, cracked one eye open in a withering feline glare, and dropped right back to sleep. She groaned and mashed her pillow over her face, shouting into the goose down. "The only good thing about this situation is that I get to sleep in, and I can't even do that right!"

Grumbling, she flopped and repositioned herself, but by five thirty, she admitted defeat and rolled out of bed, shuffling into the kitchen to dump a heap of coffee into a filter.

As the machine burbled to life, she plunked herself down at the kitchen island and propped her feet on the stool next to her, picking up her phone.

Mabel: *Don't you dare be too funny without me.*

Ten seconds later, Dave's reply zipped back: *Weird in here without your hideous face.*

She immediately pulled a cross-eyed grimace, snapped a pic, and hit Send. It was almost like being there with him.

Except that it wasn't. Like, not at all.

With a self-pitying sigh, she filled her mug and hesitated in front of the radio in her kitchen. Listening was masochistic. Not listening was wallowing in denial.

"Go big or go home," she announced to her empty kitchen as she pressed the power button.

She listened to every minute of Dave's first solo show. It was *awful.* Not the show, of course. It was solid enough. She thought he did better matching wits with another person, but then again, she was probably biased. But she and Dave had been a broadcasting duo since they'd been paired up on a group project their sophomore year. Not being in the studio with him that morning felt wrong. So she sipped her coffee and nurtured her loathing of Brandon, the cause of her misery. She moved from the kitchen to the living room couch, where she ate handfuls of dry cereal out of the box; to the bathroom so she could shower; then back to the living room, where she stared at the wall as Dave thanked the listeners for putting up with his first solo outing and signed off.

"Well, the world didn't end after all," she informed the cat snoozing on her lap as her phone buzzed.

Dave: *Guess the world didn't end.*

She barked out a laugh. That Arrogant Asshole could separate them, but it didn't mean they weren't still psychically linked.

She arrived at the station around eleven and parked in one of the available slots on the shade-free side of the lot.

Yet another grievance to add to Brandon's pile: no longer having her choice of parking spots. Nerves propelled her through the parking lot and into the studio, where she'd left herself plenty of time to prep. A solo show was a whole different beast, and she'd be radically changing her usual presentation. She felt like she was standing at the edge of a cliff while her evil new boss stood behind her with a hand on her back, nudging her toward the edge.

She claimed the new desk in the greenroom and list-lessly read through Google news while Skip ran his show on the other side of the glass. Until now, she hadn't fully appreciated the talent it took to make talking to yourself for hours entertaining. Skip was a master, rattling away about the finer points of the weekend's White Sox game. Lucky him; sports would be a disaster for her.

Frustrated, she slammed her laptop shut and opened the door to the booth as soon as the ON AIR sign turned off. She dropped into the chair opposite Skip and wilted dramatically over the side. "I can't do this."

He glanced up from the computer screen where he was searching through songs. "You're gonna have to, sister. They already sold the ad time."

"Oh. Well, in that case, anything to make Lowell Consolidated a little richer." Mabel shifted to drape her legs over the left arm of the chair, deciding that the early-afternoon sunlight slanting through the slats of the venetian blinds would bathe her in angelic light. Poor Mabel, martyred at the altar of profit to appease the gods of rock 'n' roll. She tossed her head back dramatically.

"Why are you squirming? That chair's wobbly, and you're making it worse."

"Fine." She grudgingly straightened herself and watched Skip do his thing for the rest of his shift. With ten minutes to go before her afternoon debut, they switched places so she could take over the control board.

"You ready for this, kiddo?" he asked, caterpillar eyebrows arching upward.

She puffed her cheeks with air and exhaled. "Nope. But I don't think I'll ever be, you know?"

"I kept a bucket next to me so I could throw up between bits during my first solo show twenty years ago."

Mabel leaned her elbows on the counter. "Wow, Skip. Thank you. That's so... disgusting."

His laughter carried him out the door, leaving her to her final prep. She needed to stop being a drama queen. She'd flown solo plenty of times in the past when Dave was sick or when she filled in for vacationing deejays. She knew how to work a board, and she knew how to fill the hours on air.

"You'll be fine," she muttered. "You can do this." God, was talking to herself round-the-clock her new solo-show persona?

With three minutes until airtime, she nervously clenched and released her fists a few times and reached for her headset. Before she settled it around her neck though, the greenroom door burst open and Dave marched into the studio, wordlessly pulled her out of the chair and into a tight hug, then spun around and left.

That's what she needed to slow down her heartbeat and boost her confidence. She was alone, but she wasn't *alone*, and the thought wrapped its soft, fuzzy arms around her as she queued up her opening song—"All by Myself," natch.

She flipped on the mic, shuffled her notes, and was hit by a bolt of inspiration so stupid, so ridiculous, so oh-my-

God-Brandon-will-hate-this, that every part of her recoiled. She couldn't do *that*, obviously.

But when she opened her mouth, it rolled out, unbidden. "Good afternoon, Beaucoeur! It's Mae Bell here to take you through your commute home. As always, I'm joined by my partner, Dave."

She let dead air sit for six seconds, about the length of time Dave would take to introduce himself and throw it back to her.

She picked up as if he had. "That's right, Dave, it *is* weird to be on the air this late in the afternoon. What's that big glowing yellow ball hovering over the horizon?"

Silence.

"Wait, I *shouldn't* look directly at it? Well, I wish you'd warned me earlier."

More silence.

"Hospital? I don't think so. I'm sure this blindness is just temporary."

And then she really committed to the bit, intentionally knocking over a stack of CDs on the desk to her left. They tumbled to the floor with an audible clatter.

"Ummm, Dave? Tell me I didn't just knock over one of the fancy pieces of equipment that our new station owners bought us."

Siiiiileeeence.

"Uh-oh. Guess I'd better play some Soundgarden in honor of this strange and confusing time of day."

Mabel hit Play on "Black Hole Sun," then leaned back in her chair, smiled, and waited for the next break.

After twenty more minutes of talking to imaginary Dave, she ducked beneath the counter, stretching the cord on her headset to the limit to rummage in her purse for some ChapStick. When she righted herself, she shrieked and grabbed her chest.

"Jesus! What if I'd been on the air?"

Brandon leaned against the doorway. "Yes, what a shame to ruin such an entertaining show."

She yanked the cans off her head. "What the hell do you— Um, what can I do for you?" She'd been expecting him at some point, but his appearance still had her heart thundering.

He pushed off the doorframe and strolled into the small room, stopping at the cluttered counter along the far wall to poke at the big magnet that erased the now-obsolete carts the station had used for commercials once upon a time. He straightened a tottering pile of fast-food napkins on the counter, then turned to face her.

"Knock it off," he said.

She widened her eyes. *Who, me?* But he just looked steadily at her as the Yeah Yeah Yeahs played in the background, warning them that heads will roll. Man, he was good at the silent rebuke thing.

She broke first, muttering like a sullen teenager, "Fine. Whatever."

"I don't want to hear the name Dave even one more time on your show. Clear?"

Her lips twitched as a new idea hatched in her brain. He narrowed his eyes, obviously seeing something on her face he didn't like, but she pasted on an innocent smile and said, "I'll stop referring to my former cohost. Promise." She traced a dramatic X over her heart, and after one last glare, he left the booth with a scowl. Well, he should be frowning. He'd just handed her her next move.

When the song ended, Mabel was back on, this time talking in standard deejay patter, no invisible cohost this time. But she spent the next hour introducing every song she could think of with Dave in the name. The Dave Matthews Band was low-hanging fruit. Then Joan Baez's "A Song for David," and her personal favorite, "David Duchovny" by Bree Sharp. She had to do a deep dive into the station's archives to come up with "Dave" by the Boomtown Rats and "David Watts" by the Kinks, but it was worth it.

It took longer than she expected, but an hour into her all-Dave rock block, Brandon appeared outside the studio window, legs planted and arms crossed.

She flashed him a delighted smile as she flipped on the mic and said, "After the break, I've got David Bowie's 'Heroes.' Hey, do you think David Bowie ever went by Dave?"

She maintained eye contact the whole time she spoke, not bothering with any fake contrition. When she was finished, Brandon dragged a finger across his throat, then turned and left.

Oh well. She'd made her point for the day.

By the end of her shift, she was *bored*. Was she supposed to spend the rest of her career locked alone in a booth? How did Skip stand it? A social creature like her shouldn't be cooped up like this.

Her phone buzzed, and she dove for it.

Dave: *Ana says u done good.*

Mabel: *Sorry, but you need to leave her immediately. She's obviously lost her mind.*

Dave: *I also say u done good.*

Mabel: *Then you've lost your mind and she should leave YOU. Don't worry, you can stay in my spare bedroom until the divorce is final.*

She tucked the phone into her bag, feeling lighter

than a moment ago. Maybe it wasn't boredom she was feeling, but loneliness. And now she'd be headed home to an empty house. It never used to bother her, before...

Before nothing. Before nobody. This off-kilter feeling certainly wasn't about the man who didn't want her in his life at all. She was in a temporary weird spot, that's all. She'd get through it.

She powered down the nonessential equipment and made sure Dave's prerecorded voice track was set to play overnight. Then she grabbed her purse and left through a greenroom made otherworldly by the dim glow of the nighttime security lights.

TWENTY-TWO

Three weeks into the second stage of his life in Beau-coeur, Jake had resigned himself to the status quo. Weird how alternating work and sleep didn't have the same appeal for him that it used to. So what if he was spending another of his Friday nights working on the Kriegsman file? It's what he would've been doing in Chicago. Of course, there he'd be surrounded by the plush rugs, sleek sofas, and carefully selected architectural prints deco-rating his Gold Coast condo. Not that he was too good for the Formica and microsuede. Hell, everything in this apartment, including the uneven kitchen table that doubled as a desk, was miles nicer than the stuff he grew up with.

The problem was Mabel of course. She'd been in this place only once, yet he felt her absence everywhere.

He pushed back from the table with a snarl and stalked to the fridge to snag a beer. He was so fucking tired of himself. He was moping around like some kind of Howard Hughes-ian recluse when in fact his partnership was closer than ever. With an angry twist, he pulled off the cap but ended up staring into the neck of the bottle, unsure if he had the strength to even perform the simple task of bringing it to his mouth.

A pounding on his door shattered his pity party, and he braced himself to turn down yet another invitation to whatever social event Thea was jetting off to this weekend. Instead, he was shocked into silence by the sight of Milo on the doorstep with a duffel bag over his shoulder and a six-pack of beer under each arm.

"I sensed moping from all the way up in Chicago and came to make that stop." He pushed past Jake and plunked the six-packs onto the kitchen table. He did a slow turn around the room, taking in the nondescript couch, bare walls, and tiny television, then gave a low whistle. "Love what you've done with the place."

Jake ignored the insult, too flabbergasted by his buddy showing up unexpectedly in Beaucoeur.

"What the hell are you doing here? And how do you even have this address?"

"Weaseled it out of your assistant at BPS." Milo dropped his duffel bag on the couch. "She should probably be more careful about your personal information, but I brought her a muffin and overwhelmed her with my charm."

Milo took one look at the Budweiser bottle in Jake's hand and groaned. "It's worse than I thought. Here." He pulled a bottle from one of the six-packs he'd arrived with, pried the Bud from Jake's fingers, and replaced it with a Sliced Nectarine IPA from Moody Tongue.

The gesture blew the rest of the cobwebs out of Jake's brain. "Thanks, man." Moody Tongue was one of his favorite Chicago microbreweries, and Milo's thoughtfulness was the first nice thing to happen to him today.

"You're welcome." His friend grabbed a beer for himself, kicked off his shoes, and stretched out on the couch. "I'm yours for the weekend, here to take your mind off whatever's ailing you."

"What makes you think anything's ailing me?" God, was his bone-deep sadness sending invisible SOSs all the way to Chicago?

Milo grabbed the remote and clicked around until he found the Cubs game. "I bumped into Greg McDonald at a charity golf thing last weekend. Man, you work with some douchebags."

"Did he look smug? I bet that fucker looked smug." His grip tightened on his bottle as he imagined McDonald's beady, entitled eyes.

"Dude's got resting smug face," Milo pointed out. "I guess he recognized me from that bachelor auction we did last winter, because he asked me if I'd heard anything from you during your 'prison sentence down south.' I said the last report I had was that you were doing amazing work for your fancy new media company and living the good life in Beaucoeur. But I thought I ought to come see for myself."

Jake's anxiety spiked, and it propelled him to take a lap around his apartment. "Good life. Yeah, something like that." Then he shut up and picked at the edge of the IPA label with his thumbnail.

"Wait a minute." With a rustle and a clink, Milo pushed himself into an upright position and set his beer bottle on the coffee table. He even muted the game. "I remember that tone from all those years ago. You went and caught a bad case of emotions. There's a woman, isn't there?"

Jake cursed softly. This was the problem with people who'd known you for years. "There's no woman."

"Bullshit," Milo gleefully shot back. "You've been gone for a couple of weeks, and somehow Chicago's most eligible demisexual found a girl in Beautiful Cow, and now you're sitting around your apartment listening to love songs. I'm... Well, I'm astounded, frankly. Who *is* she?"

"Nope. We're not doing this." Jake spoke with finality designed to shut Milo down. His friend had the start of it right, but Jake didn't have the strength to tell him that it wasn't love songs he was listening to but Johnny Cash's "Hurt" on repeat.

Milo raised his hands in surrender. "Fine. Shut down my supportive questions. But if you're not gonna spill your guts, I need you to shut up. The Cubs are down by one, and I have to focus." He clicked the sound back on and reclaimed his beer. "And I *am* going to use this weekend to do some research and find out all about the girl."

Research. Jake plucked that word from Milo's jokey threats and held it up to the light. *Research.* There was something there, something he could use. If he could just...

He straightened with a start as the idea materialized. "I've got to handle a few work things. You good here?" he asked Milo, who waved him off without tearing his eyes from the screen. Jake shut himself away in the bedroom, blocking out the announcer's voice from the TV, and selected a number on his phone.

"Well, well, well. You're calling *me* for a change."

"Hey." Too restless to hold still, he paced the tiny length of the room. "I need to borrow your marketing genius. Got a minute?"

"For you, brother of mine, I've got all the minutes," Finn said. "Let me just put my glamorous life on hold for you."

He snorted. "Glamorous? It's Friday night, and your boyfriend's next to you on the couch, reading something nonfiction, isn't he? Oh God, please tell me that's all you were doing."

His sister responded with an identical snort. "Actually, yes, Tom *is* reading a book on macroeconomics while I'm immersed in a magazine. A trashy one. Much sexy. So glamour."

"Well, put it down. I need your help on a research project, and knowing you, you'll want to take notes. It's a, uh, a personal thing."

He heard rustling, as if she almost dropped her phone. "Personal? Like, *personal* personal?" He grunted, and Finn stifled a gasp. "Jake, did you meet someone?"

His heart lurched at the delight in his sister's voice—delight that he had to crush. "No. I mean yes. I did. But it didn't..." He sighed and pinched the bridge of his nose to hold back any further words.

"*Oh.* Oh, I'm sorry," Finn said softly. "Do you want to talk about it?"

Jake's younger sister was one of the people who knew how uniquely challenging his relationship situation was. Well, she knew most of it anyway. She'd helped him through the worst of his depression after he ended things with Asha, but what she didn't know was that the only woman since then who'd sparked similar interest was her best friend Josie. Jake had seriously considered it, thought long and hard about pursuing the flirty redhead. But in the end, the possibility that it would create friction between him and Finn, and between Finn and Josie, had been too much, so he'd turned away from that possibility even though it felt a little like he was turning away from romantic relationships forever. Until Mabel.

"Yeah, I guess I do need to talk about it," he said.

Finn listened raptly as he sketched the broad strokes of radio-station events in Beaucoeur, his spirits plunging as he neared the end of the story. He concluded with "I don't know that Mabel will ever forgive me, but I want to at least try to make things right for her job-wise."

Finn was quiet for a long moment. "And my marketing genius might help with that."

"You tell me. Will commissioning a focus group work? Have them listen to the old morning show and the new, non-Mabel one?" Everything else might be fucked up, but he could at least try to help Mabel with this.

Finn laughed softly. "Oh, my quantitative-minded brother, how it does my heart good to hear you asking about qualitative methodologies. Yes, focus groups provide rich data that could help convince the new boss in a situation like this. Assuming the show actually was better before."

"It was. So you'll help?"

"Of course I will, Jake."

Her simple statement of support overwhelmed him, and he swallowed thickly. "Thanks." He was used to feeling like he had to take care of *her*. How strange to be the one taken care of for a change.

"So," Finn said briskly, tender sibling time apparently over, "I'll type up an outline for the focus group moderator and research what local firms might be able to run it. Check your email on Monday."

"I will. Give my best to Tom, okay?"

"Oh, I *will* give my best to Tom," his baby sister

purred, then hung up before Jake could groan over the wrongness of that. Actually, no. Nothing was wrong with his sister finding happiness with a guy who adored her. In truth, he envied her the joy she'd grabbed for herself.

Envy. Jealousy. Frustration. Of course those feelings hit him from time to time, but he always buried them under work and gym and good-guy Jake. He was the person who toasted his friends at their engagement parties before hopping into a cab to finish up some work at the office before going home alone, and *fuck*, he was tired of it.

When he wandered back out to the living room, Milo spared a glance at him before zooming back to the game. "So what are the plans for the rest of the weekend?"

Jake settled on the couch. "Work. Maybe stream a James Bond movie later. I could give you a city tour, I guess."

Milo gave him a dramatic Roman-emperor-style thumbs-down. "I don't want a tour. I'm talking bars. Ladies. Nightlife. You may or may not have found your person, but I'm still on the prowl." He scratched his stomach and took another pull of his IPA. "Come on, man, what do you do for fun around here?"

"I don't," Jake said flatly, then reconsidered. "I guess there's a thing with the radio station I'm down here for. They're auditioning women at a bar tomorrow to be station ambassadors." The words were out before he could call them back.

Milo perked right up. "*Sexy* station ambassadors?"

"That's the idea, yes," Jake reluctantly confirmed.

Milo grinned. "There's our plan then. You're working for the station, so you have some say in the auditions, right? And I'm obviously qualified to be an auxiliary judge. So we kick around here tonight, then tomorrow you give me the five-minute tour of whatever passes for scenery around here, we eat a solid dinner primarily composed of red meats and cheeses, and then we drink our faces off with the pretty ladies of Beautiful Cow. I like it. Who else should we call to join?"

Leave it to Milo to orchestrate a night out in a town he'd never visited before. "The only one I can think of is Robbie, the new station receptionist. I think you two'll get along."

"Call him. Let's do this," Milo commanded.

As Jake tapped out a message to Robbie, he assured himself that he wouldn't bump into Mabel tomorrow since she'd undoubtedly be steering clear of the Brick Babe auditions. Plus he was taking concrete steps to help her, and he had the promise of a night out with friends. His weekend suddenly looked a tiny bit less bleak.

TWENTY-THREE

"Hello!" Mabel called out as she let herself into Dave and Ana's house. "I'm here for the lasagna!"

"In the kitchen, Garfield!" Ana called back.

After almost a decade of spending every morning with Dave, it was weird having to schedule a dinner in order to hang out. At least Ana knew how to capital-c Cook, and spending time with their two adorable kids always made her count her blessings—her "blessings" in this case being her diaper-less, LEGO-free home.

She strolled into the kitchen, brandishing a bottle of Ana's favorite shiraz and nearly swooned at the scent of tomatoes, garlic, and oregano. "I hope you're prepared to feed me until I'm dead."

"I wouldn't have invited you if I wasn't," Ana said.

Her friend looked far more collected than a woman toiling away at the stove should. Not a strand of her shiny black hair was mussed, and she wasn't covered in sauce or flour or any visual indicators of kitchen endeavors. At this point in dinner-party prep, Mabel was generally sweaty, cursing, and covered in at least five different ingredients.

"Grab a tomato and help Aiden with the salad stuff," Ana instructed.

The drummer for the Moo Daddies looked up from where he was slicing a cucumber and cheerfully waved his knife at her. "Miss Mae. How's tricks?"

Mabel grinned. "Well, hey, Adonis! I had no idea you were so handy in the kitchen."

The sharp blades of Aiden's cheekbones turned pink. "Come on, you've gotta stop calling me that. I will get so much shit if that catches on with the rest of the band."

Ana looked up from where she was layering the lasagna to chide him. "Language! And Adonis, you must admit that you're a beautiful man. Let us womenfolk gaze upon you without any backtalk."

She and Mabel both stopped what they were doing to moonily stare at Aiden until he was red all the way to the tips of his ears and the two women couldn't contain their laughter any longer. He shook his head and kept slicing.

"Where are Thing One and Thing Two?" Mabel asked as she started on the tomato. "I was hoping to get in a little auntie time tonight."

Ana held out a glass of wine, which Mabel accepted.

"Dave's putting them to bed. If we're very lucky, they'll sleep through the evening so we can speak as adults."

"I work in a radio station. I'm deprived of adult talk," Mabel said. "Tell me things about the world where actual grown-up people work."

"My job is nothing but staff meetings these days," Ana said. "Aiden?"

"Don't look at me." He shrugged. "I work with incredibly competent craftsmen, but the one thing we don't do is have deep, meaningful conversations. Mostly we grunt about who took the ladder and what radio station to listen to for the day."

Mabel gasped and dropped her tomato. "You don't automatically tune to the Brick?" She and Ana hit him with a double dose of stink eye until he raised his hands to ward them off.

"When it's my turn to pick, of course! But other dudes have musical preferences too."

"Adonis, your father owns the construction company. You can be a little prince and demand it," Mabel reminded him.

He pointed the knife at her. "Just for that, I'm switching over to the Top 40 station next week."

She clasped a dramatic hand over her heart just as Dave strolled into the kitchen.

"Everybody's asleep. If we can keep the ruckus down tonight, they all might stay that way."

Ana greeted her man with a kiss and a bottle of beer. "You need to have a talk with Aiden. He's not exhibiting the on-the-job loyalty to the Brick that one might hope."

Dave took a long pull of his beer, then leaned across the counter until his face was even with Aiden's. "Get out of my house, asshole."

"Language!" Ana thwapped Dave on the butt with a kitchen towel.

"Hey, the kids are in bed! Let me work blue tonight."

Ana's stern expression dissolved as she leaned in for another kiss that left Mabel a wee bit jealous of their easy affection.

As soon as Dave's lips left hers, Ana warned Aiden, "You're still not off the hook."

"It'll be all Brick all next week, I swear," he said.

"Although it's not the same with this one gone." He inclined his chin in Mabel's direction.

Look at that. She could bounce from envy to misery in a few short seconds.

"Don't remind me," Dave said glumly. "The Brick Babe auditions are tomorrow, and then I'm gonna be stuck with a rotating cast of bimbos."

She'd just have to joke her way out of her dark mood. "Hmm. Kind of like Aiden's dating history," she mused, enjoying the return of his flushed cheeks. You'd think he'd be un-embarrassable about his sex life, but apparently not.

"*Anyway*," Aiden said loudly, "Ana would you tell us more about the grown-up world of social workers so the rest of us heathens can understand what it's like to work a respectable job with respectable people?"

They all settled at the dining room table as the lasagna baked. While Ana described a coworker's trip to the ER after getting beaned in the head with a softball during a home visit, Mabel studied Aiden. Pretty face, lean build, workman's muscles, rumple-me hair. And not a single bit of it attracted her in the least. What was wrong with her?

She sighed heavily into her wineglass, and Ana glanced over.

"Still upset over Jake?" she murmured.

Mabel slouched forward and spoke quietly, hoping Dave and Aiden were fully immersed in their own conversation. "No. Kind of. A little. But that's okay. I'm okay," Mabel said, doing her best to convince herself along with Ana. "I haven't seen him since he told me he didn't want to see *me*. It's fine. It's easier for both of us."

It wasn't though. It was dreadful, and she missed him. But maybe if she spun the same story over and over, she'd start to believe it. "Anyway, he'll be back up in Chicago before I know it. I mean, where were we headed, realistically?"

Ana raised her brows. "I saw the way he looked at you when you were onstage during the last Moo Daddies show. You were headed to the nearest horizontal surface that night, for sure."

"Up against a wall actually," she muttered, then laughed when Ana slapped her a high five.

"But you forget that I also talked to him that night. He likes you, Mae."

Mabel shifted in her seat and swirled the last of the wine in her glass, then jerked her head toward the kitchen. Ana followed her. Once they were safely out of earshot of the men, she picked up her last thought.

"I liked him too. But at this point, it's best if we don't have anything to do with each other."

"Is that what you really want though? I thought—"

"Please don't make this harder," Mabel begged. "Long story short: I let myself forget that relationships are a bad idea for me, and it bit me in the ass. Now I just need to get over him."

Ana tapped her chin thoughtfully, then looked pointedly at the dining room. "Hmmm. If only you could find a *different* guy who thinks you're hot."

Mabel whipped her head toward the dining room, then back to Ana. *"Dave thinks I'm hot?"*

"Ha." Ana lowered her voice and leaned in. "Aiden and I have had conversations. He's made allusions."

Mabel glanced into the dining room and ran her eyes over him again as he laughed at whatever Dave was saying. "Unfortunately, we've always just been pals. No chemistry there at all." She poured herself more wine and automatically reached for Ana's to refill too. But Ana slapped her palm over the top of her glass.

"No more?" Mabel asked, waving the half-full bottle at her. "Really?"

"Just one glass for me."

"But you never do dinner without wine, unless... Oh my God!" Mabel's mouth fell open. "Are you pregnant?"

Ana bit her lip and tried not to smile.

"You are! My partner got you good and knocked up again!"

Ana's smile bloomed across her face. "I'm still in my first trimester, so we're not telling anybody yet. We had another appointment this afternoon."

Mabel whooped and twined her arms around Ana's neck. "Mum's the word. But you're going to name this one Mabel, right? Dave promised me you would last time, and then you guys let me down and had a boy."

Ana's smile dimmed a bit. "We haven't started talking names yet. Honestly, this one's been rough. More nausea and fatigue than usual, that kind of thing. Poor Dave's basically turned into a single dad with all the puking and sleeping I've been doing. Today's the first good day I've had in ages. Take my advice and stick to heavy petting, just in case."

Mabel hugged her friend again. "As we just discussed, sex is so far from happening that it's not even funny. But you'll let me know if I can help out with anything? Cook you dinner sometime?"

"Cook? You?"

Mabel laughed. "Okay, order you a pizza."

Three hours later, Mabel and Aiden were both moaning in discomfort over their full bellies as they headed down the Chiltons' driveway. She studied his profile as they walked. He was hot. He was nice. He wasn't Jake. And maybe that's exactly what she needed.

"What are you doing tomorrow?" she blurted.

He raised his eyebrows in surprise. "Why? Looking for a good time?"

If she was doing this, she owed him honesty. "Actually, no."

"That's... not what women usually say to me."

They'd reached his Murdoch Construction pickup truck, and he leaned against it with a puzzled expression.

"No offense," she said. "I'm sure you're a very good time, but I'm actually thinking about hitting the Brick Babe auditions." The very thought of it threatened to smother her in despair, but at the same time, she felt compelled to witness the shitshow. See how obnoxious Brandon got with it. Test the limits of what she'd be able to survive during this awful time.

"And you think the hit-it-and-quit-it guy's going to make that better somehow?"

"That's a far worse nickname than Adonis." But the skepticism in his voice surprised her, and she asked, "Who wouldn't want to just hang out with you?"

One shoulder lifted in a shrug. "Again, that's not what most women are looking for from me."

"I thought that was your perpetual mission. 'Get in, get *in*, get gone.'" Had she been reading Aiden wrong all this time?

He shifted from foot to foot, considering his answer. "Yeah, it's... it's getting old." He ruffled a hand through his hair, the glow from the streetlight falling across the flat line of his mouth.

"Whoa. Aiden Murdoch's ready to settle down?"

He grimaced. "No. God no. I have no idea how to do

the adult dating thing. But fewer man-whore jokes would be nice." His smile didn't quite reach his eyes. "It's a big thing to live up to."

His confession surprised her, but she could fold it into her plan. It was the act of a mildly desperate woman, but it could work. Jake had made his wishes clear, but she might need some help honoring them.

She straightened her shoulders and made the ask. "I need a babysitter. For me."

He tilted his head like an adorably confused puppy, and she sighed.

"I recently ended a sort of relationship and need some help not drifting back into it. For my own sake, and for the guy's."

Aiden crossed his arms over his chest. "So I come along to your thing tomorrow to keep you occupied and to stop you from sending any tipsy texts."

"Exactly. Totally platonic, and everybody keeps it in their pants."

"Good thing you look good in those pants." A slow grin spread over his face.

"No thinking about my pants." She pointed a warning finger at him, not trusting the gleam in his eyes. *Damn.* Why couldn't her solution be as simple as getting under Aiden to get over Jake?

"So are we trying to make this guy jealous?"

"No!" The startled response burst out of her. She tried again more calmly. "No. And besides, he won't be there tomorrow."

"Okay then. I'll be your babysitter." His lips curved into a smile. "What time should I pick you up?"

TWENTY-FOUR

They were quite a trio that night. Robbie in a tight black T-shirt, cuffed jeans, skinny suspenders, a belt with a huge devil's-head buckle around his waist; Milo in slacks and a blazer because he was convinced women liked a man who wasn't afraid of dressing up; and Jake in jeans and a navy button-down, sleeves rolled up. They started the night at a steakhouse overlooking the Illinois River and consumed enormous amounts of beef—the better to soak up the alcohol later on, Milo had argued—and arrived at the bar a little after nine.

Brandon was holding the Brick Babe auditions at a place called Draven's, which Robbie described over dinner as a sticky-floored nightmare that catered heavily to the Rayman College crowd. Of course Brandon would choose a place known for its cheap draft beer and vomit-covered parking lot. By the time they arrived, the place was wall to wall with bodies, and the music was so loud they had to shout. Robbie dove through the crowd like a salmon swimming upstream to secure them all beer while Jake tried to locate Brandon in the midst of the throng. He didn't particularly want to be a part of the auditions, but he ought to say hello since he was there.

He and Milo edged around the crowded room toward a raised platform in the back where the station booth was assembled for the night. Robbie found them there and passed around the beers dangling from his fingers.

By then they'd made it far enough along the circuit of the room that Brandon spotted them and waved them over to the booth. Naturally, he was surrounded by women with numbers pinned to their admittedly impressive chests.

"Jakehammer! I didn't think you'd come!" Brandon waved a clipboard full of notes, his grin euphoric. Apparently, ranking women based on their looks agreed with him. Brandon explained his evaluation methods to a bemused Robbie and an enthusiastic Milo. "We're looking for women who'll show up to station events, mingle with the crowds, make sure everybody's having a good time and buying plenty of alcohol," Brandon hollered over the music and the chatter. "Feel free to tell the applicants that you three are with the station, and let me know which numbers impress you. This may be the best perk of the job, fellas!"

"I've been training my whole life for this," Milo deadpanned.

A woman with a bright red Bettie Page haircut and floral tattoo sleeve covering her left arm stood on her tiptoes to holler at Robbie, "Hi, I'm number seven! Want to know why I'd make a good Brick Babe?"

"Uh, sure?" Robbie tilted his head down to the tiny grinning woman.

"My conversation skills, of course!" she said with a wink. Then she stood on her tiptoes to whisper something in Robbie's ear that made his eyelids flutter shut. He turned to Jake with a sheepish smile. "Sorry, man. When a beautiful woman wants to go someplace quieter to talk, you damn well go someplace quieter to talk. It's only polite." Then he and Bettie Page disappeared into the crowd.

"I guess number seven gets his vote." Milo inclined his chin at numbers fourteen and twenty-one, who were eyeing him appreciatively from a few feet away.

"I'm way too married to be here," said a voice in Jake's ear. He swung around to see an uncomfortable-looking Dave Chilton trying to blend in with the wall. His thin fingers clenched a beer bottle, and he looked ready to bolt. "They're like ravenous wolves, and I'm the haunch of beef."

Jake hid a smile at Dave's hunted expression and introduced him to Milo, whom Dave greeted with a gloomy, "Hiya."

"They're going to start trying some of the women on the morning show with Dave," Jake explained to Milo. "I don't think he's looking forward to it."

"Emphatically not," Dave said. "And I wish they understood that I have no decision-making power. I've had my neck licked three times tonight. *Three times.*"

Milo perked up at that. "Which numbers?"

Jake and Dave pretended not to have heard him.

"She's here, by the way," Dave told Jake in a quieter voice.

He stared at Dave for a beat, certain he'd misheard. Mabel was *here?* For *this?* He'd avoided her for weeks, and now they were under the same roof, which was packed with alcohol and throbbing base and college kids making out in every corner? Fucking *great.*

"She?" Milo asked. "So there *is* a girl?"

Jake groaned as a delighted smile spread across Milo's face. Ears like a bat, that one, even in this overstuffed, overloud bar.

"No," he said quickly at the same time that Dave said, "Mabel."

"Iiiiinteresting. There's a girl named Mabel," Milo said, but when Jake didn't brush away his comment, the teasing smile fell from his face. "Wait, is this somebody you're serious about?"

Jake cut his eyes to Dave, then nodded. "Yeah."

"Like Asha serious?" Milo's eyes widened.

"Bigger than that even." Jake sighed and tilted his head to the ceiling to keep his thoughts in check. Getting over Asha had been hard. Had been almost impossible. Getting over Mabel was going to be... *Fuck.*

When he looked back down, Dave was watching him curiously, and Jake offered the simplest explanation he could in this overly hot, overly loud bar. "I don't date."

"Understatement," Milo said. "Jake's had exactly one girlfriend in the decade I've known him, and that was years ago."

Dave's brow creased. "So you hold out for a relationship that's worth it."

"Kind of, yeah," Jake said. He had no problem explaining his situation to Dave, but he'd be goddamned if he'd do it with Brandon assigning scores to women's bodies ten feet away.

"That's why I'm dying to hear all about this paragon who managed to lasso my buddy," Milo told Dave excitedly. But when Jake growled, Milo held up his hands in surrender with a laugh. "Fine. I won't ask another question about her tonight if you'll tell me the number of the hottest licker."

Jake turned pleading eyes toward Dave, who sighed and said, "Number five."

"Thanks! But don't think I'm leaving town without meeting your girl," Milo said. And with that he vanished, leaving Jake and Dave to try to disappear into the crowd.

"I know she's not my girl," Jake muttered. God forbid Dave took away the impression that he felt some kind of claim on Mabel when she'd made it clear that wasn't what she wanted.

"Yeah, well, I wish she was." Dave nodded toward the dance floor, and Jake lifted his eyes to see the tall blonde that he definitely hadn't been watching for all night. She wasn't here alone, and the whole bar seemed to tilt sideways.

When Dave turned to give him a sympathetic look, Jake realized his indrawn breath had been louder than he thought.

"That's Aiden Murdoch," Dave said. "He's the drummer for the Moo Daddies."

"I remember," Jake said shortly. "You don't forget a guy who looks like an underwear model."

Dave snorted. "Oh, he'll hate that. I can't wait to give him shit about that later."

But Jake wasn't listening. "I thought she liked to keep a low profile about guys she's seeing." He spoke more to himself than to Dave, but his friend answered anyway.

"I was as surprised to see them together tonight as you are," Dave said. "Maybe she needed something easy. Aiden's not relationship material, if you get what I'm saying."

"Afraid I do." Jake's hands curled into fists as he

watched Mabel and Aiden playfully grinding on the dance floor. Mabel's over-the-top shimmying only lasted about thirty seconds before she burst into a peal of laughter that was audible all the way across the room.

Hearing her maple syrup laugh almost broke him. His muscles burned with the need to grab her, kiss her, demand she tell him why she decided to go public with some new guy so quickly after the two of them crashed and burned. But they'd both set limits on their new dynamic, and well, he did have a *few* shreds of dignity left.

When she tugged Aiden off the dance floor, their trajectory took them right past where Jake and Dave were lurking in the shadows. She stopped short when she noticed him. He sardonically lifted his bottle toward her in a greeting, and her jaw fell open. She turned and whispered something to *goddamn Aiden*, who gripped her shoulder briefly. Then they walked over together.

"Professional coworker," Mabel greeted Jake. Then to Dave: "Mole person."

The underwear model held out his hand to Jake. "Aiden Murdoch."

"Jake Carey." He tried not to turn it into a strength contest, but somehow in the course of that endless handshake, fingers were squeezed and masculinities were tested. Both men surreptitiously flexed their hands once they broke their grip.

"So how are the auditions going?" Mabel asked brightly.

"You don't have to fake it with us. We all know this is soul-crushing," Dave said.

Her smile vanished. "I bet Brandon's being a complete pig."

"He's got a clipboard for notes," Dave said. "At least he hasn't taken their measurements."

"Yet," Jake said.

At Mabel's frustrated groan, Aiden looped a casual arm around her shoulders while Dave glanced over at Jake and Mabel dropped her eyes on the floor. This had to be the most awkward four-way conversation since the Virgin Mary explained her situation to Joseph and her parents.

Mabel pulled away from Aiden, and her gaze flitted over each man's face before she declared, "Restroom. Be right back."

She spun on her heel and vanished into the crowd, and no, this time Jake would *not* be following her.

Desperate to think about anything except the first time he kissed her, he turned to Dave and made aggressively mundane conversation. "Ana stayed home tonight?"

"Yeah, how weird that she'd want to miss this." Dave cast a fearful gaze around the crowded bar.

"You're lucky, you know?" Aiden said. "You and Ana, you've got this great, comfortable relationship. She trusts you out here with the minidress brigade, and you're obviously dying to get back home to your family. It's nice."

Aiden stopped talking when he noticed the shock on Dave's face.

"I'm sorry, is Mr. 'A Groupie in Every Port' envious of my domestic life?" Dave's brows lifted above the top of his glasses, and Aiden took a pull from his beer.

"Nah. It's not for me. But it's a nice thought." He ran a hand through his hair, then abruptly changed the subject. "I'm empty. Anybody else need another drink?"

Dave accepted, Jake declined, and Aiden went to brave the crowded bar.

"Maybe not so fun and uncomplicated after all." Dave whipped his glasses off to polish them.

Jake grunted. As bad as fun and uncomplicated sounded, something more serious sounded even worse. He leaned against the wall and rubbed a hand over his eyes. When he opened them again, Mabel was standing next to Dave.

"So, you scoped out my replacements yet?"

"I'm leaving that to *il Duce* over there." Dave jabbed his thumb to where Brandon was laughing with two pneumatically gifted women.

"He's certainly some kind of *Duce*," Mabel grumbled.

"Damn straight," Dave said.

"Hi!"

All three of them jumped at the chipper voice behind them. It was Thea. Of course. Because this night wasn't spiraling down the toilet quickly enough.

"Hi, Jakey!" She stretched up to give him a quick hug, which Jake accepted with all the pliability of a two-by-four.

Sliding his eyes to Mabel, he gestured toward the brunette pixie in the barely-there black dress. "Guys, this is Thea. My neighbor."

"Hi, everyone!" She waved, then clapped her hands together and twisted them nervously. Three seconds later, she looked down, seemed to notice the movement, and forced her palms down against her thighs.

Mabel stepped forward. "Hi, Thea. I'm Mae Bell." Her dangerously syrupy words poured from an insincerely smiling mouth. "Since you know *Jakey* already, can I introduce you to my former cohost Dave?"

Thea gave an excited shriek and tossed up her arms. "You're Dave! You're as cute as I pictured! I soooooo hope Brandon gives me an on-air tryout with you!"

She beamed up at him, and Dave, who apparently had never gotten the hang of the insincere radio personality smile, gave her a weak approximation that made him look like a man contemplating extensive dental surgery. But he recovered his composure and dodged Thea's outstretched arms before they could wrap him in a hug too.

"Brandon's the man with the plan, so you'll have to chat with him about that," he boomed in his most obnoxious Big Time Radio Host voice, pointing her in the direction of the booth. "Nice to meet you! Bye now!"

"Oooh, thanks!" Thea called, scanning the bar like a Terminator before heading off to seek new prey.

Once she was gone, Dave turned to Mabel in desperation. "We have *got* to get you back on the morning show."

Aiden rejoined the group in time to hear Mabel say, "Yeah, all that exposed flesh so early in the morning will be really distracting."

"Doesn't matter. Mabel's the hottest woman here," Aiden announced.

Mabel rolled her eyes and smacked his arm while Jake drained his bottle. If he didn't exit this situation immediately, his jealousy might just bubble over until his fists made Aiden's face a lot less pretty.

"I'm going to circulate," he announced. "Dave, Mabel, good luck getting through the rest of the auditions."

When he cut his eyes to Aiden, his hands curled into fists, and he turned and stalked away, plunging into the crowd to track down Milo and Robbie. He was willing to interrupt any amount of licking if it meant he no longer had to be part of the couple he'd just left behind.

He found his buddies standing near the station booth, Brick Babe contestants circling like june bugs. Milo hooked an elbow around Jake's neck. "Best night ever! I think I'd like living here!"

Jake half-heartedly clinked his empty bottle against Milo's, but before he could respond, a woman wiggled between them, shoving Milo aside so she could wrap her lean, tan arm around Jake's waist.

"Hey, handsome! Are you with the station?" She pursed her glossy peach lips and leaned into him.

"Ah, no—" he started to say, but Robbie jumped in and hollered, "Hell yes, he is!"

"Great!" She fluttered her lashes like she was trying to kick-start a tidal wave. "I'm Wendy, and I'd be a great Brick Babe. Wanna know why?"

"No," Jake said flatly, looking over her head at Milo. An undercurrent passed between them, one forged in the fires of countless crowded Chicago bars at which Jake had perfected the art of tactfully directing any woman approaching him with a gleam in her eye to his eternally receptive friend. But tonight Milo seemed to be the only one with any tact.

"Tell me instead, beautiful," Milo said, smoothly leading the blonde toward the opposite end of the station table where Brandon was, in fact, making notes on a clipboard in the middle of a dozen or so number-sporting women. Jake's old roommate sent him a sloppy smile and an even sloppier salute, and Jake grimaced in return. He turned to look for Robbie, but as he did, he spotted a different blonde. Mabel, frozen in place across the room.

Their gazes locked, and all the sound in the bar

dropped away as he stared into her wide eyes. His old friend panic came roaring back as he considered how this must look. He was standing in the middle of the hot-girl applicant pool, and Mabel undoubtedly thought he was an enthusiastic participant. He hadn't taken the chance to explain himself to her, hadn't tried to make her understand why an event like this didn't have the power to move him at all while one single word from her lips could make him tremble.

His first instinct was to cross the room and lay it all out for her: how rare his attraction to her was, how devastating it had been to lose her before they'd even begun, how much he still wanted to be with her. But he forced his feet to stay planted on the sticky floor. She wanted to keep things polite and professional? She wanted to hit the bar with some new guy? Then she could goddamn well deal with him trying to pick up his life and move forward too.

When the crowd around him shifted, it broke the spell, and Mabel blinked and turned her head sharply to laugh at something her date said.

Her fucking date.

Screw politeness. This was a hot, crowded nightmare, and nothing about his night would be improved by sticking around. "I'm going," he called to Robbie and Milo over the bass thumping from the speakers six feet away.

"You sure?" Robbie swiped his sleeve across his sweaty forehead and gestured around them. "Lots of ladies here. Lots more fish in the sea."

"Nah, not for Jake. He's picky," Milo said lightly, and a slight bit of tension in Jake's chest eased at having a friend in town who got him without the need for a long conversation. Then Milo followed Jake's gaze across the bar to where Mabel was whispering with Aiden.

"Is that her?" Milo moved to stand next to him. When Jake nodded, Milo looked back at her and her date. "Christ. No wonder you haven't wanted to talk about it." Then he turned to Robbie. "Hey, man, we're gonna call it a night. Maybe grab some burgers on the way home. You good here?"

"Oh yeah," Robbie said, casting his eyes toward Bettie Page, who smiled back shyly from a few feet away. "I'm good. You guys go ahead."

Without bothering to say any additional goodbyes, Jake and Milo weaved through the press of sweaty bodies to reach the cool evening air. Once they were buckled into his Jeep, Jake rubbed his ears, which still throbbed from the blaring dance music.

"So do you want to talk about it now?" Milo asked as Jake put the car in drive and left the parking lot.

"I chose work when it mattered." He kept his eyes on the twin circles of yellow his headlights splashed on the road. "I wasn't wrong to do it, but at the same time she wasn't wrong to be hurt by it." He clenched the steering wheel until his knuckles whitened. "I guess in the end, she was my person but I wasn't hers."

Milo exhaled but said nothing, and Jake was grateful. They drove through the dark streets of Beaucoeur in silence.

As Milo snored on his couch that night, Jake tossed his phone from hand to hand, then tapped out a message and hit Send before his better instincts could wave him off.

So that was awkward.

The whoosh sounded, and he dropped the phone on

the mattress as if it had burned him. So much for keeping his distance. But it was the only way he could think to say, "I didn't like the way tonight went down and also please don't still be with that guy."

Just when he was starting to worry that she'd blocked his number, the phone buzzed, and he snatched it up.

Mabel: *Nah. Seeing you surrounded by women just reminded me of a joke.*

Jake: *A joke?*

Yeah, tonight *had* been a joke, and not a very funny one. But that's not what she meant.

Mabel: *What do you call an accountant who's spotted talking to someone else?*

Jake: *What?*

Mabel: *Popular.*

Triumph burned through his veins. If she was texting him, that likely meant she wasn't still with Murdoch. And he could play this game. He could play this game all night.

Jake: *Okay, Bowen. How many deejays does it take to change a light bulb?*

Mabel: *How many??*

Jake: *None. Nobody wants to turn on a light and see their faces anyway.*

Mabel: *Gasp! How do you drive an accountant insane?*

Jake: *Text him bad jokes?*

Mabel: *No! Tie him to a chair, stand in front of him, and fold up a map the wrong way.*

He groaned. He actually groaned out loud in his bedroom, not from the corniness of the joke but from the thought of Mabel and ropes and a chair. Instead of begging her to do just that, he returned fire.

Jake: *You asked for it: Knock, knock.*

Twenty minutes later, he couldn't stop smiling because Mabel wasn't spending the night with her date. She was spending it texting with him.

Not very professional. But he didn't care.

TWENTY-FIVE

Mabel was stretched out on the greenroom couch on a Monday in early November when Dave slouched in wearing a rumpled shirt and a weary expression.

"What's up?" She put down the magazine she was reading. "You look like hell."

Dave batted at her legs until she lifted them enough for him to slide underneath. "Just tired."

She craned her neck to look at him more closely. The skin under his eyes was dark, and lines bracketed his mouth.

"It's more than that." She nudged his side with her ankle. "What's up?"

Dave's hands tensed around her shins, and he dropped his head against the couch and closed his eyes. "This Brick Babe cohost situation has been such a time suck. Each Babe who's interested gets a one-week tryout, but I'm spending at least a couple of days beforehand showing them around the studio, explaining the equipment, running down how you and I always prepped. And then they get in front of the microphone and malfunction like faulty droids."

She waved her arms like C-3PO and intoned, "*Danger. Dave. Robinson*" in her best robot voice.

But the topic wrapped its arms around her and refused to let go. Brandon had selected fifteen women to be Brick Babes last month, and they'd all been quickly outfitted with a variety of tiny WNCB T-shirts and slapped across the station's social media sites. Of the fifteen chosen, only six were interested in an on-air tryout once they learned about the wake-up call for a morning show. The tryouts had been disasters so far, and each one had Mabel feeling worse than the last, so she changed the subject. "Did Thing Two ever shake his cough?"

Dave scrubbed his hands through his hair. "No. He's still hacking all night, and now Thing One's caught it. I can't remember the last time Ana and I got more than three consecutive hours of sleep."

Mabel made a sympathetic face at him, then got distracted when her phone vibrated. She fished it from her pocket and smiled at the *Barbarian Time Brigands* meme Jake had texted her. Over the past few weeks, they'd fallen into a texting relationship—light, funny stuff and jokes about their favorite TV show, none of it serious —and somehow the buzzing of her phone had turned into the highlight of her day.

She turned her screen to show the image to Dave, who was also a huge *BTB* fan, but he only offered a thin smile.

"Seriously, what's your deal?" she asked, setting her phone down.

"Nothing. It's just... life is so short, you know? I want to spend it being happy."

The huge sigh he gave might as well have come from the soles of his feet, and Mabel swung her legs around so she could sit up and face him. "I know. We'll get me back on the morning show somehow."

Dave squeezed her shoulder, then deftly maneuvered behind her to swipe her place on the couch.

"Mmmm. Warm spot." He crossed his ankles and assumed his favorite napping position, nudging her to the edge of the cushion.

She rolled her eyes. Apparently sharing and caring time was over.

That afternoon she stepped into the studio to devise the latest plan for her upcoming shift. She'd been doing her best over the past month to do such a subtly shitty job that Brandon wouldn't be happy with her performance but he wouldn't be able to complain about anything specific. She was actually pretty proud of herself. It took skill to bring the wrong type of energy to an afternoon show by keeping her voice just perky enough and her delivery a shade below frenetic. She knew damn well people should be winding down at the end of the day, not ramping up with a manic pixie radio girl, but Brandon didn't know she knew it.

And then there was her second wave of attack: playing the worst music in the universe. Last week she'd worked through the unknown B-sides and deep cuts of every one-hit wonder of the past three decades, which absolutely nobody was clamoring for. She didn't have a good idea yet for this week, so she browsed through the music list, hoping inspiration would strike.

In the end, she was stuck with a plan she came up with that wasn't her best sabotage attempt to date, but hey, you couldn't win 'em all. She just needed to keep her ratings low so Brandon would acknowledge that he'd made a mistake and put her back with Dave. Any little bit would help.

At the top of the hour, she fired up the microphone and modulated her voice for extra chirpiness.

"Hey, hey, hey, Beaucoeur! It's Mae Bell here, and can you *believe* I'm starting my second month flying solo in the afternoons? Cuh-*razy*! So as you've noticed, you're hearing a little less from me and a little more music. Now that I'm free of Dave's morning-show music monopoly, you're definitely hearing some different tunes. So let's kick things off with Filter's cover of 'One' from *The X-Files* movie soundtrack followed by the Black Keys' "Lonely Boy." Then we'll see where the afternoon takes us."

She hit the button to start the song and sagged back into her chair. Five minutes down; two hundred and thirty-five to go.

At the start of her third hour on air, she received a visitor as she pondered which version of "Space Oddity" to play.

"Mabel." Brandon, impeccably turned out as always, lurked in the doorway. "Just coming to check on my programming brainstorm, make sure you're properly motivated to succeed in this time slot."

"Look at me, motivated as heck." Mabel beamed. "Hey, which lost-in-space-all-alone song do you like better, 'Space Oddity' by Bowie or 'Major Tom' by Peter Schilling?"

He smiled thinly. "'With or Without You,' 'Alone' by Heart. I see what you're doing."

"Don't forget Whitesnake's 'Here I Go Again (on my own)'!" she singsonged.

"Stop being cute."

Mabel's eyes glittered. "Stop trying to dictate my playlist. I have two more hours' worth of music scheduled and your word that we're free to choose our music."

Brandon started to speak, but Mabel brandished a silencing finger and held his gaze as she flipped on the mic. "Thanks for tuning in tonight, my besties! I'm keeping the music going for your drive home, and right now here's Har Mar Superstar with 'Alone Again (Naturally).'"

She turned the mic off. "I'm sorry, you were saying something about going back on your promise to let us program our own shows?"

All traces of patience fell from Brandon's expression, and he moved to face her over the soundboard. "I get it. The shitty music, the chipper-bimbo delivery. You don't want the show to work. But the thing is, I *do*." He sighed. "You can be great in this slot. I want that for you. But if you truly don't want it, I'll replace you with somebody who does. Please don't make me do that."

Her throat grew tighter and tighter as he spoke. He saw straight through her. Of course he did; he'd grown up around his family's radio stations, he knew the business inside and out, and he had the money and influence to crush her like a bug if that's what he decided to do. She didn't want this shift, but she sure as hell didn't want to be out of a job either.

But to admit a single fault to this man who'd blown up her life was unfathomable, so she responded the only way she knew how: by lifting her chin and blustering through it. "You don't like my on-air style? I'm wounded."

Brandon drummed his fingers on the countertop and stared at her until she squirmed. "I honestly don't know if you really can't see all the potential you're squandering here or if you're just too stubborn to admit it. Whatever the case, this is your last chance to do your job."

"Hey, I—" Mabel was about to argue that she *had* been doing her job, but that was a lie. She'd abandoned her professionalism the moment she'd started broadcasting solo.

Brandon was right. She was wrong. *Shit.*

"Okay." She sucked in a deep breath and forced out an apology. "I'm sorry. I'll play it straight from now on."

"Glad to hear it." Brandon leaned down so their heads were level. "For what it's worth, I think you'll be dynamite on your own."

Then he smiled, a real smile, and the expression was so shockingly open that she was startled into offering him a real smile of her own.

"Thanks," she said, then narrowed her eyes. "But I'll be playing Beck's 'Go It Alone' next."

He threw back his head and laughed. "Fine. But it's your last free pass, and I'm only allowing it because damn, do I love that crazy Scientologist. Oh, and you've given away too many free tickets to the I Love the 90s music fest next month. Any more and they're coming out of your paycheck."

With that, he turned and left the booth, shaking his hips a little in time with the music as Mabel stared after him in confusion. A reprimand, a pep talk, and another reprimand in a six-minute span? Her head spun. Still, she kept her word, playing it straight for the rest of her shift and refraining from awarding any more free tickets. She relaxed her delivery style, letting a little languor creep into her voice. She took listener requests and picked music she actually enjoyed listening to. And throughout the show, all she could hear were Dave's words from earlier that day: *Life is so short, you know? I want to spend it being happy.*

She wasn't sure what happy looked like anymore. She'd thought she had it there for a hot second, working with Dave and spending time with Jake until—

The vibration of her phone interrupted the dangerous path her thoughts were wandering. It was Aiden, probably calling about dinner. She didn't know how it was possible, but their relationship had gotten even *more* platonic over the past few weeks. Maybe it came from watching him lose the battle to eat spaghetti gracefully.

"Hey you," she said. "We still on for tonight?"

"That's why I'm calling. I've got a situation at home."

The strain in his voice gave her pause. "No worries, we can reschedule. Everything okay?"

"Yeah. I..." He sighed. "I'll get it sorted. Catch you later." He hung up without elaborating further.

Poor guy. She suspected part of the reason he'd been spending so much time with her was to avoid something malfunctioning in his own life, but he wasn't inclined to share what that was, and she wasn't inclined to push. And hey, it freed her up to head straight home and take a long bath. It was her favorite relaxation spot to text with Jake— and only a little because it allowed her to imagine him there with her in the bubbles.

TWENTY-SIX

Dave pushed back from the table with a groan and patted his stomach. "You burn a mean steak, even when you have to do it in the snow."

Jake saluted him with his beer bottle. "Thank you. I wasn't expecting an early November blizzard when I asked to use your grill."

He and Dave had been chatting at the station on Wednesday when the subject of fire-kissed meats came up, as it often does when two men are speaking. Jake was struck with homesickness for his own grill, wasting away unused in Chicago, Dave joked that his Weber was available for conjugal visits, and the conversation led to him turning up at the Chilton house the following day with steaks, enormous potatoes for baking, and a box of mac and cheese for the kids.

Ana tried to collect their dirty plates, but Dave pushed her back into her chair and started clearing. She gave him a grateful smile. "The kids are fed and asleep, and we're all full and happy. Is it wrong to take myself off to bed too?"

Dave stood behind her, hands full of dishes, and leaned down to press a kiss into the top of her head. "Go on. I'll clean up."

She didn't waste any time excusing herself from the kitchen, and Jake was glad to see her go. Not that he didn't enjoy her company, but she looked exhausted. Happy, but exhausted.

Dave though? Dave just looked exhausted. That was another reason Jake had invited himself over. At the very least, he could provide a meal and a place to vent if necessary.

He picked up the empty meat platter and followed Dave to the kitchen, where he was finishing loading the dishwasher. They talked about inconsequential things while they scrubbed the rest of the dishes, then retired to the living room with fresh beer.

Dave collapsed on the couch, and Jake looked over at him with raised eyebrows.

"Is this where I spill my guts?" Dave cradled the bottle in his hands but didn't bring it to his lips.

"Hey, no head-shrinking here. But Ana seems a lot better than the last time I was here."

A soft smile touched Dave's lips. "She does, doesn't she? This pregnancy's been hard on her, and I don't want her to have an extra ounce of stress to deal with. She's already got enough at work with the layoff rumors at her agency. So I'm trying to handle the laundry, the cooking, the shopping, the kids..."

So that explained the bags under Dave's eyes.

"And then there's *your* work stress."

Dave grimaced. "I don't think I can take another week of on-air tryouts. They've broken me. I'm a shell of a man."

"This last one was the worst yet," Jake agreed. He'd caught bits and pieces of the train wrecks that were the previous five auditions. "I don't think she said a single word the whole show. It was nothing but giggling."

Dave burst into a frighteningly accurate impression of the high-pitched screech, and Jake winced.

"Nah, Michele the giggler was better than Ashley," Dave said.

Ashley had been Dave's first guest host, and she hadn't even made it through an entire show. She'd been so nervous just to be in the studio with him that she'd barely been able to choke out her own name before bolting from the booth and locking herself in the ladies' room, too rattled to continue. A bemused Dave had kept right on going, hosting solo as if he hadn't planned four hours' worth of two-person bits.

"And then we had Mary Beth, the blonde with great tits," Dave said.

"Huh." Jake hadn't noticed of course; he only had eyes for Mabel. But he took a stab in the dark. "Her bra size was bigger than her IQ?"

Dave cringed. "She turned everything she said into a single-entendre, which in itself was impressive but not particularly entertaining."

"You're on the last one though. And it's Thea," he said. "I can promise she's not shy at least."

Dave shuddered and held the cold glass against his forehead. "I'm not going to make it."

"Sure you will. She's going to be a spectacular flame-out, and your hell month will be over. You can do this."

Dave grunted. "Okay. I can do this. Thank you. I needed a pep talk from someone who doesn't weep when the subject comes up."

Jake froze. "Mabel? She cries?" This was the first time Dave had brought her up all night, and he was ravenous for any information Dave wanted to share about her.

"Not quite. But it depresses her. Seems like she's sad a lot these days, not that she'll admit it."

"Even with a new man in her life?" Acid burned in his gut at the thought of them together.

"Funny that. And honestly, I'm not sure what that's about. She keeps saying they're just friends, but I didn't think Aiden *had* women friends."

Well, didn't that make Jake feel like yakking up his baked potato? Dave worked his mouth like he might go on —and oh, how Jake wished he'd go on—but instead of continuing, Dave finally took a sip of his beer and sagged back against the couch. He closed his eyes and said tiredly, "Anyway, how 'bout them Bears?"

THE CHIRPING of Jake's phone pulled him out of sleep at 6:25 on Monday morning. He fumbled to locate it on his bedside table, knocking over a glass of water in the process.

"Shit," he yelped, lunging to mop up the liquid with a corner of the sheet. But the chaos was worth it when he saw the name on the screen.

Mabel: *You up?*

Forgetting all about his now-damp bedding, he tapped the phone against his palm a few times. What did he have to lose? He snapped a picture of himself in his still-dark bedroom, sleepy eyes, rumpled hair, balled-up pillow and all. And he made sure to include his bare chest in the shot since he knew Mabel liked the view.

Jake: *I am now*.

Mabel: *Sorry*.

Immediately another text flashed on his screen.

Mabel: *But morning looks good on you*.

Seconds later, she replied with a picture of her own. She was still in bed too, propped against her headboard with an enormous pillow, her cat dozing next to her. She looked warm and relaxed in a thin, low-cut tank top. Was the angle of her shot as intentional as his had been? He'd love to believe that was the case, just like he'd love to be lying there next to her in that big bed.

Then a horrible thought struck him. What if Murdoch had just left? Dave had seemed skeptical about their just-friends claims, and Mabel never brought him up when the two of them were texting. From what he could tell, they'd been spending plenty of time together since the Brick Babe auditions. But if Mabel was texting with him, she must be alone. He looked more closely at the picture, searching for any signs of recent occupation: an extra indent on the pillow, masculine clothing tossed on the comforter, a book left behind on the nightstand.

Nothing visible. Nothing obvious. Not that it was *professional* of him to care.

So why did his fingers tap out such an unprofessional response?

Jake: *That goes double for you*.

Mabel: *Who, me?*

She sent another picture, this time doing an exaggerated duck face like she was a thirteen-year-old sending her first Snap. But she'd moved the camera closer and had shifted in a way that pulled her tank even tighter against her breasts so Jake could make out every line and curve and, yep, nipple. He groaned and knocked the back of his skull against the headboard. She probably wouldn't appreciate a shot in return of the massive erection he was now sporting, although he was briefly tempted to send her something more realistic than the eggplant emoji. She had to have chosen that angle on purpose, right? For reasons passing all understanding?

Then her next text was a virtual bucket of ice water in his lap.

Mabel: *Your dear friend Thea's pretty good.*

Jake: *Can't say I set my alarm to catch my "dear friend's" radio debut.*

He opened the station live stream on his phone and heard Dave's voice followed by a surprisingly confident female one.

"New research out of the University of Connecticut says that even a fifteen-minute nap during the day can boost memory and productivity," Dave was saying.

"Well, that's what I tried to explain to the traffic cop, but he insisted on writing me a ticket anyway!"

He gave a huff of surprise. Thea was quick. Still, she couldn't compare to his favorite radio personality.

Jake: *She's no Mae Bell.*

Mabel: *But she's not bad.*

Jake typed, *Meet me in 30 minutes for coffee,* then deleted it. Next he typed, *I started falling for you in July, and I'm still not over it.* Delete. *I wake up every morning dreaming about your lips.* Delete. *Pick me over him.* Delete, delete, delete.

He finally settled on *Bet her Jerry Seinfeld impression's not as good as yours.*

Mabel: *WHOSE IS??*

He snorted and rolled out of bed, ready to start his day. Okay, ready to start his day after a quick jack off in the shower. That night after the Moo Daddies show, he'd stumbled back to his hotel room, almost dizzy with lust and desperate for the release he'd walked away from when he'd tucked a drunk Mabel into her bed alone, then fucked out his frustrations with his own hand. But that night he'd had the promise of a relationship with Mabel as he pictured her wrapping her lips around his dick while he worked himself. Now he was that creepy guy obsessing over a woman who didn't want to be with him.

Still, he was getting by as best as he could these days, and if that's what it took to sand down his Mabel-related rough edges and keep it *professional*—a word he was truly coming to hate—then he'd do what he had to do.

TWENTY-SEVEN

Thea was Dave's new cohost, and Mabel felt like vomiting *all the time*.

She was being replaced. It was actually happening.

"The thing is, she's not *that* good," she grumbled to Aiden the Monday of Thanksgiving week. "She's just better than anybody else who tried out."

With Dave off doing who knew what and her treacherous mind constantly threatening her with thoughts of Jake, she'd welcomed the distraction of Aiden's laid-back company when he offered to bring lunch to the station that day.

"They definitely don't have the same timing you and Dave did," he agreed.

"Yeah, that we *did*." She speared a tomato with unnecessary force, showering her spinach with a spray of pulp.

"Easy there, tiger." Then his amused expression vanished when his phone exploded with a series of text messages.

"Trouble?"

"Maybe. They need me at a job site." He wolfed down the rest of his sandwich in three quick bites and grabbed his Murdoch Construction coat from the back of the chair, mouth tight. "Dinner tomorrow?"

"Sure. Text me."

He left without further explanation, and once she'd cleaned up their lunch trash, she headed to the recording studio. But instead of working on a new commercial for a local dentist, she imagined Brandon falling to his knees and begging her to come back to mornings. It was the most satisfying non-Jake fantasy she'd had in ages.

"Oh! I'm sorry! I didn't know anyone was in here!"

She snapped back to reality to find Thea hovering in the doorway, wringing her hands.

"Yeah, I've got some ads to record." She gestured at the ad copy on her desk and asked stiffly, "Did you need something?"

Thea bit her lip and did a little fidget-dance. God, did that woman ever just hold still for fifteen seconds? "I was going to, you know, practice."

"Practice?" Did she mean practice stealing Mabel's life?

"On the board," Thea clarified. "It just seems like I'd be a little more useful to Dave if I knew how to do all that stuff. I can't even spell him when he has to run to the bathroom." She edged out the door. "I'll just come back some other time."

Mabel swallowed hard. Thea actually *was* practicing to replace Mabel in her own life. And yet the words spilled out unbidden. "Actually, do you want to stay?"

Thea stopped, hand gripping the edge of the door. "Why?"

Inwardly, she agreed. Helping train Mabel 2.0 wasn't

smart. In fact, she wanted Thea to fail spectacularly. But at the same time, she wasn't a supervillain.

"Want some lessons on running the board? I can walk you through the basics. We could even toss some banter back and forth to give you a little more practice."

Thea's eyes widened. "Really?"

Mabel shrugged. "Sure. Everybody starts somewhere." She wasn't doing it for the station or Brandon or the ratings. She was doing it for Dave and his drawn, tired face. Whatever was up with him these days, he looked like he could use some help.

"Oh. Okay," Thea said. "I didn't think you'd want to, um..."

She shifted uncomfortably, and all Mabel could do was shrug again. "Yeah, I know. It's kind of like talking to your ex's new wife. Not a comfortable situation."

"The new wife isn't comfortable either."

They exchanged small smiles.

"So this is hella awkward for both of us. Great," Mabel said. "Pull up a chair."

An hour later, Thea was flipping mics on and off and queuing up songs like a champ. They'd even managed to defrost the ice enough that Thea invited Mabel to a beginner's yoga class that weekend.

"It's a new gym, and I don't have anybody to go with," she confessed.

Mabel wrinkled her nose. "I've never done yoga."

The other woman immediately backtracked. "It's okay. No big deal. You've probably already got weekend plans with Aiden, right?"

Lord, exactly how many people were invested in their non-relationship? "Uh no, we don't have plans for Saturday. We're not dating or anything. Just friends."

Thea didn't seem to hear Mabel's disclaimer. "He's always been that good-looking, even when we were kids." She sighed and propped her chin on her hand. "I always wondered what I'd do with a guy that pretty. I'd probably spend our time together just petting his hair."

"Yeah, he's a nice guy," Mabel agreed, vaguely uncomfortable discussing Aiden's charms.

"Nice guy?" Thea scoffed. "'Nice guy' is not the first descriptor that comes to mind. 'Intimidatingly attractive.' 'Temptation on two legs.' 'Boyfriend goals.' Not 'nice.'"

"Eh." Mabel knew exactly which temptation on two legs she wanted. Compared to Jake, Aiden was just... a guy. Eager for a new topic, she asked, "Hey, want me to show you how to voice track?"

THAT EVENING, Mabel and Dave climbed into the station van following their public appearance at the Toys for Tots kickoff at Beaucoeur's outdoor mall. Dave had been unusually terse throughout the event, so Mabel propped one booted foot on the dashboard and attempted to talk him out of his bad mood. At least the van had started on the first try, so she had that going for her.

"Hey, how do you think the new hire's doing?"

The one area where Brandon had come through was in finding a new deejay for late nights, but Dave shrugged off her question and kept driving in silence.

"I mean, Javier could be babbling in Aramaic on the air, and I'd still be thrilled," she said. "Anything to get us out of voice tracking nights, right?"

Still nothing from the driver's seat, so she plowed

ahead. "We always chat a little when we do the handoff. He seems nice enough."

Dave nodded, finally joining the conversation. "Yeah. I'm pretty sure he's a vampire though."

A laugh exploded from her throat. "He is *so* a vampire! Pale, quiet, thin. Are we sure Brandon found him in Arizona and not Transylvania?"

"Wouldn't surprise me."

She waited for Dave to continue their game with another quip, but he didn't offer anything, so she picked back up with her one-woman show. "I bet he carries a little graveyard dirt in his pocket."

His lips quirked, but he didn't return the volley.

"I mean, he definitely orders his garlic bread with no garlic, if you know what I mean." She would've pushed on, but when her phone buzzed in her pocket, she dug it out to read the incoming text.

"That from your boyfriend or your other boyfriend?" Dave asked.

"Neither. It's my mom asking what time I'll be home for Thanksgiving," she said absently. Then, "Hey! I do not have two boyfriends."

Dave shrugged. "If you say so."

His easy acceptance of her denial needled her. "I don't have *any* boyfriends. I've told you a million times that Aiden and I are just friends. And Jake and I are keeping things professional."

Even before Dave's scoff was fully formed, she admitted to herself that the last part was a lie. She and Jake's daily texting had abandoned professionalism ages ago.

"You need to quit using Aiden."

Mabel's head snapped back at Dave's sharp tone.

"Excuse me? Aiden's a big boy. He can take care of himself."

His fingers tightened on the steering wheel. "Right. Does he know you're just killing time with him because you're too chickenshit to admit that you'd rather be with Jake? Who, by the way, is still hung up on you. Have you considered that you might be hurting him every time you send another 'professional' text?"

She swiveled to look at him, her head wobbling on her neck like it might topple off her body in shock. Dave *never* got angry, least of all with her. But the grim set of his mouth and the shoulders up around his ears told her that he was angry right now. So she got angry right back.

"You're serious," she snapped. "You're going to jump my shit because I'm hanging out with our friend—the one who's slept with the majority of the single women in this town, by the way—and you don't like it? And how do you even know what Jake's thinking?"

Dave didn't take his eyes off the road as he turned into the WNCB lot and pulled the van around back. "He's come over for dinner a couple of times. We talk."

"You talk?" Mabel was sputtering now. "You *talk* to my..."

Dave's laugh wasn't friendly. "Your *what*?"

She leaned away from him, pressing her back against the door, shocked by the venom in his voice. It left her off-balance and on the defensive.

"Oh yeah? How is this any of your business?" Even as she said it, the words tasted wrong on her tongue. Dave was her business, and she was his. Had been for years. But he'd never *ever* spoken to her like this.

He turned the van off but wouldn't meet her eyes. "Look, I'd be thrilled if you were actually happy, but you're not. You mope around but pretend everything's okay. You claim your texting with Jake is all innocent, but that's bullshit and it's fucking with *him* too."

She swallowed hard and blinked back tears. "Dave, I... Why are you saying this?"

Now he looked at her, his jaw set. "Oh, poor Mabel, sad because she won't date the guy she's crazy about. Why don't you worry about something real for a change? Because you don't seem that worried about your job even though I know you've been intentionally fucking it up like it's some sort of game."

She shook her head, tempted to tell him that she wasn't—at least not anymore. But "not anymore" was a shitty defense.

And Dave still wasn't done. "In the meantime, all I do is worry. I worry about Ana having to go on bed rest or, God forbid, losing the baby. I worry about my useless new cohost. I worry that my ratings are falling and I'm going to get fired. And then I have *you* acting like a child because you're too scared to go after what you want. God, just save the angst for those of us with real fucking problems."

When his torrent of words died away, the only sound in the van was the ticking of the engine as it cooled down.

He deflated against the seat, pushing his fingers under his glasses to rub his eyes. "Sorry," he mumbled. "I shouldn't have... I'm sorry."

But she was already scrabbling for the door handle, desperate to escape the van before the tears started. Her stomach roiled as she walked to the recording studio on autopilot, not bothering to turn on the lights. The room was small, and the egg crate insulation was like a cocoon. It was the perfect place to cry. She dropped into one of the chairs behind the control board and pulled her knees up to her chest, sobbing out her anger and hurt and guilt in the dimness of the room.

The worst part was, Dave was right. She wasn't being fair to either guy in her life. If she stopped spending time with Aiden, she was afraid the loneliness that she used to tolerate in her own life would rise up like a wave and drown her. And she'd been so wrapped up in convincing herself that her life was A-okay without Jake that she'd completely ignored the fact that Dave was floundering. She'd seen the signs; her best friend was sinking, and she'd been too selfish to do anything about it. That piddly hour she spent training Thea was too little, too late.

She was mopping her face with a crumpled Kleenex she'd found in the bottom of her purse when the door opened to reveal Dave's lanky frame silhouetted in the hall light.

She scrambled to her feet, swiping at her eyes. "I haven't been there for you. I'm so sorry."

He was already shaking his head as he stepped into the room. "No, *I'm* sorry. I shouldn't have said any of that." His face was drawn and miserable, and the ache in Mabel's chest expanded.

"No, me. I'm the shitty friend. I can't believe I didn't know how much stress you've been under. I should've—"

Dave cut off the rest of her apology with a grimace. "Let's agree we were both terrible and move on. But you need to stay pissed at me for at least a week."

She gave a watery laugh. "How about I stop being pissed at you right now, and you tell me when I can come over to watch Thing One and Thing Two so you and Ana can have a night off. Go out to dinner, see a movie, get a hotel room so you can make out or take a nap or whatever you married people do."

Dave exhaled a gusting sigh. "That would be amazing. Thank you."

"You're welcome. Ana and Mabel Junior will be fine, and we'll get through this work nightmare together." She twined her arms around his waist and gave him a squeeze.

"Love you, monkey face." He squeezed her back.

"Love you too. And I miss being your partner."

He released her and sank into one of the studio chairs. "Hard same. You know, the last time I talked to Brandon, he looked almost regretful. Part of me thinks he's starting to see that there's something useful about actual broadcast training for radio personalities in one of the state's biggest markets."

"If only there was a way to rectify that mistake..." She plopped into the seat next to him.

"Fall ratings come out in January."

She nodded because *of course* she knew when the ratings were due out. From the bottom of her heart, she hoped they'd be so abysmal that Brandon would see the error of his ways. And in the meantime, she had Dave's voice echoing in her head, accusing her of being too afraid to go after what she wanted.

Maybe it was time she shook off that fear.

TWENTY-EIGHT

Jake stepped off the elevator on the fourteenth floor of the Capital Bank Building and unwound the scarf from around his neck. Part of him was astounded to find himself still living in Beaucoeur as winter knocked on the door of the city, and he was grateful that he'd grabbed cold-weather gear on his last trip to Chicago.

He was unlocking his office door when another elevator opened and disgorged Mitch, a lawyer at the firm across the hall.

"You beat me in this morning."

Jake glanced at the clock in the hall. "Shit, it's after seven. What will your boss say?"

"He'll say it's two days before Thanksgiving and all the judges are on vacation anyway. Speaking of, no poker tonight. Let Robbie know, wouldja?"

"Sure thing. I'll enjoy hanging on to my cash this week." Jake wasn't much of a gambler, but when a few of the attorneys across the hall invited him to join their regular game, he figured he'd be gambling with his sanity if he didn't say yes because he'd been living like a hermit.

He dragged Robbie along with him the first night and was relieved to discover that the big guy had an even worse poker face than he did.

"If I don't see you again, enjoy the holiday," Mitch called before disappearing beyond the double glass doors of his firm's suite.

"Same to you." Jake stepped inside and flipped on the lights in his closet-sized office, dropped his briefcase on the desk, and walked over to the floor-to-ceiling window running along one wall. The space was tiny, but he had to admit that his view, showcasing the renovated warehouses of downtown Beaucoeur and the Illinois River sparkling just beyond, was superior to the one in his Chicago office, which showcased the west wall of the building next door.

Turning back to his desk, he checked his email and ignored the rest of his inbox to click on the one from Finn right away. As he hoped, it was the focus group results, and although she'd presented him with an organized document, he wasn't sure he was reading it correctly. So he did what any sensible person would and called his brainy younger sister.

"Help me understand this," he said by way of greeting.

She didn't even have to ask what he meant. "Okay, so basically, your girl needs to be back on mornings," Finn said. "At least that's the conclusion of the focus group."

"Good. That's good news." He sagged back in his chair in relief.

"Also, I have to ask: Does Mabel look the way she sounds like she looks based on these demos?"

He pictured his sister sitting at the desk in her chic Chicago office, pointy little nose twitching in excitement over the opportunity to grill him about this relationship.

It's what he used to do to her, after all. "How does she sound like she looks?"

"Like Lou Dobbs."

"Hey!" he protested.

"Oooh, so touchy," Finn laughed. "Actually, she sounds witty and smart."

"You forgot gorgeous."

Finn was quiet for a moment. "Is she also the reason you're still living three hours south of your condo?"

"No. That's because of my job," Jake said. Sort of. In truth, he suspected he could make a strong case to move back to Chicago and finish the Lowell Consolidated work from there, but for some reason he just hadn't pushed for it. Inertia maybe. Or misplaced optimism.

"Is this going to help you get her back?" Finn's question was tentative.

"That's not why I did it. She didn't deserve to have her life uprooted, and I'm just trying to fix that."

"You're a nice guy."

"And we all know where they finish." God, he was depressing himself.

"Stop. She could come around."

"Negative. Nothing's changed between us." Just because they were constantly texting didn't mean she wanted anything more than casual friendship. Time for a new subject. "Speaking of change, any chance you changed your mind about me writing you a check for the rest of your student loans?"

Finn's response was immediate. "Negative."

"Finnie—"

"Grown woman. Financially solvent. Living with her even more financially solvent boyfriend. I don't need your money, Jake."

"Right, but it's smart to have a cushion." He tapped his pen on his desk in irritation.

"For the last time, I have a cushion!" The snap in her voice meant she was equally irritated. "When are you going to stop worrying about me and focus on yourself?"

"When one of us is dead," he muttered. Lifelong habits were impossible to break, and he didn't know *how* to stop worrying that his sister might lack for some creature comfort.

"You're a pain in my ass, and I love you," she said matter-of-factly. "I'll still see you for turkey, right?"

"Wouldn't miss it," he said. "Love you too."

"WHAT'S UP, MAN?"

Robbie's greeting from the reception desk slowed Jake's attempt at an in-and-out mission to stash some paperwork in Brandon's WNCB mailbox and be gone before anyone noticed him. His call with Finn had left him melancholy. She'd be at Thanksgiving on Thursday with Tom, along with his mom, his stepdad, and his favorite cousin Brandy, who'd bring both her knitting and her husband with her. He loved his family, but for the first time ever, his stomach hollowed out at the thought of facing it all without someone by his side.

Without *Mabel* by his side. Mabel, who was in this building, one room away. Mabel, who'd texted with him earlier in the day about their favorite Thanksgiving foods. Surely that was an invitation to say a quick hello since he was there in person.

Decision made, he pushed the door open and went inside, where the lights blazing from the studio illuminated the woman inside. She was playing the Rolling Stones' "Honkey Tonk Women," and she was dancing. Hair wild, head back, arms up, hips gyrating. He stood still and watched her, content to drink in the fierce joy on her beautiful face. When she noticed him, her lips split into a grin, and she crooked a finger at him, gesturing him into the studio.

Okay. That was friendlier than he expected. He stepped into the booth, curious about her mood.

"You caught me!" She laughed. "It's my favorite Stones song. How can you sit still while it's playing?"

Her hips still twitched along with the beat, and Jake raised his eyebrows at her. "Don't let me stop you."

She smiled again and performed a little pirouette, tossing her hair. "You coming to the Moo Daddies show on Friday?" she asked, still shimmying to the music.

Jake actually had to close his eyes at the memory of what had happened at the other Moo Daddies show he'd watched. Mabel's singing; the softness of her skin; the pounding, unslaked lust she'd unleashed in him. It had been one of the best and worst nights of his life, all rolled into one.

He leaned against the doorway, tipping his head to study her. "Do you want me there?"

She met his gaze. "Yes. I'd like that."

A silence settled between them, and he was pretty sure they were *both* thinking about the last show now.

He nodded once. "Then I'll be there. Because you asked me to."

Their gazes caught and held, and with a nervous little laugh, she asked, "Does that cut into family turkey time?"

"Not much, but I can't miss the main event. Mom

relies on me to mash the potatoes. Nobody else can match my silky texture."

She moved around the soundboard to stand in front of him, her movements slowing to a gentle sway. "Handsome, smart, *and* he cooks." She tipped her chin up to look him in the eyes. "Be still my heart."

Jake froze. This sounded dangerously like flirting. As he considered his response, the next song kicked in.

"'Wild Horses,'" she said. "I was on a Stones kick when I programmed today's music."

She bit her lower lip, then stepped forward and sought out his hand with hers. He immediately seized the opportunity and the woman, snaking his other arm around her waist and pulling her toward him. They started to move together, and she relaxed against his chest, the top of her head just brushing his chin.

They danced in silence; Jake didn't want to say anything to break the spell. She was warm against his body, her curves pressing into him, and he could feel the vibration as she hummed along to the song. And God, it felt *right*.

Unable to hold his tongue any longer, particularly because he was thinking about other things his tongue could be doing, he drew a breath to ask Mabel what exactly was going on. But she anticipated his question before he could speak.

"It's just dancing, Jake." She turned her head to nestle into his collarbone.

"It's full-contact dancing, Mabel." God, she had to feel how hard he was, pressed against her hip, didn't she? But he didn't let her go, and she didn't move away.

She gave a tiny sigh, her breath ghosting across his

neck. "Sorry. I'm in a weird place. I fought with Dave yesterday."

"Really? You and Dave?" The heat in his veins receded at the thought, and he pulled back to look at her.

"Yeah. We never fight. It was bad."

Jake didn't say anything, just tightened his arms around her and wished he could chase away the sadness from her voice.

"But he also got me thinking. And I guess... I guess I'm tired of fighting it."

His pulse kicked up. Could she possibly mean what he thought she meant? "By 'fighting it,' are you saying—"

"Just a second." She slid out of his embrace and moved around to the control board, plopping on the headphones, flipping on the mic, and talking over the last bars of the song.

"That was a Rolling Stones rock block to get you home on this blustery Tuesday before Thanksgiving. Coming up, I've got new tracks from the Pretty Reckless and Radical Face, but right now here's the Foo Fighters."

"Everlong" thumped from the speakers, and Mabel flipped off the mic and removed the headset.

"Sorry. Where were we?"

"You were about to explain—"

Her buzzing phone cut him off, and she frowned at the screen. "Sorry. It's... Aiden."

He felt like she'd dumped cold water on his head. "Right. Your boyfriend." He shoved his hands into his suit pockets and stepped away from her.

She shook her head, cramming her phone into her own pocket. "No, it's not like that. He's not my boyfriend. We're just—"

He couldn't bear to hear her describe it. He had to get out of there.

"Cool. Okay. He's just another guy you text with. I've got to go anyway." He moved out of the studio and though the greenroom, angry at himself for once again letting her knock him off course.

Mabel followed him. "Wait! Let me just— I'm sorry."

He turned around, arms spread wide. "For what? We're all just *professionals* here, right? Nothing to apologize for."

Without waiting for her response, he pushed the door open and let it fall closed behind him. What bullshit. He wanted her as much as he always had, no matter how much he pretended to be fine with his all-work life. And sometimes he let himself believe she felt the same way about him too. But if that were the case, she wouldn't be spending so much time with someone else, would she?

He left Mabel and the frustrating mix of emotions she caused behind in the studio and headed toward the exit.

"Hey, neighbor!" Thea called Jake over to where she was chatting with Robbie.

"Hey." Jake's response was more subdued. "How's it going?"

"Great, but you look sad," Thea said. "Come here." She grabbed his shirt and dragged him forward so she could wrap her arms around him. He was startled to find himself cradled in the vee of her thighs as she hugged him.

"Uh, what's up?" He rested his chin on the top of her head and shot Robbie a look that screamed *Help!* Robbie just shrugged. When Thea's hands started to stroke down his back, Jake broke her hold and took a big step backward.

"Did you hear? Mabel coached me on how to run the boards, and we've got a yoga date on Saturday morning! This has been the best week I've had since I started here."

Her smile was so broad that he had to return it. "That's great. Pretty soon you and Robbie'll be running this place."

"Oh, I already am." Robbie's massive feet were propped up on the desk, one crossed over the other, and his hands were linked over his belly. He was every inch the master of the station.

Thea sounded a little more unsure. "Yeah, I don't know about that. It's a lot harder than I expected. But it's fun to try."

Jake lingered for a bit to chat about Thanksgiving plans before excusing himself to pack for his trip home. The emotional mess he was leaving in Beaucoeur would be here when he got back.

TWENTY-NINE

In a few short years, the Moo Daddies' Turkey Coma Concert on the day after Thanksgiving had become a bit of a local legend. It was a highlight of the long holiday weekend, and the crowd at the Elephant was either contented and well fed or desperate to escape the clutches of their loved ones. Either way, everybody in the audience that night would be excited to drink and listen to good music.

Everybody except Mabel.

She'd tried not to obsess over Jake while she'd been home for Thanksgiving, but it had been almost impossible not to. She'd been thinking about Dave's advice to chase her own happiness, and then she'd looked up to see Jake watching her through the studio window. The mix of heat and affection in his gaze had caused her heart to leap and her thighs to clench. What woman wouldn't give in to the long-simmering temptation to touch the man who looked at her as if she were the most important person in the universe? And then when she'd followed him into the hallway to reiterate that she wasn't with Aiden, she'd found Jake with Thea. *With* her. Hugging her, pressing into her body, letting her hands smooth down the muscles of his back.

Proprietary. Comfortable. Coupled.

Her stomach churned every time she thought about it. In all their texting and in-person interactions, the one thing she and Jake didn't talk about was how he was spending his free time in Beaucoeur. He'd apparently honored her request to keep it professional between them and started seeing someone else. And why wouldn't he? He was a smart, attractive man with a good job and a sense of humor. And kindness and patience and a sense of style and an ass that wouldn't quit.

God, she was an idiot. An idiot who'd forced Jake to dance with her. Great.

Worse, nothing had changed in their texting routine over the holiday, which drove home the fact that Jake was happy with their relationship the way it was. In fact, he sent her a selfie on Thanksgiving of him holding a ladle while wearing a pink gingham apron and a sheepish grin. It had been both the best and the worst part of the day for her, and she'd peeked at it countless times over the past twenty-four hours, disappointed with him for moving on and angry with herself for letting him.

So did she pick out clothes for the Moo Daddies show to please herself? Of course not. She pulled on a gauzy blouse, imagining the heat of Jake's hand through the sheer material. She shimmied into a short red skirt because she knew damn well he liked her legs. And she went for broke with the spiky, knee-high boots that she never wore because they left her practically hobbled by the end of the night, hoping they'd make him crazy.

Which made *her* crazy, because he was apparently dating someone else.

Unlike most shows, she was driving herself to the Elephant so she could make it an early night; she and Thea had an early-morning yoga date the next day, and boy, wasn't she looking forward to *that*. She could've canceled, but it didn't seem fair to punish Thea for having the good sense to scoop Jake up when he was available. Mabel was trying out the whole "personal growth" and "being the bigger person" thing with the perky woman. So far, she hated it.

At the Elephant, Ana spotted Mabel as soon as she entered and enthusiastically waved her over to their usual table. She squeezed between clustered groups and tightly packed tables to reach her friend up front, where she was seated with Skip's boyfriend Chris.

"Well hey, Julia Roberts in *Pretty Woman*," Ana said when Mabel finally reached her.

Chris gave a long, low whistle that made her flush.

"Oh God. Should I go home and change?"

"Are you kidding? It's criminal that I haven't those boots before." Chris eyed her ensemble as he took a long sip from his gin and tonic.

"Or it means that I'm trying too hard," she said nervously, forcing herself not to look around the bar to see who was or wasn't there.

"It might also mean you don't try hard enough on a regular basis," Ana said brightly. She paused to let Mabel gasp in fake outrage before gesturing to Chris. "Then again, none of us ever looks as sharp as this guy."

The older man adjusted his bow tie, which was as crisp as always, and tugged his striped sweater vest over his round belly. "Well, I certainly didn't dress up for you hussies," he said primly. "Speaking of, I should go wish my fella good luck and get back to my table."

He gave them each a peck on the cheek and disappeared into the crowd.

"Sit," Ana said, tugging Mabel into the just-vacated seat. "You really do look fantastic."

"Thanks. But more importantly, so do you. I'm so glad to see you out. How are you feeling?" She peered at her friend, looking for any signs of fatigue in Ana's brown eyes.

"Better. I think I'm over that early rough patch. But it's been hard on Dave."

Mabel squeezed her hand. "I know. Hey, I love that scarf."

"It's my fiery Mexican heritage emerging," Ana said dryly, adjusting the beige-and-cream chevron print scarf around her neck. "How was Thanksgiving?"

Mabel tried to covertly scan the room as she and Ana chatted about their respective feasts. Unfortunately, Ana was too observant.

"He's here with Brandon and a handful of Brick Babes, so keep your eye on that quadrant." She pointed to a large table on the opposite side of the room.

"Brandon's here?" Mabel was surprised he cared enough to show up.

Ana shrugged. "Maybe he's supporting his deejays?"

"Sure. That's one explanation. The other is the hot-pants brigade he's with." Mabel rattled the ice in her Diet Coke in agitation. Following the aftermath of the last show, she was avoiding alcohol tonight.

Just before the show started, she gave in to the temptation to peek at the Brick Babe table, and there was Jake, sitting right next to Thea. The last thing she saw before the lights dimmed was Thea tugging him down to whisper in his ear. Stung, she whipped her head back to the stage, and as the Moo Daddies launched into Filter's "Hey Man, Nice Shot," she tried to squash the bolt of betrayal that raced through her. Jake hadn't done a single thing she could reasonably be jealous about, and she needed to push it all aside so she'd be ready when her set rolled around.

It didn't work, of course, and she perched, tense and unhappy, on the edge of her chair for the first hour of the show, refusing to turn her head toward the other side of the room again. Thank God she was used to being her brightest self in public even when she was sick, sleep-deprived, or heartbroken, because when Dave called her up onstage, she was able to bound out of her seat with a big smile and a high five for Skip.

"Helloooo, Beaucoeur!" she caroled into the mic, and okay, she had to admit it: she loved the cheers from the audience. The radio booth could feel so isolated, especially on a solo show, and this immediate, enthusiastic feedback was like a drug.

The band launched into the opening strains of Blondie's "One Way or Another," and she lost herself to the music and the emotion and the crowd. They pulled out some of her old favorites—"Dragula," "Stray Cat Strut," "Polyester Bride." Oh, she was aware that she wasn't the best singer in the world, but she loved letting her mind fill with the throb of Dave's guitar, the pulse of Aiden's drums, the strum of Skip's bass. The stage lights were hot on her face, and she forced herself not to wonder if Jake was even watching or if he'd slipped away with Thea.

Before she knew it, her set was wrapping up. She

finished their slowed-down version of Robyn's "Dancing on My Own," and after the cheers died down and she caught her breath, she addressed the crowd.

"Okay, guys, before I go, Dave and I worked up a little song that we hope you enjoy. Aiden, Skip, you guys wanna take five?"

She and Dave settled themselves on the two stools positioned downstage, her with a microphone and him with an acoustic guitar, and Dave picked out the opening strains of Billy Joel's "And So It Goes." When they'd run through the song last week, she hadn't realized what a gut punch the lyrics were.

Tonight though, she felt every word she sang, and almost against her will, she looked for Jake in the crowd. She dredged up every bit of longing, every bit of regret, every bit of wistful hope that refused to budge from her heart, and she sang it all to him, Dave a solid presence by her side. The lights were bright enough that she couldn't make out Jake's expression from the back of the room, but she could see his silhouette, and she could sense the extreme stillness that enveloped him as she stood on that stage and offered him her heart, even though she might be too late.

The song ended on a sad, sustained note that drifted into a few seconds of silence before a shrill whistle opened the floodgates for the cheers and applause that followed. Mabel stood and turned her back to the crowd to shift her stool over, using the action as an excuse to dash away the tears trembling along her eyelashes. Dave shot her a concerned glance, but she gave a minuscule shake of her head.

When she turned back around, her big public smile was in place, and she waved her thanks. "Okay, last song of the night for me, and I'm going out on an upbeat note. Aiden and Skip, you're back on. Let's do some Kelly Clarkson, okay?"

Mabel's set did, indeed, finish strong, and she smiled and laughed and blew kisses at the end of it. But she didn't walk over to Aiden for their traditional spin-and-dip following her set, and when she hopped off the stage, she knew she wasn't up for any chitchat with fans. Ignoring Ana's excited jazz hands, she muttered, "Bathroom" and took off. In the hallway, instead of turning toward the ladies' room, she headed in the opposite direction and ducked into the first open door she saw. The manager's office was illuminated by the meager light from the floor lamp in the corner, and she leaned forward and braced her hands on the front of the desk, letting her head drop and sucking in a shaky breath. The noise of the crowd snaked down the hallway, the chatter ramping up since the band was taking a break.

"Why are you with that fucking underwear model and not me?"

She jumped at the sound of Jake's voice and spun to face him. The easygoing guy she knew was gone. In his place was six feet, three inches of aggressive, worked-up male. This was a new Jake for her, one who was closer to losing control than she'd ever seen him. His expression was dark, his hands clenched at his sides.

Fine. She could get mad too. She narrowed her eyes and injected as much ice into her voice as she could. "*God*, I've tried to say this to everybody who'll listen: Aiden and I are just friends." Jake's jaw tensed, but she wasn't done. "And I'm sorry, but did I not see you and Thea mauling each other at reception on Tuesday? You must love getting women up on desks, *Jakey*. Am I right?"

Jealousy seeped from her pores; he could probably smell it on her.

"What?" He advanced on her, eyes blazing. "I'm not seeing Thea. I'm not seeing *anybody*. And do you know why?"

She shook her head, unable to find a single word in response.

"Because the only person I think about is you. Every morning, you. Every night, you."

His gaze was so intense she considered diving over the desk just to put more space between her and the heated expression in his brown eyes.

"I've tried to stay away," she whispered, both thrilled and horrified that they were apparently having this conversation here, in the manager's office at a bar where basically all her coworkers were drinking and mingling twenty feet away. "Tried so hard. But it's not working. I want..."

She stopped speaking when he put his hands around her waist and lifted her to sit on the desk behind her. Then he turned, took three short steps to the door, and shut and locked it. The noise from the crowd became muffled, and she could hear his slow, steady breathing as he took one deliberate step forward, then another and another, stopping when his thighs brushed her knees.

"Was that song for me?"

She closed her eyes. "No." The word was barely audible, and he leaned down as if to scoop it from her mouth.

"Liar," he murmured, his lips against hers. And then he wrapped her loose hair around his fist, using it to pull her head back so she met his eyes. "You feel the way I do. You started to say so at the station on Tuesday: you're tired of fighting it. And so am I."

He bypassed her lips and moved his mouth along the line of her neck, alternating kisses and soft bites. Then the bites turned more forceful, and he nipped sharply at the side of her neck, sucking on the skin there until she trembled.

"I think if you didn't feel the same way, you'd be telling me to stop right now," he said against her skin, his voice raspy. "Am I right?"

She shuddered at the feel of his breath on her neck. His big hand landed on her solar plexus, and he pushed her gently back until she was flat on the desk. She stared at the ceiling and tried to steady her breathing, and then there were his hands, shoving up her skirt. Her boots came up almost to her knees, and the cool air against the newly exposed flesh above them made her shiver.

"If you want me to stop, you need to tell me, Mabel." His voice was thick as he dropped to his knees in front of her. "Tell me right now."

"Don't stop. *Please*," she whispered, looking down her body to where his dark head bent in front of her. With a growl and a tug, Jake pulled her toward him and ripped away the fragile lace of her underwear, then nudged her legs apart. She held her breath, anticipation mounting as she waited for the press of his mouth. But he surprised her by kissing a line down her inner thigh, almost to the top of her boot, sucking on her skin there before moving to her other leg and kissing his way back up in a pattern of licks and bites that quickened her breath. His blunt fingers slid underneath her knees to spread her open farther, and she squirmed as he took his time familiarizing himself with the softness of her stomach below her belly button and the crease where her leg met her hip.

"Jake, I..." She whimpered and shifted restlessly, pleasure and frustration mingling as his soft laughter brushed her skin.

"Is this what you need?" He ran a finger up and down her hot, slick flesh, and then she forgot to breathe as he finally, *finally* lowered his mouth to her and caressed her with long, flat strokes of his tongue, his hands curling possessively around her hips. Her back arched off the desk as he laved and sucked, pulling away only to growl, "Tell me you love the way I make you feel."

"Love it. Yes," she gasped, eyes fluttering open to catch the look of pure male satisfaction on his face. "God, I love it."

She moved against him, reaching down to slide one hand into his thick hair, savoring the feel of it against her fingers, the hot wetness of his tongue making the pleasure build and build until her breath sawed in and out of her chest and every muscle was tense and on edge. Release danced just out of reach, and she writhed against his mouth until he eased one finger inside her, then another, and blew a gentle stream of air over her hot skin before sucking her clit into his mouth. And with that she shattered, throwing her head back with a hoarse cry. Wave after hot, liquid wave crushed through her, and she rode out his steady pressure until her body was limp and satiated. Then he stood and leaned over her prone body, kissing her with salty lips.

"You are delicious," he said, stroking a hand through her hair. "And I'm leaving now so I can go be polite to women I have no interest in dating. If you finally make up your mind about what you want, you know where to find me."

He turned to leave, and before he reached the door, Mabel pushed herself up on her elbows and called out weakly, "See? I knew you had a thing for doing it on top of desks."

Jake smiled a wicked smile at her. "You have no idea. Those boots, by the way? So fucking hot."

Then he left, easing the door shut behind him. Mabel collapsed backward, not sure her legs could support her yet. After a minute or two, she sat up and pushed her skirt down, yanking off her ruined underwear and dropping them into the trash can next to the desk. Let the office's owner wonder what had happened in here. Actually, no. It was pretty obvious what had happened. Let the owner be jealous instead.

Mabel moved to the door on watery knees and stuck her head out into the corridor, looking left and then right like some kind of cartoon villain making sure the coast was clear. She aimed for her best "nothing to see here!" vibe as she walked out to rejoin Ana at their table, although she imagined her tousled hair told a completely different story.

"Hey." Ana handed Mabel a drink when she was seated. "The guys just got onstage for their last set."

She nodded and drained her glass, barely tasting the contents. It could've been soda or alcohol or diesel fuel for as much as she tasted. Her friend watched in amusement.

"Nice hickey." Ana unwound the scarf from around her neck. "Want to borrow this for the rest of the night?"

Mabel touched the tender spot above her collarbone and shivered at the memory of Jake's tongue and teeth loving the mark onto her skin. Then she wrapped the gauzy fabric around her neck and leaned to press her cheek against the wood table, letting out a long sigh.

Ana reached out to stroke her hair. "Jake?"

Mabel nodded against the table.

"And you're still determined not to be with him?"

"Yes. No." She closed her eyes, enjoying the feeling of Ana's fingers moving along her scalp. "I want to. I'm scared."

Ana kept smoothing her hand over Mabel's hair. "Too scared to chase your joy? That's not the Mabel I know."

Her friend was right. Jake had stripped her bare and, well, stripped her bare. Time to locate her bravery and chase that joy.

THIRTY

Jake strutted back into the main room of the bar. Really, that was the only word for it. The memory of the way Mabel had fallen apart in his arms; the taste of her, hot and wet against his tongue; the helpless, blissed-out look on her face; the sounds she made when she came. What man wouldn't strut a little having caused all that?

Back at his table, he dropped into a chair and inclined his chin at Brandon, who was sitting in the middle of the Brick Babe brigade. Brandon chin-nodded back but didn't make any comments, lascivious or otherwise. Hopefully that meant he was in the clear and didn't look too smug for having rounded most of the bases just now with the hottest woman in the bar.

He hadn't intended to corner her tonight to talk about their relationship, and he *definitely* hadn't planned on kissing her, let alone sliding his hands under her skirt to steal all that heat for himself.

It was just that she'd sung that song.

Before that, he'd been enjoying her performance. She was as electric as he remembered from the show in

September. He'd been content to sit back and drink in all her magnetism, but of course Brandon just had to speak up.

"Your girlfriend's good!" he yelled over the Rob Zombie song she was covering.

Thea turned and hit him with a confused glance. "Your girlfriend? I thought she was dating Aiden?"

Jake closed his eyes briefly, praying for strength. "She's not my—it's not like that."

And then Mabel and Dave moved to the edge of the stage and she sang for him. No, she'd sung *to* him, as if he were the only other person in the room. Her voice had been strong, but the vulnerability on her face and the raw yearning in her tone gutted him. She didn't move. She didn't shift her focus away from him. She simply sat on that stool and exposed her soul. And when she was done, she morphed back into rock star Mabel, laughing and waving as if she hadn't just shown him his own bloody, beating heart.

After the song, he didn't dare make eye contact with anyone at the table until he felt a gentle touch on his knee. It was Thea.

"Are you telling me that woman up there doesn't care about you?" Her soft voice was barely audible over Mabel's final song.

Jake shrugged helplessly.

"Well, it sure seems like she does. Maybe go talk to her?" When he didn't move right away, Thea tried another tactic. "If you don't track her down the instant she's off stage, I'm making a move on you myself."

That startled a laugh out of him. "For pretty much any other guy, that would be awful motivation," he said. "Thanks."

"What a lucky bitch." Thea shook her head.

So he followed Mabel when she left the main bar area. Then, seeing her alone in that dark office, something inside him snapped, and this time he didn't pull back from pouring out all his pent-up frustration that she wasn't with him.

Well. Their relationship was going to change after tonight, and he wasn't sure if he was more excited or scared to see which way it would go now that he'd finally laid it all out. He'd declared his intentions; the rest was up to her.

Suddenly he couldn't sit in the bar a minute longer, wallowing in uncertainty. He leaned across the table to make his excuses to Brandon, needing to holler to be heard over the Amy Winehouse song the Moo Daddies were covering.

"I'm heading out, man. See you Monday?"

Brandon, arm around a giggling Babe, leveled a gaze at him. "You two finally working out your issues?"

Jake didn't even pretend not to understand. "One way or another."

"Good luck with it." Brandon offered him a smile, a startlingly real one. "Believe it or not, I'm rooting for you."

Then he returned his focus to the woman hanging on his arm, leaving Jake to process one more surprise in a week full of them. Shaking his head, he shrugged into his coat, said good night to Thea, and left the bar alone. The ball was in Mabel's court now. She had his number, after all.

SO WHY HADN'T she texted yet?

Jake bounced from one room in his apartment to the next because he couldn't settle in one spot. He was too restless, too preoccupied with whether Mabel would tell him to fuck off or ask him to take her out next weekend.

He just hoped she'd tell him soon.

But the minutes dragged by, and his phone stayed silent. He finished a beer and decided against a second one. He did his dishes and was contemplating scrubbing down the kitchen, just to keep his hands busy, when a knock sounded at the door.

His heart leaped. Who else would be showing up at his apartment after midnight? But he didn't rush to answer, warning himself that it might not be her. It was probably another surprise Milo visit rather than Mabel on his welcome mat.

He opened the door to find Mabel on his welcome mat, one corner of her mouth kicked up in a smile.

"My turn," she said without preamble, walking over his threshold and kicking the door shut behind her. She wasted no time shucking her coat and pulling her shirt up and over her head, dropping both to the floor.

"I'm not seeing Aiden." She shimmied out of her tiny skirt. It joined the rest of her clothes. "I'm not seeing anyone. Because all I can think about is you. Every morning, you. Every night, you."

She was repeating his words from earlier as she unwrapped the stripy scarf from around her neck, and then she was standing in front of him in an ice-blue bra and those hot-as-fuck boots, blond hair slipping over her shoulders. No underwear, of course, because he'd torn them off her eager body a few hours ago. All the blood rushed from Jake's head straight to his dick. He'd never seen anything hotter in his life than Mabel Bowen standing almost naked in his living room.

"You're right; I'm tired of fighting it. You're what I want."

She pushed him back until he bumped into the living room wall. Her hands, cold from the November night, pushed under his shirt, dragging it up his torso as her fingers skimmed along his skin. He helped her by raising his arms so she could pull it over his head, and she gave a purr of appreciation as she took in his bare chest, trailing a finger over his collarbone and down the ridges of his stomach. Then she dropped to her knees, glanced up at him with a knowing smile, and squeezed his throbbing cock through his jeans.

Nope. *This* was the hottest thing he'd ever seen: Mabel on her knees in front of him, breasts spilling over the top of her bra, hair wild down her back. And then he stopped thinking entirely because she'd undone his jeans and pushed them low on his hips.

She didn't tease her way down his stomach or kiss a path up his legs. No, Mabel—his bold, direct Mabel— opened that gorgeous mouth and took in the full, straining length of him, hard and fast and firm.

"Oh fuck, Mabel," he groaned, reaching forward to twine his fingers through her hair.

He didn't guide her movements but let her take control as she moved up and down his shaft, sucking and stroking him with her tongue. *Fucking finally.* After months of imagining this, she was actually here, and it was better than his dirtiest fantasies. She used her hands —warmer now, thank God—to work the base of his cock with a twisting motion as she increased the suction in her eager mouth.

"Fuck, yes. God, that's good." He clenched his hands in her silky hair as she hummed her pleasure, and it vibrated along the length of him and straight into his blood as she continued to work. And finally when the heat and the wet and the pressure got to be too much, he gritted out, "Mabel. God, Mabel, I'm so close."

She paused long enough to smile up at him. "Good." She curled her tongue around the crown of his cock and increased the suction and speed until Jake's hands fell from her hair and slammed against the wall, his hips bucking forward as his nerves ignited and he came with a shout. Afterward, his limbs trembled and his veins felt hollow, and he let himself slide down the wall, pulling her with him down to the questionably clean carpet.

They ended up on their sides, facing each other, and Mabel gave him a satisfied grin. "Hello, by the way. May I come in?"

He flopped an exhausted arm around her and pulled her closer so he could kiss her, long and soft and sloppy. "Yes, Mabel. Please come in."

They didn't stay on the living room floor for long though, because as Jake's ability to reason returned, he remembered that this hot woman was practically naked and he'd barely touched her.

Tracing one finger along the skin of her right breast where it met the top of her bra, he asked, "Can you give me a single good reason for us not to spend the rest of the night in bed?"

She tipped her head to one side, spilling her golden hair across the carpet. "Do you still work for Lowell?"

He reached for her hair and twined a strand around his finger. "Technically, I work for Black, Phelps, and Suarez." In Chicago, no less, but he didn't add that part.

This... whatever they were doing... was too early to be worrying about *that* wrinkle. Then he saw the look she leveled at him and said, "But yes, Lowell is one of my clients."

She nodded and flicked her hair out of his grasp. "And do I still work for WNCB?"

"You do," he said. "You're burning up the airwaves on the afternoon drive." His fingers moved down the slope of her left breast now, and he savored the warmth of her skin through the thin material.

Her breath started coming more quickly. "And do you still sit in your office, looking at numbers that impact my job?"

He ran his palm over her bare hip now, marveling at the softness of her skin. "At this particular moment the only numbers that matter are you and me."

"That doesn't even make sense," she said with a bemused shake of her head.

"Come to bed with me, Mabel," he whispered. "*Please.*"

And then he held his breath, hoping to God she'd say yes.

THIRTY-ONE

Mabel was starting to feel a little self-conscious. She'd barged into Jake's apartment, stripped, gotten him off, and was now basically naked on the floor. And they still had some things to discuss.

"I'll come to bed with you, but there's going to be some talking first."

Jake's eyes were heavy lidded as he studied her, a small smile playing across his mouth. "Fine by me. I could listen to you talk all night."

She nodded and sat up, trying to look as businesslike as the situation would allow.

"First things first: no distractions." She reached for his discarded T-shirt and shrugged into it. It was too big, but the cotton was soft, and it smelled like him. She wanted to hold it to her nose and give a cartoonishly huge inhale, but she restrained herself.

Next, she twisted around to unzip her left boot, then her right one, wriggling out of them as if she were a snake shedding its skin.

"Oh, thank God," she groaned, stripping off the thin socks she wore underneath, then flexing her feet and wiggling her toes, trying to get the blood flowing again.

Jake, who'd shucked his jeans and was now seated with his back against the wall, had one ankle crossed over the other and looked perfectly at home lounging in nothing but boxer briefs. "Beauty is pain?"

"When I wear those, yes." She leaped to her feet and reached for his hands to pull him up. "Take me to your bedroom?"

He rolled to his feet, smooth as a jungle cat, and grinned down at her. "Do you know how many times I've dreamed of hearing you say that?"

The idea that he'd imagined it made pleasure curl through her belly, and she followed eagerly when he grabbed her hand and pulled her down the tiny hallway to his room. He skipped the overhead lights, instead flipping on the bedside lamp. It cast a mellow amber glow around the room.

"Wow," Mabel said, turning in a circle. "You sure you're not a serial killer? This is really... stark."

The room was immaculate, the bed crisply made, the nightstand clutter-free, with no stray socks or discarded undershirts in sight. There were also no pictures on the walls and no personal items on top of the nightstand or the bureau. It might as well have been a hotel room.

Jake stretched out on the bed, hands behind his head. "I'm a man of simple tastes."

Mabel gestured to his closet. "If I opened this right now, would everything be disgustingly organized?"

Jake swept his arm toward the mirrored doors. "Keep in mind that you've just sprung an unannounced audit on me, but go ahead."

Too curious not to, Mabel slid them open and saw, as she suspected, a neat line of suits carefully positioned on hangers alongside a row of starchy dress shirts.

She wrinkled her nose at him. "You have a special hanger for your ties?"

"Oh, that's nothing; the rest of my collection's back home."

Mabel resolutely ignored the reminder that Jake's actual home was in Chicago and joined him on the bed, rolling to her side and propping her head on her hand. Jake in nothing but underwear was spectacular, and she took her time studying the slopes and dips of his arms, his chest, his abs. He had that abdominal V pointing to his groin that she'd never actually seen in the wild before this. "The time you spend at the gym is *so* worth it."

"If you like it, then it's worth it," he replied, rolling to face her. "Time for talking now?"

She looked down at where she was tracing a pattern on his comforter with her index finger. "I need you to understand that I was never dating Aiden. Never even interested in him like that."

Jake laid his hand over hers, stilling her restless movements. "The night of the Brick Babe auditions—"

She cut him off, embarrassed to admit this part. "I... may not have vetoed the idea of making you a tiny bit jealous that night." She was startled to feel a growl rumble through his chest, and she bit her lip to hide her pleasure at his reaction. "But it's only been you since the week you pulled me up from the gross old greenroom couch and then jumped the station van."

A slow smile spread across his face. "Poor Murdoch." He shook his head in mock pity. "If only he wasn't such an ugly bastard, maybe he'd have stood a chance."

Mabel gave his shoulder a little shove, remembering her own distress over Thea. "You're not off the hook here. Why were every one of my replacement's limbs wrapped around you Tuesday at the station?"

"I can't believe you saw that." Jake groaned and mashed his face into the comforter, which did a world of good at dissolving the ugly knot of jealousy lodged in her chest. "She was excited because you taught her to run the boards, and I guess that manifested itself as an enthusiastic hug. If you'd watched for another two seconds, you'd have seen me take three big steps back. I promise you, I'm *not* interested in Thea like that."

Then his smile fell, replaced by a creased-brow expression that she usually only saw when he was contemplating long rows of numbers. "Something you should know about me." He drew a deep breath and exhaled slowly. "This"—he gestured between the two of them—"doesn't happen for me often."

Her own smile slipped as his serious tone sank in. "What do you mean?"

His shoulders tensed. "I mean sex. I need an emotional connection with someone before I take them to bed." He held up a hand as if he anticipated the question forming in her mind. "And not in some old-fashioned courtship wait-until-marriage way. I mean that sexual attraction just doesn't happen for me if I don't feel strongly about someone."

She blinked, frowned, processed. "Emotions first, then sex?"

"Yeah. Demisexual, if you're trying to come up with the word. I had one serious girlfriend just after college, and one friend who sparked something for me that I didn't pursue, but hookups and casual relationships aren't my thing." He rolled to his back, a trace of bitterness creeping into his voice. "It's what makes me such a good corporate drone actually. I rarely have the time or opportunity to get to know anybody well enough to see if those feelings develop. So I work long hours and weekends without complaint. Until you."

He turned his head to flash a small, secret smile at her, and she struggled to wrap her arms around the tiny miracle that *she'd* been the person who drew those feelings to the surface for him. The new information joined the Jake-puzzle she'd been assembling in her brain and her heart over the past few months, and this piece fit right in the center, filling some gaps. But she still required a bit more clarification.

"So sex for you is...?" Uncertainty colored her voice, but God, everything he'd done tonight had turned her on and made her want him more. What if she couldn't return the favor for him in the same way?

"It depends. If the person isn't right?" He shrugged. "I can take or leave it. It's not something I need."

"And with the right person?"

"With the right person, I love sex." He smoothed his palm down her waist with a wicked smile. "Fucking love it."

His hand was heavy on her leg, and her breath was heavy in her lungs. She was scared to ask the next bit, but she had to. "And—"

"And you're the right person." His eyes scorched her, and his fingers clamped down possessively on her hip. "You may be the rightest person I've ever met. You're perfect for me here." He pressed his hand to his forehead, then moved it downward, pausing briefly over his heart before it landed on his groin. "And here. And now I need to make up for lost time."

Fire surged in her veins at the strain in his voice. Need. Not want, *need*. Jake needed her and only her. And she needed him too. Now it was time to show him how much.

"Hmm." She turned onto her stomach and wiggled a bit, feeling the shirt ride up her thighs. "What else do we need to discuss tonight before we do this? International trade policy? The city's new ban on leaf burning? Which Taylor Swift album is the best?"

Jake grinned, and his big hand traveled up the back of her leg to cup her butt. "I'm sorry. Were you talking?"

She shot him a laughing glance over her shoulder, and he flipped her onto her back and rolled on top of her in one smooth motion. Her heart battered against her ribs; this was *finally* happening.

"Keep talking," he murmured against her neck. "I fucking love your voice."

"Really?" She sounded breathy all of a sudden.

"Really. Your voice is *everything*. I've wanted to get you naked since I picked you up and put you on a desk in that furniture store. But your voice? I haven't been able to get enough of it since the first day I met you." His hands slid up her sides until his thumbs rested just below her breasts.

"Jake," she breathed, putting as much weight to his name as she could, and his eyes burned into hers.

"I'm just going to start kissing every part of you now. Lost time, remember? Keep talking."

When he claimed her mouth with his and nibbled at her lower lip, she wondered how he expected her to say anything at all. Then he moved down her body, pulling off the T-shirt and unhooking her bra. He tugged it down her arms and tossed it to the floor, inhaling hard at the sight of her breasts. She felt a surge of power at his speechlessness.

"Like what you see?" Her normal speaking voice never sounded that decadent, but she was pouring as much rich honey into it as she could and was rewarded when he looked up at her with naked want in his eyes that made her blood churn.

"Fuck, you're hot." His voice was reverent, and his dark hair fell over his forehead as he leaned down to swipe his tongue across her nipple.

She hissed at the sharp bolt of pleasure, and his cheeks curved into a smile.

"I don't hear you talking, sweetheart," he said against her skin, rolling the pad of his thumb across her other nipple. "I thought you had words for days. Tell me about Taylor Swift burning leaves."

He was right; all her words had failed her. He sucked her nipple into his mouth, and she moaned, raking her fingers through his hair.

"That's not talking either." He trailed his hand down her body to a different wet heat. "Use your words, Mae."

Mabel arched her back off the bed as he ran two fingers along her slickness. His thumb circled her clit with the perfect amount of pressure, and when his teeth grazed her nipple, she found the words she'd misplaced.

"Yessssss, just like that, Jake, please like that, please don't stop." The words rushed out in a throaty, frantic voice she barely recognized as her own.

And good man that he was, he chuckled and followed her commands, continuing at that delicious pressure and speed while she hovered for an eternity just beyond paradise. Finally, *finally* he bit down gently on her nipple, and the bolt of pleasure/pain combined with the motion of his thumb below brought her orgasm crashing down on her, leaving her gasping.

When her eyes fluttered open, he kissed her gently and whispered against her mouth, "You're gorgeous when you come."

Mabel ran one hand along the hard muscles of his chest, enjoying the sheen of sweat there, and whispered back, "Are you *ever* going to stop talking and fuck me?"

He went comically still for a beat and then exploded into a flurry of action, kicking off his boxer briefs and rolling to the bedside table to grab a condom. Mabel stilled his hand before he opened the packet, running a delicate fingertip along the wetness beading at the tip of his cock.

"Who's speechless now?" She couldn't help teasing him.

He responded by rolling the condom on and pulling her to the edge of the bed, positioning himself between her legs. "No words. That's how desperate I am to be inside you."

Mabel smiled and trailed her fingers down over her breasts, pinching her nipples. "Then do it already."

It had the desired effect. He groaned and pulled her legs around his waist. Then, with one quick thrust, he plunged into her. She sucked in a breath at the delicious intrusion and hooked her heels together to pull him even closer. He stilled for a moment, hands tight on her hips, eyes closed, face tense.

Mabel wanted to reach up and smooth away that pained expression, but before she could, he began to move. The delicious friction chased every other thought from her mind, and she let him set the pace. When her head lolled to the side, the mirrors on the closet doors reflected them back, and she saw herself spilled across his bed like a pagan offering, hands clenching the covers and hair pooling around her head. She saw Jake's muscled body tense and thrusting, watched the globes of his ass as he pounded into her. She saw the two of them finally, finally joined.

"Jake," she murmured. "Oh God, baby, look. Do you see how good we are together?"

He turned his head and met her gaze in the mirror. "Fuck. Oh fuck, Mabel," he ground out.

Then he lifted her as if she weighed nothing and rolled onto his back on the bed, positioning her so she could ride him, so they could both watch her move along his cock. The new position allowed him to penetrate even deeper, and it provided intriguing new views in the mirror.

But as Mabel's orgasm drew near, she turned away from the mirror, locking eyes with Jake and reaching down to twine her fingers around his.

"So perfect. So perfect for me," he panted, fingers tight around hers.

He freed one hand so he could caress her where their bodies were joined. As she shuddered around his cock, he gave a guttural groan and joined her in tumbling over the edge. After a suspended moment, he pulled her down next to him and kissed her, deep and slow. She curled into his big body, and their heartbeats slowed together.

MABEL WOKE EARLY OF COURSE. As soon as her eyes snapped open, the entire night flickered through her head like a highlight reel from someone else's life. A much braver someone else. Had she really started the night by getting her underwear torn off in a bar and ended it by riding Superman to her third orgasm of the night while they watched their sweaty, naked selves in a mirror?

That should really be the lead sentence in her obituary.

The clock in Jake's bedroom read 6:15 a.m., and she felt a flutter of unease clawing at her throat. The only clothes she had with her were the *Pretty Woman* gear, and no way were she and Jake going out for a cozy breakfast with her in knee-high boots. Also, he hadn't actually asked her to breakfast or made any plans at all beyond last night. *Also* also, she'd promised Thea she'd meet her at the gym at eight for that damn yoga class, which at the time had sounded like a dreadful idea but now gave her a plausible excuse for running away from a situation that seemed a little bigger than she knew how to handle at the moment.

She cautiously shifted to her side and allowed herself the luxury of staring at the man lying next to her. Jake was sound asleep on his stomach with an arm splayed across her waist. His handsome face was slack, lashes resting on his cheeks. The needy part of her wanted to smooth down his thick, ruffled hair and run a hand along the muscles of his back, but instead of waking him, she inched out from under his arm and quietly slid out of bed. She snatched her bra from the ground and tiptoed to the living room to collect her tiny skirt and slinky top. Her hair was a snarled mess, and she couldn't bring herself to shove her feet back into the torture boots, so she pulled on her thin socks, slid her arms into her coat, and resigned herself to a frigid dash to her car, which was at least parked near the main door.

A quick glance around his kitchen didn't yield a notepad or even a piece of junk mail to leave the neat freak a message on, so she fished an old Starbucks receipt out of her purse and scrawled, "Early appointment. Call you later. —M"

She placed the scrap of paper on the kitchen table and frowned at the message. It was impersonal, but it was the most she was able to articulate at the moment. The intensity of their pairing last night was too much, too fast. She needed to clear her head.

Easing open his front door, she shut it behind her as quietly as she could and hustled to the elevator and out to her car. The sock-clad dash to her car in the visitor's slot was as unpleasant as she'd feared, and once she made it home, she threw herself gratefully into the shower, then pulled on her workout gear and was fifteen minutes early to meet Thea, who, bless her heart, had actually beaten her there.

"Hi!" She looked like a tiny, spunky badass in her stretchy pants, workout tank, and hoodie, but her expression was nervous.

"Hi yourself. What's up with you?"

They'd parked themselves on one of the comfortable-as-a-wooden-log couches in the gym lobby, which was swarming with people there for their Saturday-morning workout. Thea bit her lip and stared down at her hands, which were fidgeting with the strings of her hoodie.

"Oh my God, *what?*" Mabel asked. "Is somebody dead? Am *I* dead?"

That, at least, pulled a smile out of her. "You're not

Bruce Willis, no." Then she took a deep breath. "Okay, I'm not sure whether I should even bring this up, but were you with Jake last night?"

How could she possibly have guessed that? Mabel's surprise must've registered as a no, because Thea covered her face in her hands with a wail. "Oh God, I shouldn't have brought it up."

Mabel gripped Thea's knees to get her attention. "Brought *what* up?"

She lifted her head slowly, then her words tumbled out in a rush. "Okay, so in that case, I don't know if I should tell you, but I bumped into the lady across the hall on my way out this morning, and she complained that some, and I'm quoting here, 'trampy tramp' snuck out of Jake's apartment a few hours ago." Thea leaned forward and squeezed Mabel's shoulder. "I'm so sorry. I guess she was barefoot and her hair was absolutely wild. And, well, he and I share an apartment wall, and last night I did hear some, um, things..."

Thea's voice trailed off as Mabel collapsed sideways into a quivering mass of embarrassed horror. "Oh my *God*. You guys share a wall?"

"I'm so sorry!" Thea cried. "I *knew* I shouldn't have told you. Maybe she made a mistake and saw somebody leaving a different apartment."

"No, it was Jake's." Mabel clapped her hands over her face and spoke from between her fingers. "I'm the trampy tramp. And oh my God, *you heard us?*"

Thea's mouth formed a perfect O for a solid twenty seconds before she dissolved into giggles. "You trampy trampy tramp!" she crowed, nudging Mabel's shin with her toe. "So? How was it?"

Mabel's whole body melted into boneless satisfaction,

and she grinned dreamily up at Thea. "So good. So incredibly good. So unbelievably, brain-meltingly good."

"Uggghhh, jealous." Thea stood and matter-of-factly zipped up her hoodie. "Come on. Today is not a day for yoga. Today is a day for donuts and coffee and gossip. I'm buying."

THIRTY-TWO

Jake wasn't terribly surprised to find himself alone in bed on Saturday morning. Disappointed, yes. But not surprised. He'd hoped Mabel would stick around after they both dropped to sleep exhausted; Mabel first thing in the morning was something he was dying to see. And kiss. And touch.

Okay, he was also dying for a repeat of the previous night, although maybe less frenzied this time. He wanted more savoring.

But her side of the bed had long grown cold by the time he woke up. He tamped down the hurt that bloomed in his chest; she'd been resisting the pull between them for so long that her bolting at the first opportunity made a weird sort of sense.

It still stung of course. But he wasn't going to take it lying down, although it did take a slight struggle to disentangle himself from the mess they'd made of his sheets. He wandered through his apartment, looking for any sign that last night had actually happened and hadn't been an especially vivid fantasy. He found his T-shirt crumpled on the bedroom floor and his jeans in the living room. Nothing of Mabel's though, not until he spotted the note on the table. Barely a note actually. A few terse words that did nothing to ease his growing concern.

The last time he'd had skin-to-skin contact with Mabel, he hadn't sought her out the following day, and on Monday everything exploded. He didn't think they had any remaining undetonated grenades lurking in their lives, but just in case, he wasn't going to leave their next meeting to chance or put it off until he bumped into her at the station. He needed to see her. Today, if she'd let him.

He sat on the couch and spent way too long laboring over a text message that conveyed the right amount of warmth without crossing into desperation.

Jake: *Missed you this morning. Free for dinner later?*

He hit Send and stared at the screen, relieved when her response zipped back almost instantly.

Mabel: *Yes to dinner. Yes to missing you too.*

Good. That was friendlier than her note at least.

Mabel: *Will you wear your pink apron?*

She remembered the apron. He grinned down at his phone. His cousin Brandy had draped it around his neck and snapped that shot during the lead-up to their family Thanksgiving, and he almost hadn't sent it to Mabel because they'd left things in such a weird place, but God, he was glad he had.

Jake: *Your place okay? Mine lacks kitchen supplies.*

Mabel: *And mine doesn't? But sure, come by whenever. Can I pick anything up?*

Jake: *Nope. See you around 5.*

He didn't want to wait until five. He didn't want to wait at all. But she clearly needed space, and he'd give it to her. He'd just have to fill the interminable hours in between with busywork so he wouldn't claw his way out of his skin.

At the grocery store, he wandered the aisles and snagged the ingredients he'd need for dinner, then made a few more stops when he couldn't find the final ingredient for the evening. At last, after the longest afternoon of his life, he pulled into the driveway of Mabel's one-story brick home. He hadn't been back since he'd taken her home after that first Moo Daddies concert, and now that he was seeing it in daylight, he was able to appreciate the way the aquamarine shutters mirrored the personality of their owner: attractive with a flash of the unpredictable.

He gathered his supplies and slipped an item on over his coat before walking up her front steps, laden with bags. He rang her bell and was rewarded with a delighted laugh when she opened the door.

"That is the pinkest apron I've ever seen." She grabbed him by a frilly strap and hauled him inside. "Just had this lying around, did you?"

He followed her into her house and set the grocery bags on her white-tiled kitchen countertop. "What, this old thing? Yeah, had it for years."

"Years," she repeated, reaching behind him to fiddle with the price tag on the neck strap.

"You asked for a pink apron, and since the original's with its owner a little north of here, I had to find a replacement," Jake told her. "This is not an easy thing to find in Beaucoeur, I'll have you know. I had to try three different stores. The saleswoman assured me that my wife would love it. I couldn't bear to tell her it was for me."

They both looked at the cotton-candy-pink apron that barely covered his thighs and the lacy, heart-shaped pocket sewn directly over his groin.

"I may not be your wife, but I love it." She hooked her fingers around the straps and pulled him close.

He responded by wrapping his arms around her and kissing her soundly, enjoying the soft sweetness of her mouth.

The last thing he wanted to do was pressure her, but he also wanted to let her know where he was on the events of the day so far. "I was disappointed to wake up alone," he said against her lips. Not accusatory, just a statement.

She colored a little and pulled back. "I promised Thea I'd meet her at the gym, so I needed to go home and get changed. Although I guess I could've just knocked on her wall. By the way, I recently learned that when you said she's your neighbor, you literally meant *neighbor*."

"Aggressively friendly literal neighbor, yes." He ran his thumb along her jaw. "And that's the only reason you snuck out?"

She turned her head to catch the tip of his thumb between her teeth, then let it go. "I needed a little time to process. Last night was..."

Her voice trailed off, and Jake rested his hands on her shoulders. "I'm desperate to hear what adjective you come up with."

She laughed and dropped a tiny kiss at the corner of his mouth. "Amazing." Another small kiss, this time on the opposite side. "Fantastic." One more kiss, directly to his mouth. "Intense."

His enjoyment of her lips on his skin was interrupted when she gave him a little shake. "And? I'm desperate to hear your own adjectives about last night."

"Mind-blowing." He kissed her cheek. "Life-changing." He kissed her jaw. "And yes, intense." None of that was an overstatement. She'd opened doors for him last night that he'd never walked through in terms of physical pleasure from an emotional connection.

He was hooked on her now, so he kissed her throat and kept kissing down to the neckline of her soft, long-sleeved shirt, scraping his teeth over her collarbone. She dropped her head back to give him access to the soft skin there, and he could've stood in the sunny kitchen and kissed her for hours.

But he pulled back and said, "Mabel, I've got to ask you something incredibly important."

She froze and asked warily, "Yes?"

"Tell me, and please be honest: Do you own a zester?"

Her lips twitched, but she kept her voice flat. "I like grated cinnamon in my hot chocolate. Of course I own a zester."

"Okay then," he said. "Step back and let the master work. Your mission, should you choose to accept it, is to provide the music for the afternoon."

"I've been training for that my whole life. Zesting, not so much." She connected her iPhone to the speaker in her kitchen and thumbed through her music list, settling on Kate Nash. She then seated herself on a stool at the countertop and hooked her bare feet around the rungs to watch as he prepared a chicken for roasting, sliced potatoes for a gratin, and put the zester to good use on lemon-infused asparagus.

"No dessert?" Mabel faux pouted. "Slacker."

"As if I would leave you with no dessert," Jake scoffed. "Check the bag to your left."

"Is this...?" Mabel extracted a glossy white box with the words Have Your Cake Bakery printed on the top.

"Cupcakes from my friend's bakery in Chicago, yes. I brought some back with me for a taste test."

"You remembered!"

"That you once described cupcakes as orgasmic? I did. That kind of imagery tends to stay with a guy." Jake turned away from the stove. "Okay, the chicken and potatoes go in the oven now, and we hit the asparagus at the very end. Want to give me the official tour of the house?"

"Yeah, you didn't get to see very much other than the homeowner being a hot mess the last time, did you?" she said wryly, hopping off the stool.

"A cute hot mess." He followed her out of the kitchen and through a house that proved to be cheeky and comfortable and perfectly Mabel, with its explosion of purples and greens, corals and blues. At her bedroom door, she gestured to the cat sleeping at the foot of her bed. He cracked open one yellow eye, stretched, and repositioned himself for more sleep.

"You remember Tybalt?"

"I do," Jake said gravely. "He and I bonded that night. Oh hey!" He gestured to the pot of delicate purple orchids on her bedside table. "I truly thought these would've been mulched to fertilize your garden the day you got them."

She tucked her loose hair behind her ears with a rueful laugh. "They almost were. I sent them home with Dave, and he kept them safe until I asked for them back a few weeks ago."

A spurt of pleasure raced through him. She hadn't trashed them, and when she got them back, she put them where she'd see them as she began and ended her day. She really had been thinking about him as much as he'd been thinking about her.

They left Tybalt to his nap, and Jake ducked into the kitchen to check on the food. Then they ambled back to Mabel's living room, where she settled cross-legged onto one end of the couch and pulled him down onto the cushion next to her.

Now was as good a time as any for a big pronouncement.

"I didn't come right out and say it last night, but just so we're clear: I'm all in." He draped an arm over the couch and watched her absorb his words. Too much, too soon, too demanding—he didn't care. They'd been doing this dance for far too long for him not to lay his cards on the table.

Still, his whole body tightened as she looked down for a long moment at her fingers laced together on her lap before taking a deep breath.

"Yeah. Me too." Then she looked up and smiled, and his breath caught in his chest. "Let's see where this goes."

Before he could respond, she launched herself at him, latching her arms around his neck and sliding down his body until they were both reclined on the couch with her warm weight on top of him.

"Wait. Wait, Mabel," Jake said through her kisses. It killed him to stop, but he was doing things right this time, dammit. "If we're going to do this, I don't want to keep anything from you about your job."

"It can wait." She slid her hands under his shirt and scratched his stomach lightly with her nails.

He grabbed both her wrists. "No. No surprises this time."

She stilled, body sprawled on top of his, hot eyes on his.

He gulped and made it quick. "As part of my oversight of the station's financial health following the buyout, I asked my sister to commission a marketing company to do a focus group on the different shows at your station. That will provide some qualitative data to go along with the listenership numbers being released in January."

"This is weird pillow talk," she muttered, pulling herself upright to straddle him.

It took effort, but he ignored the hot pleasure of her pressing against his fairly serious hard-on. "Long story short, because you're killing me with your wiggling, we've convened the focus group four times so far, and people chosen to participate rate your morning-show performance incredibly high, and they hate the rotating cast of women on the air with Dave. I haven't shown the results to Brandon yet, and I don't know if it'll do any good, but it's something."

Her lazy movement stilled. "Four times? How long has the research been going on?"

"Since October," he said, wrapping his hands around her hips. "They listened to shows with you and Dave, with Dave when he was solo, then Dave with the other cohosts. They listened to the other shows too. They like you on afternoon drive, but not as much as on mornings."

She blinked. "Since October," she said slowly. "So when I was ignoring you and keeping it professional and being generally obtuse, you were still fighting for my old job?"

He tried to keep his shrug casual. "Somebody's got to look out for the financial health of the station. And taking initiative looks good to the partners."

Of course, if he impressed the partners too much, he'd find himself back in the Chicago office with a promotion and a raise. But that was ages away, and who could say what would change in his life between now and then? He'd find a way to make it work, but at this moment, Mabel's glassy eyes were his priority, and his heart clenched when a tear broke loose and streaked down her cheek.

"Oh, sweetheart, no. I didn't mean to make you cry." He sat up to brush the moisture away.

"I'm not sad." She sniffled. "Nobody's ever commissioned research for me before! This is the nicest thing, Jake."

He started to repeat his warning. "Again, I don't know that Brandon will—" But her lips cut him off as she renewed her assault on his mouth.

Being honest in a relationship was a good gambit, he decided thirty minutes later as they shrugged back into their clothes and devoured their dinner at Mabel's kitchen island, talking nonstop and eating the food right out of the pans.

"You're staying tonight, right?" She licked a dollop of cupcake icing off her lower lip, and his eyes followed the movement of her tongue the whole way.

"Yep. And I'm planning to be here in the morning when you wake up."

"You'd better be." Then she stood and led him by a belt loop to the bedroom.

The next day he learned that Mabel was as warm and pliant in his arms first thing in the morning as he'd always imagined. He moved poor Tybalt off the bed and made love to her slowly, languishing attention on every millimeter of her body.

Afterward, he tucked her against his side, but thoughts of work that day, and all the days moving forward, crowded his brain and pushed aside the post-sex glow.

"What gives?" She stroked a hand lightly over this chest. "You're supposed to be basking."

"Oh, I am." He pressed a kiss into the top of her hair, relishing the warm weight of her against him. "It's just work. I think... I've used it as an excuse over the years."

She looked up at him with a frown that matched his own, so he elaborated.

"Nobody asks questions if you say your long hours are the reason you're not going home with that girl from the bar. 'Sorry, my dick's just not interested' is a much longer conversation, and it's not one that most women appreciate having. People expect men to always be up for it, and if they're not, it becomes an issue. It's exhausting." He sighed. "And sometimes it was easier to tell *myself* that work was more important than investing time in..."

He didn't finish his thought, and Mabel reached out to twine her fingers around his.

"Time in yourself?" she asked softly. "In finding a person to care about?"

He nodded and squeezed her hand.

"I do it too," she said after a moment of silence.

"Yeah?" He faced her again, some of the bleakness draining from his heart to be talking this easily about the things that had made sex and love so complicated for him for years.

"Yeah." She kept her eyes on their hands as she spoke. "I lost my first radio job when things went south with the boss's son, and I haven't seriously dated anybody since. For my own protection, and for Dave's, right? Except..."

He rolled over and wrapped his free hand around

their entwined fingers, pressing tight so she'd know he was listening and he wasn't going anywhere.

"Except I was terrified of getting hurt again. Of trusting anybody again. And then you came along."

He raised their joined hands to his lips and pressed a kiss to her knuckles. "I'm so glad you took a chance on me."

When she looked at him, tears danced along her lashes. "I'm so glad you took a chance on *me*." Then she smiled and tossed her hair over her shoulder with a flourish. "So are we going public with this or what?"

"Hey, I already let you parade me around the food carts downtown like a piece of meat. How much worse can it get?"

She huffed out a laugh. "Well, there's somebody who's been rooting for you this whole time, so if we're letting people know..."

She reached over him to snag her phone off the table on his side of the bed. It put her in the perfect position for him to suck one of her rosy nipples into his mouth, which of course he took advantage of, which of course distracted them both for longer than they expected. When they came back up for air, he pointed to her phone.

"Got plans for that?"

"Hmmm," she said dreamily, then snapped out of it. "Oh yeah. Something tasteful."

She turned the phone toward them and snapped a photo of their grinning, tousled heads sharing one pillow.

"I may as well let Dave know that his lobbying on your behalf finally paid off." She hit Send on the picture only, with no explanatory text added, and her phone immediately buzzed with Dave's typically understated reply: *About time.*

Jake kissed her temple, thrilled that she'd told her best friend about them. "Tell him I owe him a beer."

"One beer? That's all I'm worth to you?"

Jake kissed along her neck as he amended his offer. "A six-pack. A case. A keg. A lifetime supply."

She shivered. "Lifetime, huh? I'll let him know."

"He can wait." Jake grabbed her phone and dropped it on the bedside table. "Now get over here and make your case for why I should buy him something fancier than PBR."

Laughing, she pushed him back on the bed and did just that.

THIRTY-THREE

"Are you asleep?"

The sun wasn't up yet, but Mabel was, and she wanted Jake to be too.

In response to her whispered query, his arm snaked around her waist, pulling her backward to nestle against his chest.

"Of course I'm asleep," he finally said, voice creaky. "No normal person is up this early."

Mabel gave a *humph* and tucked her feet under his leg. Her habit of waking up at five a.m. was much more tolerable with Jake lying next to her. They hadn't spent *every* night of the past three weeks together, but it was often enough that on those mornings when her eyes snapped open without the benefit of an alarm, she usually found all kinds of lovely ways to fill her time with the willing man next to her.

"I was thinking we should host another dinner party," she whispered. Her bedroom was dark, but she felt his chest quake in a laugh. "What? I was a great chef!" she huffed.

Jake brushed aside her hair and pressed his lips against the nape of her neck. "Correction: *I* was a great chef. My pork loin was a hit. But I don't think Robbie's recovered from your curried vegetables yet."

"He liked them," Mabel grumbled.

"He was being polite. Now hush. One of us is trying to sleep." He made a show of snuggling deeper under the covers.

Oh, he thought so, did he? She wiggled and gave a little stretch. "Hmm. What do you think about hitting the gym?"

In truth, gym wasn't the kind of cardio she was angling for that morning. Her pestering paid off when a pair of strong hands clamped around her waist and hauled her on top of him, where she discovered that at least a part of Jake was wide awake. She rocked against him once, and he responded with a gentle bite to her shoulder.

"Too early for the gym. I'm thinking breakfast in bed. French toast?" he asked hopefully.

"You know you lost your french toast privileges."

Jake had gotten creative with maple syrup during a breakfast delivery last Sunday, which resulted in Mabel having to wash every last scrap of her bedding. Worth it though.

"No gym, no french toast," he mused. "Good thing I have a couple of other ideas for how to pass the time."

An hour later, Mabel left a well-satisfied Jake in bed and went to forage for coffee. While she waited for the Keurig to heat, she glanced around her kitchen, taking in his stack of work files on the counter, his tie folded on top, his running shoes neatly placed in the corner. He'd invaded every corner of her house, and she loved it. In fact, sometimes she had to remind herself that this beautiful life was *her* beautiful life.

She was grabbing the creamer from the fridge when the man in question padded into the kitchen, Tybalt twining around his ankles. He yawned and settled onto a stool at the island.

Mabel set his coffee in front of him and kissed his bare shoulder. "Wanting to get into the office early, as per ushe?"

He looked her up and down with warm brown eyes. "Say the word and I'll blow off work to take you back to bed for round two."

"Deal," she said. "But after coffee."

They sipped in silence until Jake gestured at the radio on the island. "Do you want to...?"

She sighed and flipped it on, tuning in just as Dave and Thea greeted the early-morning listeners.

"She's gotten a lot better," Jake said. "All that coaching paid off."

Mabel stirred her coffee but didn't answer. Every scrap of her soul still hated hearing someone else with Dave, but at the same time, she'd spent hours working with Thea to get her more comfortable on air. Her protégée had taken to the morning show like a perky duck to water, and Mabel felt a weird mix of pride and resentment every time she tuned in. How confusing.

Thankfully, Jake recognized the conflict on her face and hustled her into the shower, where they used up all the hot water until he was forced to rush out the door so he wouldn't miss his first scheduled call of the day.

THAT EVENING the chime of Jake's phone interrupted their post-dinner viewing of a *Barbarian Time Brigands* rerun.

"It's my mom," he said. "Do you mind?"

"Not at all!" Mabel paused Netflix and hopped up to carry their empty plates to the dishwasher.

But when she returned to the living room, the sight of a sixty-something woman's face on Jake's phone screen halted her in her tracks in the doorway.

"Where are you right now, sweetie? I don't recognize the background."

He caught Mabel's eye and silently asked the question they hadn't discussed yet: *am I telling my mom about you?* To her surprise, the answer that clawed its way to the surface was *hell yes*. She nodded, and he rewarded her with one of his big, for-her-only smiles, which was fast becoming one of her favorite things in the world.

He turned back to his phone and said, "I'm, uh, I'm at Mabel's actually," and the tiny bit of bashfulness in his voice traveled straight to Mabel's heart.

It clearly had the same effect on his mother too, because she gasped and pressed her fingers to her mouth and breathed, "You're at *Mabel's!*"

Jake had inherited his brown eyes from his mother, and hers were busy scanning the parts of Mabel's living room visible over Jake's shoulder. Hmm. When was the last time she'd dusted?

"C-can I say hello to her?" his mother asked tentatively.

Another questioning glance from Jake, but this one found her straightening in alarm. "I'm not cute!" she mouthed at him, looking down in dismay at her sloppy sweatshirt and leggings and slapping her hands over her makeup-free face.

But he looked at her with his usual steady warmth and murmured, "Always beautiful, remember?"

Then he jerked his head to summon her over, and she joined him on the couch without a second thought. He wrapped his arm around her and kissed her temple, and then she turned to the face on the phone.

"Hi, Mrs. Carey. I'm Mabel." She gave a little wave.

"Call me Shannon, honey. I'm so glad to meet you. *So glad*. Jake's told me..." She blinked rapidly and swiped at her eyes. "Well, let's just say that Jake's been waiting for you for a long time."

Mabel felt tears threaten too, and she turned to look at the man on the couch next to her. "I can't tell you how glad I am that he found me."

He smiled back at her, and for a moment she forgot that they had an audience as she let the warmth of his gaze wash over her. But his mother's sniffle pulled her out of the moment, and she looked back at the screen to find Shannon beaming at them.

"I'm just so happy. So happy he's happy, that you're both happy." The older woman sniffled once more, then brightened. "So Jake says you're a deejay?"

"I am!" Mabel chirped, nervously aware that this was her first chance to impress the mom. "Face for radio and all that."

She laughed a little awkwardly, and Jake nudged her. "Yeah, such a burden to look at every day."

Shannon's own face, ruddy-cheeked and creased with lines under her brutally short salt-and-pepper hair, glowed as she looked between Mabel and her son. "Are you joining us for Christmas? We'd love to have you.

Have you met Jake's sister yet? She'll be there with her boyfriend. I'd love to have all of you come."

Excitement colored Shannon's voice, but Mabel wasn't about to crash the Carey Christmas without a longer discussion with Jake. "Oh, um, we hadn't really talked about—"

"If I can talk her into it, yes," he said firmly.

She turned her head to whisper, "Really?" He looked back at her like that was the most ridiculous question about a foregone conclusion he'd ever heard, and she melted. "Okay, it looks like I'm joining you for Christmas."

"Well, that's..." His mother drew a deep breath and placed a hand over her heart. "That's just wonderful."

Shannon looked to be on the verge of tearing up again, but Jake steered the conversation toward practicalities. "I bought the turkey, so that'll be delivered along with a couple of pies on Christmas Eve."

"I keep telling you, you don't have to take care of that every year." Shannon's exasperated voice made Mabel think this wasn't their first conversation about the topic.

"You know I want to." Topic closed, based on Jake's tone. "Oh, and I just had a conference call with my BPS bosses, and they're thrilled with the work I'm doing down here. Things are looking great."

"That's nice, sweetie. I know that's important to you," Shannon said before turning to Mabel again. "But I want to know all about the beautiful girl who makes my son smile like that. Where are you from? Do you want kids?"

"Mom!" Jake groaned, but Mabel lightly flicked his ear.

"Hush. Your mother and I are talking."

As she answered all Shannon's questions, Jake's

comment burrowed into the back of her brain. "Things are looking good." Was he referring to the partnership? And what did that mean for the two of them? As Shannon peppered her with questions, Mabel glanced at Jake, who watched their exchange with such contentment that it eased the tension in her chest. He was in this, just as much as she was, and she trusted him to let her know if there were any bumps on the horizon. If he wasn't worried about their future, then she wouldn't worry either.

THIRTY-FOUR

"We're going to be late!"

"We are not!" Mabel's voice floated from the bedroom, which she'd booted Jake out of half an hour earlier after upending the entirety of her closet onto every available surface. One raised eyebrow as she held up every pair of shoes she owned next to every scrap of fabric she owned, and he'd been exiled to the living room.

In truth, he was content to laze on her couch while she spun like a top, getting ready for the Brick's New Year's Eve party. Then again, he hated being less than punctual. Maybe he should check on her progress.

He dropped his feet from their perch on the coffee table, and Tybalt, who'd fallen asleep on his lap, gave a *mrrpt* of irritation at being jostled. The orange cat grumpily resettled himself on the adjacent cushion and allowed Jake to give him an under-the-chin apology scritch. The cat appeased, Jake headed down the hall to brave the feminine prep zone. When he stuck his head around the doorframe, he was again reminded that he was the luckiest son of a bitch on Earth. His woman stood in front of the mirror, flushed, adorable, and draped in a tiny black dress.

"What do you think? Too basic?" She smoothed her hands down her sides and pivoted, giving him a good look at the plunging neckline. Then she turned around and leaned over to put on her shoes, letting him ogle her long, bare legs.

He swallowed. Swallowed again. Cleared his throat. Shifted to accommodate his suddenly interested dick where it pressed against the zipper of his pants.

"Nothing basic about any of that," he managed.

She straightened with a pleased smile and fluffed her hair, which she'd styled in a mass of curls for the night. "Thanks. I'm worried I'll freeze outside, but—"

"I'll keep you warm." He crossed the room and wrapped his arms around her, kissing her hard, and she didn't even bat his hands away when they slid into her hair. If anything, she pressed herself even more tightly against him and returned his kiss ferociously.

When his hands crept to the hem of her skirt, she pulled away with a laugh. "Now who's going to make us late?"

"Worth it," he murmured, pulling her back to him. "Some things are *so* worth it."

An hour later, they arrived at one of Beaucoeur's posh riverfront hotels where the station-sponsored New Year's Eve bash was in full swing in the ballroom. All the deejays were expected to give a few short live broadcasts throughout the night, and Mabel must've been feeling anxious, because she tapped her way across the parking lot as quickly as her heels would carry her. Jake's longer legs allowed him to keep up, and when they finally made it inside, the first person they bumped into was Brandon, without a date on his arm, surprisingly.

He eyed them with a smirk. "You're late. Wonder why."

Just like that, Mabel's happy, I've-been-sexed-up glow vanished, and Jake bit back a curse. She might have adapted to her new work situation, but her interactions with Brandon usually left her a little snarly. He rested his hand briefly on the small of her back before pulling it away, aware that she was still uncomfortable with PDA and not wanting to push his luck. She flicked a smile up at him before returning her glare to Brandon, but it just bounced off the man's Teflon skin.

He pointed a thumb over his left shoulder. "We've got the live remote booth set up in the far corner. Skip's already done two cut-ins, so go let him know you're here. I'm sure he'll want you to take a turn making the unwashed masses feel bad that they're not here hanging with the slightly more-washed masses tonight."

She rolled her eyes, nodded curtly, and stalked across the room toward Skip, who was no doubt about to get an earful about their nightmare boss.

Jake sighed. "Why do you get off on antagonizing my girlfriend?"

"Nothing I said was antagonistic, was it?" Brandon asked innocently. "Other than implying that she just had good sex—in the most HR-friendly way possible, of course."

"Nothing about you is HR friendly."

Brandon plucked a glass of champagne off a circling waiter's tray and saluted Jake with it. "You're damn right. But let's jump back for a second. The delectable Mabel's officially your girlfriend now?"

"If we're doing this, I need something stronger than *that*," Jake muttered, gesturing to Brandon's champagne flute. The other man shrugged, drained his glass, and followed Jake to the bar.

Once they each had a tumbler of scotch in their hands, Jake felt capable of venturing into this conversation. "To answer your question: yes. Things are going well between us."

The information pulled a wolfish grin out of Brandon. "So a woman finally got you to look up from your precious spreadsheets."

Jake's hackles rose at the amusement in Brandon's tone. "What's so funny about that?"

Brandon pointed at him with his glass. "You, dude. We had hot-and-cold-running sorority girls in college, all of them dying to have sex with you. 'Oh, Brandon, fix me up with your friend Jake.' 'Oh, Brandon, why doesn't Jake ever come to these parties or hook up with any girls?'" He grimaced at the memories and took a sip of the amber liquid in his glass. "But no, no, the scholarship student had no time for women. Then you get out of college and start making some money, and all you can see is that partnership."

Jake stiffened. "There's nothing wrong with ambition."

"Of course not," Brandon said impatiently. "What's hilarious to me is that you relocated down here for a temporary assignment, your last one before making partner, and what happened?"

"Wait, are you complaining about my work? I've been laser focused on the Lowell accounts." It took a little more juggling of his time, but he was making it work, and he was damn proud of the balance he'd achieved. But if

Brandon was sending negative reports to his superior at BPS... The thought made the blood pound in his ears.

Brandon dismissed his fears with a lazy wave of his hand. "You worry too much. Your work is good. In fact, my old man just played a round of golf with one of your bosses at Augusta and sang your praises for the first five holes."

His relief at that unexpected news vanished with Brandon's next words.

"I'm just commenting on the irony of it all."

Jake raised his brows. "Irony?"

Brandon saluted him with his glass. "Of you, stopping to roll in the hay when you're only five feet from the finish line you've been running toward for twenty years."

"I'm not sure that's how irony works," Jake said distractedly as his stomach twisted into a knot. He *was* working fewer hours than he ever had in his life, yet he seemed to be closer to his goal than he'd ever been. A year ago, he'd have laughed off the idea that becoming less of a workaholic would win him a partnership, but he was still on course, even if he answered his emails a little more slowly these days. He was still in it for the career, the partnership, the financial stability he'd craved his whole life. He'd just made a little room for Mabel alongside it all.

Still, his expression must've betrayed some of that inner turmoil, because Brandon clapped him on the back. "Not fucking with you here. I'm genuinely trying to pay you a compliment. You found your person and fell in love, and you didn't worry about your self-imposed life sched-ule. That's brave. Now"—he drained his drink—"if you'll excuse me, I'm going to see if I can find a woman or two to *not* fall in love with tonight, if you know what I mean."

With one more hearty back slap, Brandon disappeared into the crowd, leaving Jake frowning into his glass. Something about their conversation itched along the edges of his brain, probably to do with Mabel and his partnership. God, if he could just jump ahead to their Jamaica trip, where he wouldn't have to think about work or the future or anything he couldn't control. It'd be just him on a beach with the woman he—

In a flash, he realized what was needling him. He ditched his glass on a vacant high-top table and set out across the room to find her at the WNCB table next to Skip, holding a mic, ready to do her live spot.

"Hi!" She waved him over. "Give me two minutes."

She slipped the headphone on and raised her voice to be heard over the buzz of the crowd. "Hey there, Beaucoeur! This is Mae Bell, coming to you live from the ballroom at the Samuel Clemens Hotel. I'm here with a couple hundred of my closest friends, ringing in this glorious New Year, and good news, there's still time for you to join us before we do our final countdown to midnight." She paused and shot Jake a quick wink before turning her attention back to the mic. "This year I've got my somebody special picked out to kiss when the ball drops. And maybe you've got somebody picked out too, or maybe you don't. Either way, get on down here and join us! We're having a blast."

He was hit with a surge of joy. Hats-in-public, no-PDA Mabel had mentioned their relationship on air. That was important. That let him know that he was doing the right thing.

Skip signaled her that they were out, and she dropped her equipment on the table. "Thanks, kiddo," he said. "I'll pull in Dave for the next one."

She shot him a thumbs-up, then spun to Jake, who rested his hands on her waist and backed her into the corner behind the station table until they were as alone as they could be in a packed ballroom.

"Did you just announce to the world that you're a taken woman?"

She laughed breathlessly and pressed a hand to her chest. "Did I?"

"You did." He tugged her closer. "And I need you to know something too."

The teasing expression dropped off her face when she noticed how seriously he was studying her. "Oh God. What did Brandon do this time?"

She glared over his shoulder, angry gaze scanning the room until he caught her chin and turned her attention back to him.

"Nothing bad, actually." He released her and smoothed his hand down her neck. "He said something to me just now, about how brave I am to have..."

She looked up at him expectantly, and he swallowed hard and tried again.

"How brave I am to have fallen in love with you." He watched her expression, searching for any hint of panic or rejection, but her face only registered surprise. "And the thing is, as soon as he said the words, every part of me knew it was true. And then I got pissed at him."

She gave a shaky laugh. "Join the club. But why over that?"

He moved his hands down to rest on her hips. "For saying it out loud to me before I could say it to you."

"Then you'd better officially say it to me," she whispered, eyes bright.

"I love you." It felt so good to say that he repeated it, louder this time. "I love you, Mabel."

Then, thank God, she said it right back. "I love you too. I love you so much that I'm only slightly annoyed that Brandon was involved in this."

Jake laughed and pressed his forehead to hers. "Does that mean I'm allowed to lay my unworthy hands on you in public now?"

"Oh, absolutely." She reached up to wrap her arms around his neck. "And you should probably kiss me a couple of times too, just so everybody here knows we're together."

Who could resist? He kissed her soundly and offered a silent thank-you to the universe that he'd looked up from his spreadsheets and found her. Now if only the universe could show him the formula for landing his partnership and keeping his girl.

THIRTY-FIVE

Mabel walked into the greenroom and found Dave slumped on the couch with his guitar on his lap.

"It's Monday," he said when she dropped on the couch next to him. "The third week in January."

"Yup." A tiny spark of hope flickered in her belly. The Nielsen ratings were due out any day, which meant they'd soon know about any listenership changes that happened in October, November, and December—in other words, the months following the morning-show split. No amount of stern internal commands had been able to quash her foolish optimism. Because what if? What if the station's audience numbers dropped? What if Brandon changed his mind?

Dave moved his fingers through silent chord progressions, his favorite activity to channel excess energy, as Mabel watched Skip through the glass going through the motions of his show. "My numbers'll be down. It's inevitable."

"But that's good, Eeyore," she said. "If you improved, then That Arrogant Asshole was right all along."

"But if I haven't improved, it means I'm a shitty deejay."

"Right, but we already knew that."

His small pained noise was a tiny rebuke.

"Oof, sorry." A closer look revealed the strain around his eyes. "You're really worried, aren't you?"

The strings squealed as Dave slid his fingers over them. "We both know the show isn't as good without us working together. I just hope that doesn't mean I'll be out of a job if the book really is that bad." He kept his eyes on his guitar.

"Please, they'd never fire you. You're Mr. Beaucoeur Radio." She leaped off the couch and started pacing. "I just want the wait over with already! Who the hell knows what the ratings will be? Plus there's Jake's focus group research, and God only knows what Brandon'll do with that. Gah!"

She flung herself back down, and this time Dave actually strummed his guitar, plucking out an ominous riff suitable for the drama of the situation, at which point Skip whipped the studio door open.

"Take it somewhere else, you two. Your palpable anxiety's seeping under the door."

Their wait ended at noon on Wednesday when Robbie stuck his pompadoured head into the secondary studio where Mabel was working on commercials. "Ratings are out. Brandon wants to see you and Dave in his office in two hours. Book's in the greenroom."

He hadn't even finished speaking before she ripped the cans off her ears and bolted out the door. Dave was already holding the book and scanning the results, so she stood on her tiptoes to peer over his shoulder.

"Hoooooooleeeeeey shiiiiiiit," he said.

He wasn't wrong. The spring numbers had placed the Brick at number three in the Beaucoeur market, with their morning show as the second-most listened to. Not so in the fall results Dave was holding. Ratings for the past three months now had them trailing the Top 40 station and the country station like usual, but the all-talk station had bumped the Brick down to number four by a fairly large margin.

"We went from an 8.7 percent audience share to a 5.1?" Mabel asked, horrified. "How did that happen?"

"My fault," Dave said flatly. "Look."

She inhaled hard at the morning-show numbers. The spring ratings had Dave and Mae in the Mornings at a 9.3 audience share. The new numbers had the Mae-less show sitting at a 4.0. She'd never seen a drop that big before.

"Not your fault." Her voice was harsher than she intended it to be, but she hated the shell-shocked look on Dave's face. "You were struggling to keep all the oars working in the right direction with a new copilot at the helm every week. Of course the numbers are rocky."

Dave shoved the report at her and collapsed onto the couch, running his fingers through his hair.

"Not good, not good, not good," he muttered, then looked up at her. "Well, *you're* good."

She flipped to the afternoon-drive numbers. Sure enough, she was pulling in more of an audience than Roman had been at the same time in the spring, up from 5.6 to 6.7. Surprising, since she'd been intentionally sucking for two of those three months. Not that she'd say that in front of a panicking Dave.

"I told you you'd be fine without me," he said. "You make me funny, and you're great on your own. *I'm* the train wreck."

She dropped the papers on the desk and stalked over to him, leaning down to put both her hands on his shoulders. "David Winnebago Chilton—"

"Winston," he muttered.

"David *Winnebago* Chilton," she said, raising her voice, "if you don't shut your pity hole, I will shut it for you. You hosted what should be a two-person show solo for a month, and then you had to parade a group of ill-prepared, marginally talented party girls though on-air auditions. Of *course* your numbers are wonky."

He leaned forward, his head lolling. "Tell that to my unemployment officer."

She was saved from answering when the greenroom door opened and Jake strolled in. He crossed to her and, without a word, pulled her into his arms, bent her dramatically backward, and kissed her hard. They broke apart when Dave pointedly cleared his throat, and Mabel, fanning herself a little, said, "I didn't know you were stopping by the station today!"

"Brandon just called so we could go over the most recent ad-revenue numbers. I don't know what he's thinking, but I know he's not happy."

"Great," Dave moaned.

"I just hope he keeps it short. I've got a last-minute conference call with the Chicago office in an hour," he said, checking his watch.

"The drudgery of the upwardly mobile." She winked.

"It's the only way to the top, and you know that's where I wanna be, baby."

She kissed him again because his work ethic was damn sexy.

"Anyway," he said when they separated, "between the

numbers and Finn's focus group research, I've done all I can."

"I know," she purred. "And you'll be rewarded with displays of my gratitude tonight, whatever happens."

Dave's moaning morphed into a retching noise, which she ignored as she tugged Jake's lapels back into place. "By the way, you really need to start packing, friend-o."

"I cannot wait to be on a beach with you where I don't have to spend a second thinking about work," he said. "I've already got my swim trunks and my sunblock laid out. Do I need anything else?"

She stroked a hand down his abdomen, covered in layers of office-wear. "Not on my account. In fact, if you forget to pack any shirts, that's fine by me."

The seventy listeners who'd signed up for the station's Jamaica trip were departing the next morning for the five-day, four-night resort vacation, and Dave, Mabel, and a handful of Brick Babes, including Thea, were going along to mingle with the fans and do periodic broadcasts from paradise. A still-safe-to-fly Ana was also going, but more importantly for Mabel, Jake had managed to swing the time off from BPS, so the two of them were looking forward to their first trip together even if it would be work-adjacent.

"I'll leave all my shirts at home, I promise."

Home. Was he thinking of Beaucoeur as home? The thought warmed her as much as the sunny Jamaican beach no doubt would, and she kissed him until she was breathless, flustered, and unconcerned about anything, including the ratings.

THAT AFTERNOON, Mabel and Dave walked side by side to face Brandon.

"Have a seat." He smiled his oiliest smile and gestured to the guest chairs in his office. "You've reviewed the Nielsen numbers by now?"

They both nodded, and when Dave drew breath to speak, Brandon held up a hand. "Save it. Your morning numbers aren't where I'd like them to be, and the ad people are having a harder time selling for the show. Even though Thea's doing relatively well, the feedback we've gotten from advertisers is that they miss the old partnership the two of you had."

Mabel's heart started to trip in her chest as Brandon looked from her to Dave and back again. Then he shrugged. "I'm not perfect, and I do admit my mistakes. We could let it ride until the next book comes out, but between the ad revenue and lover boy's focus groups, I see that I was wrong."

Mabel groped for Dave's hand and squeezed it. Was this really happening?

"So congrats," Brandon said, rubbing a hand over his brow. "The week after Jamaica, Mabel, you're back on the morning show with Dave. No more solo show, no more guest hosts. Full-time Dave and Mae. We'll find somebody new for afternoon drive."

Dave let out a shaky breath as Mabel breathed, "For real?"

Brandon nodded. "Numbers don't lie."

She gripped the arms of the chair, terrified this was some kind of cruel joke. "Really? Really and truly?"

"Really and truly." He tapped his pen on the Nielsen book sitting on his desktop. "And Lowell Consolidated's going to pay for an advertising blitz about our return to morning-show greatness. What do you say, team? Think we can rebuild the show, take it to number one in the market?"

Elation filled her chest, and she scrambled to her feet, whooping. Dave joined her, and they both jumped and hollered like kids while Brandon winced at the noise.

Her joy kept expanding in her chest until she felt like she might burst with it. She had her job back and her best friend grinning like an idiot next to her, and when she got home from work that night, an amazing man would be waiting at her house for her. Could any one person handle this much happiness in life, this much love filling her heart?

She guessed she'd just have to get used to it.

THIRTY-SIX

That night, Jake sat in Mabel's kitchen and waited for her to get home. He didn't have the radio on like usual. No TV, no iPad, no newspaper. Nothing but the cold silence of the empty house and the cold knot in his stomach.

Tybalt scruffed himself against Jake's ankles before leaping onto the stool next to him, where he tucked himself into a cat loaf and tried to drill a hole into Jake's forehead with his Sphinx eyes.

"I know, buddy." He sighed, running a hand down the cat's back.

They stayed like that until Tybalt's ears perked up and he hopped off the stool with a grunt to mince toward the front door. A few seconds later, Jake heard Mabel's steps on the porch. He stood and tried to calm his pounding heart.

The door creaked as she pushed it open, and he heard her stomping snow off her boots and baby talking to Tybalt.

"Hey, sexy man," she called from the front hallway as she dropped her purse and shrugged out of her coat. "It's freezing out there! I cannot wait to be on a beach with you. Less than twenty-four hours now!"

She walked into the kitchen and joined him in front of the island, wrapping her arms around him for a quick hug. "Wow, do I have some things to fill you in on." She pulled away to move toward the refrigerator.

But Jake finally unfroze and grabbed her wrist, pulling her back against him. When he spoke, his voice was low and desperate. "I love you."

She looked up at him, a slow smile melting across her face, and she tightened her arms where they rested around his waist. "And I'm wildly, stupidly in love with you too." She leaned her head against his chest and continued her bright monologue. "This may be the best day of my life because not only are we disgustingly in love, but guess who's back on mornings? Brandon admitted he was wrong and put it all back."

"Seriously? He didn't tell me he was going to do that." He pressed a kiss into her hair and held her close. Her joy was a tiny bright spot in the middle of the darkness. "I'm so happy for you, baby."

"Right? Once we're home from Jamaica, I'm back to mornings, so you and I will have to find some new time to go to the gym together unless you want to start getting up at, like, three thirty, which I definitely don't. Is that okay with you?"

She pulled away from him and grabbed a bottle of Prosecco from the fridge, then selected two glasses from the cabinet. But Jake couldn't take her heartbreaking cheerfulness anymore.

"Mabel, I can't go to Jamaica with you." His throat constricted as he watched confusion move across her face.

"But you've got the time off work. We leave tomorrow."

He shook his head. "Not anymore. And..." He forced himself to spit it out. "Sweetheart, they want me back in Chicago as a partner. Full time. Immediately."

Now Mabel was the one who froze. "So soon?" she whispered. "I thought we had more time."

"Me too," he said miserably. "I thought..."

He'd thought it would all work out somehow. His friendship with Mabel had crept up on him, and then their relationship had intensified from see-how-it-goes to... this.

They had aggressively never talked about what would happen once he was back in Chicago, probably because neither of them wanted to believe this period of blissful happiness would come to an end. He'd thought he'd have a few more months with her at least. More months to come up with a solution that didn't end up with the two of them living in different cities. More months to get a better handle on what this relationship actually was. But fucking Greg McDonald couldn't fucking handle the fucking Kriegsman account, and it was Jake's life that got blown to fucking smithereens because of it.

She set her wineglass down on the island with a clink and stared into the liquid as if she might find answers in the swirling bubbles. Her shoulders rose and fell as she drew in a breath, and he watched her struggle to conjure a smile.

"A partnership. That's... that's great! Congratulations. I know how hard you've worked for this." She blinked rapidly, and he hated that this was hurting her. But when he took a step toward her, she shied back. So he kept his distance and tried to explain.

"Things blew up with the BPS guy who was handling one of my biggest clients, and they've threatened to pull their business if I don't come back to manage their accounts full time. That's what today's call was, my boss telling me I'm needed back in my office as soon as possible, and Brandon okayed it."

Mabel nodded once, sharply. "Yeah, that sounds about right. I was just starting to get smug about how great my life was, so this was inevitable." Her laugh was bitter.

"I did try. I told them I couldn't just walk away from the Lowell accounts. But they refused to budge, said if I wanted the partnership... Mabel, you know how hard I've worked for it. What it means for me. What it means to be able to support my family if it comes to that."

She swallowed hard. "I do. I know. I'm proud of you."

Her voice broke on the word *proud*, and they both fell silent.

It had been so easy to let himself forget about his old goals, his lifelong goals, while living out this dream life with her. Then the real world had come calling. The forever he'd spent his adult life chasing was here, and it was fucking up the forever he'd just started building with Mabel.

"So when do you need to leave?"

"I'll pack up my apartment and leave in the morning."

They stared at each other from opposite sides of the island. He wanted to reach across that vast expanse of countertop and take her hand, but she'd retreated into herself.

"And you won't have much reason to come back to Beaucoeur after that." Mabel's voice was as flat as her eyes.

He rocked back on his heels at her words. "I have *every* reason. I'll come on the weekends, or you can visit me." What was she saying? Did she not want to keep seeing him once he was gone? "It's only three hours away, and we can Skype during the week."

The corners of her mouth tightened. "And your work hours in Chicago, they're nine to five and no weekends, right?"

He squeezed the back of his neck, not wanting to answer. When he was in Chicago, he worked into the night and weekends too. Beaucoeur had kept him busy, but it hadn't come close to the grind that Chicago was.

She swirled the wine in her glass but didn't take a drink. "And good thing my job at the station never involves weekend work either." A cold was creeping into her voice, an awful chill far worse than the subzero temperature outside.

"I don't suppose you'd want to move up there with me?" He kept his tone light, but her annoyed *tsk* told him that even as a joke, it wasn't something she'd consider. And he already knew that anyway. He'd thought maybe if she was still unhappy with the afternoon-drive shift, she might consider a city change. But now? Her work was here. Her life was here.

With a sharp motion, she brought the glass to her lips and drained it. "It's not fair," she said, her voice low and furious. "It's a shitty situation, and it's not fair."

She turned her back to him to rinse the glass in the sink. "We'll try the long-distance thing for a while, but it'll never be the same. Three hours each way doesn't seem like much now, but it'll start adding up. We'll end up visiting each other less and less, and then we'll start talking less and less, and eventually everything will collapse."

"It won't." His heart raced as he fumbled for the words to change her mind. "We're stronger than that."

"No. I was right all along." She addressed her reflection in the window over the sink. "I should've followed my own rules."

Her own rules? Her rules against relationships?

"Are you saying you regret us being together?" His voice swelled to fill the room, and when she didn't answer, he walked around the island to stand in front of her, desperate to reach her. "It's too late for that. I love you too much to just walk away."

She shook her head and pressed a hand to her mouth, stopping whatever words might otherwise have tumbled out. His fingers twitched to smooth out the line between her eyes, but he was scared that if he touched her, she'd crumble.

She leaned against the sink, her eyes focused on some object just over his shoulder, and the longer he waited for her to speak, the heavier his heart sat in his chest. Why wasn't she putting up a fight? Was she just going to shrug and let him walk away?

When she finally spoke again, it was to say in a hollow, remote voice, "It's been a big day. I'm going to bed."

She brushed past him, but he stayed rooted to the spot, unsure if she wanted him to follow.

Then she paused in the doorway and looked back. "You coming?"

He nodded and walked with her to the bedroom, where they undressed in silence and made love with an intensity that felt like goodbye.

When he woke up the next morning, she was already gone.

———————

PACKING up his apartment was too grand a description for what Jake actually had to do. He crammed his clothes and the contents of his bathroom cabinet into a duffel and zipped his suits into a garment bag, then stripped the soft sheets Mabel had gotten him for Christmas off the bed and stuffed them on top of one of the boxes with his files and books. And that represented the totality of his life in Beaucoeur. When he left, it would all fit neatly in his Jeep. All except his heart, of course, which rested in Mabel's hands.

After he dropped his key with the property manager, he pointed his Jeep toward the radio station where he had a few more files to pack up. He was also hoping he'd find Mabel there, but just his luck, he found Brandon instead.

"So you're actually leaving?"

Jake glanced up from the stack of paperwork he was sorting through. "Yeah. Of course. Have you got an extra banker's box?"

Brandon didn't answer, and Jake braced himself for whatever snideness he was about to be hit with.

But Brandon only shook his head. "I'm surprised. I mean, we both know you could've gone back to Chicago months ago if you'd really wanted to."

Jake clenched his jaw but said nothing as Brandon crossed his arms and leaned against the door.

"I mean, have you ever wondered why I'm still in Beaucoeur when this place basically runs like a machine whether I'm here or not?"

"The sketchy midwestern sushi?" Jake asked tightly.

"That's one reason," Brandon said. "But mostly it's because I've got nothing in Detroit to go home to. Empty house, angry ex, nightmare father."

Had Jake been talking to any other human on Earth, he would've described Brandon's tone as lonely, but that didn't track with the guy he'd known for a decade.

"What's your point?" he snapped.

"Me? I'm just enjoying some different scenery for a while. But you? You've got something to go home to."

"Yeah. My partnership," Jake said, intentionally misinterpreting what Brandon was getting at because *fuck*, it hurt too much to open the door to anything else. "Don't worry; I'll stay on top of Lowell's books no matter where I am."

Brandon's face fell. "Can't say I didn't try." And in a blink, that flash of disappointment was gone, replaced by his usual smirk. "Well, no worries, Jakehammer. I'll make sure to keep everybody so busy down here that they'll barely know you're gone."

And with that he vanished, leaving Jake feeling even lower than he had ten minutes before.

It got worse when Dave knocked on the door.

"*Il Duce* said you needed a box," he said, handing one over. "Gotta say, this is a weird way to pack for the beach."

Jake swallowed back the bile creeping up his throat. Dodging questions from Dave would be much harder. "I'm not going to make the trip after all."

Dave tilted his head in a question. "Come again?"

"I'm headed back to Chicago."

"For the weekend?"

"For good."

At Jake's terse explanation, Dave's brows met over the bridge of his nose. "Wait, you're *leaving*?"

Christ, why was this so hard for people to understand? "That's where my job is. What else am I supposed to do?"

Dave folded his arms over his chest and frowned. "Sure, and nothing changed between July and now. No reason to try to renegotiate your job terms or anything."

Jake felt a welcome rush of anger at Dave's sarcastic tone. "I *did* try. Believe me. But I've been working toward a partnership with BPS for years, and I'm not just walking away from it."

"But you are just walking away from her," Dave sneered. "Got it."

He wasn't doing this. He wasn't going to argue with Dave about the thing that threatened to crush his heart. Haphazardly tossing the rest of the stack into the box, he slammed the lid closed. He'd go through the fucking paperwork in Chicago, where nobody there would hurt him.

He grabbed the box and turned to leave. "We'll figure it out."

"Convince yourself first, because you're sure as fuck not convincing me."

No way was he letting that be the last word. "She gave up on *me*!" he roared, wheeling around to face Dave. "I was already scheduling weekend trips. I was planning on wild phone sex and taking whatever vacation time we could steal together. But she just... she just rolled over and took it. Didn't even try to fight for us. She all but helped me pack."

Somehow, watching Dave's anger morph into pity made him feel even worse.

"Whatever. It's been great. See you round," he muttered, storming down the hall and out the door before anybody else could rub more salt in his already painful wound. He threw the box into the back of his Jeep and slammed the door shut, anxious to get on the road. If he had to leave, he wanted to do it now before he lost the strength to uproot himself from Mabel's life.

As he drove out of Beaucoeur, he called her, but it went straight to voicemail. So he left a message, not bothering to hide the pleading in his tone.

"I love you, Mabel. Stay with me on this. We'll make it work, I promise."

He didn't know how though. He didn't have a clue.

THIRTY-SEVEN

Had anyone ever been this miserable on her way to paradise? Mabel pondered the question. Napoleon traveling to Elba maybe. Wait, was Elba considered a paradise? And wait, why was she thinking about Napoleon in the first place? She was in the middle of a rowdy group of travelers at the Beaucoeur airport, getting ready to board a plane to take them to Atlanta, where another plane would deposit them all in Montego Bay. She bet nobody else here was thinking about despotic French history.

"You look gloomy for someone trading Illinois in January for a beach for the next five days," said Thea, straightened her Brick T-shirt as she scanned the sea of humanity milling around them. "I thought Jake was coming with you."

Mabel reached deep for her big radio smile, but it was low on wattage that morning. "He got stuck at work. You know how he is."

Thea's "right" sounded skeptical, so Mabel excused herself to make the rounds with the fans, greeting them, thanking them for coming along, whooping excitedly along with them. Then she retreated to sit next to the Chiltons and Aiden, who'd decided at the last minute that the trip sounded too good to pass up. By the time they lined up to board the plane, she was exhausted from the forced cheerfulness. Yes, the Chiltons were lucky to be on an adult's-only vacation. Yes, this *was* a great chance for Aiden to escape his work and family stresses. Yes, a week of sun and sand was exactly what she needed. Smile, laugh, keep your chin up.

And then she shuffled onto the plane, sat down next to the empty seat that was supposed to be Jake's, and started to come unglued. The tears she'd been fighting all morning trembled along her eyelashes, and she was scrounging through her purse for a tissue when Thea plopped down next to her and handed her a drink napkin.

"Do you mind? I cannot sit next to Brick Babe Kimmie. She's already drunk and suuuuper into hugging. And if the hugging's bothering *me*, you know it's bad."

Mabel sniffled and shook her head, gratefully clutching the napkin in her fist. "Go ahead."

Thea crammed her carry-on under the seat in front of her and turned shrewd eyes on Mabel. "So here's the thing. I think whatever's going on with Jake is more than a work issue. We've got hours and hours, so you may as well spill it."

When Dave had tried to talk to her about Jake that morning, she'd threatened to play nothing but Kenny G when their partnership resumed, but being crammed into a metal tube preparing to hurtle through the sky must've weakened her resolve.

She heaved a shuddery breath and exhaled the words on a long sigh. "I panicked. He told me he was going back to Chicago, and I wasn't prepared. So I freaked out and ripped off the Band-Aid."

Thea cocked her head. "Explain."

So for the next hour, Thea nodded in sympathy as Mabel poured out the whole story: Jake's sudden return to Chicago when she'd thought they'd have more time to grow in their relationship. Her fear that another bad breakup would hurt her professionally. Her certainty that watching their love slowly dwindle would be more painful than a clean break now. The only thing she omitted was the way Jake had made love to her the night before. With each thrust, he'd whispered into her ear "I love you" with so much tenderness that she'd almost wept. She'd wanted to say it back, to tell him that she'd never loved anyone the way she loved him and couldn't imagine the shape of her life without him. But the words had clogged in her throat, so she kept her eyes shut and turned her head away, already willing herself to forget the sweetness of his touch.

"How did you leave things?"

"I figured it would be easier for both of us if I didn't make it some big, dramatic goodbye, so I just... left." She blinked furiously to hold back the tears. The rest of the plane didn't need to know how heartbroken she was, particularly since she needed to be radio babe Mae Bell this week. "And..."

Thea waited for her to keep going. When Mabel didn't, she gently prompted, "And?"

Mabel took a deep breath and confessed what she hadn't spoken out loud to anybody, not even Jake. "And I can't just pack up and go be a deejay in Chicago, and he's not going to chuck his career out the window for me. He shouldn't! I'm so proud of what he's accomplished. He's been working toward that forever. Besides, we *just* started dating. How can you be sure after a few months?"

She fiddled with the fold-down tray in front of her, not looking at Thea. "But... I think he was *it* for me. I felt like I'd finally found him."

"And did you tell him any of this?"

Mabel shook her head. "No. I couldn't do that to him. Everything he's done over the past decade has been to land a partnership. How can I ask him to blow it off and stay in Beaucoeur with me? It's better to just end it now."

Thea furrowed her brow. "No, I don't think so. You should call him. You should explain all this—"

Mabel pressed the heels of her hands into her eyes, hard. "Nope. No more deep relationship talk for the rest of the trip. From this point on, I never want to be without a glass of rum in my hand, and I'll only entertain fun conversations." Then she was struck by a thought that made her shift uncomfortably in her seat. "Oh, but first, did Brandon talk to you about—"

Thea nodded. "No worries. We're all good. I'm so glad you're going back on the air with Dave."

"You're sure?" How weird that she was worried about hurting Thea's feelings, but there it was. Joining her for yoga had become one of the highlights of her week. Okay, they usually skipped yoga to get donuts, but it was still a highlight.

"Very sure. Turns out those morning hours are not for me. Of course, that means I was maybe a *little* hasty in quitting the hotel job." She grimaced and held up her plastic cup of white wine in a salute. "But I'll find the next thing before long. I always do!"

She drained her cup, then said perkily, "Okay, so let's move on to a fun conversation. Ummm... which of our traveling companions should I hook up with this week? Or should I wait until we get there to find somebody who's *not* from my hometown?"

For the remainder of the flight, Thea kept up a mostly one-sided conversation, and if someday she'd be forced to testify under oath, Mabel couldn't have come up with a single one of the topics Thea covered. But it didn't matter. She was pathetically grateful for the wave of chatter that didn't require any response on her end except a dull *uh-huh* every five minutes or so.

By the time the crew of their second flight collected all their empty cups and instructed them to return their tray tables to an upright position for their descent into Montego Bay, Mabel was torn between guilt and gratitude.

"I don't deserve this."

Thea paused in the act of unwrapping a stick of gum. "What do you mean?"

She looked down at her chipped manicure, which she hadn't cared enough to touch up after the heartbreak of the night before. "I mean that I wasn't very nice to you at first. I definitely didn't *think* nice things about you. But you just made this whole flight tolerable for me. Thank you."

Thea freed the gum and popped it into her mouth. "No worries. I've been told it takes a while to warm up to me. I can come on a little strong."

Mabel's lips pulled into a smile for the first time all day. "Maybe a little," she said, giving Thea a nudge.

Thea held her thumb and pointer finger a fraction of an inch apart and squinted through the gap at Mabel. "That's okay. To know me is to grudgingly tolerate me."

Miracle of miracles, Mabel actually laughed at that,

and before she knew it, she was being herded off the plane and onto a hotel shuttle with the rest of her group. She shuffled obediently through the check-in process at a hotel that was full of sunshine and ocean breezes, and when she got to her room, she walked out on a balcony overlooking the azure water and white-sand beach to find fresh-squeezed mango juice waiting in a carafe. Maybe she could find a little peace here for the week, away from the sorrow waiting for her in Beaucoeur.

Then her eyes traveled to the massive bed in the middle of the room, made up with crisp white linens, and the tears started again. She was a single in a double-occupancy room. Six months ago, it might not have bothered her much, but now? It felt like an arrow through her heart.

She turned back to the balcony and poured herself a glass of juice. She was in paradise, and the man she loved was thriving. All in all, it could be worse. She was happy for him.

She'd try to be happy for him.

THIRTY-EIGHT

Chicago looked vast from where he was standing.

The jagged skyline sprawled across Jake's vision, glittering with lights and motion, and he should be reveling in it. He had the office. He had the window. He had the view. All of it came with the partnership he'd officially been handed that morning, along with respect, stability, security. Everything he'd ever wanted.

So why the fuck did he feel so empty?

He was struck with the sudden urge to laugh. To drop onto his new plush carpet and howl with laughter until he had no more breath in his body. But nothing was funny about his current mood. Mabel liked to tease him about his Clark Kent appearance, but it turned out he was actually Bruce Wayne: handed the world, yet stuck glowering at it alone from on high.

Clark Kent. Mabel. His broken heart.

With a growl, he spun on his heel, turning his back on the view. He snatched his phone from his desk to confirm what he already knew: she hadn't texted. Of course she hadn't. He hadn't texted her either. He'd had no contact with her since his unreturned voicemail. And if they ever did talk again, he wasn't even sure which of them should be the one to apologize. Him, for taking the partnership? Or her, for letting him go without a single argument?

"Fuck!" He dropped the phone and leaned his hands on his desk. It was shined to such a polish that he could see his reflection. He looked like shit.

"You look like shit."

He snapped his head up at hearing his thoughts spoken out loud to see Milo in the doorway. "How'd you get in here?"

His friend sauntered into the room and took a lap around the perimeter. "I told you. Your assistant thinks I'm dreamy." He paused in front of the floor-to-ceiling window, giving a low whistle. "Sure beats the hell out of my office." He dropped into the guest chair in front of the desk.

"Your office is three times this size," Jake reminded him.

"It's on the third floor of a glorified warehouse. I *wish* I could see all the way to Navy Pier."

Jake only grunted, but if Milo thought his lack of enthusiasm was strange, he didn't mention it. Instead, he reached into his bag and produced a bottle. "Here. Congratulations on the partnership."

Jake accepted it without much enthusiasm, but when he read the label, it startled a laugh out of him. "You remembered."

A corner of Milo's mouth tilted up. "Of course I remembered."

Jake wrapped careful fingers around the bottle of Suntory whiskey, touched at the reminder of their long-ago conversation. "What were we drinking that night?"

"Old Crow," Milo said with a grimace. "Celebrating you moving into your own apartment. Eight years ago, right?"

The memory brought the first real smile to Jake's lips in days. "That's right. Old Crow was all I could afford after I'd put down a deposit and last month's rent." He shook his head. "God, we were babies. So excited to take on the world."

"So excited to have enough cash to swap Old Crow for Suntory someday." Milo looked pointedly at the bottle in Jake's hands.

"Right, right. One minute." He scrounged through his drawers until he located the coffee mugs where Marissa had stashed them after his possessions had been transferred into his new space. He'd have to get some barware for his office soon. Maybe he and Mabel could—

Fuck. Including her in his plans was going to be a hard habit to break. It was a habit he didn't *want* to break.

With an impatient motion, he cracked the bottle open and inhaled the sharp scent, waiting to feel... something. But the pride over his new place in the world didn't materialize as he'd hoped it would. He poured a healthy portion into both mugs and offered one to Milo.

His friend clinked his cup against Jake's and took a long sip. "Worth every penny," he sighed.

Jake imitated Milo's action, letting the expensive Japanese alcohol roll across his tongue. It tasted fine; the smoky burn was what he expected from an aged whiskey. But it left him disappointed. This expensive bottle of alcohol was supposed to *mean* something. It was supposed to bestow a grander meaning to the events of the day, to be the ceremonial capper to this lifelong achievement. Instead, he tasted... alcohol.

He took another sip, this time seeking numbness instead of elevation. He'd made it. He wasn't the kid with the closet full of thrift-store clothes anymore. He could stop worrying about the future. So why did the years stretching ahead of him seem so empty?

Milo stared down into his mug, still lost in the memory of their younger selves. "I thought we were going to die of alcohol poisoning that night, or at least go blind." When Jake didn't reply, Milo sighed. "Okay, dude, something is clearly bothering you. You should be fist-pumping and gloating about your success. Instead, you're"—he waved his arm to encompass Jake's whole sad-sack body —"whatever the fuck this is. What gives?"

Jake set down his mug and dropped his head into his hands.

"Oh. Oooooh. It's the girl. Got it."

Jake lifted his gaze. "How the fuck do you always know?"

"You think I don't recognize breakup misery when I see it?" Milo tilted his head in sympathy. "I've never seen you that gone for a woman before. What happened, man? Did you dump her? Did she dump you? Did you propose and she said no? Oh God, is she pregnant?"

"What? No!" Why was Milo talking about marriage and babies, and why did the thought of that fill Jake not with panic but with yearning? "No, we... we decided the long-distance thing wouldn't work."

"So don't do long distance."

Jake laughed humorlessly at Milo's overly simple suggestion. "Yeah? How?"

"Um, it's pretty simple." Milo set down his mug and held his hand out toward Jake, jabbing a finger to the base of his palm where it met his wrist. "You." Then he slid his finger to the tip of his fingers. "Move here to be with the most important person in your life."

Like it was that simple. "Sure. I just walk away from this place after I finally got my—"

"I swear to fucking God, if you say *partnership* right now."

The disgust in Milo's tone caught Jake by surprise, and he shot back, "I'm sorry, have we not both been working our asses off for years for exactly this kind of promotion?"

"Sure," Milo said easily, pouring another splash of whiskey into his mug. "But I turned down an offer from New York last year because I want to stay close to my folks, and I never would've made that choice when I was straight out of college. Ask yourself this: Have you let your goals change over the years? And if not, why not?"

"My goals are fine. Why would they need to ch—" Jake's voice died in his throat as his brain finally caught up with the things his heart and his gut had been screaming at him.

His priorities *had* changed. They'd started shifting months ago when Mabel walked into his office and asked for help with the station van. They'd kept shifting as he'd fallen in love with her, as he'd started valuing time with her over checking another box on his work to-do list. But when the time came to choose between her and the job, he'd been too scared to admit that he wanted something different after so long.

"Oh fuck." He looked at Milo in horror, realizing everything he'd said and done wrong. His mom and Finn were fine. They didn't need him to take this partnership for the money; all they needed was for him to be happy. "I think I screwed it all up."

Milo nodded sagely. "I have no doubt you did. You don't have much practice using your brain as anything other than a calculator."

Jake lurched to his feet. "I have to fix this. I have to get her back. I can still get her back, right?"

Milo reached for the bottle of Suntory. "Hope so. Here, you're going to need some more of this while we plan."

THIRTY-NINE

Saturday. Three days in paradise. Three days of Mabel shuffling around the island, wrapped in her own personal gray cloud.

This should've been an amazing week. The first night of the trip, Dave had announced at dinner that she'd be back on the morning show with him when they got back, and everyone in their group had cheered and raised their glasses. She'd stood in the center of a group full of warmth and enthusiasm and thanked them all for their support, but inside she felt as steady as the crumbly sand under their feet.

The following day, she established a system that allowed herself three minutes to cry in a bathroom stall before emerging to hide her puffy eyes behind big sunglasses for her next on-air segment. Thank God for the relentless Jamaican sun that made them a necessity. Turned out her closest companions in Jamaica were her mirrored sunglasses and her thoughts. Her bitter, heartbroken thoughts.

At least she didn't have to force her plastic cheerfulness on Ana and Thea, who were stretched out next to her under the early-afternoon sun. They knew she was a shambling wreck and didn't expect anything other than gloominess from her.

"If you sigh one more time, I'm going to make you eat my sunglasses," Ana said. "My baby bump and I are absorbing all the UV rays we can, and you're bumming us out."

"Sorry." And then she sighed again. She couldn't help it.

Ana propped herself up on her elbows and looked at her over the rim of the enormous tortoiseshell frames that Mabel really didn't want to have forcibly shoved down her throat. "I'm on day three of this beautiful beach vacation. My children, whom I love dearly, are in Iowa with Dave's parents. I have the finest, fruitiest alcohol-free drink in my hand and eye candy from one side of the beach to the other. Quit raining on my parade."

"Seriously." Thea lifted the edge of her floppy hat to squint at the part of the beach where Aiden and Dave were emerging from the ocean. She'd been letting her pixie cut grow out, and she impatiently brushed the dark strands out of her eyes. "Jake's the idiot who's missing out."

"I doubt Jake's sobbing in his beer over not witnessing a bunch of pasty midwesterners in swimsuits." There, saying his name didn't make her cry that time. Progress. Trying to keep it light, she pointed to the two men racing up the beach like puppies. "I mean, there's exhibit A and B. Nobody's missing anything with those two."

"Mmm. If you say so," Thea said, her eyes pinned on

Aiden as he jogged across the sand. And yeah, true, his chest was nice, but it wasn't the chest Mabel was missing.

Once the guys joined them on the towels, they shook water over everyone to get them all moving toward a restaurant for a late lunch. Ana and Thea both accepted, but Mabel refused to budge.

"Not hungry. I'll stay in the sun a little longer. I've got a book." She gestured at the paperback on her lap even though she hadn't been able to focus on a single paragraph for long enough to understand it.

"Suit yourself," Dave said with a shrug. "Don't cry to us when you turn into beef jerky."

She lazily kicked sand in his direction as the four of them gathered their belongings and headed toward the hotel.

Alone finally, Mabel let the book slip from her lap and noticed that Dave had left his flip-flops on the sand next to her. Here's hoping they were headed to a "no shoes, no problem" kind of place. Laughter erupted from the cluster of bikini-clad Brick Babes down the beach, and Mabel had to admit she was glad they were here. They took the heat off her to entertain the fans, and they all really did seem to be having a great time. Somebody ought to be anyway.

She settled back against her chair and closed her eyes behind her sunglasses. She hadn't slept well last night or the night before that—or the one before that, come to think of it. Now that she was alone, she was able to turn a newish thought over in her mind. Chicago had radio stations, after all. It wouldn't hurt to just look. That didn't mean she'd be leaving Dave or making any major life changes. But looking at job postings? She could do that.

The thought brought a measure of peace to the storm in her heart, and she'd almost slipped into a light doze when a shadow fell across her face as someone stepped between her and the sun.

Not opening her eyes, she gestured toward Dave's sandals. "Forget something?"

"Yeah, I did."

The familiar voice had her bolting upright in her chair. She whipped off her sunglasses. "Jake?"

"I forgot to tell you something."

She blinked up at him, wondering if she was suffering from sunstroke. But there he was, barefoot in a rumpled business suit, carrying his shoes in one hand and his suit jacket in the other.

"Are you really here? On the beach? In a suit?"

His shirt was partially unbuttoned, tie loose around his neck, and he squinted down at her as the ocean breeze ruffled his hair. "I'm really here, and I'm in a suit because finding a last-minute flight to Jamaica is harder than you'd think." He ran a hand down his face. "I left the office yesterday, went straight to O'Hare, and booked the first flight I could find. I had a few layovers, I've been traveling for twenty hours, and I haven't had anything but airport food for an entire day. But quit changing the subject. I forgot to tell you something on Wednesday."

He dropped his shoes and grabbed her by the hand, pulling her up to face him. Stubble darkened his jaw, and shadows darkened his eyes. He'd never looked better to her.

"What?" she asked, barely daring to hope.

"I forgot to tell you how much I don't want to leave Beaucoeur."

"You don't?" Her heart squeezed.

He dropped his jacket and grabbed her other hand, running his thumbs over her knuckles. "My Chicago apartment that I wanted to get back to so badly five months ago? It's empty without your socks and dirty coffee mugs everywhere. When they showed me to my new office at BPS, all I could think was how I prefer the view of downtown Beaucoeur from my closet in the bank building. And the only thing I felt when my boss made the official partnership announcement was how wrong it was that you weren't there with me. So, no. I don't want to leave Beaucoeur. You're in Beaucoeur, and I don't want to leave you. It's that simple."

She gave a short sob and squeezed his hands back, so full of love for this man. "I didn't want you to leave. I wanted you to stay with me. You're *it* for me," she choked out, finally saying the words to the one person who needed to hear them.

He smiled at her then for the first time since he'd found her on the beach. "You're it for me too," he said. "So I quit my job yesterday."

"No!" Mabel gasped.

"I told BPS I'd be working in Beaucoeur from now on. If they want to keep me on, that's great. If they don't, I'll open my own firm."

What he was saying made no sense. Not for the Jake she knew. "But all that work, all those years you put in—"

"—don't matter if my heart's in Beaucoeur. I'm good at what I do. They'll either accept that and make me a partner remotely in charge of the Lowell account, or I'll be my own boss. I'm good either way. As long as I have you?"

The last bit ended on a question, and Mabel realized what he was asking.

"You have me. You've got all of me. No more pulling away when it gets rough. I love you. I love you so much. I love you." She would've kept saying it, but he scooped her up to kiss her, stopping her words.

"You've got ten seconds to gather whatever stuff you brought with you," he warned her, "because after that, I'm taking you to our room, and we're not coming out until we're forced to seek sustenance. Or until you have some radio thing to do, because *one* of us needs to keep their job."

Mabel abandoned her paperback and Dave's sandals on the beach. She had more important things to think about.

She and Jake held hands as they stumbled across the sand and burst into the tiled lobby of the hotel, making a beeline for the elevator, which moved upward at a glacial pace. They used the whole trip to communicate with kisses instead of words.

When it finally disgorged them onto her floor, she led him to her room. "Do you want to shower, or—"

"Later." He cut her off, kissing her as he simultaneously backed her toward the bed. "I was afraid I'd never get to touch you again."

"But wouldn't you—"

"Seriously, sweetheart, you're in a bikini, and it's making me crazy. Showers and talking can wait. I promise we can talk all you want in the shower later."

He tumbled her to the bed, and they shucked their clothes, desperate to be skin to skin. Mabel was almost dizzy with relief that Jake had come back for her, that he'd chosen her. She pushed him onto his back and climbed over him, kissing his throat, his shoulder, his jaw.

"Don't ever leave me," she said, licking along his chest.

"Never again," he panted, moving his hands up her sides, curving them over her breasts. "I'll never leave you again."

She positioned herself over his erection and sank down, too desperate to feel him moving inside her to be patient. His hands gripped her hips as he drove up into her again and again. She rocked against him, moaning at the electric friction and the thrill of Jake's warm skin against hers.

"Can't last, sweetheart," Jake gritted out. "Love you so fucking much."

Mabel responded by leaning forward and sucking his lower lip into her mouth. "So make me come."

He groaned and slipped a hand between their bodies to caress her, tipping her gasping over the edge. He followed soon after, shouting her name, and then pulled her down against his chest so he could whisper sweet nothings into her ear as their breathing returned to normal.

They eventually untangled and, wrapped in the sheets they'd ripped from the bed in their frenzy, moved out to the balcony to let the breeze cool their sweat-drenched skin.

Mabel was tucked against Jake's chest, feeling the steady rise and fall as he breathed and marveling that she'd get to experience the simple joy of that forever.

Jake broke the stillness by clearing his throat.

"So, uh, Mabel?"

"Yes, uh, Jake?" she replied sleepily.

"It occurs to me that I don't have any place to live in Beaucoeur since I gave up my apartment."

Ridiculous man. Perfect, wonderful, ridiculous man.

"I thought we cleared this up on the beach. Your home is with me." Then she tapped her chin in thought. "Well, as long as you bring that pink apron with you."

EPILOGUE

SIX MONTHS LATER

"Good night, Robbie!"

Mabel's cheerful voice floated in from the lobby of his office, and Jake smiled to himself and hit Save on the Lowell Consolidated documents he was working on for Brandon. If his fiancée was here, that meant it was time to wrap up and head home.

Moments later, Mabel poked her head around his office door. Her golden hair caught the glow of the late-afternoon sun, and his breath hitched in his chest. Her beauty still startled him sometimes, shocked him with the knowledge that this woman was his. He suspected he'd always feel that way.

"Robbie says good night, and he wanted to express his thanks yet again for his position as junior accountant at Carey and Associates, CPA."

Jake shook his head. "At some point he's going to get tired of thanking me. Until then, I'm letting that junior accountant bring me an extra coffee in the morning."

She crossed the room and dropped into the chair in front of his desk, her short skirt creeping up when she crossed her tan legs. "So Cheryl's also gone for the night," she said, referring to the assistant he'd hired to keep his growing office on track. "It's just you and me here."

Jake raised his brows, recognizing that note of invitation in that maple syrup voice.

"Just you and me," he said. "And our plans to have an early dinner so you can wake up at that ungodly morning-show hour."

"Yep." Mabel swung her foot, dangling her sandal off one pink, polished toe. "Early dinner is one of the things we could do tonight. But, I mean, we're here *all alone*."

Jake liked where he thought this was headed and, not wanting to discourage her, repeated, "All alone."

"And"—she hopped up and leaned across his desk —"for all that talk about your desk fetish when we first started dating, you have never once ravished me in your office, despite the fact that we are newly affianced."

She had a knee up on his desk now, that utilitarian metal desk he'd picked out in a haze of anger and despondency after she'd crushed him the previous summer. He was grateful now for his foresight in selecting such a sturdy piece of furniture, because Mabel was on top of it now and kneeling in front of him, playing with the hem of her shirt.

"And we're *all alone*." She smiled that Mabel Bowen smile at him and inched forward across the surface.

Jake finally snapped into action, slamming his laptop shut and shoving it into the top drawer, then sweeping all the pens and notebooks and files onto the floor.

"*All alone*." He stood and pulled her toward him, eager as always for her mouth and hands and body. "And look, we've got a perfectly clean desk right here."

Mabel laughed and kissed him as if she'd never stop, which suited Jake just fine.

If you're not quite ready to say goodbye to Mable and Jake, head here for a sassy bonus epilogue!
www.sarawhitney.com/talk

*Can good-girl Thea and playboy Aiden pull off a fake relationship without catching any feelings? Find out in **Tempting Lies**, the toe-curling fourth book in the Tempt Me series. Available now!*

Dear reader,

I'm so honored that you trusted me with your precious reading time, and I hope *Tempting Talk* transported you to a funny, sexy, and all-around joyful place for a few hours.

Many, many years ago, I worked as a deejay at my hometown radio station, so when I started writing the Tempt Me series, I wanted to set a book somewhere similar. Although I would sometimes sneak in catnaps on the cold, hard station floor during my 5 a.m. shift, I thought I'd spare Mabel that indignity. Other than that, though, the energy of the stations are similar.

Creating The Brick and all the people who inhabit it was a pure delight, and you'll see them all again in my fake-relationship romp *Tempting Lies*, which is out now. And be sure to sign up for my mailing list to keep up on all the Sara Whitney news: **sarawhitney.com/newsletter**

Stay sassy, and stay in touch!

Sara Whitney

The Tempt Me Series

Tempting Heat

Tempting Taste

Tempting Talk

Tempting Lies

Praise for Sara Whitney

Tempting Taste

"Sara Whitney has pulled together the most fun you'll have in a bakery with this one! I loved the cupcake-baking, cinnamon roll hero who looks like the God of Thunder. Hello to my new book boyfriend." *Christina Hovland, author of the Mile High Matched series*

"Sexy, sassy, and downright delicious! Whitney's pint-sized heroine and strong-but-silent hero make for the perfect pairing. Tempting Taste brims with her trademark wit, humor and warmth." *Kate Bateman, author of This Earl Of Mine*

"A fun, sexy read full of humor and heart." *Sarah Hegger, author of Positively Pippa and Roughing*

Tempting Lies

"Sweet and funny and sexy all at once. I couldn't put this down." *Marianela Aybar, Mari Loves Books Blog*

"This book kept me laughing. I am super excited to check out more books by Sara Whitney." *Stevie, Book Obsessed Reviews*

"The roller-coaster ride the author takes us on getting to their happily ever after left me feeling slightly broken but so happy and hopeful. Even though I've only just closed the cover on this book, I'm already looking forward to what the author has in store for us with the next installment in the series." *Kristen Lewendon, Renaissance Dragon Book Blog*

Tempting Talk

"This story made me laugh, sigh, shout in triumph and blink away tears." *Faith Hart, author of Another Try*

"The interactions are hilarious, while the sparks are flying everywhere. I was all in cover to cover." *Jennifer Pierson, The Power of Three Readers*

"A sweet, witty, and engaging story featuring likable, complex characters." *Laurie, Laurie Reads Romance*

Tempting Heat

"It made my heart squeeze and my cheeks flush. Finn and Tom are 100% guaranteed to make. you. swoon." *Blair Leigh, author of What Comes After*

"A brilliant read. I adored it from beginning to end." *Sandra, Jeanz Book Read & Review*

"The perfect amount of tension, smoldering heat, unexpected twists, and satisfying conclusion." *Sarah, Paranormal Peach Reviews*

ABOUT THE AUTHOR

Sara Whitney writes sassy contemporary romance that's always sunny with a chance of sizzle. An RWA© Golden Heart© award finalist, Sara worked as a print journalist and film critic before she earned her Ph.D. and landed in academia. She's a good pinball player, a great baker, and an expert at shouting her TV opinions to anyone who'll listen. Sara lives in Illinois surrounded by books, cats, and half-empty coffee cups, and she loves hearing from readers! Be sure to connect with her on social media:

f facebook.com/sarawhitneyauthor

a amazon.com/author/sarawhitney

⊙ instagram.com/sarawhitney_

BB bookbub.com/profile/sara-whitney

g goodreads.com/SaraWhitney_

🐦 twitter.com/sarawhitney_

9 781953 565020